ELVISH

S.G. PRINCE

ISBN: 978-1-521-43548-9

First Edition

Cover design by Damonza

"She wanted to reach out to the little girl she had once been. She wanted to tuck that child into her arms and tell her that it would be hard, chasing this dream. It would be long. But it would be worth it."

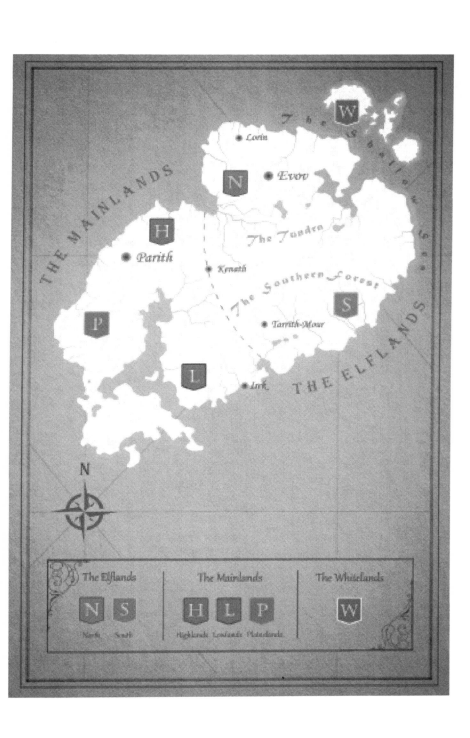

ONE

Venick was not ready to die.

He lied about this often. To himself, to others. It was easy to believe a man like Venick did not fear death. He was tall, broad. A fighter. Built to die bravely, in battle maybe, or during the hunt. Venick battled and hunted often enough, but he always emerged the victor. He was sword-touched, people said. God-touched, too. Venick didn't believe it. If the gods were watching him, he wouldn't be where he was now: with his foot caught in a bear trap, the pain so bright it snagged his breath, turned his mind sharp and hot.

And the bear.

She was nursing. It was late in the season for it, but Venick knew the signs. Her cubs were nowhere to be seen, perhaps hidden deeper in the forest, lost somewhere in the thick brush. Not that it was any comfort. The snap of the trap had frightened the bear, but it was Venick's knife that made her angry. There, stuck in her shoulder. It missed her throat by mere inches. If the gods had been watching him, they might have steadied his hand. Might have helped him see through the pain, helped him ignore the smell of blood around him as he hurled his knife in a desperate attempt to *live*.

They hadn't. The knife missed its mark. It riled the bear instead, her teeth baring in a sharp grin. Hell and damn. Maybe the bear *was* the god's blessing. Maybe this was their mercy, to give him a quick death rather than let him bleed out slowly. Venick let out a laugh that sounded nothing like a laugh. He dug his nails into gritty forest earth. His bones felt tight and wrong. His whole body did, as if he was made of his injury, his entire being condensed into sharp iron prongs dug through boot and flesh. And a panic, too, that ran even deeper.

The bear reared and Venick was suddenly glad for the pain, the way it fuzzed things. It would be easier to die with a hazy mind. Easier to forget that way. He didn't want to remember all the things he had yet to do. All the things he had done.

Memories came anyway, a tide of them all at once. The bay where he had spent his boyhood, where his mother still lived. The ocean, the salty smell of it. Later, the crags where he had been exiled. Those mountains, their rocky caves and keening winds. The feel of his toes over the edge, wondering if a banished life was worth living, imagining what it would be to jump. But there was no one to lie to on those cliffs, no one to pretend to be brave for. No one who cared whether he lived or died.

He had chosen life. Chose it again and again, every day since.

And now.

The bear roared. Lifted a massive paw to swipe. Venick's eyes locked on the curved claws and he felt the first pulse of fear, *true* fear, the kind that warned of certain pain.

Certain death, you mean.

Death. But Venick was not ready to die.

The bear clawed the air and Venick ducked, then scrambled backwards. The trap dug deeper. Reeking gods. He imagined the clansmen finding his body, the humiliation of that. Caught in a bear trap. Killed by the bear. His cheeks heated even as he knew the people of the mountain would not think to look for him in these forests. He doubted they would come looking at all. Venick was not a clansman, would never be a clansman, no matter how many years he had lived and slept among those people. He was a lowlander, raised in a little city by the sea—and an outlaw, wanted for murder.

Murder. The word never failed to bring bile to his throat, a horrible twist in his gut at the reminder of everything he had loved and lost.

The people of the mountain didn't know it. They didn't ask who Venick had been or what he had done. He was an outsider. That was explanation enough. Ever since the day he stumbled upon their camp and begged for refuge, they tolerated him, but he would never be one of them. They would sooner launch a hunt for one of their missing goats.

But then, a noise Venick recognized. He froze. Listened.

A hiss on air.

A thud.

An arrow, right through the bear's eye.

The force of it jerked her head and she stumbled, then fell. Leaves scattered, breezing over Venick's boots as he stared, shocked. A moment passed, then another. The bear lay motionless. Dead.

Venick should have felt relief. He should have stood one-legged and greeted his savior, offered his life's price, whatever that was worth. Maybe asked for a hand out of the bear trap, and did they have anything to stitch up a wound while they were at it? Except at that moment he spotted the arrow—green glass shaft, currigon feathers for the fletching—and he knew he had not been saved.

That was an elven arrow.

Reeking *gods*.

They came quickly, five, six in all, fully armored and armed. They were like ghosts with their milky skin, their moon-white hair, except ghosts did not carry weapons, ghosts did not glare with golden eyes. Venick remained motionless on the ground, thinking himself the hunter and they the skittish prey. If he moved too quickly they might startle. Might strike out of fear.

Except Venick was not the hunter here, and these elves were certainly not the prey. They surrounded him, a perfect circle. Or maybe a six-pointed star. Venick knew elves liked stars better, and liked circles not at all. They may not believe in gods, but every race had their superstitions. He touched the thin silver chain around his neck and thought of his own.

Concentrate, Venick.

On what? Their lean bodies perfectly honed for fighting? Their swords and seaxes forged in green glass that never chipped, never dulled? Venick met their eyes and felt the stirring of some old anger buried long inside him. He was in their lands. No matter *why*. It didn't matter why. They didn't care that Venick could not count on the clansmen to share the meat of the iziri goats they herded, that he had no choice but to hunt on his own. They didn't care that aside from those herds, food in the mountains was scarce, that winter came early there, and so each season Venick was forced to go farther and farther south to hunt. They didn't care that *south* for Venick meant *home*, or that he was banished from returning home, so he must either hunt in the elflands or starve. Men were not allowed in these forests. They would kill him for it.

And indeed, the center elf gave the order.

"*Ynnis.*" Kill it.

It'd been years since Venick had heard the language of elves. Once, he'd thought that language beautiful. Not anymore. Not now as he translated the word, the insult. Not kill *him*. Kill *it*. Venick was nothing to them. No better than the bear.

The single female of the group nocked another arrow and pulled her bow tight. And again, the fear of certain death, the shower of memories. Again, the cliff. The wind tickled his cheeks. He peered over the edge and saw the drop yawn wide. He felt the hollow swoop of his stomach as he stumbled backwards, gasping, heart pounding and still very much *alive*.

No. Venick was not ready to die at all.

"Wait," he choked out in mainlander, his native language. "Don't."

"You are in our lands," the male said in the same language. Though most humans could not speak elvish, all elves knew mainlander. "The penalty is death."

"I didn't know."

"Liar."

But Venick's mind was spinning now. He had not expected them to pause, to reply. Either he had stumbled upon a benevolent group of elves—

Not likely.

—or they had cause to hesitate. But why?

"A reason," Venick forced himself to say. He spoke past the dry mouth, past the pain in his leg that had run from hot to cold. "There's a reason I crossed the border. I was sent to Evov."

Had he not spent time around elves, Venick would not have known to look for their earrings, to spot the small golden loops that marked this group as northern. He would not have chosen Evov for that reason.

Indeed, he would not even *know* about Evov. But Venick had spent time around elves.

Had loved an elf, once. Be honest now.

And so he knew that Evov was a little elven city nestled deep in the heart of the north, and that it was hidden, so difficult to find that its very existence was a rumor. He knew it was where elves mined green glass and raised their young, who were both precious and rare. He knew it was where the queen went during times of war.

He watched the elves stiffen. The change was subtle. A slight shift in posture, the sharpening of their gazes. Even for all his knowledge of their race, he might have missed it. But Venick was desperate, was ready to find meaning wherever he could, and so he watched the elves become still and translated it.

The queen was in Evov.

The elves were again at war.

And *these* elves were northerners in southern lands, enemy territory. So they did have cause to hesitate. Venick could be important. Oh, they might still kill him, but not right away, not until they knew for certain who he was and what he knew. Venick's pulse beat a double rhythm, his courage swelling with this new knowledge. If he played this right, he might survive yet.

The female of the group stepped forward. She didn't ask him *who sent you to Evov?* or *what business do you have there?* Asked him instead, "How do you know of this place?"

Typical, for an elf to worry over secrets first.

"My mission is important to the queen," Venick said.

"The queen."

"Yes."

"And you expect us to take you to her?"

"No." Calmly, because that could lead nowhere good. Venick smoothed his expression, trying to match their stillness. It was impossible how still an elf could hold herself. Even without one foot stuck in a trap, Venick couldn't hope for an ounce of that control. And with the foot. Well. "I just expect you not to kill me."

She hesitated.

"Ellina," the male said. "You cannot tell me you *believe him.*"

She clicked her teeth, an elven sign of impatience. "*Ivisha,*" she replied, switching from mainlander to elvish. "*I do not.*" She didn't realize Venick understood, though. Few humans did. "*But we will not kill him.*"

"*He is a liar. And in our lands.*"

"*He knows about Evor.*"

"*He will not, once he is dead.*"

"*Who told him about that city?*" She became stony. "*What else does he know?*"

The male paused. He tilted his elegant face. "*You think he is a spy for the south.*"

"Yes."

Venick blinked. His courage slipped away. An enemy spy?

"*We cannot take any prisoners.*"

"*I am not asking to take him prisoner, Raffan.*"

Raffan made a noise, frustrated. "*An interrogation? You cannot torture a dead man, and this one is as good as. Look at that foot, Ellina.*"

"*A bargain, then.*"

"*Ah, as you are making with me now?*"

Ellina clicked her teeth again, but seemed to glean something from the exchange that Venick had not. Permission, he assumed, as she turned back to face him. She didn't take another step forward, didn't raise her voice. She didn't need to. She had his full attention.

"Who sent you to Evov?" she asked in mainlander. "What is your mission?"

"The queen is in danger." A guess. "I have information regarding your war." A lie.

"I do not believe you."

"That doesn't change the truth." It was unwise to bring up that word. *Truth.* Elves hated it as much as they hated circles. They would hate it more that he might have it when they did not. Venick watched the female's anger hollow her. He knew what she would say before the words were out.

"Man knows no truth—"

"—and cannot be trusted." He finished the elven saying and tried for a smile. It came out a grimace. "Let me prove my honesty."

"You cannot."

"Then leave me. Let fate take things from here." Not that he believed in fate, but the words sounded genuine enough. The pain in his leg even thinned his voice, made it sincere. A nice touch.

"Fate is not—" but she faltered. That was odd. Elves rarely stumbled over their words. "You cannot prove your honesty," Ellina said instead, "because you speak the language of men."

Venick understood her meaning. Men lied, but it was impossible to lie in elvish. Neither humans nor elves could break the rules of that language, the ancient binding that forced the speaker to tell the truth. Venick knew too well the way it was with elvish. To attempt to lie was to come up short, the words stuck, hovering just out of mind's reach. Try harder and face a pounding headache. Harder than that: suffocation.

It was the reason Venick continued to talk in mainlander, continued to play on their ignorance. If they discovered he knew their language, they would force him to speak in elvish, and then he would have no choice but to admit the truth: that he was not a messenger, not anyone who mattered, that he'd crossed the border illegally for no better reason than that he was hungry—starving—and the elflands were his best chance at a decent hunt. This silver thread of a lie he was weaving would unravel, and then he would have no hope at all.

"You want me to prove myself in your language," Venick hedged.

"You do not speak our language."

"No." Another lie. And an idea. "You could teach me," he said, and ignored the way she recoiled. As if the thought of teaching a man their language was repulsive.

"You are a *man*."

But she weighed him. She seemed to consider what he might know, the difficulty of the task. Venick again felt that spark of hope, because he saw it clearly: a way out. No matter that learning a language took months, *years*, and she would be a fool for agreeing to teach him. If only she agreed to *try*, it would buy him time to form a real plan. To escape.

"Enough, Ellina," Raffan said. He stepped between them. "He is stalling, and we are out of time."

But at that moment came another noise Venick recognized. One that made his insides sink, his whole body harden to stone. Those were wanewolf howls. Alerted to the smell of blood, no doubt. *His* blood, which stained the leaves around where he lay, pooling up to his fingers, thick and wet.

"We go," said Raffan, and motioned for his comrades to sheath their weapons.

"The trap," Venick said, and hated the desperation in his voice. "Please. Help me out."

"We will—how did you put it?—let fate take things from here," Raffan replied. They turned to leave. All but Ellina.

She stood frozen. Her golden eyes met his. It was foolish for her to hesitate. Foolish, for her to ignore her leader's command. And anyway, Venick was a dead man. If the wolves didn't get him, fever and rot would. *Look at that foot*, the male had said. *He is as good as dead.*

But.

But. If they couldn't help him, maybe they would give him the mercy of a quick death. Venick's eyes went to her arrows, the blood-red currigon feathers. She followed his gaze and understood.

She nocked an arrow and pointed it at him.

So this was it. Venick blinked and tried to feel glad. An arrow to the heart. Not a bad way to die. Better than the alternative, which howled again, closer now.

Venick looked up into the canopy. He saw the afternoon light filter through the trees. The leaves glowed, their veins thrown into perfect relief.

He heard the twang of the bowstring. The whiz of the arrow.

It hit the trap's spring, which shattered and released.

His foot came free.

TWO

They ran.

Venick didn't make it far.

His foot was useless, the blood-stained boot swollen so tight he thought the leather would rip. He hobbled after the elves who went deer-swift through the forest, who were soon out of sight. Except Ellina. She hovered back, uncertain, watching as he heaved and stumbled. Venick saw her calculation. He saw her gaze shift behind him to the fresh trail of blood there.

"Go," he told her through clenched teeth. But she did not.

Venick was glad not to remember much of what came next. How the wanewolves appeared, a young pack of females. How Ellina descended upon them, killing them swiftly with arrows and a shortsword. The high cry of the animals as her green glass found their soft bellies. The silence of death. The way Ellina's face became sorrowful, and a slow memory tugged on Venick's mind. Different elves, different arrows, another forest. But he had no time for memories, no time to think of anything but the elf with him *now* as Ellina crouched beside him and cut away his boot. As she used needle and thread that she got from—*where?*— to stitch together the wound. Quickly, in a way that might worry him, might warn that the danger was not over yet. There was no poultice to numb the pain, no salve. Not even a swig of ale. Not that he would ask.

Proud, are we now?

Stupid, more like. The pain became overwhelming, every dig of the needle, warm blood peeling over exposed flesh. Light popped across his vision, which tunneled and darkened. Venick struggled to hold to consciousness. He knew what would happen if he didn't. He had imagined this moment, the way it would feel to cling to the ledge. The dark chasm spanning beneath. How he would spend all his strength, and the pain of holding on would became worse than the pain of letting go.

But he *had* let go. He had let go of his old life, his dreams. Whom he'd loved, who he had been: a warrior, a lowlander, a son. Honorable. Venick remembered the feel of honor, how he'd worn it like a cloak. Proud. Capable. That was who he had been.

And now?

Now Venick had only the stretch of empty days, hunting when he could, scavenging when he couldn't, warding off the bitterness with thoughts of ending it all for good. In the mainlands, the penalty for murder was banishment or death. Venick had escaped death. Three years later, he wasn't sure banishment was the better choice.

There was, of course, a third option: redemption. Soldiers who committed crimes otherwise punishable by death could redeem themselves by making a sacrifice. The nature of the sacrifice was up to the soldier to choose, and the outcome—whether that soldier was absolved of his crimes—was determined by those he had wronged.

Venick thought of his mother. He wondered what sacrifice would be enough to absolve him in her eyes. If any sacrifice would be.

"Stay with me." Ellina's voice broke through the haze. Her face swam in his vision.

But Venick wasn't with her.

He was again hanging from the cliff. Again, feeling his muscles strain, peering down into the void. He began to lose his grip. His fingers slipped loose, one by one.

• • •

Venick cracked open an eye, then the other. The campfire burned low. Its golden-red light spread just far enough to touch the first ring of trees. Beyond that: black, as if the world only existed inside the fire's halo.

Venick shuffled upright. He gave a cough, heard it rattle in his chest. Heard his captor—

Savior, you mean.

—shift on the ground beside him, alert. Her eyes moved to his foot, then to his face. Her expression darkened. He knew that look and didn't like it.

"I'm alive," he said, though he wasn't sure if he meant to reassure her, or himself.

"Hmm."

He found it hard to hold her gaze. He didn't want to read her thoughts, which said *stupid human* and *look like hell* and *worried*, too. He looked at his leg instead, at the fire. The first was painful and swollen, bandaged in what appeared to be packed leaves. The second, burning wood. Venick took the fire to mean they were safe. Safe enough, anyway, if she would risk an open flame. He touched his leg and searched his memory, trying to recall what had happened, trying to piece it all together. He was rewarded with hazy pictures and a headache for his efforts.

He blinked bleary-eyed into the forest and noticed for the first time that they were alone.

"Where are the others?" he asked. She didn't answer. "What happened?" She didn't answer that either. Gave him a long look instead, one that might have silenced a wiser man. "How long have—" But then he noticed something in her fist. A silver chain. His hand shot to his neck and touched only skin.

"Who gave this to you?" she asked, holding it up. Her words were delicate, silvered like that necklace. She spoke in a combination of his language and hers. Venick mentally parsed out what she'd said in elvish, deciding if any other man might understand her. He would, Venick thought. But *hell* if she wasn't testing him.

"No one."

"You stole it?"

He let out a breathless noise. "No. I meant *no one important*. No one you know. It doesn't matter, anyway."

"This is elven silver."

Venick was silent, his body stiff. When had he become so stiff? It must be the hard forest ground. His injury. Not the sight of his necklace in this elf's hands, not the weightlessness around his neck where it usually hung. He watched her trace a thumb over the links and forced himself not to snatch it back.

"You are a mystery, human."

"My name's Venick. And I'd like that back."

"This is *elven silver*," she said again, ignoring his outstretched hand. "It belongs to an elf. Where is she?"

"Gone."

"Gone, or dead?"

"Dead," he said, and practically spat out the word. Ellina raised a slender brow.

"Did you love her?"

"Stop."

"Did you kill her?"

"*Enough.*" His anger came quickly, thick and hot and too big for his body. And behind the anger, a flash of memory. An elf he'd loved, a secret revealed, a murder. His entire history condensed into a blink. He pushed those memories away, forced them out of his mind. He wouldn't think about that right now. He certainly wouldn't explain it to *her*. He let out a growl and tried to get to his feet, but Ellina was there in an instant, pushing him back with a strong hand.

"You will tear the stitches," she said.

"*Damn* the stitches."

"I did not mean to anger you."

But she was an elf. Gods, he *knew* elves. And she did mean to anger him, meant to push him at all angles to see what snapped. She was fleshing him out, baiting him into revealing something vital. It was a test. Lay the plank. Hammer it down. See if it would hold his weight.

And then another thought occurred to him, a nagging suspicion that broke through the *anger* and *pain* and forced him to *think*. Forced him to see each piece of this moment. The fire blazing. Her missing comrades. And now, an attempt to bait him.

"I have been thinking about our bargain," she said. She released his shoulder and sat back on her heels. Firelight danced across her face, drawing dark shadows. It was odd, that fire. Venick had assumed fire meant safety, but they couldn't be safe. Not this far south, not if she was a northern elf in enemy territory. And her gaze. The careful way of it. The way she drew *his* gaze where she wanted it, to her, to his necklace in her hands. Not at the trees. Not into the dark. As if there was something there she didn't want him seeing.

Venick looked anyway. He peered into the night and found nothing. But he heard Ellina's breath hitch, and his suspicion took root, blooming into full-blown certainty. Even if he couldn't see the other five elves beyond the bright ring of firelight, he knew they were there.

So they were interrogating him after all.

Hell and damn.

"You say you have information for our queen," Ellina went on.

"Yes." Voice flat, because he knew how this would go. They would prod him for information, torture him when they became impatient. He would admit in elvish that he didn't truly have a message for their queen, that he knew nothing about their war, and then they would kill him for trespassing as they should have done from the start. Or for lying. Or because they were elves, and he was human, and that was simply the way these things ended.

"And since I cannot trust anything you say in mainlander," Ellina said, again studying his necklace, "I might teach you elvish in exchange for the truth. For proof that your information is valid."

"Yes."

"Do you speak elvish already?"

Venick hid his discomfort with a frown. "You know that I don't."

"I know nothing for certain." The chain swayed gently in the light. "The elf who gave this to you. What was her name?"

"She was from the south. You wouldn't know her."

"Tell me anyway."

Venick could lie. He would have, if only because saying that name was difficult, impossible, sometimes, and because he didn't owe Ellina the truth. But he caught the shape of her mouth, the slow breaths, and some unknown instinct urged him to tell her. "Lorana," he said, and this time it wasn't pain that thinned his voice.

"Common name."

"Yes."

"I know many Loranas."

"Know any who were killed by their own kind?"

Ellina was silent for a long moment. "We elves do not kill our own."

"I hadn't thought so either."

"You are a liar, human."

"Am I?"

She darkened. There was anger in her gaze now that she didn't try to hide. No, she *wanted* him seeing she was angry. Wanted him afraid for it, which he might have been if not for the ache in his foot, and his exhaustion, and the fact that he understood elves. He understood them better than humans, sometimes, and so he knew that her anger was meant to cover all the rest. Her uncertainty. Her worry. The train of her thoughts.

"I will teach you," Ellina said.

Venick blinked. "What?"

"We are traveling to Tarrith-Mour. I will teach you elvish along the way."

"I don't—"

"You have until we reach that city to explain what you know in our language—in *elvish*—to prove that your information is true."

Hope flared. Venick searched her face for some sign that she was joking, even though elves rarely did. She handed the necklace back and stood. "If you fail, human, you will die the way the bear did."

THREE

The sun broke clear the next morning, the stars blinking out one by one. A liralin bird arrowed through the trees, calling out high and sweet. But Venick didn't see the sun. He didn't see the bird. He didn't see the elves—six again—who hovered over him, or the grim lines on Ellina's face. He didn't see anything at all.

His condition had worsened. It should bother him that he could no longer feel his leg. That he couldn't feel anything but the dull throb of his heart and the heat of fever, like wildfire on his skin. But Venick was not bothered. Not as Ellina argued with Raffan about leaving him there to die. Not as she forced him to stand and walk—*That is it, just over this ridge*—to the caverns on the other side. Not as one day turned into two, into three, into *many*.

He mostly slept. He didn't dream. Not really, not in the usual way. Sometimes, though, in the deepest quiet of the night, he would open his eyes to the dark cavern ceiling, and blink, and be somewhere else. Back on the shores of Irek, back where he belonged, the wind laughing across the wide ocean, gulls dipping low. He watched the waves swell, felt their salty spray. The water misted his face and dried on his skin, sticky. He closed his eyes and touched his tongue to his lips. Freedom had a taste, Venick thought. Like this, he thought.

He heard a voice. Female. Lorana? He saw her face then, the curve of her mouth as she smiled and begged him back to bed. Venick smiled too. He reached out to take her hand.

Do not die, human, she said. *Don't you dare.*

"I won't," he murmured. "I wouldn't."

But then, the smell of her. Warm, woody. Elven, certainly, but not Lorana. It couldn't be, could it? Because Lorana was…

His heart thumped hard as this dream melted into another. Black night. Moonless. Screams that clawed into his skin, angry shouts, a desperate plea. He ran toward her voice, kicking the door open, ripping it right off its hinges. And there, Lorana in the corner, a broken vase clutched in her bloody fist. It was pitiful, that makeshift weapon against green glass swords and the trio of elves who wielded them.

Venick's heart was in his throat. He'd forgotten how to breathe.

Let her go.

An elf nocked an arrow.

No.

He pulled it tight.

Lorana. Lorana, look at me.

She did, and held his gaze for every moment after. As Venick reached for his sword. As the elf released his arrow. As it pierced her heart and the life raced out of her, *that* quick. Gone.

Gone, or dead?

Say it Venick. Go on.

Dead.

Venick had killed men before. Men were soft, slow. A sword to the gut, the throat. He knew the way it felt to press steel into a man, to feel the resistance and then the give, to see the warm gush of blood.

Killing elves was not like killing men.

They were faster. Stronger. Well-trained and honed for the purpose. Their green glass weapons were light as air and held a wicked edge. But elves, like men, were afraid to die, and in that moment Venick was not.

He killed the three elves with frightening ease. Then he went home and killed his father.

• • •

It was the rain that woke him.

He heard the first light drops across the ground, the soft patter that grew into a steady hiss. There was no thunder—it was too late in the season for it—but the rain was *like* thunder as it echoed through the cave.

The cave. Venick blinked and pushed himself up. He blinked again, this time to clear his head from the last of the dream.

Nightmare, you mean.

Memory, he meant. He had fought three long years to keep those memories away. He fought again now as he took a quick survey of his surroundings. There was a tiny fire that couldn't possibly be for cooking or heat, but maybe for light to illuminate the dark cavern, which was small and empty save for him. And Ellina.

She sat with her back against the wall opposite him. Her shoulders were bare, her armor propped on a nearby stone. She looked different without it. Smaller, somehow. Less predatory. Her hair, too, gave this impression. It was dark, almost black, which was different than the usual moon-white of most elves. Her face, though, was classically elven: high cheekbones and golden eyes that narrowed, now, as she caught him staring.

He cleared his throat. Didn't say *I'm alive*. Wasn't sure that he was. He sat up farther and tested his leg instead, rolling it this way and that, and was relieved to see that the swelling had gone down. He tested the rest of himself, too. He flexed his hands, felt along his jaw and ribs and found, with a blink of surprise, that his knife had been returned to his belt.

"I cannot have you completely helpless," Ellina said. Her lip pulled back in what might have been a smile, and was that—*humor?* Gods.

"You could have let me die."

"Could have."

"But you didn't."

"No." Amused. "Is that what you want? To die?"

Had she asked him that earlier, he would have said no.

And now?

No, gods, *no*. It was the dream that made him hesitate. Venick swallowed hard and forced himself to say it aloud. "I want to live."

"You have been sick," Ellina said. "You still are."

"I am better."

"Better, but not *well*. You would be were we in Evov and I had proper supplies. But." She didn't shrug. That was too human.

"You are *eondghi*. A healer," he said, and made sure to fumble the word.

"It is pronounced *eh-nod-gee*. And no, I am not. I am *joiujon*. A soldier." Which meant whatever she'd done to his foot, she'd learned from the legion. Venick glanced at her armor—light, leather—and then at her face. She was young, he thought, for an elven soldier.

"And the others?"

"Also *joiujon*. Say it back to me." He did. "They are part of my troop."

"And where are they now?"

"Ahead. We will have to catch up."

Ah. Well. That was unlikely, given the speed at which elves traveled and the state of his foot. Venick knew this, and *she* certainly did, and so: "That's not your true plan. Catching up."

"Oh?"

"You're glad to stay back. You have something else in mind."

"Like keeping you alive?" There was no humor in her voice now. Just that steady-eyed stare, the slight lift of her chin. Venick looked away. Down at his hands, which were empty, then out into the rain.

Thank you, Venick. That so hard to say?

Yes, it was. She'd saved his life—what was it? Twice? Three times? Elves didn't deal in life prices, but there was no doubting Venick's belonged to her anyway. And yet, Venick wasn't sure what to feel.

Grateful. Think of that?

Only *grateful* didn't explain the unease that clamped his heart, or the suspicion. The journey from here to Tarrith-Mour would take a fortnight, maybe less. It was not enough time to learn a language, and certainly not *elvish*. He should know. He'd done it once already. Theirs was a language built not just on words but on intent. Words meant themselves and also their opposites, questions could be commands. The language was frustrating and confusing and *poetic*, gods help him. Venick always thought that the only way anyone said what they meant in elvish was because lying was impossible. He thought of his own lies.

They saved your life.

Maybe. Maybe just prolonged it. Elves weren't stupid. Ellina would have already rummaged through his meager belongings—threadbare pack, flint, an empty flask—and guessed that he was not truly a courier for the queen. That he was not a spy, either, as she had suspected. It was true that humans sometimes became involved in elven affairs, but not lone humans, unarmed and half-starved and looking more lost than anything. And yet, instead of leaving him to die Ellina had stayed.

He wondered what reason she would give for that, if asked in her language and not his.

"We have camped here too long," Ellina said. "It is not safe anymore. We will need to move."

"Soon?"

Her eyes slid sidelong out the cavern's mouth. "Tonight."

"Ah."

"I would rather have waited until morning, but our position has been noted."

"And not by wolves, I assume."

"Can you walk?"

No. "Yes."

"There is a trail not far from here. It leads to Kenath."

He knew of it, a border town on the edge of the elflands and the mainlands. "What's in Kenath?"

"Horses. Food. A place to sleep."

"And it's safe?"

"For you it will be." Which meant that for her it wouldn't be. Venick wondered how much to ask. He filtered through a dozen questions before settling on the simplest.

"Who wishes you harm?"

And there again, that not-quite-a-smile. "No one you need to worry about."

"If we're traveling together, I should know."

"No. I will handle any threats. You focus on keeping yourself alive."

Venick dropped his gaze back to the fire: small, hot. Like his shame. And when had he become so helpless, anyway? Venick wasn't used to being helpless. He wasn't used to being *indebted*. A life's price. It didn't matter that Ellina might kill him yet. By the laws of man, that was her choice to make.

So be thankful she wants you alive.

Right. *Thankful*, that was the word. Be *thankful* she knew how to mend a foot, well enough that he wouldn't lose it. Be *thankful* for a trail and a nearby city where he could resupply, maybe find a weapon. A real weapon. A sword, preferably, or an axe.

Then what?

Venick imagined—the image quick, shining—that the clansmen *would* notice his absence. That they would come looking for him. But the thought was so absurd, so impossibly stupid that he hated himself for even considering it. There was no one west of the border to question his disappearance. No one to come after him, no hope of help. He was an outlaw, and unless he could offer his mother a worthy redemption sacrifice, he had no home or family, either.

Maybe he was no better than the bear after all.

He glanced again at Ellina. Elves didn't trust humans, wouldn't trust anything Venick said about their queen or their war unless he spoke in elvish. She'd agreed to teach him, to let him live in exchange for the information he claimed to have. It was a delicate bargain. Unexpected, unstable—and unlikely to end well for Venick, unless he found a way to escape.

And yet, beneath it all there was something else. A small feeling. She'd saved him, cared for him, no matter what her reasons. Venick had forgotten what that was like. It was warm, unfurling under his breastbone. He looked at Ellina and felt his heart sidestep their bargain and his lies. It beat an unsteady rhythm as he gazed at her face, the shadow of her neck, the smooth skin of her shoulders.

She met his eye. Something in his expression changed hers.

Venick blinked. He was thinking—he didn't know what he was thinking. He inhaled a deep breath, held it between his teeth. He forced his mind back to the task ahead, to their destination. Kenath. The city was a half-day's walk to the north. Not an easy feat on an injured foot, but he could make it.

And then?

His gaze drifted to Ellina's weapons. He was lucky to have made it *this* far. If he wanted to survive, he'd have to escape, plain and simple. It was his only option.

FOUR

Ellina did not expect the human to live.

The fever had passed, but his foot was swelling again now that they were forced to walk, and she did not like the look of those stitches. Liked less, the empty-eyed stare, the tight lips. Ellina knew pain when she saw it. She knew determination too, and grit, and a fierce will to survive. He had all three, but simply *wanting* to live was not enough. Not in these lands.

She scouted ahead and behind as they followed the forest trail. She tried not to push him, tried not to say *hurry*. It was still raining, which might have been lucky had she been alone. Heavy rain meant better cover. Rain also meant slick earth and wet clothes and a human who did not need either.

He was younger than she had first suspected, maybe somewhere in his second decade. It was difficult to tell with humans; they did not age as elves did. She glanced at his face, the unshaven scruff, strong jaw, hair pulled back and loose. He did not wear armor and carried no weapon save for that hunting knife, which was not a *real* weapon. He did know how to wield one, though. She could tell by his hands. That particular pattern of calluses was not from chopping wood.

Young, yes, and lost, *yes*, but maybe not so naive. She had seen that in his grey eyes, heard it in his voice in the heat of fever. She had touched his skin and felt its razor burn, had seen his expression morph in pain and anger that had nothing to do with his injury.

Steady, human, she had said to him. She knew better than to wake a man from a dream, and especially a fever-dream. It was said that when men dreamed they walked another earth, and to wake them was to meddle in that other realm. Ellina could not know for sure. Elves did not dream. Still, she had stayed close, and sprinkled the fire with berrybough to ease his mind, and waited for him to wake. She was glad then that the others had gone ahead. She imagined what Raffan would say could he see her now.

You are getting soft, Ellina. He is human. He does not deserve your pity.

But then, pity was not what she felt, was it? He was strange for a human. It was his eyes. Most humans had a way of looking at elves. Quickly, then away, as if they were afraid to stare too long. But this human did not dart his glances. He stared at her full on as an elf might, without a whiff of fear on him.

She kept waiting for it. Waiting for him to show some sign that he feared her. He should. She had pointed her weapons at him, threatened him. She had him at her mercy, but he simply gazed at her with that too-long stare and waited for whatever came next.

Maybe he did not fear her, Ellina thought.

Maybe he was a fool, she thought.

He seemed to sense her gaze and lifted his eyes. Grey, like a winter storm. A wintery smile, too, that he flashed at her now.

Yes, Ellina decided. She was glad that Raffan was not there. Glad, that he did not see her turn away from that smile, the dark resolve that settled into her. And something else, too. The air piqued with some unknown feeling. Uneasy, a little somber. Raffan would know it. He would feel it. He heard and saw and felt *everything*.

Ellina's skin prickled. She suspected Raffan already knew she was hiding her real reason for saving the human. He had to know. And it was obvious, was it not? The human was a liar, their bargain a charade. No elf would believe a human had been sent to Evov to speak with their queen. *She* certainly did not. Ellina was an elite soldier, a scout trained in the art of deceit. That had been their mission before this diversion: to investigate the rumors of southern elven resistance, to observe their enemy. To *spy*. The north and the south had never been allies, but only recently had tensions between their two sides sharpened into something like a weapon, capable of doing violence.

Ellina was not afraid of violence. And yet, she also understood the power of stealth, of gathering evidence, of watching and waiting for a plot to play out.

She thought of the human's plot. The story he told about who he was, the way he lied to convince her to spare his life. Ellina did not have much experience with humans, but dishonesty had a certain flavor, a certain color. She knew it well.

She used it herself.

But Ellina could not let Raffan know her real reason for saving the human. She could not let anyone know. If they found out...

She clamped down on her mess of worries. She was thinking too much. Better not to think at all. Better to watch the shadows, listen to the trees, the rain.

She forced her gaze to the path ahead and marched on.

FIVE

Venick smelled the city before he saw it.

He had never been to Kenath, but he recognized that smell immediately. It was chimney smoke, cooked meat, the sour odor of animals and people shoved together in too-close quarters. A city smell. Different from what he was used to, which was open sea air and mountain. It might have been unwelcome, too, if not for the alternative: a wet forest and an aching leg and a chill that might be the wind. Might also be his fever returning. He tried not to worry over which.

They'd trekked through the night and into the morning without any sign of the not-wolves. The forest was quiet save for Ellina's soft footsteps and Venick's uneven gait and the motherless *rain*. It had frothed and swelled into a true storm, battering them in a way that made Venick wonder if rain could be vengeful, and what he'd done to cause offense. It wasn't until dawn that the rain finally retreated, rolling back into clouds that parted and drifted away.

To reveal Ellina in stark daylight, there, ahead. Venick had only seen snatches of her through the night. She flitted through the trees, finding him long enough to say *keep going* or *watch the path* before disappearing again. Venick might have assumed she was covering their trail if not for the storm there to do that for them. He considered asking, then thought better of it. He didn't expect her to walk with him. He didn't want her to. It was bad enough that he was limping, his bandaged foot sucking and popping in the mud. It took all his concentration just to keep that leg under him without having to pretend otherwise.

No room for your pride, Venick.

And who was he fooling, anyway? Act like he hadn't got his foot caught in a bear trap, act like the metal hadn't sunk into flesh and muscle. It was a wonder he was walking at all. He had considered asking her about that, too. She'd said she wasn't *eondghi*, but she was more skilled than the average soldier. He remembered pieces from the cave, but they were foggy, half-dreamed. The medicines she'd used, something thrown into the fire, leaves wrapped and rewrapped around the wound. How she knelt over him, her dark braid falling across one shoulder. How her hands brushed his cheek, checking for fever. The warmth of them.

"The city," Ellina said from where she stood at the edge of the trees. Venick—damn his stupid pride—forced himself to walk normally as he came to her side. He watched her expression, which was carefully impassive. Her hand, though, had dropped to her sword.

"Trouble?"

"No. No trouble." But she wouldn't quite meet his gaze.

He arched a brow. "Really?"

"Look for yourself if you do not believe me."

He squinted across the meadow towards the city, trying to see what she saw that might cause that stiffness. Kenath was built on a river, a wide valley to the south, sloping hills to the north, grey and red buildings stacked to either side. It was a border city, sprawled across the invisible boundary between the elflands and the mainlands and one of the few places where elves and men could meet freely. It was also north of the southern forests and therefore in the north's domain. Ellina should be safe in such a city.

And yet, her hand on her weapon. And yet, the set to her shoulders, the tightness behind her eyes.

Venick didn't understand it. He scanned the watchtowers, the rooftops, but he couldn't make out much else from this distance other than that the city was bigger than he had imagined, and tightly packed. But that was nothing unusual.

"I don't see anything," he admitted.

"Then there is nothing to see."

But Venick was unconvinced. He remained alert as they followed the trail down into the meadow, as the soft earth turned into paved road, which led them through the gates. The city was human-built, the stone and slate set over the hills rather than dug into them as elves would have done. The river was high and swift from the recent rain, the streets slick. Crowded, too, as Venick had imagined, but mostly with humans. For a border city, there weren't many elves.

None at all, now that he looked, except for Ellina. Venick peered around, searching for the telltale golden eyes, the white hair. Nothing.

And yet, that couldn't be right. Because here: a horse wearing an elven-woven blanket. Here: elven glyphs carved into the side of a cart. And here: the sliding eyes of strangers, too keen. Had they been back in Irek, Venick might have understood that suspicion, but Kenath was no small town to worry over newcomers.

Ellina led them through the streets, which followed no obvious pattern. Some were wide and straight, others curved, slanted, paved in brick or stone or some combination of the two. That was typical of manmade cities, especially on the border. There were no quarries this far east. No reliable overlords, either, to see a project through. This city had likely been built bit by bit, perhaps mauled down during a war and rebuilt differently after. Some would argue all cities should be built in such a way. It made them less susceptible to attack when there was no clear path in or out.

It made the citizens susceptible, too.

It made Venick's skin itch, is what it did, as he peered up and behind. It might have been his imagination, the shadow sliding behind the window overhead, another on the roof above. His imagination, the way the crowd seemed to part for them, keeping distance, making room. But he didn't think so.

"Ellina," Venick said, perfectly calm. "Want to tell me why you've led us into an ambush?"

"It is not an ambush."

"Want to teach me elvish for *the hell it's not?*"

"Elves do not curse. And stop looking around. We are almost there."

There turned out to be a tavern wedged between a whorehouse and the river. The exterior had been painted and then painted over again, the edges cracked and peeling in the sun. The door slid smoothly when pushed. Silent. Well-oiled. Ellina led the way upstairs, past a few empty tables and the bartender who glanced up, then away. As if he didn't see them. As if he'd been bribed not to.

Venick swallowed and wondered, for the first time, who Ellina really was.

He wondered if he was an idiot for not wondering sooner.

The stairs led to more rooms. Dark, musty, mostly empty. Ellina strode to the one at the end, pulling him through and closing the door behind them. She crossed to the window and drew the curtain shut, then knelt to pull up a floorboard with a twist and a *snap*. She retrieved a dagger and a coin purse from the space underneath. Which she pushed into *his* hands.

The realization cracked open inside him.

"The southern elves have seen you with me, but you are human," she said. Fast. A little breathless. "They have no reason to harm you."

"Ellina."

"If they stop you, you tell them you know nothing. You *lie*, human. That is what you are good at, is it not? Wait a few days. Act as if you are just passing through. And then you leave. *Home*, back on your own side of the border."

And where is home, Venick?

He didn't know. It didn't matter, either. Not right now. No, what mattered now was that gaze, two golden eyes waiting for him to respond, to tell her he understood.

And do you?

That she never had any intention of taking him to Tarrith-Mour, yes. That she never planned to kill him, yes. That she knew he didn't have information for her queen, that she lied to her troop to save him, *yes*. Remember that conversation now, Venick. Remember the male's question—*You think he is a spy for the south*—and her answer, in *his* language.

Reeking gods.

"You said the city would be safe," he said.

"I said the city would be safe for you. And it is."

A wise man wouldn't ask questions. A wise man would take the money and the dagger and hope never to see this elf again. A wise man certainly wouldn't argue. It didn't matter that she had lied for him and mended his foot and asked for nothing in return. Elves didn't deal in life prices, didn't think in terms of debts paid.

But.

"I don't understand," Venick said. "*Why?* Why help me?"

"Consider it a blessing from one of your gods."

"Elves don't believe in gods." Venick pushed a hand into his hair. He should be dead. He'd trespassed into the elflands, and lied about his reasons, and Ellina *knew*, and she saved him anyway. He owed her his life. Three times over he did. "You risked yourself for me."

"I risked nothing." Her chin lifted, eyes flashing. Damn him if that wasn't pride.

"That so?"

"Yes." She ghosted a smile, already turning to leave. "Be thankful, human, that you are not the only one who lies."

• • •

Venick decided he would count to one hundred, then he would follow her.

One.

He could still see that flicker-smile on her face, the one she'd given him before turning on her heel and striding back out the way they had come.

Two.

He could see everything the smile was meant to hide. The tension. The worry.

Three.

He watched her touch the hilt of her sword. Her fingers traced its edges.

Four.

Venick went to the bedroom window. He beat a light fist against the glass, then opened his palm to feel its cool surface. He could not understand why she'd chosen to help him. Why she'd lied to her comrades, created excuses to bring him to safety. She *had* risked herself.

He thought again of the shadows in the windows, on the roofs. He imagined who might be following her. Who might wish her harm.

He shouldn't care. He was an outlaw. He had no duty to anyone, no reason to honor his life price. He was not honorable. Maybe he had been once, but that was before he'd murdered his father and fled into exile. Three years in the mountains had hardened him, severed all loyalties, made him forget what it meant to fight for someone else.

Except, Venick felt the pull of it. Rusty, stiff like an unused muscle. A desire to help, to *do*. An unease at being indebted, a shame that he would even consider ignoring his debts. A memory of a time when he'd befriended an elf, loved her, would have done anything for her. Another memory, this one of Ellina in the forest, the gentle way she had touched his face when he was fever-dreaming. The surprise at discovering her gentleness.

Venick understood that his exile had hardened him. But as he gazed out the window, a plan taking shape in his mind, he thought maybe it hadn't changed him. Not really.

Five.

Count to five, then. Close enough.

He tucked the dagger into his belt and went out the door.

SIX

Ellina forced herself to walk.

It would do no good to run. Running was for open spaces. For when you knew the city, knew the streets and the slopes and the tide of the crowd. For when you had somewhere *to* run. But Ellina did not know this city. She did not know the hidden paths or alleys like she knew the ones in Evov. If she ran, she would meet a dead end. She would become stuck against the river. And then she would be trapped.

No. Better to walk and wait. Count her steps, count the arrows at her back. Count the shadows trailing her.

Four, so far as she could tell. Two behind, two on the roofs above. She did not need to see their faces to know they were southern elves, the same ones who had hunted her in the forest. She could tell by the way their shadows seemed to follow her, peeling away from windows and corners in pursuit. That was not a trick of the light. That was conjuring.

And a skill Ellina did not possess. No northern elves did. Usually, she felt glad that she did not have that witch-magic inside her. It was bad enough that her hair was dark, almost as black as the shadows that followed her. Black hair was rare among elves and rarer still among northerners. If not for the certainty of her heritage, she might have been called a bastard fledgling and cast out to the wild for it.

Now, though, she would not mind some of a conjuror's skill. To weave the shadows over herself and disappear.

Ellina took a hard right, moving under a sky of merchant flags. They fanned in the wind, the sound of them filling the air. There were other sounds, too. The bay of a goat. The angry burst of a child. The hush of a crowd sensing danger, an almost imperceptible change.

Ellina risked a glance behind her and caught sight of golden eyes.

She pushed forward, through bodies, past guards. They were a false comfort. The crowd was. Humans did not intervene in elven affairs and could not be counted on to help. No. Better to escape back to the forest. There, she knew how to cover both her scent and her trail. There, her troop waited for her. There, she could disappear.

She turned back towards the river, skirting down a narrow alley. She trailed her hand across the brick and stone. Smooth, no crevices for climbing. The only option was forward. She wished she had thought to wear a hood. She wished she had *thought*. But she had been busy, her mind full of the human. Keeping him safe, keeping him alive. There was no room for anything else. Raffan would skin her could he see what she risked for him, let alone *why*. It was bad enough that she had broken ranks and chosen to stay behind with false promises to question the human further. She made those promises in the language of men, a testament to her dishonesty. But Raffan had let her go anyway.

He would punish her. In front of others, if she was lucky. In private if she was not. Ellina outranked him in blood titles, but he outranked her in the legion. And now that they were bondmates, he outranked her in *both*. He could exact whatever punishment he wanted and be well within his right. And he would enjoy punishing her, no matter in public or private. It was why he said nothing of her obvious lies. He let her disobey him. He wanted her to.

Ellina could hear the river now. It churned, a low hum. She flexed her hands, touched the sword at her hip. She could draw it. *That* might gain her some human attention. Or it might prompt her pursuers to act faster, to subdue her before she could cause a scene.

As they seemed to intend now. She could sense them close behind. Moving closer. A too-long shadow flitted across her vision. Another angled beside her.

She wrapped her fingers firmly around the hilt of her sword. Fight, or flee?

One breath. Another.

She turned and drew her weapon.

SEVEN

Venick had never liked the sound of green glass.

It wasn't like the clang of steel, which was hard and cold and solid. Not like the swoop of an axe or the strum of a bow. Green glass said *shh*, a mother to her child. It was low and soft. Animal.

And clear, now, as it hissed through the air.

Venick cursed. He ignored his bad leg, the way the stitches pulled. Ignored his pounding heart, which had vacated his chest and clawed up his throat. He darted glances through the crowd, moving as fast as space and injury would allow, praying his leg wouldn't give, praying he wasn't too late. He didn't imagine what he would see if he was. Didn't imagine the reason green glass echoed through the streets, Ellina backed into a corner, her pupils blown wide, an arrow through her heart. He did *not*.

And yet, Venick couldn't quite help but hear Ellina's words, the surety in them. *We elves do not kill our own.* She might have spoken in elvish, how certain she was of that truth. Yes, elves would maim and fight and torture, but this was old law, one she thought was never broken.

She was wrong.

The memory slipped inside him before he could stop it. Lorana's screams. The flash of an arrow. His own voice, hoarse, desperate. The way he'd fought to reach her. He felt panic rising, and couldn't tell if it was true panic or the memory of panic. Time layered over things, made his mind foggy. He remembered Lorana's panic too, the way it gripped her, a black claw sunk into flesh. But then that terror had calmed, vanished, replaced by steady silence as she realized she was going to die and there was nothing Venick could do to save her.

Venick clenched his jaw and forced those thoughts away, forced himself to see the *now* and not the past.

Ellina is not Lorana.

But she wasn't no one, either.

Venick turned a corner, then another, hating Kenath's streets for being too narrow and too winding and too crowded, so packed full of people that no one noticed him until he was shoving them aside with a *move* and a curse.

And still too slow.

But then, there. A flash of green. And *there*. Ellina. He saw her in plain sight, caught between the market and the river, surrounded by four elves with weapons drawn.

Venick's fear vanished then, anger crowding in its place. At the human guards who watched but did nothing because it was not their race and therefore not their problem. At the elves who had her cornered. And at Ellina, who had drawn her weapon but was doing a worthless job of using it. Venick had seen Ellina when she wanted something dead. He remembered how she'd killed the wolves in the forest, the skilled strokes, effortless and without hesitation. But she was holding back now, speaking in low tones as the four elves advanced, parrying their strikes but attempting none of her own. As if she was afraid to hurt them. As if she refused to kill.

And all Venick had was a dagger.

And an idea.

A lousy one. But there was no time to think of anything better.

He pushed towards her. He caught the surprise in her eye as she spotted him, the confusion and then the fear as she realized what he intended. She shook her head once, quickly. *Don't.*

Too late.

Venick stepped into the space created by wary onlookers. He didn't pull out the dagger. Four long strides brought him to the closest elf, who spun at the look on Ellina's face, who wasn't expecting an attack and therefore didn't raise his weapon.

Venick heaved a punch. He aimed for the jaw and missed. The blow struck the elf's windpipe instead with a *thump* and a whoosh of air. Crushed it. The elf heaved, then stumbled, clutching his neck. And now Venick did draw Ellina's dagger, which was useless against swords but made a fine distraction as he cocked his arm as if to throw. And yes, three pairs of golden eyes on him, weapons up and exposed as Ellina took the opportunity he created for her, folding into the space and swiping her blade across another's calves, ripping flesh and muscle. Crippling but not deadly.

Venick threw the dagger then and missed. He drew his hunting knife into his hand next. No good history of hitting things with that weapon either, so Venick didn't try. He held onto it as one of the two remaining elves came at him, green glass flashing, and *damn* he was fast. Venick dodged the first strike, then the second, but not the third.

The sword slashed his chest, flayed open the skin. A pain that broke his vision.

Stay on your feet.

He did, somehow. He managed to stumble backwards out of reach as Ellina stepped between him and the elf, as she parried another strike, hissing in elvish, and then just *hissing*, angry and gritty and fending off the attack with a skill that was beyond any of them, that could have ended in four southern elves dead had she only chosen it.

Venick lurched sideways under a swipe of green glass and up by Ellina's side. He felt the spray of the river at his feet. He saw the shadows of buildings on either side, the white eyes of the crowd who watched the fight in fascination, who by doing so blocked any easy chance at escape. There was no way they would win, not unless Ellina decided to start *killing*, and she wasn't.

Venick spun then. He wished to offer an apology, an explanation, but he managed only a grunt as he grabbed Ellina around the waist and swung her into the river. Time seemed to slow. It stretched thin. Venick could see each piece of the moment, every beat of seconds passing. He saw Ellina's hair in the wind. The sword still in her hand. Her eyes wide, shocked. She hit the water and her head disappeared under the surface.

There was a moment of terror. Venick felt it under his skin, down between his ribs. Because elves couldn't swim.

Ah, Venick. But that's the point, isn't it?

He didn't look back to see if the other elves understood what he had done or if they would follow. He knew they wouldn't.

He sucked in a lungful of air and jumped in after her.

• • •

The river was exactly as Venick knew it would be: cold and furious. It slapped the breath out of him and whipped him under, pulling him feet-first through the black water. Venick let it. He relaxed and didn't struggle, waited for the current to bring him up for air.

Which it did, briefly, before sucking him under again. Venick held his breath until it ached. He pretended he was back home, pretended these were Irek's currents, the ones he knew by heart. Venick had grown up in those waters. He understood the way the tides came in and out, how to recognize a rip in the current, the way the water would heave and buckle. The way his pulse would jump before he remembered not to panic, to time his breaths and wait for the ocean to release him, which it always did safely near the shore. Venick had learned that all water was like that: conquerable, if you knew what to do.

He waited for the river to toss him up a second time, then a third without making any attempt to swim. But then the river turned a bend. It widened and slowed just a bit. Enough. Venick kicked and brought himself to the surface.

It was easier to stay afloat now. He let the water propel him as he looked for a head of black against brown waves.

And saw nothing.

Dread kicked him in the gut. He beat it away, forced himself to focus. It occurred to Venick that Ellina might not have made it this far. It occurred to him that *she* didn't know how to relax into waves. Even if she did, he'd given her no time to prepare. Instinct and cold would make her inhale. Fear would make her struggle.

The waves rolled. Their silvery reflection in the sunlight blinded. They lapped against the seawall on either side. There was nothing to hold onto out here, not a single boat in the water, no one to see her and pull her to safety. Had this been Irek, the river would be teeming with rowboats, maybe a few larger vessels. Not here. The people of Kenath weren't fishermen. The elves certainly weren't.

The current began to strengthen again. It roiled, pulling at him on all sides. His ears were full of water. His eyes were. And still no sign of Ellina. He began to lose the reins on his own composure, began doing everything he'd been taught not to. He swam against the current. He called Ellina's name, shouting himself breathless. He had no way to know how far the river had taken her. No way to know if she had swallowed a lungful of water. If she was floating somewhere under the surface.

Until he spotted her just ahead, clutching the vertical bars of a sewage grate with one white-knuckled hand. In the other hand, her sword, which she'd somehow managed to keep hold of. Relief flooded him, hot and heavy. He used much of his remaining strength to swim to her. "Ellina."

"You are a *fool*." Anger rolled off her in waves, more violent than the current.

"We're still too exposed. We might be seen. We need to move."

"I told you to *leave*. But does the human listen? No. The human follows and tries to get us *both* killed."

He didn't bother responding to that. There would be time for her anger later. Now, though, they were losing warmth and energy and needed to move. "I'm going to get you out."

"No." She bit off the word, hard and flat and maybe a little frightened. Venick softened.

"It's just water, Ellina. It can't hurt you." Which wasn't true, not for elves who could hunt and fight and climb better than any human but who couldn't swim to save their lives. It was meant to be a secret among their race, not something they wanted humans knowing. As it was, Venick did know. And he could swim well enough for the both of them. "I won't let you drown."

He was asking her to trust him. There was no reason she should, not after he'd thrown her down here in the first place, even if it *was* to save her. But he saw her study him, saw her wet and cold and yes, there, *frightened.*

Hell, Venick.

Better than let her die.

Which she would have, had that fight gone on a moment longer, and damn her elven laws.

"Ellina," he said. He moved closer and pretended not to notice her flinch away. A quick glance downstream confirmed his suspicion: each end of the river was blocked by a tall metal grate where the city wall crossed the water. They could not escape that way. But: "There's a ladder not far from here. Near your hideout. We just have to make it there."

"We cannot go back there. We were seen."

"The whorehouse next door, then."

She wanted to refuse. He could see that refusal in her every fiber. But he saw the quality of her gaze, the way it changed from firm denial to something more reluctant. And then, finally, she gave a tight-lipped nod that he took for a *yes.*

Venick wanted to be gentle. It was important, suddenly, that he did not frighten her more, that she understood what he was doing as he moved closer, as he wrapped a strong arm across her body and carefully, so carefully, pulled them back into the water. He watched Ellina's face, measuring her reaction. *Trust me,* he wanted to say, but didn't. He thought the words instead. *Trust me.*

And he saw it. He saw the way her shoulders relaxed, how her eyes lost their glazy fear. Her breath tickled his neck. Her hair ribboned along the water's surface. And there, like he promised, a ladder that brought them to safety.

EIGHT

Venick entered the brothel soaking wet. His slopping footsteps left smears on the hardwood, shining patterns in the dim light. Just water. Not blood. Not a cut reopened and bleeding again.

Believe that.

He refused to look at it. He refused to look at his chest where the elf had sliced him, either. He looked instead into the dim room, through the plume of perfume and smoke that stung his nose and eyes and throat. It was made to be hazy on purpose, he thought. The smoke was bad for guests, but it was safer for the mistress to be able to appraise him first, to size him up, check for weapons, note the quality of his clothing, glean whatever she could from that.

Which she did now, shifting shadow-smooth towards him from across the room. She was his mother's age. His mother's height. But she had light skin, light hair, a white smile that was anything but motherly.

She took in his threadbare clothing drenched in water and blood and did not like what she saw. Venick was prepared for that. "I can pay," he said, and pushed Ellina's coins into her hand. She glanced at the money. Her smile changed.

Next came the women. They were mostly flatlanders with fair eyes and silky hair, but a few were small and dark, from the coast, Venick thought, or the mountains. They were all human. All half-clothed, too, in golden chains and sheer fabric that hid nothing.

Venick cleared his throat and remembered Ellina's words, muttered hastily as they'd darted through alleys to get here. *Pick the youngest. The shyest. Someone who looks easily frightened.* As if they were discussing which deer to fell, the weakest link. Only, none of these women looked easily frightened. And they were all young.

He pointed at the one he thought most modest and tried to look anywhere else, which got the girls giggling.

"He's shy," the mistress tutted. "Aza will fix that."

The woman named Aza stepped forward. She had long black hair woven in thick coastal-style braids and a smile that looked almost genuine. Her bracelets clinked as she reached for his hand. Venick jerked away without thinking.

Idiot.

Aza gave him a curious look, her eyes lingering on his blood-stained tunic. "You have had a—*stressful* day," she decided after a breath. "Let's get you out of those wet clothes. Come, I will help you."

This time Venick forced himself steady, forced himself to relax as she slid slender fingers through his. Her skin was velvety smooth, impossibly so. Or had he simply forgotten what a woman's skin felt like? He thought of Ellina, of her hands on him in the forest, then again in the river. He tried to remember what *her* skin was like.

Enough, Venick.

But he couldn't quite help the burn that crept into his cheeks as Aza led him up the stairs and into a private room. Couldn't quite help his nervousness, either, as she started to undress. She watched him with dark eyes, flashing a lazy smile that had him wondering how he ever thought her modest.

"No," Venick managed as she reached a hand for his belt. "I'm not— I don't—"

Ellina chose that moment to appear. She came through the window, the loose glass panes shuddering in their sockets as she forced it open. Aza and Venick both jumped as Ellina stepped inside, surveying the room and the whore and Venick's half-undone belt in one swift glance. Venick swallowed and stayed silent, feeling as if he had been caught doing something he shouldn't, and never mind that this was the plan all along.

"Say nothing," Ellina ordered Aza. Her hand fell to the weapon at her belt. "If you scream, I will—"

Too late. Aza opened her mouth and sucked in a lungful of air. She would have rattled the walls with that scream had she managed to get it out. She didn't. Ellina was there in an instant, dagger out, ramming the hilt into the girl's temple. The scream was cut short, breaking into something that sounded more like a shriek of delight, and no shortage of those around here. She crumpled to the floor where she lay motionless.

Venick might have thought her dead, had Ellina been another elf. She *would* be dead, had Ellina been another elf. But Ellina was not another elf, and so Venick caught the shallow rise and fall of Aza's chest and knew she lived.

It was uncertain how much time they had, then, before she woke and screamed for real. Venick had paid the mistress handsomely, more than enough to cover the room for the night. They would be safe to hide here until nightfall, assuming Aza stayed unconscious. If she *did* wake, though, and if she *did* scream, the mistress would surely come to investigate, and then they would have to kill them both, or run.

Venick wondered how far Ellina's charity would stretch if it came to that.

Not far, given her expression as she turned to face him. He expected anger, which he got, a full-on glare that felt like a slap. He expected argument, too, but she said only: "You are bleeding again."

Venick touched a finger to his chest. It came away sticky. "The southerners would have killed you," he said in answer.

"Elves do not—"

"Enough with that. Elves *do*. I told you already. I've seen it."

She drew a sharp breath in through her nose and her anger deepened, spread and darkened like a bruise. "You are wrong."

"So maybe they won't kill you." Venick heard the way his own anger—sudden, unexpected—graveled his voice. "Maybe they'll just capture you. Torture you. And don't tell me *that's* against elven laws. I know it isn't."

"I can handle the southerners."

"Is that what you were doing? Because from what I saw your sword was barely up. You forget how to use it?"

Her gaze cooled. "You ran into a swordfight with a dagger."

"And I would again."

"You *are* a fool."

"Next time, you fight back. You *defend* yourself."

"You are not responsible for me."

Which caught Venick under the ribs, a dagger-sharp twist of pain that felt like *hurt* and *truth* all mixed together. It was what she had said from the start. What he had known all along. *I will handle any threats. You focus on keeping yourself alive.*

He hadn't listened. Hadn't wanted to listen. But here was the truth. He saw it in Ellina's golden eyes, in the animal grace that made her what she was. She was an elf, and he was a human, and whatever debts he felt he owed her were not truly his to pay. Besides, he'd seen her skill with a blade. The northern legion was known for it. She could have killed her attackers in a few quick moves, could have ended the whole chase in a breath.

Only, she hadn't. Only, she *wouldn't*. He'd seen the way she clung to law and honor and whatever other ridiculous notions she valued over her own life. But she had to know, didn't she, that not all elves could be trusted to do the same?

She did know. He'd seen the worry on her face in the tavern. He'd seen it again as she fended off the elves by the river. He thought of those elves, how they'd trailed them through the forest, into the city. He imagined Ellina captured, Ellina tortured.

He shouldn't care. But he did.

"I couldn't just leave," he said.

"You would if you had any sense of self-preservation. You would if you understood."

"Enlighten me, then."

He didn't think she would rise to that bait, and she didn't, not at first. She walked back to the window to draw the curtains closed, then to the door, which she cracked open to peer into the hall. A split-second glance, then sliding it shut. The lock was silent when she bolted it.

She turned back to face him. Her eyes shifted to his chest, then to his foot, her gaze narrowing as it had that first day in the forest. "You should sit."

Venick shrugged that away. "It's just a little blood."

"It is not just a little blood. Sit and let me look, and I will answer your questions."

A bargain. He'd made one of those with her before.

Venick looked down at himself. He saw the river mud and soaked clothes and yes, blood. Bright red and fresh, but not so painful. Not like before, which gave him hope. Maybe the cut on his chest wasn't so bad. Maybe the stitches weren't torn.

Maybe you should sit and let the eondghi do her job.

He sat.

She had no supplies this time, no fresh leaves to heal the wound. He sat on the bed and she knelt beside him, examining the swollen flesh. Then, one by one, she began picking out the ruined thread.

Venick made no noise. He clenched the sheets and his breath as Ellina loosened the stitches and the wound reopened. As she pulled a needle from her braid and threaded twine through it, then began at it again.

Needle and thread and a wound sewed tight. They'd done this before, too.

"Do you know why we elves do not kill each other?" Ellina asked after a time. When Venick didn't reply, she said, "It is because our race is dying."

Venick blinked. He drew his gaze back to her. "That's only a rumor."

"*Ish nan amas*," she replied in elvish. *It is no rumor.* Then again in his language. "More elves die each year than are born. Elven children are rare. Elven partners are. We live long lives. Elves do not marry like humans do. To commit to one elf for hundreds of years…" She shook her head. "We do not. And a child? For two elves to form that sort of commitment is…complicated. A child is *like* a marriage for us. And so elves do not do that either. During the hundred childless years, only a handful of elven fledglings were born. Our queen began to worry, so she *made* us have children. She forced bonded pairs, arranged births. And she prohibited elves from loving humans."

Venick had gone very still. Ellina paused to look up at him.

"It was easy for elves to love humans," Ellina went on. "With a human, there is no fear of a lifelong commitment, because elves outlive humans. There is no fear of siring a child, because elves and humans cannot bear children. It became more common for elves to find human partners than elven ones. And so the law was changed."

"I know the law." His voice was like ice. His heart was.

"Then you know it is nearly impossible to enforce. The best chance is to keep humans and elves separate. You understand the border was drawn for that reason. And you understand the danger."

"No. I understand why I'm not allowed east of the border, which I knew already. But you still haven't told me why you were attacked."

"I am a northern soldier. I was caught in southern lands."

"That's hardly a reason."

"Maybe not. Unless we are at war."

"And *are* you at war?" No sense in pretending he had answers now. She knew he didn't.

"Yes." Ellina didn't smile, not quite, but he heard the irony in her tone. "This time, though, it is not a political war." And now she definitely wasn't smiling. Her brow knit, face suddenly somber. "The north and south both agree that these laws—the ones that keeps elves and humans separate—are for the best. What we do not agree on is what happens to elves who break them. In the north, if you pursue a relationship with a human, you are banished."

"And in the south?"

"You die."

"But you just said—"

"An honor suicide," Ellina interrupted with a hand. Venick drew back.

"An elf will kill herself?"

"Yes, but often under pressure. And that is the issue. Forcing an elf to commit suicide—it is no better than murder. And it makes no sense. Why create laws to protect our race, only to kill elves who disobey them? The southerners are working against their own goals. Honor suicides help no one, but the south…" Ellina let out a breath. "They are unstable. They have no ruler, no sovereignty. That is why our queen chose to step in. Queen Rishiana does not rule the south, not truly, but she has always had power over the southerners simply because the north is strong. She threatened to act unless the southerners stopped pressuring each other into suicide."

"Which they haven't," Venick guessed.

Ellina nodded. "Reports of these suicides have continued to rise. That was our mission here. To investigate the rumor of another honor suicide in Tarrith-Mour, to spy on the southerners, and to stop them where we can." Simply. Which it wasn't.

It would be easier to leave it at that. Easier to nod and say *I see* and go back to not asking. Harder, to imagine what forced honor suicides meant for elves. Harder, to picture Lorana, to see her face in his memory. Terrible, impossible, to remember the way she had died, to know exactly the price of these elven laws.

Venick's anger returned, not bright like before, but dark, serpentine. He hated to remember that night. Hated that no matter how he tried to forget, he couldn't forget *this*: that Lorana had been a southerner, and she had loved a human, and she was dead because of it. Venick remembered the broken shard of glass she'd held in her hands as the elves surrounded her. How it cut into the meat of her palm, bled down her wrist. He had always thought that weapon was a last attempt to live, but Ellina's story made him see things differently. Maybe Lorana hadn't intended to fight.

Maybe she'd been forced to make a different choice.

Venick closed his eyes. He was unraveling, coming apart at this new and frightening thought. He remembered that night, suddenly, starkly, but also other nights. Lorana on Irek's shore. Lorana handing him a little pressed flower. Lorana in the market, dodging the playful nip of a horse. Venick couldn't imagine her taking her own life. He was repulsed. He repulsed himself, that he would even consider it.

And yet, the shard of vase. And yet, the law. He remembered the look in her eye, the hopelessness that was too much like resolve. As if she knew she was going to die. As if she accepted it.

Venick opened his eyes, tried to pull himself out of the syrupy web of his own feelings, tried to keep his voice calm as he spoke next. He reminded himself that whatever Lorana intended, she *hadn't* ended her life. A southern arrow through her heart did that.

"You can't know what the southern elves would do," Venick insisted. Ellina raised a brow. "If they capture you." He closed his eyes again. Opened them. He saw Ellina's face, which was elven, which wasn't so different from Lorana's. "You said it yourself. You are a northern soldier spying in southern lands. You are their enemy. And the southerners don't honor your queen's laws. You can't know that they won't kill you."

"It is too politically risky. They would not."

"Still." He shook his head. Venick understood that elves did not fight wars like humans did. Their battles were usually political, waged with cunning and compromise over steel and blood. Regardless, war was war. It could be messy. The rules only worked if both sides chose to obey, and they wouldn't. They weren't. "Coming to Kenath, exposing yourself to these southern elves who hunt you. It is wrong for you to take that kind of risk." He met her gaze. "It was wrong for you to take it. For me."

Ellina dropped her eyes, suddenly busy at her task. There was a long stretch of silence. Venick became conscious of her hands on his skin. He noticed that her hands were not like Aza's but like his: hard, callused.

Ellina finished the stitching, then stood. Venick stood too, aware that the air had changed between them. He flexed his foot, needing something to do. The stitches pulled but held. He looked at his chest next, feeling the cut's edges, the nerve-dead skin. The bleeding seemed less. The cut was long but not deep.

"It will be dark soon," Venick finally said. "I don't think it's safe to return to the market for supplies, but we can search these rooms for food and fresh clothing." And weapons. Ellina had her bow, dagger and sword and he his hunting knife, but Venick was useless with a knife in a fight. Better to have a sword of his own, or an axe. A hammer, even. Something he could heft and swing. "We'll hide out here until nightfall."

"The southern elves will not be hindered by nightfall."

"Then we'll search the rooms and leave now."

"They will be watching the gates."

"There is more than one way out of a city." Ask how he knew that. Ask when *he'd* ever had to escape a city. Well, he had, and with more than a few elves at his back.

But that wasn't why Ellina was hesitating. Venick knew this even before she turned away from him, even before he caught a glimpse of some quiet emotion on her face. "I have told you already," she said. "You owe me no debts."

But Venick smiled. "By my reckoning, I still owe you two."

NINE

Dusk came anyway, shifting quickly to night, reducing Kenath to splotchy black shadows cut only by yellow pools of light from lanterns and windows. After a quick search of the upper rooms they'd found nothing of use, save for a row of boots, shirts, and a drawer full of jekkis. Venick eased his bandaged foot into one of the boots and traded his torn shirt for a fresh one, and Ellina stuffed the jekkis into her pocket.

"To trade," she'd told him in response to his raised brow. "Elves do not smoke."

There were a lot of things elves didn't do, he'd wanted to say back, but didn't. He nodded instead because she was right. Jekkis was illegal on both sides of the border, and that meant it was valuable. They might be able to sell it or trade it for things they really needed: weapons, shelter.

Black market thief, are you now?

Whatever got them to safety.

After, they'd returned to their room to find Aza gone, her clothing still heaped in a bundle on the floor. Venick stooped to pick up the garment. The thin fabric was liquid between his fingers. A moment later, shouts erupted downstairs. He glanced up at Ellina in alarm.

Time to move, then. Quickly.

Venick followed Ellina out through the window and back into the streets, which were empty. They would not have been, had this been any other human city. Even Irek's people stayed out past dark, drinking or telling stories. But not here, not in a border city. It was too easy to get caught where you shouldn't be, too easy to wind up missing or dead. People were wary, and so everyone went in at dusk, closing shutters and drawing curtains and waiting for dawn to wake again.

There was a time when Venick might have been grateful for empty streets. Might have welcomed the quiet dark, the way he could see whole spans of the city without the crowd to block his view. But not now. Not as he heard the chime of the bell tower sounding the alarm, the bay of dogs that followed.

Venick gritted his teeth. They couldn't have been gone from the room for more than a few minutes, which meant Aza had likely woken long before, had lain in wait for the right moment to flee and call the guards. They should have tied her up while they had the chance. Should have—

"*Meit lai,*" Ellina hissed, tugging him sharply down an alley. *This way.*

They turned a corner, then another. The darkness consumed them. There was no moonlight here, no lanterns. Venick was painfully aware of his bad leg, awkward and stiff underneath him. It would be easy to trip in this dark, to become cornered with nowhere to run. Easy to imagine the dogs following their trail, closing in on them like the wane-

rest.

ile consumed by that vision, to forget to watch the path

k didn't see the elf. Didn't see Ellina skid to a halt or throw out her arm until he was crashing into her. But then Venick did see. A sudden figure appeared, tall and waiting at the end of the alley. Venick's heart lurched as he pulled his hunting knife into his hand. Ellina stepped towards the elf, and of course *she* didn't draw her weapon, hell and *damn* her stupid—

"Dourin," Ellina breathed. "I told you not to come for me."

"I am glad I did not listen," the elf snapped, closing the gap between them. "They have the whole kennel on the hunt. What did you *do?*"

"Later," Ellina said, then turned to Venick, who was lowering his knife, who was quickly coming to understand. He didn't recognize this elf, not at first, not in the dark, but Venick did recognize the leather legion armor and realized this must be one of the six members of Ellina's troop.

"You still have the human with you," Dourin said as if noticing Venick for the first time.

"He is coming with us."

It was difficult to make out Dourin's features, but Venick didn't miss the scowl, the sudden stiffness that was elvish for *the hell he is*. "The southerners have seen him with me," Ellina explained. "He helped me escape. They will kill him."

"And? He was not supposed to live anyway."

"They will interrogate him."

"Like you did?"

"Careful." Ellina didn't change her tone, but Venick saw the sudden shift of power, the way Dourin dipped his head and flicked his fingers. It was a gesture with many meanings. *Apology*, it meant now. *Deference*. "He comes," she repeated as they began moving again. Quickly, worried that they'd wasted too much time already.

"I do not suppose he knows how to scale a city wall?"

"Ask *him*, Dourin."

It was only then that Venick realized they'd been speaking in elvish. Realized, too late, that he looked as if he understood. He turned his face more deeply into the shadows, hoping that if they'd caught a glimpse of his expression before, they would look again now and see nothing.

"Well, human?" Dourin asked in mainlander. "Can you climb?"

"We cannot leave over the wall."

Dourin made an impatient gesture. "So says *you*."

"They've rung the bells," Venick said, attempting to keep the frustration from his voice. The urgency, though, he let ring clear. "That means a full party search. Whatever the dogs miss, the watchmen in the towers will catch."

"It will not matter. I have horses waiting on the other side. By the time they see us, we will be gone."

"Maybe. Except it's not just men we're running from." Which brought him to his next thought, the one that had tugged on the corner of his mind since he'd heard the first bell ring. Since before then, even. He remembered walking into Kenath, the suspicious eyes of the crowd, the way the streets had emptied of elves. He remembered the shadows in the window, on the roof, how quickly the southern elves had caught their trail. Like they'd been waiting. Or told.

And now, the sound of a hunt. Full party searches were rare. Guards—especially *border city* guards—were happier to let citizens sort out their own justice. But now they had launched a search, and for what? Because Ellina had assaulted a wench? And since when had guards ever cared about that?

And then, another memory. Venick had been young, a child of six or seven the first time his father brought him into his study and began teaching him tactics of war. Venick remembered his father's heavy hand on his shoulder, the smell of leather and oil. And in himself, a pleasure, a desire to please. His father had retired from the military after a knee injury left him with a permanent limp, but he was determined to instill in his son everything he knew.

Here is how the people of the grasslands won the city of Aras, his father said. *Here is how we won it back*, he said.

The story was fuzzy in Venick's memory. An uprising. Stealth attacks. Poisoned horses, burned supply wagons. The people of the grasslands were weaker, but they had somehow managed to bribe or kill their way into positions of power within the city of Aras. They infiltrated it from the inside and took it for their own.

There are no rules to war, said his father's voice, *except the ones you imagine*.

Venick fought a well of bitterness. He didn't like to think of his father in this way, or to remember that there had been a time when he'd admired—hell, *worshiped*—the man. And yet, this memory had power.

"I think—" Venick started, then stopped, struggling to put his thoughts into words. It would have been easier had he understood more about these southern elves, had Ellina given him something other than *I will handle it* and *it is not your concern*. But now all he had were cries of alarm quickly gaining ground and a hunch. Well. Spit it out then, and let them figure the rest. "The southern elves have taken the city."

Dourin shot Venick a skeptical look. "And you know this how?"

"Those are *war* bells. The guards wouldn't sound those, not for us. The southern elves are behind this. They've infiltrated the guard, and now they're heading this hunt."

"That is absurd."

Venick caught Ellina's eye. "Do the southerners have anything to gain from overtaking this city?"

"It is irrelevant," Dourin answered. "The southerners do not have that kind of power."

"Anything at all?" Venick insisted. Ellina pressed her lips together. "They already chased Ellina through the city, attacked her, lost her. They won't risk that again. If they have control of the guard and a tip about Ellina's whereabouts, why *wouldn't* they launch a hunt?"

Dourin clicked his teeth in frustration. "What makes you think—?"

But the answer was given for Venick as shouts became clear over the growing howl of dogs. There were hollers in a mixture of his language and theirs, which made it clear, so painfully clear that what Venick had said was true. The guards should all be human. Elves didn't protect border cities, and elves and men didn't work together. Not like this.

"We can use the sewers," Venick said, turning from one side street down another. He glanced up in dismay to see the glow of lanterns lighting from behind curtained windows, citizens roused by the sound of the bells. "There are grates along the river wall, entry points. Do you remember them?"

Ellina matched his pace. Her eyes flashed as they locked on his. "And they lead out?"

"Yes." Gods, let that be true.

"*Wait.*" Dourin moved to block them. "Ellina." His face was ghostly-white, his eyes two dark holes. "How do you—this could be a trap. How can we be certain he is telling the truth?"

Venick thought he'd begun to learn all of Ellina's faces. The way her eyes would narrow when she was about to argue, the proud set to her jaw, the way she tried and failed to hide her thoughts. But the look on her face then was nothing Venick recognized. It was hard and soft at once. Honest, which she wasn't usually, not with him.

She met Venick's eye and gave her answer. "*Beuro en imastha.*" Because I trust him.

This time, there was no mistaking what language she spoke.

TEN

Ellina stared at the rush of water below. It roiled red and brown, the waves lulling up the seawall. The smell of it touched her nose, a smell she had not noticed the first time, had not had time to notice. But she noticed now.

The human—*Venick*—stood to her left, Dourin to her right. If Dourin was nervous, he did not show it. Neither did she. She schooled her face into calm indifference, as if the water did not terrify her, as if she was not haunted by visions of drowning, washed ashore pale and swollen, her lungs filled with water. As if that image was not overwhelming her thoughts now.

She felt Venick's eyes on her and let out a breath. It did not matter what she did or did not hide. He knew. He had known the first time, too, that she could not swim, that she was afraid. It should bother her how well this human could read elves. How well he could read *her*. But she only listened to his low reassurances and tried to stay calm. *We'll use the ladder. I'll be right here, Ellina. It won't be like last time, you won't go under.*

But how could he be sure?

Because I trust him.

Ellina watched the water. It churned darkly. Her thoughts did. Had Dourin asked her this morning, she would have answered differently. Ellina trusted no one save Dourin and her eldest sister. Trust was something to be guarded, to cherish, but Ellina had spoken those words in a language that did not allow lies. They *must* be true.

They could not be.

Could they?

She glanced sideways and caught a glimpse of winter eyes. Venick was watching her. Patient. Too patient, given the precariousness of their position: butted up against the river, out in the open. She might have counted on a sharp word from Dourin—*You need a push?*—to get her moving, but Dourin had gone silent and dark by her side. That was resentment.

Because I trust him.

"Ellina." Venick's voice was controlled. "We have to go."

"I—" She blinked back down at the water. She gripped her sword's hilt hard enough to hurt. And again, the vision of drowning. She saw herself swallowed up by the river. Glassy eyes, blue lips.

If you slip, I will come for you, Venick had said to her. Dourin scoffed at that.

She is not a maiden in need of saving.

Dourin was right to resent her. He was her oldest and closest friend. They had joined the legion together, trained and traveled and fought together. Back in the forest, Ellina had told no one her true plan but him, and even then, she had not told him everything.

I am taking the human to Kenath, she had said. *Raffan has agreed to give me until first moon to question him, but I—will be late. I will catch up with you and the others after. Do not wait for me.*

She had trusted Dourin not to ask for details. He had not. Had instead chosen to risk himself to come for her and her unknown mission. And now she had pulled rank on him, shoved the knife deeper by putting him second. To a *human*.

"Ellina," Venick said again. His fingers brushed her back. Lightly, almost not a touch at all. She did not look at him. Could not. She clenched her sword harder to intensify the pain, to try and distract herself from the human and the water and *everything*.

She could hear the clatter of boots over the high chime of the alarm bells. The telltale hiss of a sword drawn. It seemed impossible that they had not yet been spotted. If she did not move soon, they would be. Her heart was a bird in flight. It fluttered in her chest. She ground her teeth and urged it to *quit*. She was a legionnaire, highborn, a warrior. She would not be disarmed by this human, or Dourin, or the coming guards, or *water*.

She spun and lowered herself down the ladder's first rung.

Then the next.

Then another, until she was even with the sewage grate's wide bars. The water lapped at her ankles. She stared into the black tunnel and did not think of becoming trapped inside. Did not think of the water rising to take her. She clutched the ladder tightly with one hand as she reached out the other to catch the sewer's metal grate. A deep breath. Another.

She crossed the small distance between them, slipping through the bars to safety.

ELEVEN

Venick was right about the sewers. They led under the city, winding a path through a pitch-black maze that might have been a danger itself, had Venick not remembered doing this in Irek. That had been three years and a lifetime ago, but he would never forget that sewer water flowed in one direction—*out*—and so could lead the way. The water pooled up to their calves, their knees, deeper than that, even, in some places. It reeked. They did too by the time they felt the first hint of fresh air and then, finally, the outer grate.

Moonlight leaked between the black bars, drawing patterns on the water's surface. Venick waded forward and watched the pattern ripple. He came level with the grate. He curled his fingers around the metal.

There was a moment of raw fear. That the grate would be locked. Rusted shut. That the southern elves knew where they'd gone and were waiting to ambush them on the other side.

He shoved hard. The hinges gave an angry creak that echoed through the sewers, followed by a swell of relief and a door swinging wide. It spat them out into a shallow pond not far from the forest. Venick hadn't known where they would emerge, not exactly, but this was the best he could hope for. Kenath was a smudge in the distance. The bells distant, faded. There were no elves. No one at all.

Venick looked at Ellina then. He scanned her wet clothes, her hands, her face, then realized what he was doing.

She's here. She's fine. Stop staring.

But he couldn't. Not as he caught her doing the same to him, her eyes raking his foot and the cut along his chest which had clotted, most-ly, but seeped along its edges. Her eyes met his.

"Raffan and the others continued on to Tarrith-Mour," Dourin cut in. "They will stay as long as it takes to investigate the honor suicide. Not past first moon, and if we are not back by *then*—"

"I know the plan, Dourin," Ellina said.

Dourin's eyes slid in Venick's direction. "We will not make it back by first moon."

Venick didn't expect gratitude from the other elf. Didn't expect a *thank you*. He didn't expect irritation either, which he got, a dark gaze, lip hitched in what amounted to an elven sneer. Venick had the sudden vision of a dagger in the elf's hand, a flash of green thrust into Venick's belly. There was nothing Venick could do if Dourin decided he was bet-ter dead after all. Not much Ellina could do, either.

Venick could get used to Ellina's mercy. He could learn to read her tells, could see that she wanted him *alive*. Could get soft from that know-ing. Because Venick didn't know how to read Dourin. Even if he did, Dourin was an elf, and Venick was a human, and nothing had changed between them. There was no reason for Dourin to let him live, not now that they'd escaped the city.

But instead of reaching for his weapon, Dourin said only, "Raffan will be displeased." And then, voice low, "I know how he is with you."

"I will handle Raffan," Ellina replied.

Venick thought Dourin must look exactly how he did when Ellina pulled that on him. *Let me handle it. I do not want you involved. This is not your battle.* Dourin's lips pressed tightly, a shadow crossing his expression. But then, gone. His face emptied as he dipped his head in a nod. *As you say.*

Venick didn't fully understand the relationship between these two elves. He did understand rank, though, and there was no doubting who gave the orders between them.

And you? Where do you rank?

Venick didn't know. It was strange, not to know. He had always been aware of his place in the world. In Irek, then as a soldier. Even in the mountains, he'd known where he—

Belonged, Venick? That what you think?

Where he was safe, at least.

Which he wasn't now. He glanced back toward the city and tried to envision the southern elves following them, finding them. He let his hand rest on his hunting knife, which was hardly a comfort. Let his eyes slide to Ellina, to *her* weapons, which weren't a comfort either.

Believe that.

"Tarrith-Mour is a forest city," Ellina said. "To the south. Not so far from the border." She hesitated, a hesitation he didn't understand until she added, quietly, "You could travel with us and cross back into the mainlands once we arrive. You would be safer."

Venick blinked. Did not—by some grace of the gods—let his mouth fall open. Her offer shouldn't have surprised him. She'd saved his life, then he saved hers. Their fates had become entangled somehow. And he wasn't her prisoner. Never had been.

Yet Venick was uncertain.

"The northern edge of the border is closer," he said carefully.

"The northern edge sits behind Kenath and the southerners. You cannot go that way."

"The western edge, then."

"Longer and more dangerous."

Venick aimed a glance at Dourin. "I don't think—"

"It is your choice to make," Ellina interrupted. "Whatever you decide."

He should refuse her offer. Cut all ties and turn around and journey back to the mainlands alone. Ellina might not be his captor, but she wasn't his safeguard, either. Not his partner.

And yet, when he looked at Ellina he felt the same pull of desire he'd encountered in the forest, then again in the tavern when he'd decided to follow her. It was the desire to act, to *protect*.

Which was idiotic. Venick wasn't there to fight for Ellina. He shouldn't be there at all. No matter how he'd begun to think of himself and Ellina as allies. No matter that small, strange twist in his gut at the thought of leaving her.

"Thought we didn't owe each other any debts," Venick said.

"That is not why I am offering."

Then why are you offering? on his lips, which he swallowed. The fact was that it didn't matter. The fact was that *he* wanted to protect *her*, too, and didn't have a good reason, either. Venick squinted back towards Kenath, then into the black woods. It was true that he would be safer if he traveled with her. That he might be able to keep her safer, too.

Finally, he met her eye and nodded. "To Tarrith-Mour, then."

Ellina set a brisk pace back towards the southern forest, letting Venick and Dourin fall in behind her. This seemed second nature to Dourin, who drew his weapon and covered their flank, pausing long enough to give Venick another hard look, his eyes lingering on the hunting knife as if to say, *that's it?*

Venick ignored him. He moved up beside Ellina, who threw him a look of her own, though for once he could not read its meaning.

Her eyes skipped away. She scanned the ground, the trees, the darkness ahead and behind. Venick did too. He watched for movement, for any sign of an ambush. The twitch of a branch. The crunch of a twig. But the forest was still.

After a time, however, Venick noticed Ellina's gaze drift. Not back towards the city, not ahead into the trees, but above and below, in crevices, tree hollows. Odd places.

"What are you looking for?" he asked.

"Shadows."

Venick left off the obvious—they were being pursued by elves, not shadows. He said nothing of the fact that it was night and everything was shadowed. He looked instead at her face, the hard mouth. He read what he could from that. "Not regular shadows."

"No."

He waited for her to explain and got nothing. Typical, for an elf to offer no more than what was asked.

So ask her then.

"Why are you looking for shadows?"

"Because southern elves can weave them."

Which was not something Venick had ever heard of. He scowled, shuffling through his memory but coming up blank. "Like magic?" he asked.

"Like conjuring."

"I didn't know elves could conjure." Didn't know anyone could, not anymore. Not since the purge, when human conjurers had been rounded up by the elves, beheaded and burned. That had been centuries ago, but even then, magic had been a human skill.

"Northern elves cannot conjure," Ellina said. "Most southerners cannot, either. Some, though…" She let the thought trail.

"You might have mentioned that sooner."

"I did not think it would matter." She didn't think he would still be with her, was what she meant.

"Tell me what to look for."

She looked ready to argue. Her brows pulled together, her mouth tipping into a frown. *I will handle any threats. You focus on keeping yourself alive.* But after a breath, she told him. The shadows cannot hurt you, she said. They might blind you. They will certainly follow you. If they catch and hold, they can trail you long beyond their conjuror. They can slip into your own shadow, can take its place without you even noticing.

"And has a shadow slipped into ours?" Venick asked. The alarm bells in the distance had halted. Moonlight shone through the trees, drawing strange shapes. He remembered the moonlight through the sewer grate too, and wondered.

"No." Certain. Unblinking. Venick didn't know if that was true confidence, or the elven mask of it. A mask, he thought, and was about to say so when—

"Ellina." Dourin's voice cut through the night. They turned. He looked pale in the dark. "The horses."

Ellina shook her head. "We cannot go back for them."

"It is not that." Stiffly, quietly. "They were homing horses."

Venick did not immediately understand, but he felt Ellina harden beside him and followed her gaze back through the trees toward the city, barely visible in the distance. He didn't see them, not at first, until he noticed a ripple in the tall grass, two black blotches heading their way.

The memory came then, blurry and ragged. Lorana in Irek's woods, the sturdy mare underneath her. How she dismounted the horse, leading Venick to the river. They had walked back on foot, never minding whether the mare would follow. Lorana knew she would. Venick had never asked how.

"Homing horses," Ellina said.

"I did not think—we left underground. The sewers. Our trail should have been lost to them." Dourin's face remained calm, but his eyes were intense. "They are loyal. They found us anyway, but…it appears they are alone."

"Which means nothing," Ellina said. Venick thought he understood. If the southern elves recognized these as homing horses, if they saw the horses leaving the city—alone, in the middle of the night, so soon after a certain northern spy had escaped capture—they would know better than to *ride* them. More likely, the elves would crouch out of sight, trailing the horses from a distance. More likely still, the elves would weave their shadows onto the horses. They would follow them straight to Ellina.

Several long seconds passed. Ellina reached for her bow.

"Ellina." Dourin's voice was a hollow shell. "No."

She nocked an arrow. "Your horses will give away our position. It is possible they have already."

"They are innocent."

She aimed. "The southerners will shadow-catch us. Do you know how to shake a shadow binding? Because I do not. They will be able to follow us *anywhere*. We will never escape."

"Ellina, please." Dourin took a step. "I summoned the horses to me and they came. Do not punish them for my mistake. They will follow me if I lead them away. Let me lead them away."

Venick remembered Ellina's face in the forest when she killed the wanewolves. The way a storm had settled into her, the dark set to her mouth, the sorrow followed by fierce resolve as she let her arrows fly. She looked that way now. Dimmer, the usual glow in her eye replaced by—something else. Grief, perhaps. Regret. Venick's eyes grazed her slender hands, pale skin, hair as dark as the sky above. Her fingers held the green glass arrow in perfect form. She aimed through the trees with both eyes open.

She released the first arrow. The beat of a moment, then a break in the horse's stride, the sound of him stumbling, crashing into the ground. Dourin made a noise. His eyes were wide, wild as he watched her nock another.

"Ellina." Venick spoke before he could pull the word back. This was not his business. And he knew about sacrifice. He knew how to make hard decisions for the greater good. He had seen it and done it. And yet: "Is there no other way?"

Ellina glanced at him. He read the answer in her eyes.

Venick remembered Ellina's mercy in the forest that was not truly mercy, but a single thread in the web of her larger plot. He remembered how she questioned him in the circle of firelight, threatened him, bargained with him, only to shove a dagger and coins into his hands and set him free. Just as he was beginning to understand her, she would draw a jagged line across the picture he'd painted. He had seen her ruthlessness and her kindness. Had been on the receiving end of both. He thought of her words spoken over the metallic clang of the alarm bells. *Because I trust him.* The warm pleasure, followed by confusion. He had not asked her to trust him. Did not understand what he'd done to deserve her trust. He thought of all the truths and lies they'd been laying at each other's feet, all the things still left unsaid. He remembered their conversation in the brothel, and as Venick watched her aim, he felt as if there was something missed. Some vital truth hovering just out of reach. Because if he had learned anything about Ellina, it was this: she did nothing without reason.

She released the second arrow. The horse screamed as he fell, a terrible, keening sound that carried through the night.

• • •

Venick understood the silence that followed was not the kind to be broken.

He understood that Ellina was worn thin. He saw it in her hunched shoulders, the line of her brow, the way she met his eye, as if she was asking for *his* apology and worried for his answer.

Venick swallowed and let the silence hold. She needed space. She needed time to mend things with Dourin, who hadn't spoken to either of them since that last arrow was drawn. Venick did not fully understand the bond between elves and their horses, but he did know the heartbreak of loss. He knew the cut of betrayal.

He knew the pain of watching someone you loved die.

• • •

There had been a time when Venick could still remember Lorana clearly. He would recall the lilt of her voice, the way she smiled, the gleam in her eye when she was after something and determined to get it. He remembered the ache of loving her so fully, so deeply he could hardly bear it. She made his chest hurt. The memory of her did. Venick used to worry he would forget pieces of her. He would tunnel his fingers through his hair and the ache would turn to true pain, the kind that kept him up at night, that changed a fond memory into a living, breathing nightmare.

As the years went by, he did begin to forget. The exact color of her eyes. The feel of her skin under his hands. It plagued him, the way he struggled to remember these things and could not. But there was one memory he could never forget. Screams. A trio of elves. The bright flash of blood as the arrow struck her chest. The night of Lorana's death crawled through his thoughts, his dreams, relentless in its clarity.

Their relationship had been a well-guarded secret. Lorana knew the penalty for loving a human. Venick knew it, too. But they were careful. It was not uncommon to see elves in Irek. The city sat close to the border, and their seaport was the only one between the elflands and the capital. The crossover wasn't legal, technically, but elves were the ones who made those rules, and if they chose to break them, who were the people of Irek to tell them otherwise? Besides, Lorana was well-liked. Too much time spent around humans, people said. It turned her soft. But *soft* for an elf meant *happy*, and no one could fault her for being *nice*. So people grew used to the elf who lived among them, whose dark hair made them forget, sometimes, what she really was. Made Venick forget sometimes, too.

There had been a night. The moon, high and round. The quiet shore, waves lulling. Venick and Lorana sprawled in the sand, tangled in each other.

She pulled away. Her eyes locked on something in the distance. Venick turned to look but saw nothing. *What is it? What do you see?* But she wouldn't say.

Venick should have known. He should have guessed. He'd seen the way his father peered at him, the slow suspicion that morphed into something darker. Fear was greedy, and his father had always been wary of elves. But Venick had not known. Not when his father's suspicion turned into spying, turned into understanding, then anger, fury.

When Venick returned home that night, he found his father waiting.

It's not natural, his father had snapped. The whites of his eyes were wide. Venick's mother cried silently in the corner. *You disgrace us. You will put a stop to this. You will not see this elf again.*

You do not rule me.

Yes, his father said. *I do.*

Venick wondered how differently things would have gone had he known then what his father planned. He *should* have known. And it was obvious, wasn't it? That his father would tell the southern elves. That they would come to kill her. But Venick hadn't known. And by the time he learned, it was too late.

Venick's heart was sore. He closed his eyes.

He wanted to tell Dourin not to mourn his horses. To forget how he'd watched them die. Because even though Venick had once wanted to remember, the truth was this: forgetting was a relief. It was a relief, not to remember how much you loved someone, how you held onto them with your entire being. How you cried into their hair as you clutched their lifeless body to your chest. It was a relief, to forget who you'd been when you were with them, to forget what you'd said and done and felt, to forget that you'd never loved anything so much, and never would again.

TWELVE

They did not stop to rest or eat. Not when the sun peeked over the horizon and brightened the day with morning. Not as the forest became dense and humid as they moved deeper. Ellina stayed close, often walking by Venick's side, which was different than before. Welcome, though, even as the nagging voice in his head warned it shouldn't be.

Dourin had gone ahead. To scout, he'd said, though they all understood this was not the only reason. There was no missing the grey pallor of his skin, the hurt hid behind anger, which pooled in his eyes and fists each time he looked at Venick. Venick pretended not to notice. He'd known elves like Dourin. That easy fury, quick to boil, quick to bubble over the brim, spill and slosh around them—*You think you are one of us now?*—at the smallest provocation.

But the anger wasn't the truth, not entirely. Underneath Venick saw the sorrow, and not merely for his dead horses. Because Venick didn't miss, either, the way Dourin's eyes lifted to meet Ellina's again and again. Searching. Distressed, too, when he didn't find what he sought.

"You should go to him," Venick said now. He could see Dourin's slender figure ahead, glimpses of white hair through the trees. "Tell him you're sorry."

"Dourin does not want my apologies."

"He wants *something*." Venick could see that clear enough. He knew she did, too.

An insect buzzed loud around them, its sturdy wings thrumming on air. Ellina adjusted her belt, working the leather until it lay flat. "He is angry about Kenath," she finally said. "I let the southern elves find me. I changed our plans. A good soldier would have done neither."

Venick had no response to that. She'd had a choice, and she had chosen *him*. A human over her kin, and never mind all the rules it broke.

"I need to know something," Venick said, "and I need the truth." Ellina stiffened at that word, wary, suddenly certain that she would not like whatever came next. "Does the law work the other way around? We are traveling together. That makes you my accomplice. Can you be punished for it?" He watched denial curl into her as she opened her mouth to answer. He cut it short with a hand, slicing through whatever lie she meant to tell. "The *truth*, Ellina."

She closed her mouth.

"The law does not mention it," she finally replied, lifting her shoulder in an almost-shrug. The movement caught Venick's attention, distracting him. Elves didn't shrug. That was a human sentiment. "I cannot say what my commander will do."

But her tone was deliberately nonchalant. Venick imagined that he and Ellina were speaking in elvish. It was a language that did not allow lies, but that might still allow you to lie. Words could be twisted, intentions muddied. Ellina might not *know* what her commander would do.

"But you can guess."

"I do not want to guess." She made that motion again, lifting her shoulder. "Raffan can be—unpredictable."

"And the others?"

"They are not a concern." She tilted her head and her mouth twitched. "Not all elves hate humans."

Which was part of the problem.

Venick felt full of something he couldn't explain, some unknown emotion that wavered between pleasure and pain. He pushed the feeling away, watched his footing instead. His injury ached, a low throb that ran up his calf into his knee. His leg felt clumsy, not his own. It didn't help that they were well off the main trail, following landmarks Venick could neither recognize nor understand.

Except, that wasn't entirely true. Venick glanced at the sun through the trees. He noted its position, the angle of the shadows. His eyes fell to Ellina. "We aren't going south," he said.

She appeared distracted. "Hmm?"

"South." Venick halted. "You said we were heading to Tarrith-Mour. That city is *south*. This," he motioned around the forest, "is east."

Ellina waved a hand. "A quick diversion."

"Ellina." Venick stood rooted. "But *where?*"

She stopped then too, turning to face him fully. "There is something I want to see. It will not take long." Her expression became amused. "You are welcome to stay here, if you like."

Venick snorted. The hell he would.

She continued onward. He went after her.

● ● ●

It was a camp. Or, it had been.

A few squat tents remained, the weathered goatskin hanging sadly on drooping poles. The space had been cleared, all underbrush cut away to reveal a swath of forest ground. It was obvious that elves had once bedded here. There were campfires spaced at even intervals, dead now, the stubs of old wood blackened by repeated burnings. Most supplies had been carried away, but a few discarded pieces remained: a waterlogged book, an iron pan, a bedroll. And a smell, too, that lingered.

Venick glanced around for Dourin, who had continued ahead without them, then looked at Ellina. "Did you know this camp?"

"It was not a camp."

He hitched a brow. "There are tents. Campfires. Places where elves—"

"It was not a camp," Ellina insisted. Her hand gripped the hilt of her sword at her belt, a habit he was coming to recognize. "It was a tent-city."

"A tent-city?"

"A city of tents. Permanent. It was here long enough to earn a name. They called it Muralwood."

And where has the permanent city moved to now? Venick almost asked but didn't, because Ellina's eyes had taken on a grey cast, her stance warning against his witticism. She began picking her way through the empty city, stopping to touch a wooden bench, a blanket, a broken clay bowl. He followed her.

Venick didn't mean to notice it. He had already decided that he couldn't make Ellina's problems his problems. Yes, they had escaped Kenath together, would avoid the southerners together, but he had one true focus: returning home. That was all that mattered.

And so he didn't mean to catch the way Ellina's mouth turned down, how her shoulders hunched, the troubled ridge between her brow. He didn't mean to take these images and shape them into a story, or to insert himself into that story. He wouldn't have, except that his thoughts still lingered on Kenath, and the words she'd spoken by the river, and her uncertain claim about whether she could be punished for traveling with him.

He moved to block her path before he could stop himself. Ellina halted, eyes lifting: *yes?*

"You're gripping your sword," Venick said, which earned him the kind of look a mother might give a difficult child. Venick explained. "You grip your sword when you're troubled."

"I—" Ellina glanced down. "What?"

"This." Venick reached for her sword-hand, brushed his fingers over hers. Felt heat—sudden, surprising—crawl up his neck at the contact. "It's what you do when you're troubled. So tell me." His voice was rough. Too rough. He cleared his throat. "What's wrong?"

Ellina stared at where his fingers lingered over hers. She didn't seem to hear him. Or maybe she did, but her mouth was unable to form any words.

Venick shouldn't be thinking about her mouth.

He shouldn't be thinking about what troubled her, or whether *this* troubled her. Him touching her.

He let his hand fall.

"You weren't expecting to find it abandoned," he guessed, taking a step back to create space between them. He tied his expression down to neutral, as if nothing unusual had just happened, as if his blood didn't feel both lighter and heavier at once. Because it didn't.

Believe that.

"No," she finally replied. Then again, stronger, "No, I did not. The south has always been unstable. In the north we have our sovereignty, but the southerners do not. They cling to the old ways. They have their clans, which are divided into houses that rule together, but there is unrest. Houses fight each other for more power, smaller houses rise to take larger ones. It is constant."

"You think this tent-city was overtaken by another house?"

"But it was not." Ellina swept her hand around the clearing. "Nothing is burnt. There is no sign of a fight. The tents are gone, packed up and taken away. These elves moved."

"But that's not so strange, is it? Elves move."

"This city was here for decades," Ellina replied. "Why now?" She peered up into the trees. The wind rustled their leaves, the papery noise of them filling the silence. "Kenath, too, was unexpected. In the past, conflict has kept the south weak. The southerners are so busy fighting each other that they cannot rally and grow. For elves to organize, to take over that city as they did, a *northern* city…"

Venick remembered the danger they had faced in Kenath. Ellina hadn't expected it. Dourin hadn't, either. *The southerners do not have that kind of power* he'd insisted as they stood in a dark alley debating whether the southerners had infiltrated the city. But he had been wrong.

"What does it mean?" Venick asked.

"For you?" She flashed a tight smile. "Nothing."

"And for you?"

"For us…" She made a gesture that was elvish for *uncertain*. She blinked, realizing what she had done. "It is uncertain," she said, then repeated the gesture. "That is what this means. The word is *tourdin*. Say it back to me."

Venick touched his necklace. "Back to that?"

"Yes." And then, as if knowing his next question, "Raffan will notice if you are not learning."

"Raffan never expected me to learn." Never expected him to *live*. Ellina understood what was not said.

"It is not safe for you to be on this side of the border without some knowledge of our language."

"I should think it's not safe regardless."

"We made a bargain."

Venick grinned, because they both knew that bargain was a farce, and now she was simply being stubborn. But he shrugged and said the word back to her, and felt no little pleasure as she smiled at his botched pronunciation.

It went on like this as they left the abandoned tent-city and continued south: Ellina teaching him a word, Venick pretending to fumble it, her correcting him. By midafternoon Venick had relearned a handful of useless words like *tree* and *mud* and *shell*. He watched Ellina's exaggerated pronunciations—*It is said zai-am-in*—as he feigned fascination. And he was, a little, but not at the words. He watched Ellina tutor him through phrase after phrase. He watched the way her edges seemed to soften, the way she would brighten when he got a word right. This was a different Ellina than the one he'd come to know.

"Stop using your hands so much," she was saying as they came upon a creek. "It changes a word's meaning. Keep them still by your side. There, yes. And stop *smiling* like that."

"I'm not smiling."

"You are." But she was too.

They dipped their hands into the creek, rubbing the cool water over their faces and necks. Venick ran a finger along the bottom, feeling the silt and pebbles he could see clearly. It reminded him of doing this as a boy, kneeling by the water, hunting for minnows and frogs, skinning naked and splashing in. There were creeks and streams and rivers all around Irek. There were lakes as well, wide pools where runoff collected from the mountains. The lakes were safer than the ocean because they had no current. Warmer, too, especially in the summer.

An idea. The seed of it planted inside him.

Venick moved downstream. The creek grew steadily deeper, twisting back and forth like a snake cut from the land. Venick remembered doing this as a child, too. *Follow the river. It will lead you home.* His mother's words. His mother's face, then, vivid in his mind. He saw her round cheeks, the tuft of wild hair, the way she would try to hide her amusement when he misbehaved. Her love for him, full and deep.

Venick rounded a bend and the creek opened into a pond. He turned towards Ellina, who had followed without question, who was gazing at him, curious. His idea grew roots, sprouted. Venick felt a sudden moment of shyness. He offered a smile. "I was thinking," he said, picking each word carefully. "It's dangerous for you not to know how to swim. You could learn. You *should* learn. And I—" he rubbed a hand across the back of his neck. "I could teach you."

Ellina blinked. Her gaze darted between him and the pond. "Elves do not swim," she said.

"All the more reason to learn."

"It is against our ways."

"It doesn't have to be."

"I—this is not done."

His cheeks heated, and he almost regretted offering. But then he remembered her facing the water in Kenath, and the southern elves, and her fear. His resolve hardened. "Will you think about it, at least?"

She was afraid. Venick could see how the very thought of water made her nervous. But she was practical, too. Elves feared water, but if she could conquer that fear it would be to her advantage. It might even save her life.

He watched her consider it. She stared at the pond and regained control of her expression, the fear rolled up and wiped away. Her face was once again a slate: blank, empty.

In the mainlands, humans told stories about elves. Venick had grown up with those stories. As a child, he had begged for them. His mother would sit him on her lap and weave fantastical tales of elves, as if they didn't walk and breathe on the other side of the border. In all the stories, elves were imagined to be wild creatures who sang and danced and drank endlessly. Some were said to be like sirens, passionate and loud. Some like fairies, magical, full of endless laughter.

Venick stared at Ellina and couldn't help but smile at the truth.

"What is funny?" she asked.

He nodded at her empty expression. "You, acting like that's hiding anything."

He pretended not to notice her mask slip. Pretended not to see the small twist of her mouth, which was better, so much better than stone-cold nothing. Pretended not to care what *she* was smiling about. He turned around and walked on and left it at that.

THIRTEEN

Dusk seemed to come early that night, shadows stretching dark fingers through the forest, shading the world grey. Venick watched those shadows and thought of the southerners. They had seen no sign of the conjurors since leaving the city the prior night. Venick knew that Tarrith-Mour was still days away, that the danger wasn't over yet. He knew that he couldn't rely on his eyes and ears to show him everything, that they might not *truly* be safe.

But he dared to hope.

He was alone for the time. Dourin had reappeared long enough to announce that he would take the night watch before disappearing back into the trees and out of sight. Ellina was out of sight, too. She had started off in her own direction, but when Venick made to follow she'd shot a look over her shoulder. *Stay here*, she had said.

Wherever you're going, I'll come.

I would really rather you not. Her brow had arched sardonically.

She left, and Venick didn't follow. He understood the need for privacy. It was something he wanted for himself. He thought again of the southern shadows, and it occurred to him that even though they'd seen no trace of those elves, he felt watched.

He trudged in the opposite direction, undressing to wash his clothes in a nearby stream. The movement warmed him, but it felt good. The water clouded, then cleared. He wrung out the fabric as best he could, then slid back into it. The damp cloth clung to his skin.

He walked back to where they'd made camp. The sky darkened. Venick looked up through the forest canopy and imagined he could see the sky, the *whole* sky, like he could from Irek. He imagined how he might peer over the ocean, find patterns in the stars. He felt the sudden wrench of homesickness.

He thought of his mother. She had not been old when he made her a widow. He could see her sitting in her favorite chair by the fire. It had been a happy place, made happy by his mother's love. That love: broken now. Warped, cast away. He saw the tears on her cheeks, rattling sobs as she watched her son kill her husband. Then, empty eyes. A blank stare, like she didn't know him, like she had no son and Venick was a murdering stranger.

Redemption was an option only offered to soldiers. Perhaps it was a way for his country to repay men for their service. Or perhaps it was simply because dead men cannot fight, and the military understands that exile and execution are a waste of a good battling body. Venick knew it was a soldier's task to choose his own redemption sacrifice, yet when Venick thought of the night he'd murdered his father, he felt a deep river of fear. Maybe there *was* no sacrifice large enough, no gesture grand enough to absolve him in his mother's eyes.

Venick loosed his hunting knife from his belt as he walked. He studied the plain handle, the filigree on the blade. It had been a gift from his mother. He remembered his surprise at that breaking of tradition. The father was supposed to gift his son his first knife, but on his sixteenth nameday his mother had woken him at dawn and pushed the heavy bundle of wrapped cloth into his hands. *This belonged to my father*, she'd said as he unwrapped it to reveal the weapon beneath. *He bore no sons of his own. He was ashamed to bear only daughters. But now I have a son, and you are of his blood. He would want you to have it.*

Venick studied the scratched steel, dried blood at its base. The handle, cracked and faded. He had not taken good care of this knife. It had not taken good care of him, either.

Maybe it's returning the favor.

He wondered if there was some unexamined part of him that still tied his mother to this knife. That he did not take care of it because he had not taken care of her. Because it was pointless to polish something he meant to betray.

Or maybe it was misplaced defiance. That this knife was a link to his old life and he wanted to sever that link.

Maybe it was simple laziness, and the knife meant nothing to him.

He decided it wouldn't hurt to oil it. Sharpen it. Maybe Ellina had a whetstone. Maybe he would return to the creek and find a rock that would do the job. He turned around, intending to look.

But then, a sound.

Venick paused. Listened. A voice. Low notes. They lifted into the air, light and sweet.

Music. Someone was singing.

Ellina.

But it couldn't be. The thought was absurd, foolish in its impossibility. Elves didn't sing. They didn't make music. Theirs was a race of minds and weapons, not to be lured by the human pleasures of laughter and song and dance.

And yet, the music.

And yet, that voice.

Venick's feet carried him towards the sound before he could think, before he could stop to consider whether this was some sort of trap, like conjuring, like the elven sirens from the stories of his childhood. But it wasn't a trap. Because there was Ellina in the small clearing where they had made camp, her damp hair newly braided, head bent over her quiver examining arrows. She was singing quietly, the words lost under her breath.

Venick stared.

Her gaze lifted. She spotted him and fell silent.

"Don't stop," he said, stepping closer. She dropped her eyes back to her arrows. "You didn't tell me you could sing."

"Elves do not sing."

"I hadn't thought so, either." But the words felt uncomfortable. Venick had the odd sensation that he'd spoken them before, the fuzzy memory of anger and desperation. He shifted, and the memory seemed to shift too, turning inside him, coming into view.

We elves do not kill our own.

I hadn't thought so, either.

"I'd like to hear more," Venick said, pushing this new moment into the place of that old one. "It helps, hearing your elvish. Maybe it would improve mine."

"To listen to me sing?"

"Why not?"

"No." She returned to her task, but her hands slowed. Her expression grew thoughtful. "A poem, maybe," she said after a moment. "I can recite one. You can listen."

"A poem."

"Yes."

Venick came to sit beside her. The earth was soft under his hands. His heart felt soft, too. Oddly light. Surprised by her offer, which was unexpected. Also unexpected: this new secret. He tried not to focus on what it meant that Ellina knew poetry when elves rarely did. He tried not to focus on what it meant that she might share such a thing with him. Instead he looked at her, the leather legion armor, long black hair, golden eyes. Quiet, in her movements now. Quiet, curious, as she looked back at him. The moment felt dipped in silver. A secret. A poem. An offer to share.

Venick smiled. "I would like that."

But when she started to speak, Venick realized it was not a poem she recited. It was a story.

A *confession*.

"*I have been thinking about the day we met,*" she said in elvish. "*My troop was not on border patrol, but it is every soldier's duty to hunt humans who wander into our lands. I wonder if you think us cruel. We are cruel. In the legion, we are taught to hate humans. Our commanders speak of your race as if you are monsters. It is what they want us to believe. It is easier if we believe it. Patrols will not hesitate to kill humans if they see them as beasts; beasts do not deserve pity.*"

He should have cut her off then, should have said something to break the moment. Venick was filled with a glossy horror. She wouldn't be telling him this if she knew he understood elvish, that he could translate *every word*. That he spoke her language fluently. That he had loved to speak it, once.

But she didn't know this. And as the words poured from her, he found himself helpless to stop them.

"*I remember a time,*" Ellina began. Her eyes were distant. Her thumb trailed a slow circle around the arrowhead in her hands. "*We found a man in the elflands. He was old. I remember he was surprised to see us, but not frightened. As if he thought we were on his side of the border. He was lost. He made a mistake. We should have let him go.*

"*Raffan was not my commander then, but he had been put in charge of our troop. He gave the order. I was young. And Raffan—I thought he knew. I admired him. So I listened.*"

Venick saw the man's story in his mind, but he saw his own story, too. The bear, the rush of elves, the flash of Ellina's arrow aimed at his heart. He heard Raffan's words and imagined how the old man would have heard them as well. But that man would not have understood, not until it was too late.

"*It felt*—" Ellina let out a breath. She looked small, suddenly. Fragile in the low light. "*It felt good to kill that human. I was serving my country. It was a task that needed doing, and I was proud to carry it out.*

"*I wanted to kill you when I saw you, too,*" she admitted. She looked at him. Her eyes blazed. "*I was angry. I wanted to kill you, and maybe I would have, if not*—" She shook her head. Venick's throat was dry. His ears roared. "*But I did not. I could not. And then in Kenath I saw your fear for my safety. Your…protectiveness. Does that make me horrible? That I wanted your death, but you did not want mine? And I think*—" She was stumbling through her thoughts. "*I think I was wrong to want that. Our laws are wrong to demand it.*" Her next words were quiet. "*I wonder what else I have been wrong about.*"

There was a long stretch of silence. Venick felt cold, a chill that cut deep. He knew he should say something. To comment on the sound of her elvish, maybe. To ask her to recite more. But Venick was gripped by the rawness of that confession, and it paralyzed him.

He had known the law when he entered the elflands. Had known, too, that he was starving, that if he didn't find food he would die a slower death. The choice was easy. It wasn't a choice at all. He crossed the border into the southern forests. For four days he hunted without seeing a single elf. That was not unusual. The elflands were immense, and elves could not be everywhere at once.

The bear trap was not his. Some other human had set it. Maybe that human had been captured and killed by the elves. Maybe he'd changed his mind and returned to the mainlands. Or maybe he was in the forest still.

When Venick thought of that bear trap now, he thought only of Ellina's mercy. He didn't think of what came before: the sharp eyes, arrow trained on him, that elven yearning to kill. But now Venick remembered it. The burn of hatred seared into her. Fingers tense, eager. The way she'd raked his injury with a soulless glance. He wondered how he could ever forget it.

And yet, he remembered everything that came after, too. Wanewolves killed. A lie and a bargain. Hasty stitches sewed in a brothel. Arguments for his sake. *Because I trust him.*

He looked into the forest. He focused on each piece of the night. He took a deep breath and reminded himself that things were as they had always been. These trees, this earth, the sky. Elves were elves. Humans, humans. Ellina used to want to kill him. Now she did not.

The hand squeezing his heart eased. He met Ellina's eye.

"What's it called?" he asked, then cleared his throat and spoke again. "The poem."

"It is—" She faltered. "It does not have a name."

Venick nodded, knowing the question he should ask next, the only question that would make sense. He forced it out. "What's it about?"

Ellina's smile was small, but true. "An elf who begins to see things differently."

FOURTEEN

He was not anything like she expected.

This was what Ellina thought as she lay down to sleep that night. But she could not sleep, not when he was so close, a mere arm's length away. She thought about his closeness. She thought about how his closeness had never mattered to her before.

It seemed to matter to her now.

She could reach out and touch him if she wanted. She imagined what it would be if she did. She would nudge him with her fingertips. She would trace the scar on the back of his hand. She might ask him where that scar came from, and he would tell her, and she would see his pleasure at being asked to share.

"You're awake."

His voice had the lusty quality of someone half-asleep. She turned to find him looking at her. He did not look sleepy.

"Yes."

"What are you thinking about?"

But this brought heat to Ellina's cheeks, and *that* flustered her even more, because she could not remember the last time she had blushed. Years ago. Maybe never. It was not something elves did.

"Nothing."

"Liar." But there was no venom in the word. He was still looking at her. He reached out a hand and touched the collar of her leather armor. His thumb brushed her skin, and her breath slowed; the whole world did. "Do you usually sleep in this?"

"No."

She did not tell him that her confession left her feeling defenseless, even if he had not understood the words. She did not tell him that she left her armor on because she felt soft without it. She did not like to feel soft. She did not like that *he* made her feel that way. She was not used to feeling anything except a strong sense of duty to her country. Anger, occasionally. Resolve. Determination. And fear. Even that, sometimes.

She thought, as Venick's skin brushed hers, she felt fear now.

Venick pulled his hand away. But Ellina felt the memory of that touch for a long time after.

FIFTEEN

He told himself not to touch her again.

Venick had seen the way her face narrowed in fear, how her eyes darted away as he brushed her collar and her skin. He remembered how she'd flinched away from him in the river in Kenath. She didn't want him to touch her. *He* didn't want to touch her.

He didn't.

Except the next morning, Ellina accidentally skimmed her fingers against his as she reached for her canteen. She met his eye. She smiled a little.

Later when they were practicing elven gestures, she cupped his hands in hers, showing him how to move his wrists, what it meant.

He brushed her with his shoulder as they walked. She didn't pull away.

He told himself it was wrong. If she didn't fear him, she should. Hell, *he* should fear *her*.

But he didn't. She fascinated him. The way she moved. Her bright golden eyes. How she insisted he learn elvish, insisted he at least try. Venick felt a stab of guilt at his lie, hastily shoved away. He instead pretended to learn in order to please her. He chuckled at the words she chose to teach him, *feign* and *closed* and *blue*. He watched the way she enunciated the vowels, how her lips curled around them, and he mimicked her movements, leaning in close. He found excuses to push into her space. Found himself wondering what would happen if he pushed a little farther. If he closed the distance between her body and his.

The vision brought him up short. The warmth fizzled out of him.

No.

No.

He wasn't thinking that. He was thinking about reaching the border, and finding a worthy redemption sacrifice to absolve him of his crimes, and returning to Irek. He was thinking about his homeland, and survival, and ending his banishment.

He wasn't thinking about how Ellina was softening, opening, warming.

He wasn't thinking about the first time he'd heard her laugh, or how it brought the world into color. What it would be like to pull her under him, to dent the earth with their bodies, to explore her with his mouth. He could never think that, because he had been here before, hadn't he? He had fallen in love with an elf, and broken her laws, selfishly, *selfishly*, and she had loved him back, and she was dead because of it.

Venick reminded himself that he would be home soon. Once they reached Tarrith-Mour, he could cross back into the mainlands. He would never see Ellina again.

He told himself it was for the better.

• • •

"That," Dourin said as Venick approached the fire, eyeing the dead rabbit on his belt, "is repulsive."

Venick ignored him. He moved across the elf's line of sight, sitting heavily on the forest floor. They were ten days out of Kenath and gods knew how many leagues from anywhere else. Ellina had promised another day's walk before they reached Tarrith-Mour and the southern edge of the border where he would be safe to return to the mainlands. She promised nothing beyond that, and gave him deliberate silence when he asked.

Venick wouldn't complain. His foot was nearly healed thanks to the medicinal leaves—*They are called isphnal, Venick. Say it back to me*—Ellina had found and the nightly salve she used to wrap it. The walking wasn't so bad now, not like before. And the path was clear, the weather warm and dry. He didn't mind sleeping under the open sky. He wouldn't mind the traveling so much, either, if it were just him and Ellina.

Venick studied Dourin. After that first night, the other elf had started walking and camping with them again. But he was still unhappy, still wary. He glanced at Venick now, his gaze settling on the new weave of bandages poking from Venick's boot. His eyes spoke of his displeasure.

Venick turned his concentration back to the dead rabbit. His stomach grumbled hungrily and gods, it had been too long since he'd had a real meal. He'd been living off moss and berries and whatever else elves ate, and *that* explained why they were all so slender.

He unwound the rabbit from its snare, then began skinning the thing. Had he been back home he might have worked slowly, careful not to nick the pelt, which he would use to line hats or boots. Not now. Now he cared only about the meat underneath, plump from easy summer living. He slid his knife under the skin, then worked his fingers through and *pulled* to reveal shining muscle. He cut off the head and legs with a *snap*, then into the belly to remove the guts.

"That is *repulsive*," Dourin repeated.

"It's good meat," Venick replied. "Where's Ellina?"

"I thought she was with you. As usual."

"She wasn't." Venick inched closer to the fire, which was almost too small for cooking, but could not be any larger less they risk unwanted attention. He began separating his catch into parts. "She told me she was going to help you build the fire."

"She told *me* she was going to help you hunt." Dourin's mouth thinned in disapproval. "She lied to us both."

Which would not have been possible had she and Dourin been speaking in elvish, but elves were careful about the way they used their language. They spoke to each other in mainlander when the conversation was casual. It was a way to trade trust—which Ellina had now broken.

"Maybe she wants us to spend quality time together," Venick said. That would be like her, lying to get her way. But stupid, utterly stupid, given the tension that had grown between Venick and Dourin these past days.

"I assure you, human, I have no interest in sharing quality time."

"Huh. And here I thought we were bonding."

Venick yanked hard at the rabbit's insides, hard enough to splatter blood. Dourin leapt to his feet, hissing.

"You. Are. *Revolting*."

"That mean you don't want to share?"

It was said that elves who spent time around humans tended to pick up human traits, becoming softer, learning to laugh and joke as men and women did. To *love* as men and women did. Venick had seen it in the elves who passed through Irek, the way stiffness would slowly peel away to reveal grins and frowns and honest emotion. Venick saw it in Ellina, too, when she smiled or shrugged. She had warmed, thawing after a long freeze.

Dourin had thawed, too, but not in the same way.

"I do not know why Ellina wastes her time with you," Dourin said.

"Dourin. There is no need for jealousy."

"I am not *jealous*." But Venick smirked. "You do not believe me?" Dourin asked.

"Say it in elvish."

Dourin darkened. Even though Venick wasn't supposed to know elvish, even though he was human, there was no softening the blow. Asking an elf to prove their truths in elvish was the worst sort of insult.

"I would gut you like that rabbit, if not for Ellina," Dourin growled.

The silence that followed was thick. It had been like this between them since the first day. The only difference now was that Dourin didn't try to hide his insults in elvish. He spoke them—*Stupid human, just wait until Raffan gets his hands on you*—in plain mainlander, as if daring Venick to object.

Venick, for his part, ignored the jibes. He instead envisioned reaching Tarrith-Mour and the border and ridding himself of Dourin for good.

Or shoving a dagger in his throat.

It was a surprise neither of them had tried. They could thank Ellina for that. She seemed always to step between them at just the right moment, before hands dropped to weapons, before insults became threats, became true violence.

And where *was* Ellina?

"You think she's okay?" Venick asked.

"She does not need you looking out for her," Dourin grumbled. He nudged the fire with his boot. Sparks showered the air.

Venick peered into the quiet dark and felt the first tug of worry. He left the carcass where it was and stood, wiping his hands on his trousers and reaching for his hunting knife, still bloody with rabbit. "Call if she shows back up here."

"You are not going out there on your—never mind. Of course you are." Dourin gave Venick a look that was neither sullen or angry, but something Venick liked even less. "You will not find her."

"Just call for me. I won't go far."

He marched away before Dourin could refuse.

• • •

Dourin was right. Venick didn't find her.

The dark pressed in on all sides. On his lungs. His heart. He knew better than to call her name, knew it might attract what *else* was in these woods. So instead he pushed through the forest, heedless to the branch-es that slapped his face, leaves and vines tugging at his clothes. Heedless to anything but his own growing worry, the twist and pull of it in his gut.

He checked all the places they had visited while making camp. The stream to the south where Ellina had filled her canteen. The little ridge beyond that where she'd watched the setting sun. The bramble of bush-es where she and Dourin picked their dinner. Venick had teased her for that—*Berries, Ellina? Is that all you eat?*—and she had smiled. The mo-ment was safe. The whole afternoon felt *safe*.

Venick returned to camp twice, just in case. The first time, Dourin crossed his arms and shook his head. The second time, though, Dourin stood. His expression, which had been unguarded, became a mask once more. Venick forced himself to see that mask, to see the blank eyes and blank mouth and remember that elven masks were only a ruse meant to cover the truth.

And what is the truth, Venick?

Dourin was worried, too.

They set out together, backtracking west, then north. The moon was not high but it was bright, arching sideways across a sky littered with stars. Venick tried to ignore the moon. Tried to concentrate on *there*, the upturned earth and *there*, that broken branch. But it was impossible not to track the moon's progress. To gauge how much time was passing. And time *was* passing. Too much time.

Venick felt his fear puddle in his chest. It gathered pressure, burned up his throat until he couldn't help it. He called her name.

"Stop," Dourin bit off. "These are southern forests. Have you forgotten what that means?"

Yes, he had forgotten. They'd seen no sign of the southern elves in days, no sign at all since the city. Venick had thought—foolishly, *foolishly*—that they had escaped. That the elves had given up the hunt.

His worry grew teeth and claws. It howled inside him.

"She is fine," Dourin insisted, but his tone slipped, let some honesty leak through. "She knows better than to find trouble." Which was a lie he could not have told in elvish. Dourin knew Ellina as well as Venick did. Better, even. It was all Ellina had done since they'd met: lie and stir up trouble. Venick couldn't begin to guess where she had gone or what she planned now, but whatever it was, she would get herself killed. The certainty of it bedded down inside him, pushed his heart aside to make room.

"Was she armed when you saw her last?"

"Ellina does not need weapons to fight." That was stone-Dourin. His lips were tight. His jaw was. His elven features were stark. Beautiful—all elves were—but harsh. He shot Venick a glance. He seemed to consider his next words for a long moment before, finally: "If she *is* in trouble, what do you plan?"

"Same as before." Pray for the best. Pray for luck.

That's not a plan, Venick.

And what sort of plan was he supposed to have? Distract the southern elves again? Hope Ellina decided to actually use that sword of hers?

"Do you have a problem killing elves?" Venick asked. He got a flat silence in answer, which meant he'd caused offense. "No need for that. It was just a question."

"It is against our laws."

"I've heard."

"We are not barbarians."

"You are at *war*."

"War can be fought without death," Dourin replied as if that were obvious. "Supply routes can be overtaken, pressure applied to southern territories, leaders captured and held prisoner."

"And tortured."

Dourin's smile was jagged. "Torture can be very persuasive."

Which might have started an argument between them—*You said you weren't barbarians*—had this been another day. Venick swallowed instead and tried a different route. "Tell me about the southerners."

"I thought Ellina already had."

He ignored that jab. "I want to hear it from you."

"They are wild. They hold to our laws, but…loosely. Queen Rishiana does not rule the south. No one does. But the queen expects the southerners to obey her. I think they are weary of that. Their disobedience— this refusal to stop forced honor suicides—is an act of rebellion. They want to remind us we do not rule them."

"And are they succeeding?"

"No." But his answer came too quickly. "There has always been tension between the north and south, but ever since the death of the queen's eldest daughter, those tensions have intensified. Some argue that our queen *should* rule the south. If she did, her daughter might still be alive."

This surprised Venick. "The queen's daughter died?"

Dourin momentarily disappeared behind a wide tree. He came out again on the other side, his white hair a beacon in the dark. "We do not know for certain. No one knows. She was traveling south on diplomatic business and the southerners were supposed to grant her safe passage, but she never returned. There has been no trace of her since, and that was eight years ago." Dourin seemed to hesitate. "Her name was Miria. She was Ellina's oldest sister."

Venick did not immediately catch the meaning of Dourin's words. They slid over him, slipped and slithered away. But Dourin's gaze became hooded, lingering a moment too long, and Venick paused. Blinked. Heard the words and their meaning all at once. The world tilted, everything shifting as he was flooded with disbelief, and then—

Reeking gods.

"Ellina's mother is the *queen*?"

"She did not tell you?" Dourin flipped a hand. "Shame."

But that made no sense. Ellina was a soldier. She could not be royalty and also be legion. Could she?

Venick's mind spun. He tried to recall what he knew about the northern elves and their county, which was only as much as Lorana had told him, but *she* was southern and rarely talked about it. Venick knew that the north was huge, twice the span of the southlands and mainlands combined. He knew the queen ruled those lands and had for the last century. He knew her soldiers took their oaths when they were young—infants, by elven standards—and served for life. But he knew nothing of the queen's daughters. Not how many she had, not the role they were meant to play.

"If Ellina is royalty," Venick said, "that means, that would make her—"

"No," Dourin cut him off impatiently. "She is the youngest of three, behind Miria and Farah. She has no place in the royal line."

"She has third. Or do elves not count now, either?"

"She is legion."

Which did make sense. Because Venick saw—clearly, painfully—what he hadn't before. He remembered the cave, the city, the sewers. The southern elves had not just attacked Ellina. They hunted her. He thought it strange, even then. Senseless, that they might target a lone elf with such determination. *I am a northern soldier*, Ellina had said. *I was caught in southern lands.*

But that wasn't all she was.

"Dourin." Venick's voice was low. Furious. He wasn't aware of becoming furious, only that he was, and the bitter well of aggression was too big, suddenly, too strong. A moment. Two. Then, forcing it out: "What are the southern elves really after?"

Dourin nodded. "Ah, human. Now *that* is an excellent question."

SIXTEEN

Ellina knew how to be silent. She knew how to step toe to heel, to avoid leaves and twigs and anything that went *snap* or *crunch*. To use the trees, to hang on their branches, become weightless. She liked the feeling of weightlessness, the way she might swing from one branch to another, her strong grip, the easy hold. She imagined she was a spider in a web. She could slip unseen and unheard, could draw her weapon if she had to, silent, deadly.

She drew it now. The green glass made no sound as she pulled it from its sheath. She watched the moonlight turn the blade translucent and felt the brimming pleasure she always felt when she beheld elven weapons. They were precise. Perfectly balanced. Sleek, not a single ounce wasted on frivolous embellishment.

She edged the tip forward to peel back a branch, shifting her eyes to peer through the brush. The elven camp was not large. Ellina counted eight elves around the fire. She counted their weapons, the number of blades and bows and axes. She counted her breaths, steady, in and out. She counted her choices.

She could return to her camp. Could gather Venick and Dourin and come back to this place together. Could risk Dourin's quick anger and Venick's silence that was *like* anger. She imagined the way he would look at her if she told him what she planned, then a stab of guilt that she had not told him. Not this, or anything.

He would learn the truth eventually. It felt inevitable, as if the truth waited there, as if it was woven into the undercurrent of every word she spoke. It would be easy to misstep, to slip over the edge, to reveal her secrets without meaning to. One wrong word. One mistake.

She thought of other words spoken by mistake, the ones she revisited over and over. *Because I trust him.* She thought of the feel of those words, the ease of them. There had been no tightening of the chest, no lash of headache that came just before a lie in elvish.

And here, the stab in her gut that was guilt, but for another reason. Because Ellina suspected that Venick trusted her, too.

He should not. She lied. About her real purpose for saving him. About who she was, what she knew. The truth was like a gaping hole inside her, a wound that wouldn't heal. She was wary of it. She was wary of what it would mean if she trusted him with it.

And she was wary of *him*, too, a little. She remembered the river in Kenath. Her panic, the shock of cold. How she had shivered from both. She had been determined, after, for him not to see. Not her fear, not her weakness. He saw both anyway. But he had not mocked her, not like Dourin or Raffan would have. He encouraged her. He offered to *teach her*.

Ellina shifted her sword into her other hand. The elves were busy around their fire. They did not sense her yet. She could leave, escape through the safety of the shadows, avoid the danger. It was what Venick would choose for her. What Dourin would.

Or she could enter the camp. She could announce herself and hope that these elves were wildings as they appeared. Ellina focused on their feathered necklaces, the pelts at their waists, bangles on their wrists and ankles that jingled softly as they moved. Wildings were clans of elves who lived in the south but were far removed from other colonies; a truly *wild* faction. Not like the conjurors who hunted her. If Ellina was right, these wildings would have no political stake in the war. They would not wish her harm.

But if she was wrong...

Ellina had been surprised by how quickly the southern conjurors found her in the caves, then again in Kenath. She thought of that coup, how the elves had infiltrated the city's guard. That sort of organized takeover should not have been possible, not from *them*. And it worried her. She worried how the southerners always seemed one step ahead. She was certain they had not shadow-caught her, but that meant they had spies. Message chains. Warriors standing by. Even if these wildings did not wish Ellina harm, the southerners were getting their information from *somewhere*. It was possible they might threaten the wildings for the knowledge they sought: information about Ellina, and her whereabouts, and her company.

But Ellina had questions of her own to ask. Questions these elves might know, like *how are the southerners gaining power?* and *where did the elves of Muralwood go?* and *what do you know about the queen's lost daughter, Miria?*

Ellina remembered her eldest sister and felt the way she always did when remembering Miria. The hitch of grief, a sharp stab under her ribs. The itch in her fingers to grab her sword and *swing*. And then the pain, the slow bloom of it in her heart. If she closed her eyes she could still see Miria's smile, the quick laugh, the easy way she gave her love.

There had been a night in Evov. The moon hung low over the mountains, a sliver of white against velvety dark. Their mother had called all three sisters into her private chambers. She had chosen Miria's bondmate, she said. He was due to arrive in a fortnight. There would be a celebration, then a bonding, and Miria would become queen. The ceremony was old tradition—and completely unexpected. Miria was young. The *queen* was young. It should have been years before Miria filled that role. But for reasons Ellina would never understand, the queen did not want to wait.

Every queen has their time, their mother had said to Miria. And then, snapped in Ellina's direction, *There are no rules as to when, daughter. It is my choice to make.*

The date was set. Miria would meet her bondmate. She would take the throne shortly after. Miria was silent through the announcement. After, she had nodded, and thanked their mother, and disappeared to her room.

Ellina's knock was soft on her door. When Miria answered, her eyes were wide with tears. *I cannot take the throne*, Miria pleaded. *It is not for me. It was never for me.*

Ellina understood. Miria never wanted to be queen. She was different from most elves, wild and full of spirit. When they were little, it was Miria who teased Ellina for her seriousness, who begged her to come to the river or ride horses or hunt for berries. The first-daughter's role was not meant for her. For Farah, maybe. Even Ellina might have grown into a queen. But not Miria.

Time had been a small mercy. There was hope that maybe Miria would come to accept her duty, would grow out of that childish laugh or her un-elven love for song. But now even time had been taken from her.

Then do not take the throne, Ellina had told her sister, full of brusque confidence she did not feel. *Leave the elflands. Make a new life for yourself.* And then, the words she would regret ever after. *I will help you.* Ellina touched two fingers to her sister's hand. It meant *love* and *comfort* and something deeper that could not be put into words.

Miria, like Ellina, had dark hair and so could easily pass as a south-erner. Ellina remembered leaning over the writing desk as she forged the southern summons, a diplomatic letter like so many Miria had received before. She remembered the smell of the ink and parchment, the way she had blown it lightly until dry. She remembered her sister packing for her escape, how they had hammered out the details late into the night.

On the day of Miria's leaving, Ellina had set a palm to her sister's cheek. It was the last time Ellina would ever see her. If this was to work, Miria had to disappear for good. It was not safe for them to write, not safe to visit. But Ellina was comforted by the thought that her sister would be free, and she would surely be happy.

I will keep your secret, sister, Ellina had said. *I will tell no one.*

Do you promise?

I promise.

Ellina had never spoken to anyone about Miria's fate. Not as the north blamed the south for her disappearance. Not as the elflands mourned the loss of their young heir. Even as tensions between the two sides heightened, Ellina stayed silent. She had promised her sister in elv-ish that she would keep her secret, and by the power of their language, that promise could not be broken.

Sometimes, she regretted that too.

Ellina lifted her eyes into the night. She inhaled deeply and thought of her choices, her mistakes, a lifetime of lies. She lowered her gaze back to the wildings and wondered what Miria would choose for her, could she see her now.

She sheathed her weapon. She stepped out into the moonlight.

SEVENTEEN

It was Dourin who spotted the blood.

He gave Venick a glance that was different from the usual side-eyed glare. This look was full of meaning. Dourin motioned toward the ground as Venick walked over. "Here," he said.

The blood was fresh. There was a long smear of it on the ground, black in the moonlight. Another a few paces away, then another, as if whatever had died took a long time doing it, had dragged itself across the ground, leaving an imprint and trail and then—nothing. The blood ended suddenly, a final patch of slick that went nowhere. Venick bent down to touch it. Thick, wet. The smell of it, like burnt metal. There was something he was supposed to glean from that smell. What was it? He tried to concentrate, tried to *think*, but his head was full of visions. Ellina hurt. Ellina captured. Her blood on the ground, crusted on her clothes and face. Dried into her hair, smeared across her pearly skin. The visions were gruesome and haunting and—

Impossible. Because…

"This is not elven blood," Venick said, sniffing again, gathering wits enough to remember what he ought to have known right away. He expected the lingering woody scent of elven blood but got a coppery tang instead. He looked at Dourin. "It doesn't have the right smell."

"And how would a human know what elven blood smells like?" But Dourin crouched beside Venick. He didn't touch his finger to the blood, didn't bring it to his nose. He simply inhaled, his eyes closing briefly before: "Hmm." He straightened. "It is goat's blood."

"Goat's blood."

"Yes."

"In the forest?"

"Nomadic elves herd them sometimes."

"I thought elves didn't eat meat."

Dourin's smile wasn't a smile at all. His lips pulled back unkindly. "We do not."

Venick opened his mouth to ask the obvious, but then he noticed it. A sudden draft on the breeze, a change in the air. Not so much a smell as a taste, a stickiness in his throat. That was, "Smoke," he said. And then, "Fire."

"I smell it too. This way."

They cut a path through the underbrush in the direction of the fumes. Venick looked up into the canopy and saw the tree's twisted fingers against the edge of morning. The sky was no longer inky black but bluish-grey, the stars a little less bright. They'd searched all night, then. But Venick didn't feel tired. He felt urgent, an urgency that hummed in his veins as he spotted the fire's light, then the clearing of trees and the cluster of elves within it.

Venick noticed the goat first. Its lifeless body lay beside the fire, cut open and still bleeding. Its legs and neck were twisted at odd angles. The skin had been peeled off its face, its eyes spooned out, ears cut off and missing. A group of elves mingled nearby, a mixture of dark and light hair, a mixture of male and female. Some were smeared with the goat's blood, swaying back and forth, their eyes closed, arms lifted into the air.

A ritual, Venick realized, and—

The hell? and—

Ellina.

There, on the far edge. Venick's pulse stammered at the sight of her, then shot high. He had the sudden insane urge to run to her, to barge through this strange elven camp and draw his weapon and *dare* anyone to stop him. He clamped down on the urge, hard. Forced himself instead to look, to *see*. He scanned her face, her wrists, her clothes, searching for any sign of a struggle, chains, a wound. Nothing. She was speaking to another elf, their heads bent low, her face gathered in the way it did when she was thinking. She wasn't a captive. Wasn't harmed.

But Venick did not relax. He glanced at Dourin. He wanted to ask *what is she doing?* and *do you know these elves?* but didn't for fear of being overheard. He studied Dourin's face instead, noticing the droop to his shoulders that was relief. The elf seemed to know something Venick did not. He motioned in elvish, quick movements Venick wasn't supposed to understand. *She is fine.* And then, a motion he *would* understand, in both languages. *We will go back.*

Venick thought of Kenath when Ellina had been surrounded by southern elves, when she'd fended off their attack with halfhearted parries, not believing herself to be in any real danger. She'd made the same motion then. A small shake of her head, a firmness behind the eyes. *Do not interfere. I can handle it. Go back.*

Venick hadn't listened then, either.

He crossed his arms. The elf frowned and motioned again, but Venick made his intention clear. *I will wait.*

Dourin looked ready to argue, then thought better of it. He shook his head, which might mean *idiot human* or *it is your choice.* Then he disappeared.

Venick turned back to the camp. The elves were dressed in furs, their weapons out and in plain sight. They didn't carry green glass; instead, their swords and axes were made of honest steel and stone. Rudimentary, though, as if carved themselves. And indeed, *everything* about these elves was rudimentary. Their bare feet. Their feathered clothing, hair unbraided. They were nothing like the elves from Kenath. Nothing like any elves Venick had ever met. Venick reckoned Ellina knew who— *what*—they were, though, and Dourin did too. He could see that clear enough. Dourin wasn't worried. Dourin *walked away.*

You can too.

Venick crouched instead, careful to stay downwind, to let the smoke cover his scent. He watched Ellina, scanning her again for any sign of distress, watching for her tells, but she was at ease. Her voice came to him in snatches over the noises of the camp. She was questioning these elves, Venick figured after a time. About what, he'd have to ask her after. Assuming she'd tell him the truth.

His anger, which had fled when he thought Ellina might be harmed, returned. He felt the beads of it crowd on a string, pulling and stretching and threatening to break. He knew better than to feel betrayed. He remembered each of Ellina's lies, all the things she kept hidden. He remembered the bear trap, the brothel. She didn't tell the truth. Neither did he. This was how it was between them.

But he'd never known Ellina to be *false.* Though their time together had been short, Venick had a sense of her. He'd never thought her to pretend to be someone she wasn't, to feel or think things she didn't.

And yet, she was the queen's daughter.

And yet, she hadn't told him.

The *why* bothered Venick. What did it gain her to keep that from him? What did she worry would happen if he knew? He wanted to ask her in elvish for the truth, all of it, bare it out once and for all. Maybe he would. Maybe he would walk into this camp right now and demand answers.

Or maybe he would stay silent. Push those questions away and re-member his life price. Remember that she was an elf, and he was a hu-man, and the secrets and lies were there for a reason. He thought of the last time he had won an elf's secrets. He thought of the last time he had fallen in love.

That what you're doing, Venick?

The thought drove him to his feet. No. *No.* Ellina had saved his life. Then he saved hers. They'd become partners, somehow, their fates en-tangled. *That* was what this was, and nothing else.

Believe that.

He did. It didn't matter that he enjoyed her company. It didn't matter that he was drawn to her strength and her cunning. Hell, it didn't matter that he cared for her, or that he had been scared, terrified, to think she was hurt. It did *not*.

The memories were there then, lightning flashes that left him blind. Static on air, the heat of a kiss, a dream. Lorana in Irek's market. Lo-rana holding his hand. Lorana's smile. But it wasn't Lorana's smile in his mind, not quite. Because Venick knew that smile. He knew the quick grin, the way it made light dance in her eyes. Sharp, though, uncertain, in the way one attempts kindness but doesn't quite manage it.

Ellina.

It was her in his thoughts. Her face. Her voice. That dark braid, her slender figure, the fierceness of her stare. The challenge in it. Him, feeling like he wanted to be good enough. Him, feeling…something else.

Venick blinked. What he was thinking…what was he *thinking?*

He spun. He could leave. Could make sure these feelings went nowhere, put distance and a border between them. He no longer required safe passage home; the mainlands were close enough. And indeed, the urge to leave was suddenly feral, the pressure of it growing large inside him.

But you won't.

No.

Venick let out a breath. He pinched his eyes shut. No, he wouldn't. They were almost to Tarrith-Mour. It was a day away. He could control himself for one more day. Ignore his budding feelings, lock them away, pretend they never were. As he turned back to watch Ellina, Venick realized that he'd known his feelings all along. That he'd nurtured it, even, this small thing growing between them.

Blame the loneliness. Blame three years of isolation, and a slow-burning grief, and Ellina, who'd shown him kindness, who *cared*, whatever her reasons. Venick watched her in the growing light of dawn and wondered how things would have been if she'd never chosen to save him. If her arrow had aimed true and sunk into his heart. If he'd died in that bear trap, like he should have.

EIGHTEEN

Venick did not at first notice the shadows.

He was watching Ellina and these strange elves and so he didn't notice how darkness seemed to rise out of corners and crevices, creeping over the forest, shifting dawn back to twilight. He didn't notice how the elves were becoming fainter, harder to see. Even when Venick did notice, he didn't understand. Thought it was the clouds moving back in, which they were. Thought a coming storm explained the encroaching dark. And listen, he could even hear distant thunder.

But then the elves seemed to still. They lifted their heads, sniffing the air like a pack of wild dogs. The hair prickled on Venick's arms, his body understanding what his mind still did not.

It began to rain. Lightly at first, a grey mist. The storm was closer than Venick thought, then. He looked up and finally saw what he hadn't before.

The shadows were moving.

All around them, a black fog descended. It crept between the trees, snaked across the ground, billowed up into empty air. Venick inhaled sharply and took a step back, hand going for his knife, eyes darting to Ellina, who had noticed the fog, too, who was barking orders at the other elves. *Go. Find cover.*

Venick abandoned his hiding spot then. He started towards Ellina as the camp disintegrated, elves grabbing hands and belongings and darting away. But then the shadows seemed to thicken, darken. The forest morphed back to night, and Venick lost sight of Ellina and the camp altogether.

His pulse doubled as he broke into a run. Overhead, the storm was strengthening, light rain evolving into something more. The wind picked up. Lightning fizzled. Venick reached the spot Ellina had been moments before, but too late. She was gone.

Venick blinked into the empty space he'd expected to find her. Blinked again through the wet and dark and dread, the same dread that had claimed him when he lost Ellina in the river: an ugly twinge in his gut, the sharp pain of nails dug into palms. The urge to call her name. The urge to run until he found her.

You know better.

He did. He was more likely to get lost if he went tearing off after her. More likely to find his *own* trouble. And there would be trouble, oh dear gods, he believed that. Venick spat rainwater from his mouth. This storm was not normal. The fog wasn't. It drew a cloak across the sun, solid black stretching between the trees, broken only by the occasional burst of lightning. But it was late in the season, too late for lightning. And this darkness. Venick didn't understand it. What *was* this? It was like a nightmare. Like magic. Like—

Conjuring.

The word came unbidden to his mind. It rose and consumed him. Conjuring. That meant southern elves. Close.

Here.

Venick lifted his knife, spinning from side to side as his mind worked, all the things he'd missed sliding neatly into place. Venick knew from his conversation with Dourin that the southerners didn't just hunt Ellina because she was a northern spy. They hunted her because she was the queen's daughter. If caught, she would make a valuable war prize. If killed, her death could be used to send a painful message. Ellina had evaded the southerners thus far, but they were getting smarter. Stronger. And now these shadows, this storm…they had found her.

Worse. They could use the darkness to *trap* her.

Venick took a step in one direction. Changed his mind, started in another. Stopped again and ground his teeth. It was suddenly again the night of his father's murder. That had been a trap, too. Venick remembered how he had stabbed his father in the gut. The gurgle of blood. His sword, oiled red. His father fell to the floor. His breath shuddered as he struggled to die.

Venick had fled north to the mountains. There was a hunt. Word of what he had done spread quickly. His father was a renowned military general. Well-loved. Venick had been loved, too, a son following in his father's footsteps. But not anymore. To kill one's own people was a terrible crime. And one's own *father?* Venick remembered the panic then, too. His people had fanned out. A chase. He was cornered in the northern foothills with nowhere to go.

Except, not *nowhere*. Venick had stared at the sheet of rock. He saw the trap, and he saw the way out. *Up.* And so Venick had climbed, sweating and shaking and dizzy with grief, with the knowledge that his entire world had changed, that he had changed it and his father had changed it. He climbed, and left his old life behind.

Venick climbed again now.

He grabbed for low branches, then hauled himself up into the nearest tree, working his way high into the canopy. Twigs scratched his face, tugged at his clothes. His hands stung raw. The darkness was no less here. He went higher still.

When he could climb no farther, Venick stopped and listened and tried to calm his pulse. He waited for the lightning.

It came, illuminating the forest. Venick caught a split-second glimpse of trees and rain and earth.

It came again. A flooded creek, ferns, the splay of moss.

Again. A glimpse of black hair. The flash of a hand.

A green glass sword, the quick sheen of it through the downpour.

Three tall figures cloaked in black.

Another figure, smaller, brown leather armor.

Ellina.

Venick was down in an instant. He dropped to the ground and sprinted in the direction of the movement, boots digging into soft earth, trees appearing and then vanishing as he flew past. He cursed his hunting knife for its uselessness, but it would have to be enough. If his aim was good—

It isn't.

—he would strike an elf first. Take his sword, go after the others.

Don't be an idiot.

But Venick was beyond rational thought. His body burned as he remembered Kenath, that battle. He knew Ellina was skilled enough to kill three southerners singlehandedly, *if* she would. But she wouldn't, of course she wouldn't, and so Venick forced his legs to move faster still, heart hammering as he came closer, as he heard Ellina's voice carry above the wind and rain.

"—get what you are after?"

Venick caught a slice of her through the trees. He could just make out her face.

"You make the same mistake that your mother makes," said another voice, unfamiliar, male. The scene flashed into view with each stroke of lightning. Three southern elves with weapons drawn. Ellina in their center, sword only half lifted. She appeared calm despite the storm and the enemy elves around her.

The southerner said, "You underestimate our growing power, Daughter of Rishiana. You do not believe we will unite."

Venick put on speed. His legs pounded the wet earth.

The southerner said, "You do not think we can *defeat you*. But we will."

No, Venick thought, hurtling forward. *No*.

Ellina lifted her sword.

Venick burst from the trees.

He threw his hunting knife. It spun through the air, catching an elf in the back of his neck. Venick couldn't hear the thump, was too far away to hear such a thing, but he imagined that he did as he saw the elf stagger, as he dove for the elf's fallen sword. He rolled to his feet with that weapon in his hand, and it felt *good*, so good to hold a sword again. Venick clutched his new weapon and felt the haze of powerlessness slip away. He could do anything. He could kill anything. The sword was a gift, a blessing from the gods.

A second elf came at him, but Venick saw her waver at the sight of his expression and he grabbed that hesitation, driving forward. Venick hailed down a series of strikes as hard and fast as the rain. And even though he was the weaker fighter, and she was a trained warrior and a conjuror, and she would soon recover from her shock and play the part she'd been born to play, Venick's pulse was humming, and he waded into the moment, too focused to care.

He parried a strike, then thrust. His sword nicked the elf's bicep, which surprised her. He could see her surprise, the foam of uncertainty that a *human* had killed her comrade and broken past her defenses, and so it was only a matter of using the momentum of that strike to bring his sword up from below, to cut a line across the elf's chest, land the tip in her chin. Her jaw split. She dropped her sword and crumpled beneath him.

Venick turned to Ellina. She was watching him and not the fight at her own fingertips, parrying the southerner's strikes without even *looking*. Venick wanted to shout at her. *Gods, Ellina. Don't look at* me. But instead he did only what he could, what his body commanded of him. He hefted his sword and *threw*.

The sword wasn't made for it. And Venick shouldn't have been able to throw a sword like that. Except, green glass was light. Except, Venick was built for it. And so the sword soared, spun once and found its mark in the elf's back.

He lurched to the ground. He exhaled a final breath.

Venick's gaze went to Ellina. His breath came in hot lungfuls, mind reeling. But she wasn't looking at him. Her eyes went to a spot just over his shoulder, her face contorting, suddenly, in fear.

He turned.

He hadn't heard the fourth elf behind him, hadn't seen. He hadn't expected, either, the looming shadow, the way it made the elf seem larger, darker, as he heaved his green glass sword up and over. Venick felt the stark absence of his own weapon. Felt his empty hands clench to fists as he stepped back, even though he knew it was too late, that he could not dodge this attack, and that death had come for him at last.

The blow never landed.

He saw the elf jolt as an arrow found its mark, there, in his neck. Venick blinked, watching as the elf dropped his weapon and collapsed, very hard and very dead. And then Venick was spinning, knowing, yet— dear reeking *gods*—unable to *believe*.

Ellina gazed back at him. Her chest heaved as she lowered her bow.

NINETEEN

Venick stared, shocked.

His mind became a wide pool. The moment dropped like a stone. He saw the surface ripple.

Ellina had made her vows. They were sacred to her. She refused to kill elves, to even believe that she could, yet here she had done it. For *him*.

"Ellina." Venick's lungs were too small. He stood there in disbelief, yet he *had* to believe it, because he was alive and the elf was not. The knowledge of what had just happened spread inside him, deep, then deeper. Around them, the rain slowed to a drizzle. The last of the shadows smeared away as the sky steadily brightened. It revealed the scene more fully, four elves slain, blood mixed with rainwater, their skin slick and shiny with it.

"He almost—" Ellina broke off. She looked as shaken as Venick felt. "He would have killed you."

"You should have let him." Venick wasn't sure he believed that, but he wasn't sure he didn't, either. He searched her face and saw it again: the flash of the elf's green glass, the certainty of death. In the seconds before the sword fell, a feeling had claimed Venick. *Ah*, said the feeling, which saw death, and opened its hands, and nodded. *At last.*

Then: the shock of Ellina's arrow. Bright blood. Disbelief.

"Your laws," Venick managed. "Elves don't kill elves. You wouldn't break those laws even for yourself. Why, then, for *me?*"

Ellina was silent.

"Ellina."

Her eyes went to the dead southerners. "Please," Venick said, then shut his mouth, because he didn't want her to see how he was coming apart, how his mind had become a scroll unfurled, and written in him was the wrongness of everything she'd just done.

He suspected she saw it anyway. Her eyes became sharp, almost fearful. Then she forced her gaze away and her expression shuttered. "There is nothing to explain," she said simply. Her hair clung to her face, water dancing in rivulets down her neck. "I agreed to see you safely home. I am not one to break my word."

"You had no reason to give me your word."

Ellina hesitated, then turned. She spoke with her back to him. "I did not need a reason."

"I don't believe you." But she was already striding away.

Venick wasn't fooled. Not by her tone or that empty expression. Not by her words, either. Because he remembered, didn't he? He remembered standing in the forest outside Kenath. The distant chime of the alarm bells, the blur of two homing horses across the dark valley. Dourin had begged Ellina to spare them, yet she killed them anyway. Venick remembered thinking, even then, that this was like her: to calculate the risk, to weigh each outcome. To choose with her head and not her heart.

But she had lost her head when it came to Venick. She must have, because it made no *sense*. It made no sense, how willing she was to throw her laws aside for him. How she put herself at risk to do it. What spurred this obligation to him? What had he done to deserve her loyalty?

Venick quickly retrieved his hunting knife and followed her through the forest. Though the storm was over, the evidence remained. Trees hung damaged and limp with rainwater, branches strewn across the ground like bones in a boneyard. It was a sickening reminder of the southern conjurors' power, the lengths they would go to capture or kill Ellina. "You risked too much to save me to not have a reason," Venick said.

She glanced at him over her shoulder. She caught his eye and her expression changed, seemed to show itself for what it was: not the careful mask of an elf trying to hide, but the slow wariness of someone who realized they *couldn't* hide. Not from him. "You saved me, too."

Venick let out a short breath of laughter. "That was different."

"I do not see how."

"You were only in danger *because* of me." Because she chose to stay behind to mend his foot while her troop forged ahead. Because she exposed herself by bringing him to Kenath. The conjurors had caught her trail, had attacked her, nearly killed her, because of *him*. Venick moved into her path, forcing her to halt. "Please, Ellina. I feel—" He dug frustrated fingers through his hair. "I just need to understand."

"I have already explained."

"Not well enough. Is there something you're not telling me? Some— secret reason you had for saving me?" Even as the words left him, he knew how ridiculous they sounded. His face heated, but he had already damned himself, so he let the rest come. "Why break your laws for me?

I'm human. Our two races have been at odds for centuries. And I'm the one who chose to cross the border. That was my decision. My risk. You are not responsible for me." It was the same thing she had said to him in the brothel. He saw her remember it, too.

A flash of defiance. The lift of her chin. "I have not done anything for you that you would not do for me."

Which was true. Venick knew if their roles were reversed, he wouldn't hesitate to give himself to her. He had already. But this was wrong. He knew it was, had grappled with the consequences of that since leaving Kenath. He feared things would be worse for her if he stayed. Worse if he left. Worse, because he couldn't decide whether to stay or go.

He *should* go. He could have left for the border already. It was close enough. Yet when he imagined leaving Ellina, he felt his heart on a string. It pulled. Tightened, dug deep.

Venick wasn't being honest with himself. If he was being honest, he would admit that this wasn't about wanting protection, not about repaying a debt. Maybe it never had been. But how could Venick explain? He couldn't tell Ellina how it had felt, when he'd woken in a small cave and she had worked to save his life, to see the fierce burn in her eyes, or to know that she saw something in him worth saving. He couldn't explain the cold agony of exile, or how his life no longer felt like a life, or how he'd wavered between a choice: live an outlaw, fight for redemption, or die and be free.

But Ellina reminded Venick that the world was not divided into citizens and outlaws. She reminded him what it felt like to fight for someone and to be fought for. What it was to *live.*

"I have a reason," Ellina said quietly.

"What?" Her words pulled Venick from his thoughts.

"You are right," she said. "I have a reason." He waited for her to explain, but she seemed unwilling to say more. Venick saw her lowered eyes, her hair coming free from its braid, the dip of her mouth.

"Look at me," he said. She did.

A feeling. It bloomed low. As Venick gazed at Ellina, he saw it in her, too. He held this shared feeling between them. It occurred to Venick that maybe Ellina did have a reason for saving him. Maybe her reason wasn't so different from his.

Explanations fell away. Thoughts did. Now there was only this feeling: a soft dawning. Its light ran through him. If Venick could have thought anything, he might have reminded himself that he was leaving. That he couldn't afford his feelings. That there were laws and a border meant to divide them.

But Venick wasn't thinking.

He lowered his mouth to hers.

His whole body flushed as their lips met, heat spreading. The kiss was breathless and heady and *impossible*. Impossible, the way her skin felt under his hands. Impossible, the way he heard her breath catch, the pulse of feeling. He pushed his hand into her hair and the kiss deepened, became something new. It was rich. He was, as he felt her mouth on his, tasting salt and rain and something sweeter, something undeniably *Ellina*.

He broke away briefly, breathing hard, then found her mouth again. The kiss became a begging thing, asking questions he refused to consider, casting words like *future* and *love* into his thoughts. But Venick couldn't think those things. How could he, when he had known the law, and broken it, and paid for the consequences of that choice every moment of every day since? Venick could still see the terror in Lorana's eyes, could feel in his hand the blade that wouldn't save her. He remembered the fury that had clung to him, and how it had been after, when

Lorana was dead and his father was dead and his world was burning.

As it would again.

He broke away.

Silence filled the space. Venick's heart thumped too loudly. His mind, too, was loud. His thoughts seemed to have taken flight.

"Venick—"

"I know." But he didn't. He didn't know. He gazed down at Ellina, her flushed cheeks, her swollen lips.

Horror filled him.

She must have seen his expression, or else understood the danger of their actions, because she took a step back, creating space. It wasn't enough. Venick could still feel the ghost of that kiss as if it lived there between them. It loomed, haunting. Venick saw its demon shape.

Lorana had been a common elf. She held no titles, owned no wealth. Yet when Venick's father turned her in for loving a human, the elves had come for her. They had killed her. What, then, would be the consequence for an elven *princess*?

Guilt swallowed him. What was he *doing*?

"Ellina." He dropped his hands. "I didn't—"

"You do not have to say it."

"Yes, I do. Dourin told me everything. I know who you are. I know the truth. You're not just a northern soldier—you're *royalty*. That's why the southerners are after you. That's why you're *valuable*." He spat out the word, hating the way it tasted. Hating all the things it meant. Venick closed his eyes, but behind closed lids he saw everything he feared: Ellina discovered, captured, forced to admit in elvish that she had killed an elf to save a human, and that human had kissed her, and she'd kissed him back. His self-loathing dipped to new levels. "You heard what they said." He opened his eyes. "The southerners are uniting. They are gaining power. If they knew about *this*…" He drew his hands between them, unable to continue.

Ellina went still. She stared at him. "What?"

"*Gods*, I never—"

"How do you know the southerners are uniting?"

"I heard them," he replied. "Just now. I heard your conversation."

"Venick." He didn't notice the anger that gathered in her face, the way her hand curled around her sword. He didn't see his mistake. His obvious, frightful mistake.

But then he did notice. The quiet that was not remorse or fear, but something else. The way she gazed at him as if she didn't know him, her whole body rigid: a weapon.

"Venick," she said again. "But *how* did you understand them? They were speaking in elvish."

TWENTY

Ellina wanted to curl into the rain and let it wash her away.

Humans did not speak elvish. *This* human did not. She heard the way he stumbled through their lessons. She watched the way he thinned in concentration, his eyes trained on her face as if he was memorizing the shape of the words, the shape of her mouth.

As if he was memorizing the shape of *her.*

Ellina flinched. Feelings butted up inside her, each one vying for attention until she did not know what she was feeling, only that she hated it. She was an elven soldier. She had sworn her oaths early, earlier than most, and she had risen quickly. First a runner, then an emissary. And then she had traded all that in to do what she did now, what she had always been best at doing. To hunt, to spy. She excelled in the art of deceit. How to use it and recognize it. How to bend any story to fit her own. She lied. She was a *liar.* But now Venick had deceived her so absolutely, so completely that she was tempted to turn in her weapons and uniform and call it dishonor.

She ached as she replayed everything she had said, every conversation he had overheard. In the forest when she lied for him. In Kenath when she argued for him, admitted her trust in him. Later, when she confessed her truths. That confession. She had wanted to tell him about the ugly jolt of surprise when she found him in the forest. She had wanted to tell him about the hatred that had oozed inside her, but also the fear. The fear that she would let hatred rule her. That she would kill him and break all her promises. She wanted to explain how she had been determined not to know him, to learn nothing about him. But how she did begin to learn. How strange that had been to speak to him, to fight beside him, to see his loyalty and his kindness. How her hatred had slowly thawed. Or maybe it was frozen still, but frozen like snow so that it could be brushed away.

And she had told him. Small pieces, the parts of her story she could bear. She had poured the words like poisoned wine so that he could see and smell but could not drink.

She had not thought he understood.

She was wrong.

"Ellina."

It was rare for elves to teach humans elvish, though it had not always been. Before the border, before the laws, elves taught humans elvish to gain their truths and to share their own. Lovers taught lovers, especially. There was a certain intimacy to it. And it was a way for humans and elves to show their commitment to one another, that they might embark on the task. If he knew elvish, it was because an elf had once loved him.

But then, Ellina had wanted to teach him elvish, too.

Her heart pounded, the quick rhythm ringing in her ears. Her hatred was not snow, she decided. It was the river in Kenath, cold and powerful.

Or maybe it was the night sky. Vast, endless.

"Ellina," Venick said again. "I'm sorry. I never meant—"

She pushed out a hand to stop him, but their eyes locked, and she saw reflected in him everything she felt. The hurt, the worry.

Fear at seeing him killed. A certainty absolute that she would never forgive herself if he was.

Their kiss. It rose into being within her.

Maybe her hatred was not hatred at all. Maybe it was something else entirely.

Her mouth had gone dry. Her lungs burned. She was ashamed. It shamed her to have stepped so completely off the edge of honor. She should never have allowed herself to get close to him, should never have allowed these feelings for him to grow. She thought of her vows. Elves did not kill elves. Ellina had sworn her life to the legion, had made oaths to her country and to herself. But Ellina had sidestepped those oaths, had allowed herself to be blinded.

"Please," Venick pleaded. "Say something."

She thought of the way Venick had burst into the clearing of conjurors. He killed for her. Maybe he would even die for her. She knew this, but the knowledge was not a comfort. It accused. It pointed its finger and pinned Ellina for what she was: the culprit. She had known his feelings and done nothing to stop them. It was wrong. *He* was wrong.

She was.

She could not bear to face her thoughts, which swirled in her mind, a bright stream of ribbons. She could not bear to look at Venick, or to see his remorse, or to know that he felt remorse at all, because what was his grief compared to hers?

She turned away so that she would not have to.

TWENTY-ONE

Venick went after her.

"Ellina."

She flitted in and out of sight. She moved through the forest with perfect grace. He struggled to keep up.

"Ellina, wait."

Venick's mind wasn't working. His thoughts crowded together. His breath came short and fast.

"*Ellina.*"

She spun to face him, and gods, her *expression*. He'd never seen her like this: stripped and angry and lost. Venick halted. Everything he wanted to say vanished. His mind became a winter valley.

She started to move away again, but Venick reached out a hand to stop her. "Please," he said. She glanced at the outstretched hand, his wordless appeal. Her eyes slid up his arm, his neck, his mouth. He let his hand fall. "Just—let me explain."

"There is nothing to explain."

"I'm sorry."

"There is no need—"

"*I am sorry*," he said in elvish. Her eyes flew to his. "*I am sorry I lied to you. Maybe I had a reason to keep my knowledge of your language a secret at first, but that was before…*" Before he knew her. Cared for her.

His heart became a hard stone. He held it in his palm, felt its heavy weight. He would have handed it to her then, would have given her the whole of him. *This belongs to you*, he would say. *You know that it does.* He would tell her how his heart had changed, how *she* had changed it, painting over old wounds, drawing him new. He would tell her what he was finally admitting to himself.

But he thought again of their kiss, and her laws, and he knew he couldn't say those things, he never could, and so he merely insisted, "*I should have told you I understand this language.*"

"*But you did not.*"

"*I know. I made a mistake.*"

"*Did you do it to gain information?*" A dark idea clouded Ellina's face. "Are *you a spy?*"

"*No, Ellina. Of course not.*"

"*Then why?*"

"*Because I wanted to live!*" he burst. "*Because you would have killed me if I had not.*"

Ellina dropped his gaze. She took a shaky breath.

It didn't matter that Venick was right. When he'd been caught in a metal bear trap and dizzy with pain, he *had* thought Ellina would kill him, so he lied about who he was and what he knew to save himself. But it didn't matter, because for reasons he still couldn't wholly explain, Ellina hadn't killed him. She had saved him. Opened to him. Tried to *teach* him. Yet still Venick kept his secret. He'd had so many opportunities to admit the truth. But he hadn't.

Venick didn't know what hurt more: the thought that Ellina had once wanted him dead, or that now he knew she didn't, and had instead given him her trust, and he had broken it.

"*Believe me, Ellina.*" He heard his own voice, wrecked and wrong. "*I am sorry.*"

"*It does not matter.*"

"*I never meant to hurt you.*"

Ellina's gaze changed. "You cannot hurt me," she said. "You did not."

But Venick didn't miss the way she switched back to his language. She seemed to realize her mistake, or perhaps she simply saw him see it. Her eyes narrowed. She turned away.

"Ellina…"

But whatever he meant to say was lost as Venick became aware of sudden movement through the trees, the slide and step of feet running. Venick turned and dropped his hand to his hunting knife, heart lurching as the footfalls became louder, the swift sound of bodies through brush. And then, one by one, they came into view. Elves. *Northern* elves.

Ellina's troop.

Venick had forgotten. He'd forgotten the stiff bodies, the stone faces, gleaming golden eyes. He'd forgotten the animal grace of elves on a hunt, synchronized like a pack of wanewolves. During their time together, Ellina had softened. Hell, *Dourin* had softened. But there was nothing soft about these elves now, nothing human. They were predators keen on their prey.

Venick recognized Raffan first. He saw the rope of white hair, the haughty eyes, smooth skin pulled over angled cheeks. Raffan spotted him, too. There was a moment of surprise—eyebrows arched, mouth loose—before he fastened it away.

"Ellina." Oh, reeking gods. Raffan wrapped the whole world into that name. There was a threat in it, no mistaking that.

"Raffan." Ellina's voice was steady as she watched the elves gather quickly around them. Dourin was there, too. If Ellina was surprised by the sudden reappearance of her troop, she didn't show it. Nor did she seem to fear what Venick did, the only thought pounding through him: that they would sense, somehow, everything that had just occurred between them.

"I thought we would meet in Tarrith-Mour," Ellina said.

"Plans have changed." Raffan looked around the wet forest, then again at Venick. A long, cold stare. "For me and for you, I see. Is this why you were late?"

"We encountered trouble."

"The human—"

"Not him," Ellina interrupted. "The southerners. They have been hunting us."

A pause. "The southerners have never been a problem for you before."

"These southerners are different. *This*," she motioned around the forest, "was of their making."

"The storm?"

"It was not just a storm," Ellina replied. "It was conjuring."

Silence, as her words settled. Venick watched the elves stifle their reactions—expressions taut, hands steady—yet he saw the truth anyway. Whatever Ellina's troop knew of southern conjurors, this was new to them, too.

Raffan alone seemed unaffected. His posture was easy, arms by his sides, shoulders back and down. A moment passed where Venick couldn't be sure what he was thinking. Then Raffan straightened and said, "The southern elves are not powerful enough to command the weather."

"But they did," Ellina insisted. "And that is not all." She told them about the coup in Kenath, how the southern elves had infiltrated that city and now commanded its guard. "The southerners are gaining strength."

"A hasty conclusion."

"Hasty?" Ellina's hand went to her sword. A habit, Venick realized, that could also be interpreted as a threat. "You said it yourself. The southerners should not have this kind of power."

"The southern conjurors are a ragtag band of rebels, and Kenath is a border city—hardly worthy of our concern. They pose no real threat to us."

"And Tarrith-Mour?" Ellina pressed. "What of the threat *there?*"

Another elf, a tall male with a hooked nose whose name Venick didn't know, answered. "We found nothing there. The city was empty."

Ellina blinked. "Empty?"

"Abandoned," the elf said. "The elves have moved."

"The entire city?" Ellina looked between them in disbelief. "But *where?*"

"We do not know," Raffan cut in, "nor is it our concern. We will return to Evov now and give the queen our report."

"I should think a vanished city raises questions."

"The south is unstable. Elves are always moving."

"Except that we passed Muralwood. It, too, was abandoned." Ellina shook her head. "Alone, each of these events could be explained away. But together? Something is not right."

Raffan seemed unconvinced. He took a sidestep, settling into commander's stance. "Our orders were clear. Our mission was to investigate the honor suicide in Tarrith-Mour. We have. It is time now to return to Evov."

"We cannot return yet."

"Would you neglect your duty?"

"My duty is to my family. To my country."

"And to me," he added.

Ellina ignored that. "Dourin and I will return to Tarrith-Mour to investigate. We will scout the other cities in the region to see if they, too, have vanished. We will meet you in Evov."

Raffan hardened. A muscle ticked in his jaw. "You are overstepping, Ellina." His gaze slid to Venick. "*Again.*"

"This is important."

"I am the commander of this troop. *I* decide what is important. And I order you to stay."

Ellina's eyes flashed, and Venick knew that look. Defiance. Pride. Then, softly, "No."

It was a small thing for Raffan to step forward. To reach across the space, his hand moving so fast that Venick didn't see a hand at all, only the flash of white. Raffan's expression didn't change. He barely even appeared to move.

Venick was slow to understand. He saw Ellina's head snap back with the force of the blow. He saw how she stumbled, how her eyes watered as she clutched her cheek. The red print of a hand swelled beneath her fingers.

Venick's blood iced over. Rage fisted inside him.

He lunged.

He barreled into the elf, forcing them both to the ground. He didn't remember drawing his knife, but that weapon was suddenly in his hand, arcing toward Raffan's neck. He didn't remember seeing the elf's counter and blocking it, heaving a punch with his free fist. He didn't—*couldn't*—see anything but the echo of Ellina's pain, Ellina's hurt, the raised mark on her cheek.

The rest of Ellina's troop descended quickly. They pulled Venick off, strong hands forcing him to his knees. He fought. He landed a kick before they were shoving his face into the dirt, pinning him to the ground. A mouthful of earth. A knee between his shoulders. Both hands bound quickly, cinched tight enough to bruise. They hauled him back to his knees as Raffan stood unsteadily. He gazed down at Venick with murder in his eyes.

And then, the cold press of green glass at Venick's neck.

The sword bit into his skin. Blood leapt from the cut. Venick didn't have time to feel fear, wouldn't have had room for it anyway. All he felt was anger, an anger so complete it consumed him. His vision pulsed. His whole body trembled.

Fool.

It was over. Some distant piece of him understood that he'd just assaulted an elf in elven lands, that he was bound and weaponless and at their mercy. But elves had no mercy, not for humans.

Except.

Venick looked at Ellina. His eyes sought hers, and when they locked he felt chilled relief, because he saw what he worried he wouldn't, even if the moment was too quick for him to understand that worry. Ellina's gaze was full of fear. Despite her angry words, despite the pain of his lies, Ellina didn't want him dead. She was afraid at seeing him hurt, because she *cared*.

Raffan took a step forward. "You would defend her?" he asked Venick. His expression was perfectly controlled. His voice, though, was a storm.

"Raffan." Ellina. She stood statue-still at the edge of his vision. Raffan turned on her.

"*He defends you,*" he said in elvish, "*at his own peril.*"

"*He owes me his life,*" Ellina answered. Her tone didn't change, but Venick saw the look in her eyes, the inward quality to her expression, which had become as smooth and clear as ice. Venick realized he recognized that expression; it was the way Ellina looked when she was scheming. "*You know about human life prices, do you not?*"

"*I care not for the ways of men.*"

Ellina almost shrugged, but stopped herself. Raffan saw it. Venick saw Raffan see it, and saw how it changed his anger into suspicion. Venick remembered his father, suddenly. The slow morph of fear, the need to control, the distrust. Raffan looked the way his father had the night he discovered Venick loved an elf.

"*It has served me,*" Ellina said.

"*But has he served you? There must be some reason he is still alive.*"

"*We made a bargain.*"

"*Yes, I remember. You would teach him elvish and he would give you his secrets.*" Raffan's voice simpered. "*And how has he performed?*"

"*He knows every word I have given him,*" Ellina said easily.

"*And does he have valuable information for our queen?*"

"*He overheard a conversation between the southern conjurors. He says they are gaining power. They are uniting.*"

True, all true. Venick should not have been amazed. This was Ellina. *This* was what she was good at. Telling lies in half-truths. Telling them with confidence. Her face might have been a looking glass: transparent, unclouded.

"*Well,*" Raffan said, "*now that we have his confessions in elvish, he is no longer any use to us."*

Venick's anger curdled. He clenched his fists, glaring.

"And now," Raffan said in mainlander, "he assaults an elf. In the *elflands."*

"He did not mean it."

"I think he did. We allowed him to break our laws once, and look at where it has led." Raffan's gaze drifted back to where Venick knelt. "This time, he will not go unpunished."

Ellina didn't hesitate. "I will take his punishment."

"No," Venick said. "Ellina, *no."*

But she unbelted her sword and threw it to the ground. Her quiver. Her bow.

"You will take his punishment?" Raffan repeated.

"It is my right as a soldier."

"It is," Raffan agreed, watching Ellina remove her weapons. "But I am wondering at your reasons." He switched back to elvish. *"I am concerned, Ellina. I do not understand what has possessed you."*

"Are you denying me my right?"

"No. I am merely questioning your motives. Why do this for him?"

"You want to punish me," Ellina replied. *"I am giving you what you want. What do my reasons matter?"*

It happened quickly. Ellina throwing down her gear. A rope. Her hands outstretched, the cord twisting to bind them. Venick's heart pounded as he watched, helpless. He didn't understand what was happening, couldn't comprehend it. The satisfaction on Raffan's face. The grim resolve on Ellina's. The sadness in Dourin as they turned Ellina and tied her wrists to a tree. Purposeful, methodic, as if this was a dance often rehearsed. Venick remembered Dourin's words to Ellina then, the somber set to his gaze. *I know how Raffan is with you.*

It wasn't until they ripped open the back of Ellina's tunic that Venick understood. His mind shut down, his whole body revolting at the sight. Scars. A maze of lines crisscrossing her back, some old, white, others pink and new. A whip was produced and placed in Raffan's hand. The elf positioned himself behind her.

Venick was distantly aware that he was yelling. He heard his own voice that sounded nothing like his voice. And then, the snap of the whip as it came down. It shredded a red line across her skin.

Venick raged against the elves who held him, threatening, then pleading as the whip came down again and again, striking new patterns across old ones. He saw the curve of her spine, the way she gripped the rope, silent, blood pouring.

His fury was a wave that frothed and swelled inside him. It crashed over his head, pulling him under.

TWENTY-TWO

Venick woke to darkness. He shuffled himself upright, blinking past the skull-splitting headache, both trying and not trying to remember how he'd landed here.

It was Dourin who'd dealt the blow. He'd come out of nowhere, his aim precise, ramming Venick's temple *just* so. Hard enough to knock him unconscious. Not quite hard enough to kill him. Call that a favor. Call it mercy.

Call it what it was, Venick: a mistake.

Maybe not. If Dourin wanted him dead, a sword through the neck would have done the trick. If Dourin wanted him dead, he wouldn't be splashing water on Venick's face now to wake him, gripping his shoulder firmly in a way that warned silence. The warning was unnecessary. Venick was not a fool.

But he had been.

He shook his head, water droplets spraying. It was night. He was still bound. He looked around, trying to get his bearings. His headache came alive with the movement. His vision swam, then greyed. He thought, vaguely, that he might black out again.

"*No*," Dourin hissed in elvish. He lowered his face to meet Venick's. There was something odd about his expression, something new. "*You understand me, do you not?*" Venick glared, but Dourin only nodded. It was his scowl, Venick realized, that looked so strange. Or rather, the smoothed brow where his scowl usually was. Dourin was looking at him differently, as he never had before. "*Did Ellina—?*" But he let out a little laugh. "*No. Of course not. You knew before. Another elf taught you. I do not know how I missed it before, but I see it now. I can tell you understand me.*"

"Understand *this*," Venick snapped, and spat in his face.

Dourin didn't flinch. Didn't even draw back. He closed his eyes as if with all his effort, bringing up a hand to wipe it away. "Maybe use your words now."

"You disgust me," Venick growled, all the recent horrors reemerging in flashes of color and sound. He thought of the way Dourin had helped bind Ellina's hands, the way he stood by as Raffan ripped her to pieces. The images all came crashing back, a shower of hurt and anger and pain. Venick felt sick all over again. "You knew what he would do to her. And you just *let him*."

"If it had been *you* tied to that tree, Raffan would have whipped you to death. Do you understand that? She saved your life. Again."

"I would rather be dead. I would rather be *dead* than this."

"You are a bigger idiot than I thought."

Venick was too angry to speak. He could still see the hot flash of the whip, cuts splitting along scarred skin, the way Ellina knuckled her ropes. He could see every moment right up until Dourin had knocked him cold. Venick didn't know how long the whipping had gone on after that. He was afraid to know.

"Listen to me," Dourin said. "Raffan is her bondmate. Do you understand what that means?"

"I don't give a *damn* what it means."

"You should." And there again, that expression on Dourin's face, strange because it was new. "Bondmates are chosen to bear children for the empire. It is their duty. But bondmates are forced pairs. Sometimes a partner is not willing. Sometimes neither partner is. There are rules. An elven child must be produced, or there are consequences. To keep elves from revolting, bondmates—" He broke off, and Venick was suddenly sure he didn't want to hear the rest. "It is more than just a coupling. Raffan *owns* her. He owns her until she bears his child. That is the law."

"To hell with your laws."

"We are elves. We are ruled by our laws."

As if that explained anything. As if that *helped*. It didn't. Gods, it made it worse.

"In the legion, commanders have the right to exact their own punishments," Dourin explained. "We have all faced beatings. But a commander knows to temper his punishments. He knows not to push too hard or he will lose his troops. It has happened before. If elves resist, the wing falls apart. But with Ellina—she resists Raffan all the time. Not just as his subordinate, but as his bondmate. She refuses him. To be with him, to bear his child. Her rejection embarrasses him, and Raffan hates her for it. Or he does not, maybe. That is not the point. He manipulates her. He lets her break the rules so that he can punish her. And she does break the rules. All the *time*." Dourin spread his fingers helplessly. "She plays into his hand. And Raffan, as her commander and bondmate, is cruel to her. But he is not wrong."

"Why are you telling me this?"

"I want you to understand." Dourin's gaze leveled. "She chose to accept your punishment."

"She should not have." He felt his anguish anew.

"No. It will make things worse for her." Dourin peered at him. "Usually, the offer to accept punishments is done between lovers. I knew Raffan would be suspicious when he saw you alive, but her offer to protect you sealed her fate. And yours."

"There is nothing between us."

"Could you say that in elvish? Could *she*?"

Venick was silent.

The agony that had gripped him since Ellina's whipping seemed to pace. It became animal, its yellow eyes glaring, ready to lunge, to swallow him whole. Venick wanted to bury his head in his hands. He wanted to find Ellina. He knew it was wrong to want it. He knew it made things worse.

He knew whose fault this was.

"Where is she?" Venick asked.

"With him." Venick stared. "After he whips her, he bandages her. It is a commander's duty."

"Untie me."

"I do not think so."

"*Untie me.*"

"You are going to do something stupid."

"I'm going to kill him."

"With what weapon?" Dourin arched a brow. "Your fists? Even if you were the better fighter—and you are not—you cannot hope to win that fight." Dourin looked up as if considering. "Ellina took your punishment. By our laws, that absolves you of your crimes. Raffan should set you free." He dropped his eyes. A hard stare. "You may have noticed that he has not."

Venick guessed Dourin's meaning. "He wants to kill me."

"Oh, surely. But he will not."

"Then what?"

"Raffan wants many things, I suspect. Ellina told some pretty lies for you. Very nice, very clever. But there is a problem. Raffan *knows* Ellina. He knows she is hiding something. He wants to understand the real reason you are still alive. Maybe he will ask her for her secrets in elvish. Maybe not. It is a delicate game we elves play. But with *you*," Dourin motioned with his hands. "You are not an elf. And Raffan will not be asking."

"Torture?" Venick shook his head slowly. "I can handle it."

"How presumptuous of you."

"All soldiers are taught how."

"And when Raffan discovers you speak elvish? What will you do *then*?"

Venick saw it again. Ellina's arrow through the southerner's neck. Her lips sealed against his. If those secrets were ever revealed, she could be banished for it. Worse. Venick dropped his head. "I never wanted to hurt her."

"Then you know that you cannot stay. It is too dangerous. If I were you, I would be thinking of escape. I would accept any chance to slip away, should it arise." Which was not the sort of answer Venick had expected. Which had the flavor of collusion.

Venick became aware of the night, the dark, his mind sharpening to fit together each piece of this moment. There was a reason Dourin had knocked him unconscious, and not just to silence his screams. There was a reason he had dragged his body through the forest, tied him far away from the others. A reason he had come for him now to speak alone. "What you're suggesting…"

"I am not *suggesting* anything."

"If you—" But before Venick could finish, Dourin pulled his sword from its sheath, and in a quick moment Venick's hands came unbound. Then, in a twist Venick never saw coming, Dourin offered out his weapon.

"Go *home*, human," Dourin said. "And go quickly."

Venick stared at that sword, at the chance that had been offered by the unlikeliest of allies. But maybe not so unlikely. He and Dourin shared a common thread that was Ellina.

Dourin was right. This was Venick's only option. He knew that it was. And yet: "I can't just leave her," he said. "Not like this. Not with *him*."

"Were you not listening to anything I just said?"

"I *can't*."

"You care about her."

Venick's throat was tight. "Of course I care about her."

"Then you need to leave." Dourin softened. "It is best. For both of you."

TWENTY-THREE

Ellina did not want to open her eyes.

She did not want to see the blush of morning light through the trees. She did not want to be reminded of the morning, or what it meant that it was day now and not night, or why that mattered. She squeezed her eyes shut and ignored the low whispers of her troop, the way they hovered around her, the burn of pain as they dressed and redressed her bandages, a salve thumbed gently over exposed flesh. She did not want to see the confusion in their eyes, or the concern, or the questions.

Mostly, though, she did not want to see her choices. They were all around her, unavoidable, laid bare in the blood that seeped down her ribs. In Raffan's gaze, his dark jealousy. In her own heart, which was restless. Insistent.

She ignored it. She told herself she did not care to know what it meant that her heart beat so incessantly. She did not care that it worried, that it begged her to wake.

She kept her eyes closed.

• • •

Dourin was there.

She heard him settle in beside her, the slide of his back against a tree. He heaved a long sigh.

She opened her eyes. It was full daylight. Sun filtered through the trees, casting everything in a haze of green. She could hear the rest of their troop nearby. Voices. The snap of canvas. A camp being broken down and packed away.

She lifted her head, and the motion sent spasms of pain down her back.

"Where is he?" The question was out before she could pull it back.

Dourin readjusted his shoulders against the tree. "Gone."

"Gone—?"

"He fled last night. I do not blame him. After what happened with Raffan, he would be a fool to stay."

The words were feather-soft. They floated around her, landed gently, a butterfly's touch. They could not hurt her. She promised herself they could not, because they were expected. Because she could not be hurt by something she already knew.

Yet *had* she known? Venick had defended her, stood by her, put his trust in her. She had done the same for him. She remembered his voice as he watched the whip fall: furious, horrible. She expected his anger. He would insist that she should never have offered to take his punishment. *Do you think I couldn't handle the sentence for my own actions?* he would demand. *You are not responsible for me.*

Yet if Dourin was to be believed, Venick was not angry. He was not going to insist on anything. He was not even there.

"That makes no sense," she said. "He would not just leave."

"Why not? He was going to cross back over the border anyway. He does not belong here."

"It is not like him to run. Not after…" She let the thought trail.

"You are seeing what you want to see."

Ellina frowned. "*I see things clearly,*" she said in elvish, and she did. She saw Dourin. She saw the little ways he had changed during their time with Venick. She saw it even more starkly when placed against the backdrop of the rest of their troop. His mouth had become more expressive. He had the habit of cocking one eyebrow. His hands were restless. Those hands. She watched them fold, then refold. She saw the way he fidgeted and felt a pinch of doubt. "*Tell me again in elvish. Where is he?*"

The challenge cut. Dourin's face became grave. "*Gone, Ellina. He is going home.*"

The words were not feathers. They were the black strap of a leather whip. They were flesh torn off her back. They were not expected. She had not known.

She had no right to feel betrayed. It had been her choice to take Venick's punishment; he owed her nothing for it. She thought again of their last words to each other. His lies. Hers. Despite all that had happened, there was no honesty between them, no real basis for trust. They were not partners. Not…something more. And it was like Dourin said. Even if Venick had wanted to, it was illegal for humans to travel the elflands. He never could have stayed. Ellina knew that.

But it hurt her all the same.

TWENTY-FOUR

It was strange, to travel alone again. Stranger: the silence. A man could get used to the company of elves. He could get used to the quiet patter of their feet, the hush of their braids trailing their backs, the conversation, when they were in the mood for it. Now silence hung over everything. It made every crunch of his steps too loud, every clink of Dourin's sword at his hip, every sigh he tugged through his nose.

Venick looked down at himself. He saw weeks of travel stains and blood stains and stains that came from he didn't know where. He saw the weariness, too, as if the exhaustion had seeped into his clothing, turned it ragged and worn. He had walked straight through the night, into the morning and deep into the next evening before hunger and fatigue forced him to make camp. Though, *make camp* was generous. He'd fallen into the first alcove he spotted, curling up under a fallen tree and succumbing to a restless sleep. He was up again before dawn, moving on.

The sky waned yellow. The air was hot and sticky. Through the silence emerged the high cry of a cicada. It was quickly joined by its brethren. Their song rang in Venick's head.

He cursed the bugs. Cursed the wet earth, the slop of it at his boots. Cursed his own fatigue, and his lingering headache, and the sweat that dripped down his brow into his eyes.

Could be worse.

Hell. Venick inhaled a deep breath and tried for patience, tried to feel glad. He managed the first, mostly. As for the second. Well. He was alive. He was free. He *should* be glad, and maybe he was, but he was also grieved. He thought about Ellina. He thought of the way the whip had cut into her skin, and how watching it cut her cut *him*, and what that meant. He remembered her lies, all of them, especially the ones she told on his behalf. He thought of how he had left.

You didn't abandon her.

But it felt like he had.

He focused on the forest. He considered his path. How far he'd come, how far he still had to go. The border was just to the west. If Venick turned and looked, he could envision the edge of the trees just *there*, and beyond it, the stretch of grasslands that marked the beginning of his homeland. Venick breathed in the stench of mud and wet forest and allowed himself to imagine crossing that tree line back into the safety of the mainlands.

But Venick was not returning to the mainlands. Not yet.

He turned south. He shaded his eyes and held his breath and *listened*, really listened, past the pitched song of the cicadas. He heard nothing else and couldn't decide whether that was good or bad.

Good, for now.

He walked. A liralin bird flashed overhead. Venick caught a glimpse of the orange throat, the dusky feathers. He imagined what Ellina would say could she see what he planned. How anger would furrow her brow. *Are you trying to get yourself killed?* The way that anger would mask her worry. In his vision, he cupped Ellina's cheek in his palm. He reassured her that he wasn't dead, he was here, right here, as he always would be.

Venick wondered if he hurt himself with such imaginings. He wondered at how cruel his own mind could be, feeding him impossible lies.

That night Venick made camp in a clearing, a *proper* camp with a fire. He should worry about southern elves. About wanewolves and bears. But he didn't. He lay on his back, watching the flames jump and bite the air. He thought about his choices. His mistakes. Old and new swirled together, clouding his mind. Hazy, a building storm.

• • •

The rain returned.

It worried Venick how the rain seemed to follow him, a somber shadow trailing overhead. It misted the earth, leaving a dewy path. The forest seemed greener. The ground, browner. Frogs chirped, their calls a cacophony of highs and lows.

Venick thought of the three southerners he had killed in the storm. That number felt suddenly small. Insignificant. Three deaths would not end this war. It would not change anything. Perhaps their deaths had already been noted. Perhaps this rain was conjuring and there were more southerners tracking him now.

The day wore on. Finally, the rain abated. Patches of blue sky appeared between the grey. But this time Venick knew better than to believe he was safe.

. . .

He missed having his own sword.

This was what Venick thought as he slid Dourin's weapon from its scabbard one afternoon, as he slashed a few practice swipes through the air. The hiss of the green glass was quiet. Hardly even there.

Venick remembered following the sound of green glass in Kenath. He had always hated that sound. The eerie whisper. Yet as Venick listened to Dourin's sword—now his—he thought maybe he had been wrong. Maybe it wasn't the sound he hated, but the feelings that came with it. Fear. Powerlessness. The knowledge that green glass meant elven fighters, who were stronger and faster and *better* than him.

He moved through an old set of training poses, learning his new sword, feeling its near weightlessness, its balance. He listened to it hiss and imagined what it would be like to fight with such a weapon. All the damage it could do.

No, Venick thought. He didn't mind the sound so much after all.

. . .

He found the camp on the fourth day.

He practically stumbled into it, catching sight of the still-warm firepit a split-second too late. Venick froze, then skidded out of sight. Hell, so much for *sense*. He had never been a scout, not a very good one, but at least he knew better than to walk with a wandering mind. He hadn't been paying attention. Hadn't even noticed the fire or the bedrolls until he was practically on top of them.

He was lucky, then, that the camp was empty.

Venick put some distance between himself and the fire. He crouched out of sight. He settled in and waited for the elves to return.

They did, after a time. Venick counted seven elves total. All southern, judging by their unadorned ears, and heavily armed, each with their own personal arsenal of swords and bows and knives. One, Venick noted with a strange stitch in his gut, even had a war hammer.

The elves settled into their camp. Dusk came. Nightfall. Venick's legs cramped. He was unbearably thirsty. But he could not risk being discovered. He stayed where he was.

When the elves broke camp sometime after midnight, Venick followed.

· · ·

The moon rose. Its light wasn't much to see by, but the elves lit no torches and carried no lanterns. Wherever they were headed, they knew the way.

Venick hung back. Twice now he had stepped wrong, breaking a branch under a clumsy foot with a *snap* that made him grimace. The elves—somehow, miraculously—didn't notice.

God-touched, are you?

He'd never thought so. Even if he was, Venick knew better than to count on that luck to hold. It was too dark to watch his footing, too quiet to hide. He hung back yet farther still. The elves became ghosts in the distance. Soon, Venick lost sight of them altogether. But Venick didn't need to see the elves to follow them.

They left a trail.

This was unusual. By habit, elves preferred to leave no mark of their presence. Yet Venick could see it clearly: seven sets of muddy tracks stamped into the earth.

Dawn came. The forest shifted from uncertain grey to brilliant green and gold. The day revealed more sets of tracks, shadowy indents in the forest floor. Venick counted ten, fifteen, twenty leather-shoe markings and more, so many more that each print became indistinguishable from the next, converging into a single, mud-stamped path.

He followed it.

The forest came to life as the day unfolded. White mossflowers opened, bending towards the sun. A dragonfly's wings purred. Two squirrels squabbled in a tree overhead. They upset branches. Leaves rained.

And then, a different sound.

Venick slowed. His thoughts did. He knew that sound. The clink and buckle of metal. The gusty whuff of a horse. Voices, the low buzz of them. They were noises he had grown up with, sounds he had dreamed of long into his exile. Venick stepped quietly forward, inching around trees, breath caught somewhere between his heart and his throat.

They came into view, and then his breath was gone.

Elves. Hundreds of them, thousands. All gathered here in the forest together. Venick gaped, his thoughts spinning away.

And he remembered.

He had served as a soldier in the mainlands as all men did. As a lowlander, his homeland was under constant threat from warring territories, colonies from the grasslands or the highlands. All men of fighting age were expected to defend their home, and Venick—being the son of a famed military general—chiefly among them. As Venick gazed at this elven encampment, the memory came clearly. He had slept in these same quartered contingents, had worn that same hammered armor, had spent countless days doing just as these elves were doing now: polishing weapons, currying horses, loading supply wagons. Venick remembered the late nights, the thrumming energy before a battle, the way he would forget himself as dawn came and war cries bellowed and he sunk steel into the men who wanted to claim his home. After, how his body became like a rippling liquid, how his arm would ache from the weight of his sword. How grateful he had been for that, that his sword had made him strong.

Venick was seventeen the first time he went to battle. Lorana had hated it. She didn't understand the human way of war. Elves warred too, certainly, but their battles were mostly bloodless.

Humans are brutal, she said to him one night, watching him buckle on his armor.

Humans are passionate, he told her.

Your fighting is endless.

We fight to protect those we love, and to keep what is ours.

If you must fight so hard for it, perhaps it was never meant to be yours.

It was common knowledge that elves did not kill each other, nor did they battle as humans did. Yet as Venick gazed at the elves working grinders, organizing horse tack, gathering crossbow quills and arrows, he knew that this was not merely a camp or a tent-city. It was an army.

Venick's mind, which had been clouded by his own remorse, by his pain and confusion and the black memory of Ellina's scars, cleared. Ellina had been right. The vanished cities of Muralwood and Tarrith-Mour were not odd coincidences. Those elves were going somewhere. They were coming *here*.

Venick watched an elf drive a stake into the ground, then raise what could only be a sigil banner. The symbol was not one he knew: a black raven between twin flames. Venick gazed at that banner and understood, suddenly, what had unsettled him at the sight of the elf with the war hammer. That was a human weapon. Banners, too, were a human tradition. These elves looked—*human*.

And this army. This *army*. Venick had never seen anything like it, even in the mainlands. There were cannons. Enormous war horses. Contraptions that looked like battering rams on wheels. A black-haired elf moved to raise a second banner beside the first. It bore the image of a female elf wearing a crown. There was a commotion among the elves. Someone produced a torch. It was set to the banner. It caught. The cloth was quickly eaten by fire. The elves didn't cheer—maybe that was too human—but they watched in silence, unified under the image of the northern queen burning.

Venick's eyes darted from elf to elf, his suspicion plummeting into dismay. He had suspected, as Ellina did, that there was something more to the vanished cities and the southerner's growing power, yet he had not quite expected *this*.

Maybe he should have. Everything he knew about the southerners hinted at deep-seated disquiet and brewing violence. Only, this army was not the ragtag band of rebels Raffan had described. Far from it.

Venick held his breath and watched and waited. The elves mingled. They spoke amongst themselves. Hand gestures were few between them. Expressions were even fewer. Damn if he could overhear conversations from this distance or glean anything from the few hand movements he did understand. *Practice. Prepare. Obey.* Nothing he could string together, nothing he could use.

Until the black-haired elf stooped to gather the scorched shreds of the banner and turned away from the camp. Until he walked towards Venick, presumably to dispose of the flag's remains. His path brought him within paces of Venick's hiding spot. The elf must have been distracted by thoughts of burning and killing. It would explain why he didn't hear the slide of Venick's step, didn't sense the ambush until the gentle touch of green glass was suddenly at his ribs. The elf froze. He did not, thankfully, scream.

No, Venick thought. Definitely not human.

"*I have questions,*" Venick said in elvish. Low, so that his voice didn't carry. "*You will answer them.*"

"*Or what?*"

Venick pressed the green glass harder. It sheared thinly into the elf's black tunic. Unlike most of his comrades, this elf wore no armor and carried no weapons. A fatal oversight.

The elf turned his head slightly to survey his attacker. Narrow golden eyes widened in surprise. "*A human?*"

"*I want to know who is leading you.*" Venick moved his sword from the elf's ribs to his neck. "*I want to know what you are planning.*"

The elf's lip curled. "*We are not coming for the mainlands, if that is what worries you. At least,*" his curled lip became a wicked smile, "*not yet.*"

Venick growled. "*And the north?*"

"*The northern queen strangles us. She has for years.*"

"*So you built an army.*"

The elf straightened. "*You should be pleased. Is war not what humans love?*"

"*We use war to protect ourselves.*"

"*As do we. We will protect ourselves from northern rule by taking back our independence. Then, we will protect ourselves by taking theirs.*" The elf was angry now. His words flew like sparks. "*The northern queen thinks she commands us, but we are uniting, and when we do, we will show her better. We will spread our power north. Take control of the elflands. Make the queen pay the price for her oppression.*"

The elf's confession was startling. Distracting, even. It was *made* to be, because if Venick was too busy reveling in the elf's threats then he wouldn't notice the flicker of black on the ground, the dark puddle forming there.

Only, Venick did notice. It was the elf's shadow, which had peeled away from its owner and was pooling like oil at Venick's boots. Venick blinked back a step. His weapon teetered.

A mistake.

The elf lunged.

Venick brought his sword up just in time, and *where* did the elf get a dagger? Blades glanced as Venick blocked the elf's blow, then swung his sword with all the force shoulder and arm could muster. A clean hit. The dagger flew from the elf's hand.

Which opened and curled.

The shadow rose.

Conjuring.

Venick slashed again as the rest of the elf's shadow sloughed away from him, face leaking of color, every crevice and corner illuminated bone-white. A skull. The conjuror's fingers twisted and his shadow obeyed, racing over Venick's skin, into his mouth and nose and eyes. The world went black. Blind.

Panic. It slammed into Venick's chest. He swiped his sword uselessly through the air.

"*Now it is my turn to ask questions,*" the conjuror said. His voice was reedy. High. "*Who sent you?*" Venick gripped his sword tightly, swiping again. "*What interest does a human have in elven affairs?*"

Venick wasn't listening. He resisted the urge to drop his weapon and start pawing at his eyes. He couldn't see *anything*.

"*How did you find us?*"

Venick tried to calm himself. He couldn't afford to panic. He drew up a vision of Ellina, remembered that crook of a smile. *The shadows cannot hurt you*, she'd said. *They might blind you. They will certainly follow you.*

"And where did you get that sword?"

Venick made his shoulders relax. The elf was weaponless now. The shadows couldn't hurt Venick. The conjuror wanted him confused, wanted him afraid.

"Answer me," the elf demanded. *"Why are you here?"*

"I wanted the truth."

Venick remembered the conjured storm. The way blackness had settled over the world. He'd nearly panicked then, too.

"Man knows no truth."

But Venick hadn't needed to see, not really. He'd let go of all thought, had simply *acted.*

He did again.

Venick thrust forward in a burst of energy, sword lifting from below. The elf made a noise as he dodged the sudden attack and Venick listened to that noise, refocusing, homing in, green glass up and swinging faster than any steel sword ever could. He heard a shuffle of earth, a surprised grunt, and Venick followed the sound with his blade, striking backhanded now, shoulder and body crowding, pulsing, pushing. His weapon hit something soft and yielding. The elf made a strange, strangled cry. The world leaked back into color.

To reveal the elf dead at his feet, neck split open like a red grin.

The fight fled Venick all at once. His sword became heavy. The end dripped blood.

He blinked into the daylight. The forest. He'd never noticed. Was it always so dappled and bright? It seemed to him like something from a dream. Hallucinatory.

He scrubbed a hand across his face, then forced himself to move, first to check to see if their fight had been overheard by the other elves—it hadn't—then to drag the body away. His thighs burned as he pulled.

He didn't really notice. His mind grew quiet. He replayed the elf's words in his head, imagining what would happen if the story played out as the elf described. This southern army would march north. There would be war. *True* war, unlike the kind the northern legion was trained for. The southerners would have the advantage of size and strength. They would have the *advantage*, because they were not bound by Queen Rishiana's laws and could kill elves freely. They would. This army would strike the north like one of those battering rams. It would devour cities in its path. Maybe it would even hunt for the hidden city of Evov. The queen herself.

The legion would be forced to act. They would leave the safety of the mountains to meet the southern opposition. They would be unprepared, untrained to battle on the open tundra. Unless the northern legion was given time to gather their own defenses, the coming battle would not be a battle. It would be a slaughter.

Venick dumped the body into a river. He watched it float, then sink.

He turned north. Ellina must be warned.

TWENTY-FIVE

Slowly, Ellina came back to the world.

Her back ached. Every piece of her did. But she could sit upright without help. She could speak, and her voice did not break. Eventually, she could stand to dress. She strapped on her boots, slung her bow across her back.

It hurt. The bow chafed her sore skin. But Ellina knew how to hide her pain.

She was good at hiding things. She prided herself on her ability to wipe her face clear of emotion. She could empty herself of emotion too, if she wished. She could close her eyes and rid her mind of feeling, could become like the forest, or the mountains: steady, still. This was the gift of an elf, this ability to tuck emotion away. It was easy. Natural.

Or so she had thought.

Sometimes, though, Ellina caught her feelings leaking free. They seeped through little cracks in the façade of herself. They billowed around her, a dark cloud, and she was forced to breathe them in. When she did, she realized that she was not empty. She was *lying*.

She knew what she felt.

She touched the jekkis in her pocket. She remembered the night she and Venick had scoured the brothel's rooms for supplies, the way he had arched a brow when he saw what she held. When smoked, the plant was hallucinogenic. When boiled and ingested, it was lethal. When chewed, however, it was effective for pain.

One night after her troop had gone to bed, she pinched off one end. It smelled ripe, a little woody. She chewed. She told herself she did not need much. She told herself it was for the pain. A little relief. She deserved that at least, did she not? A small relief.

But when Ellina woke in the morning, head pounding, she saw she had chewed everything she had.

• • •

Ellina's mind was cruel to her.

It replayed conversations she would rather have forgotten. It reminded her of things left unsaid. At night in the gooey moments before sleep, her thoughts were in the language of men.

She saw Venick in her mind. She remembered the way he had offered to teach her to swim. The shyness in him. The fear in her, the firm denial. She had thought about his offer for a long time after. Later: a river. The slow creep of water. Venick stood not far away. He felt her watching, and turned, and smiled. *Now*, she had thought. *Ask him now*. But she had not. Could not. And now she never would.

• • •

The air began to change as they traveled north towards Evov. It was crisp, its breath light on her face. Usually, the changing climate changed Ellina, made her feel free, like she could slip into the cool wind and fly high over the world.

She was not high over the world now. She was far below. She imagined she was underwater and the canopy of trees was the surface. She had the sudden desire to climb, to grab the branches and haul herself above the waves.

She touched those branches, felt their rough bark. It steadied her. It steadied the odd sense of loss that had been slowly building inside her. But it did not make sense for Ellina to feel that way. She tried to brush the feeling aside. If she had examined it, she might have said it was the feeling of want. But Ellina knew better than to want. And she had not truly lost anything.

Ellina peered to either side. She and her troop were in a star pattern, the distance between them carefully mapped. She could see Dourin's tall figure through the trees on her left, Kaji just ahead of him. Over her other shoulder, Branton and Artis, and behind them, Raffan.

He had said nothing more to Ellina about Venick since the whipping. He had said little to her at all. Sometimes, though, Ellina would catch him staring. She would see the flash of his golden eyes, the twist of his mouth when he was about to speak, and a flutter of nervousness would spread her ribs wide, as if she was certain he would say something she could not bear, or ask something she could not answer.

Ellina would drop her gaze. Raffan would lower his, too.

• • •

Raffan's suspicion did not ease.

Ellina saw the little changes in his temper. The haughty set to his mouth, the glimmer of distrust. He began to break formation to walk closer to her. He wondered aloud how her back was healing. He asked if she regretted her choices. "You took the whip for the human," Raffan drawled one evening. "Would he have done the same for you?"

"Maybe," Ellina said. She did not like the way Raffan looked at her then. As if an idea lurked behind his eyes.

"What *did* he do for you?"

"Nothing." Yet she thought of how Venick had kissed her, and fear made it difficult to breathe. Though Raffan had not yet accused her of the worst, she knew then that he would. *What happened between you and the human?* he might ask in elvish. *Oh Ellina, what have you done?*

Ellina shrunk from the thought. Yet she knew that when she was finally forced to admit the truth—that she had fought for a human, and killed for him, and given herself to him—she would deserve every punishment that confession wrought.

• • •

Unless.

Ellina lay awake. Stars flickered overhead. The clouds were shapeless shadows against the sky.

She turned onto her side away from her troop. In the days since the whipping, the danger of what she had done had morphed into something bristling and predatory. It stalked her. When she closed her eyes, she saw its grisly shape.

She thought of her mother. If Queen Rishiana learned the truth, she would show Ellina no mercy. She would banish her to the whitelands across the Shallow Sea. Maybe worse. Ellina knew now that it was not that difficult to make elves disappear.

Shame swarmed inside her. She would pay for her mistakes for the rest of her life. And Venick. Her fear spread, shook out its furrowed wings. When they discovered Venick's role in her crimes, what would they do to *him*?

Unless.

She shut her eyes. A breeze tickled her skin, but she barely felt it. She was not here. She was back in the southern forests with Venick. She was far away, where rules and laws did not bind them.

Ellina thought of the wildings. *They* had no care for rules or laws. She remembered the way they raised their hands, their bloody offerings, sacrifices to gods whose names most elves had long forgotten. Ellina had asked them questions that were not answered. But the wildings had seen her dark hair, had pulled her into their circle like an embrace. *A raven sister*, they said. *Welcome.*

Ellina's heart kicked at their words. *Raven sister.* That meant *conjuror.* But Ellina was not a conjuror, had spent most of her life rejecting that similarity. She argued with the chieftain. *I am a northerner*, she insisted. *I am not a conjuror.*

The old elf had smiled, revealing a row of pointed teeth. He laid a hand over hers, drew her close. *Let me tell you a secret.*

Ellina did not know the old stories. As a child she had not been allowed to hear them, and by the time she was old enough she was legion and did not care to ask. And yet, some of what the wilding told her stirred old memories. Legends told of a time when humans had been conjurors, and had crossbred with elves, and had passed on their genes.

But humans and elves cannot make children, Ellina had argued to the chieftain. His laugh was airless.

And why not?

Because…it is impossible.

Impossible, or illegal?

Impossible. Ellina made the word firm. *It is why we have our laws. Our elven race is dwindling. Humans and elves cannot bear children, so elves cannot waste their love on humans.*

My dear child, the chieftain had chuckled, *there are a lot of things you do not believe, aren't there?*

Ellina blinked. She saw the world blur. Its colors twined, greyed. She seemed to see herself from a distance. She saw all the rules she held dear, every pillar that propped up her life. She saw the crack in the foundation. She remembered killing humans along the border but sparing the lives of elves who hunted her. An unbalanced trade, based on *what?* Her own beliefs? Rules instilled in her from childhood? And what if those rules were wrong?

Tell me why I am a conjuror, Ellina had demanded. She was not truly ready to believe it—not yet—but she could listen.

The wilding spun an insane story. He said southerners were conjurers of the physical, but northerners were conjurers of the mental. He said it would take training, especially after a lifetime of disuse and denial. Even the most skilled northerners could not always manage the task.

What will take training? Ellina asked.

Ah, the chieftain said. *Now then. My secret.*

He leaned into her ear to whisper, his words barely breaking the air. *Northern conjurors cannot weave shadows or bend the elements. Their skill is singular, and mostly forgotten.* He pulled back to catch her eye. *Northern conjurers can lie in elvish.*

Ellina balked. *That is—*

Impossible? the chieftain had asked, eyes twinkling. *You are quite predict-*

able, you know.

Ellina shifted on the ground where she lay, glancing at the sleeping figures of her troopmates. She had spent her entire life navigating the world as it *was*. It was what made her such an excellent fighter, an excellent soldier and spy. She knew the lines of reality exactly. The difference between stabbing your opponent or missing, between throwing your knife true or missing, could come down to a hairsbreadth, but she knew it. She knew exactly how many steps it took to cross any room on sight, how far she could jump without injury, how quickly she could load and fire a dozen arrows. She counted. She was *always* counting. Ellina saw the world in black and white. There were laws, and then there was lawbreaking. There was the truth, and then there were lies. She did not touch the grey area. She did not even look at it.

But here in the quiet dark with the memory of Venick's kiss on her lips, Ellina could not help but see everything she thought impossible and watch it crumble around her.

She curled more tightly into herself. She thought of Raffan. It occurred to her that there was a reason he had not yet questioned her about Venick in elvish. Perhaps he already knew what had occurred between them. Perhaps he was waiting for their return to Evov so that her confession could be heard by her mother and the court. She recoiled from the thought. She could never speak the truth aloud. She could *not*.

But maybe. Ellina pressed a hand against her belly. A lie. She thought again of the old chieftain, the crinkle of his brow, his whispered secrets. She thought of Raffan and her troopmates, their doubts.

Ellina took a slow, steadying breath. She chose something obviously untrue. Something she worried she might be forced to say aloud in elvish.

Venick means nothing to me.

But the words quickly slid from her mind. She closed her eyes. Concentrated. Tried again.

There was never anything between us.

The pulse of a headache. Ellina had not yet even opened her mouth. She stilled, breathing deeply, remembering his warm hands, how they had brushed her mouth, her cheek. Into her hair, then at her waist. Her armor did nothing to protect her. She felt his fingers grip tightly.

I saved him because I wanted information.

She had leaned greedily into that kiss. He pulled away briefly. His eyes locked on hers. He saw her expression. The next time he moved his mouth over hers, she felt a promise in his kiss.

I feel nothing for him.

Ellina opened her eyes. Her headache reared. She leaned into the pain and tried again and again, imagining those phrases late into the night.

TWENTY-SIX

Venick emerged into the circle of trees.

The space looked no different than the rest of the forest: crooked roots and thick trunks and leaves in various stages of decomposition. If elves had ever camped here, there was no trace of it.

But elves *had* camped here. Venick reached a hand to the nearest tree, touched the fork between branch and trunk. He saw the slight change in color, as if a layer of bark had been filed away. This was where they had tied Ellina's wrists. And there, just beyond, was where he had crouched and watched the whipping, helpless.

Venick swallowed the lingering anger and turned his eyes north. He hadn't truly expected to find Ellina's troop here. Likely, they were halfway back to Evov by now. Yet he had hoped. His task had just become difficult.

Impossible, you mean.

Venick knew the legends. Evov was hidden because the *city* chose who was allowed in and who was not. It was ancient magic left over from the days when humans had been conjurors and shared their knowledge with elves. Rumor said that you may wander forever and never reach Evov's gates. Or she might guide you straight into her arms.

Venick didn't know the last time a human had entered Evov. What he did know was that if he wanted to find the elves' hidden city, he would need to start at the Shallow Sea. Every journey to Evov began there.

Journey now, is it?

He drew a hand across his face. Gods. He'd been an outlaw, last time he checked. No duty to anyone. Yet now he was contemplating making the trek north for a country that wasn't his, for an elf who *certainly* wasn't. Venick thought of his homeland. The border was still close. He could turn around, forget the army he'd seen, return to the mountains and the clansmen and the empty days dreaming of Irek and redemption. And it was like Dourin said, wasn't it? Venick had learned he couldn't trust himself where Ellina was concerned. He had caused her more pain than he was worth.

But what pain would she face if he *didn't* go?

What pain would her country face, when the south marched on the north?

And what of the mainlands, if the southerners spread west?

It had happened before. Centuries ago, during the purge, elves had swept through the mainlands and herded human conjurors like iziri goats. Slaughtered them like goats, too. There had been war. It was over quickly. Humanity had always relied heavily on their conjurors for protection, and without them, men were quickly beaten.

After, humans vowed they would never be weak again. The Fathers of War perfected battle tactics. Their sons invented cannons and crossbows. All men became soldiers, and women were trained as blacksmiths and armorers. Mankind became a beast of war.

Later, the border was drawn and the days of elven-human conflict seemed at an end, but humans would not relent their tradition of battle, which was passed from father to son to grandson. With no foreign enemy to defeat, humans began fighting each other.

Still, humans did not forget the purge. All children were taught the stories. The threat of another elven invasion was *like* a story, scaly and red-eyed. A monster. Not real. Everyone knew it wasn't. Yet the fear remained.

Our elven neighbors crouch in waiting, the story went.

First, they purged the world of conjurors.

Next, it will be all humans.

It will happen again. It could happen now.

Venick thought of Irek. His mother. He remembered how she looked each time he returned home safely from battle. The way she would hide her relief, because to show relief was to admit how much she worried, and it was dishonorable to admit she worried at all. She would smile proudly instead. *Did you fight well?* she would ask him. *Always*, he would say.

Venick thought of the black-haired elf, his coy replies. *We are not coming for the mainlands. At least—not yet.*

What would become of Irek if the south attacked the north, and the elven crown fell, and the southerners turned their attention to the mainlands? If Venick journeyed to Evov and warned the queen of the coming danger, if he had his part in helping to stop the southern army—was *this* a great enough act to absolve him of his crimes? Was this the redemption sacrifice he had been looking for? Or would his mother think him a traitor for aiding the elves at all?

He wondered, with a grim shake of his head, if the answer would change his decision either way.

He went north.

TWENTY-SEVEN

Ellina gazed up at her city.

Evov looked different than she remembered. Wider, higher. *Bigger.* She and her troop had not been gone long, but even so, Ellina felt as if she had forgotten Evov's grandeur, its immensity. She could see the buildings forged into the mountainside, the gaping windows and glittering stone. Could see elves walking along narrow streets high above, switchbacks carved into the rock. Could almost feel what it was to be up there with them: cool air on her skin, dusty path under her feet, a view that stretched for leagues.

Her troopmates were eager to be back. As they moved into the foothills and approached the city, Ellina saw their keen eyes, sensed their excitement. When they reached the wide archway that marked the city's entrance, they broke formation and pushed ahead. Dourin did, too. He brushed her shoulder as he passed, eyes soft and almond-round. "Home," he said. He walked on.

Ellina did not rush forward with the others. She hung back, her eyes again drifting upwards. A breeze tickled her cheek. The sun was a perfect orb behind a thin film of clouds.

Raffan's steps were almost silent as he approached. He stopped beside her. After a beat, Ellina turned to face him.

Raffan was handsome. Anyone would say so. He had long bones, an elegant face, lithe body. But he was too often angry, and the residue of old anger clung to him like a cloak. Ellina could see faint traces of it in the lines of his face, the muscle in his jaw.

Yet underneath, Ellina could almost catch a glimpse of the old Raffan, the one she had known as a young soldier. The one who taught her how to hold a sword, who offered to dry her armor after a hard rain, who took her side in every fight.

But that had been before Raffan became her commander. Before they were forced into a bonding neither of them wanted. Before Raffan turned cruel, and she pushed him to be cruel. They both knew why she did it. Each time Raffan punished her, it wedged the stake deeper between them, banishing the idea that their bonding would ever work, even though it *must* work.

Bondmates were to remain paired until an elven child was produced. After the hundred childless years when Queen Rishiana was most worried about the future of their race and began commanding new laws to protect them, she instated this condition because she believed it would encourage elves to act quickly, and she was right. In the years since, their elven race had regained much of its former strength. But not all elves were so easily commanded. After Rishiana's decree, some northerners did not take kindly to the idea of forced bondings. They resisted the queen's demands. Some spoke of revolt. And so Rishiana did what no one thought she would: she bondmated her youngest daughter.

Ellina should not have been bondmated at all, not unless something happened to both elder sisters and she inherited the throne. Rishiana knew this. She used it. She bondmated Ellina to prove that no elf was above the law, that even the royal family was willing to make sacrifices. Ellina and Raffan were meant to be a symbol to others.

There was a dark sort of irony to that.

Raffan's eyes lingered on Ellina now. He seemed to sense her thoughts; he had always been able to read her. Such was the way it was between elves who were close, or ever had been.

She and Raffan had been, once. Before.

"Why do you continue to fight me, Ellina?" he asked, voice soft. "Is this," he touched light fingers to her back, "really what you want?"

"You know what I want."

He did. To be freed from her duty to him. To be released from his command. Raffan did not have the power to give her either. Only the queen could do that.

Ellina had begged her mother not to bondmate her. It was rare for Ellina to question a direct order, but this went beyond mere loyalty to her country. To be...*intimate* with Raffan in that way, to bear his child... she knew she could not do it. She remembered the dim chamber, her mother in white velvet, her in legion armor, pleading. Most soldiers were absolved of their duty to bondmate, but Ellina was given no such pardon. *We must lead by example, daughter,* her mother had said to her. The queen's stare was cold. *This is your duty. You will not ask me again.*

"Rishiana would never agree to end our bonding," Raffan said now. He squinted a little. When he spoke again, his voice changed. "You should not want her to end it." A pause. A silence as wide and full as the sea. "You would not have asked it, before."

Ellina's mouth felt dry. The scabs on her back prickled, itchy. *Before*

Venick, Raffan did not say. But it was what he meant.

"I have," she insisted. "I did."

Another pause. It would be easy. So easy for Raffan to switch to elvish, to ask the questions that seemed to linger in the air between them.

What are your feelings for the human?

Is he the reason you want to end our bonding?

What is the truth, Ellina?

Ellina fought to keep her face neutral, fought to keep her hand off her sword, certain that this was it, that he would question her *now*. She was not ready. She had not had enough time to practice her elven lies, had no defense against an interrogation. She could be made to admit everything.

But as before, Raffan did not question her. He merely walked away, leaving Ellina alone with the wind.

• • •

At first, Ellina did not notice the whispers.

As she trekked alone though the city towards the palace, she did not notice how the elves around her became quiet, how their eyes followed her, hands lifting to cover mouths as they leaned into one another. Even when Ellina did notice, she did not, really. She was the queen's daughter. Famed in the legion. She was used to attention, and having just returned home, almost certainly bound to draw it.

As Ellina ascended Evov's narrow streets, however, she began to sense it: a subtle tension. She saw the way elves peered at her from under hooded eyelids, saw their interest, and it worried her.

She wondered what they were saying behind those raised hands.

Ellina quickened her pace, wending higher into the mountains, deeper into the city. The air became thin and clean. A breeze raised goose-bumps on her arms. When she finally rounded a bend and the palace came into view, she felt a ripple of relief.

The royal palace could still impress her even after all these years. It hung on a silver cloud, an isolated finger reaching up from a deep moat of skyless black. There was nothing else like it, not the glittering fortress of stone, not the endless black canyon from which it rose. The castle, like the rest of the city, had been carved into mountain rock, its spires stretching high, tiny lights illuminating windows and walkways.

There was a single wide bridge arching over the void that connected the palace to the rest of the city—the only way in or out. Ellina followed that bridge over an outcrop of rock, to the palace gates and into the entrance hall.

Where her sister waited.

"Ellina."

Farah strode forward. Ellina's elder sister looked freshly dressed, white hair woven tightly down her back, shortsword fastened to her hip. Farah was not legion, but as was a second daughter's duty, she had control over the city's guard and preferred guard's armor to the robes most highborn wore. She grasped Ellina's forearm in greeting, her eyes slightly too appraising to be friendly. "You are looking well. I came as soon as I heard you were back. Mother will be pleased by your safe return."

Just words, and most of them meaningless. Ellina doubted she looked well—not after a two-month-long campaign, a journey south and back across the tundra and a whipping—and the queen was rarely pleased by anything. But Ellina gave a nod and told a lie of her own. "It is good to be home."

The entrance hall was flooded with light, the double doors flung wide open, guards stationed here and there. A few courtiers lingered as well, but otherwise, she and Farah were alone.

And so there was no reason for the way Farah dropped her voice as she said, "I am to tell you to bathe and change. We will be dining with the queen in her private chambers tonight. You will give her your report then."

Ellina was careful to hide her surprise. She had expected the queen to summon Ellina's troop to the stateroom to report their findings, as was custom. The queen did not host meetings in her private chambers. Ellina could count on one hand the number of times she had been summoned there. Once, when she first decided to join the legion. Once, when she and Raffan became bondmated. Once, when her mother announced that Miria would take the throne.

None of those conversations had ended well, not even the first. As a third daughter, it was Ellina's right to choose her own life path. She could have become a scholar or a senator as most highborn third and fourth daughters did. But Ellina did not have any interest in history or politics. She chose the legion instead, despite her mother's insistence that this was highly unusual. It was not the role of an elven princess to live a soldier's life.

The legion will show you no mercy, her mother had said, but that only hardened Ellina's resolve. She did not want mercy.

It is my choice to make, Mother.

"Did the queen say why?" Ellina asked her sister now.

"Does our mother ever explain herself?" But there was something about the way Farah said this that gave Ellina pause. Farah's expression was carefully arranged, brows level, mouth relaxed. Her face betrayed nothing. In royal circles, Farah was known for this. She was often praised for her perfect mastery of stillness, some even going so far as to say her mask rivaled the queen's. Yet Ellina knew there was true calm, and then there was the guise of it, and she could sense there was more Farah was not saying.

"That is not an answer," Ellina replied. Her sister's eyes wavered, and Ellina took her chance, switching to elvish as she pressed, "*What are you not telling me?*"

Farah glanced around, then motioned that they should move. Together, they exited the entrance hall and started in the direction of Ellina's suite, which was located high in the south tower. "You should know," Farah said when they were out of earshot of the courtiers and guards, "that there have been rumors."

Ellina's pulse quickened. She waited.

"You were seen defending a human," Farah went on. "Fighting beside him. In Kenath."

This time, Ellina could not quite hide her surprise. She had not anticipated this. Her focus had been on Raffan and her troopmates, what they had seen, what they might suspect. It had not even occurred to Ellina that there were other witnesses—an entire *city* of them—who had also seen her and Venick together. Fighting together, like Farah said. Defending each other.

"I was in a tight situation," Ellina explained, yet inside she was reeling. She should have realized the citizens of Kenath would spread word of that fight. Should have prepared for it. For her to have missed something so obvious…what *else* had she overlooked? "He helped me escape."

"So it is true, then."

"Yes, but if not for him, I—"

"Do not *defend* him," Farah snapped, coming to a halt. They stood in an empty corridor. Torchlight ribboned across Farah's face. "*Think,* Ellina. Do you not suppose there is a reason our mother does not want to convene in the stateroom for your report? A reason we are dining in her private chambers tonight? She has surely heard the rumors, and she is displeased. She will want an explanation, and you would be a fool to answer her in such a way."

Ellina swallowed. "I have done nothing wrong."

Farah clicked her teeth, annoyed.

"We fought together to escape a threat," Ellina insisted. "There is no law against it."

"An elf died."

"A southerner," Ellina said, yet knew her mistake at once. Elven deaths—*southern* elven deaths—were exactly what the north aimed to stop. Honor suicides were the reason for this war. To defend a human who had killed an elf, even if it was to protect her...it was treasonous.

Though Farah's expression did not change, Ellina sensed her sister's disbelief. It was unlike elves to side with humans, but especially soldiers, and *especially* Ellina. She was a legionnaire first. Sworn to her country, ruthless in her devotion to its cause. She had been raised a soldier. She did not defend humans. She *killed* them.

"What," Farah asked slowly, "happened while you were in the south, exactly?"

A vision of Venick's mouth on hers. The whistle of her arrow right before it pierced the southerner's neck.

A memory of the vanished tent-city. A report from her troop that Tarrith-Mour was abandoned, too.

The coup in Kenath. The southern conjurors' strength. The way those elves had hunted her, and how Venick, again and again, had come to her defense.

It changed her. She was changed, because of him.

"Well?" Farah prompted.

Ellina and Farah had never been close, not like she and Miria had been. Ellina felt that difference starkly. She wished Miria was there now. She wished she had someone she could talk to, someone who would understand.

But Miria was not there, so instead Ellina did as she had done in the forest. She steeled herself. Lifted her chin, made sure none of her feelings bled into her expression as she met Farah's eye.

"I will give the queen my report tonight at dinner," Ellina said. "You may hear what I have to say then."

• • •

Ellina could no longer ignore the whispers.

They seemed louder here, contained between high stone walls with nowhere to escape. Courtiers and senators were braver than the citizens in the city, slower to avert their gazes when Ellina caught them staring. The echoes of their words—*The princess, with a human, did you hear?*—followed her as she walked through the palace to her bedroom suite and shut herself inside.

Her rooms brought no relief. At least, not until Ellina sent the servants away, insisting that she could draw her own bath, remove her own armor. They did not argue. Curtsied and scurried out instead, leaving Ellina alone at last.

Her suite looked as it always had: a linked series of rooms taller than they were wide, floors lavished with eastern rugs, the windows outfitted in rare glass. Ellina had insisted on that alteration after returning home from her first legion mission. That year, she had gained a newfound respect for eavesdroppers and assassins. The glass would not keep either out, not if they truly wanted in, but Ellina had her windows fitted with it anyway.

She went to the bathing room and shut the door behind her, then set the faucet and watched water pour from the pipes into the smooth basin. She unstrapped her weapons first, then peeled off her armor, which was caked in sweat and grime and two months' worth of travel. Blood, too. She examined the rust-red stains in the light of the sinking sun. Some of it was hers. Most of it not. She lingered for a moment, her fingers curling into the leather, before setting the armor aside.

The bath was scalding. Ellina hissed as she lowered herself in, hands braced against the tub's rim. The freshly healed wounds on her back felt fiery. Her whole body was stiff and sore. She held her breath and dipped all the way under.

She did not soak for long. Even here in the hidden city of Evov, even in the privacy of her own suite, bathing left her feeling vulnerable. She wanted armor. She wanted weapons. She scrubbed herself quickly, then dried and dressed in her own version of palace attire: slacks and a tunic with paneling underneath to provide light armor and to hold her weapons. Like Farah, Ellina refused to wear silken robes. Not with all those extra folds to trip over, and nowhere to house her knives.

The bathroom mirror had fogged. Ellina used a fist to wipe it clear, then caught sight of herself and wished she had not. There were bruised circles under her eyes, a fresh cut on her cheek. A new whip mark—raised and dark, not yet scarred—curled over her shoulder. And she looked thinner. Gaunt, even. Her eyebrows drew in as she examined herself.

But it was not just her eyebrows. Ellina saw that her mouth was turned down. Worry lines creased her forehead. Her eyes were too narrow, too keen.

Her face, she realized, was full of expression.

She screwed it all down. Forced her eyes and lips and brows back to nothing. Yet she could still see a hint of *something*. Some feeling lurking just under the skin. Her own frustration, maybe. Her dismay.

She *was* dismayed. It was common knowledge that too much time spent around humans could wear away an elf's mask, bringing forth new expressions and emotions. Ellina had seen it in Dourin, the little changes in his hands and mouth. She could see it in herself now, too.

She turned away from her reflection. No wonder elves were whispering. If they had not believed the rumors before, they would take one look at her now and know them to be true.

She would have to relearn how to mold her expression, and she would have to do it quickly. Ellina closed her eyes, wishing *calm* at herself until some of the lingering tension eased out of her neck and shoulders. She counted her breaths, focusing on the sound, the slow in and out. She thought of the queen's summons, then reminded herself that even if her mother did see her expression, even if she *had* heard the rumors, she did not know everything. No one did. Not Raffan or Farah or even Dourin.

And Venick...

Ellina pulled her hair into a quick braid, tugging harshly at her scalp. She considered what elves must be saying about her, their assumptions, all the many choices that had brought her to this moment...choices from the forest, and before.

No, Ellina thought. Not even Venick knew *everything*.

It had happened in this very palace. The queen's unexpected announcement that Miria would soon take her place. Miria's fear, her despair. After, how Ellina had gone to Miria, had found her alone in her suite. Ellina remembered it all again. *Do not take the throne*, she had told her sister. *Leave the elflands. There is a little city on the border. Near the ocean.*

You will be safe there. You can make a new life there. And again, those words, the ones she had regretted ever after. *I will help you.* Together, she and Miria had forged the southern summons and plotted her sister's escape: the path she would take, the things she would bring, who she would become.

Lorana. A name they had chosen because it was common and simple and safe. Irek, a city they had chosen for the same reasons.

The memory squeezed the breath out of Ellina. She remembered their hurried plans, their whispered goodbyes. The morning of Miria's departure, Ellina had smiled, even as she knew what her sister's leaving meant. She would never see Miria again. But was this not a small price to pay for her sister's happiness? Was it not what Miria would choose for Ellina if their roles were reversed?

It would be years before Ellina was to learn what became of Miria. That she would fall in love with a human in Irek. That she would die there. Word of an honor suicide traveled quickly. *Another southerner*, the rumors said. *In Irek. Forced to kill herself for falling in love with a human.*

But Ellina knew it was not simply another southerner.

When news of her sister's death had come, Ellina stormed out of the palace, out of the city, into the mountains. She pushed herself as far as mind and body would allow, then pushed herself farther. She allowed grief to rule her. Rumors of these forced honor suicides had been slowly growing for years, but she had never once thought of Miria, never considered. Her own sister.

Ellina never bothered to ask what happened to the human Miria had loved. Years later, as Ellina fought and killed humans along the border, she scarcely gave him a thought. Dead, she assumed. Gone. It was not until she saw her sister's necklace hanging on Venick's chest that everything solidified, beading to a point, a crystal drop on a razor's edge. This was the human Miria had loved. She was dead, because of *him*.

Murder gripped her. Ellina would kill him.

But then something inside Ellina had shifted. A door creaking open. Not much. Enough. And through it, another thought emerged. Miria had wanted a different life. She had chosen it, risked everything for it. And she had loved this human. Miria, who gave her love easily, who forgave, who broke the rules and defied their mother and laughed and laughed. Ellina thought of what her sister would have wanted, and she knew she could not kill him.

She hated the human, but she would spare him in Miria's name. She would save him, mend his foot, then leave and forget him. But somehow, slowly, Ellina began to know him, and hate turned into curiosity, turned into *trust*, turned into…something else.

Ellina cinched her belt a notch tighter, strapped on her weapons. It was difficult, knowing what she knew now, to reflect on her choices. She wondered, as she so often did, what Miria would have chosen for her. What Miria would think, could she see her little sister now.

Ellina finished dressing, then ran a hand down her front, spreading the fabric flat. She did not check her expression in the mirror again.

She exited the room and went to meet her mother.

• • •

Ellina hated to feel nervous. It was an emotion she avoided whenever possible. Yet as she walked the long corridor towards her mother's private chamber, she could not help but feel it: a tender sort of angst.

She inhaled a hard breath, tried to concentrate on other things. The whisper of her feet against cold stone. The twist and turn of this corridor. The sight of the chamber door coming into view, and the two guards stationed outside it.

The door was familiar. The guards were not. That in and of itself was not unusual—the city's guard numbered into the hundreds, and there were always new recruits—but there was something *different* about these two. Ellina peered at them as she approached, and for a moment she truly did forget her nervousness as she tried to place the difference. The guards stood at parade rest, boots knee-high and buckled, armor gleaming. They wore the same uniform that all of Farah's guard did. Their hair was cut the same way, ears pierced the same way…

"*Cessena,*" said the guard on the left. *Princess.* "The queen is expecting you."

Maybe there was nothing unusual about these guards. Maybe it was Ellina who was different. Maybe she was seeing that difference reflected in the guards' eyes as they looked at her.

She pushed through the door without a word.

The queen's private dining hall was located deep in the belly of the mountain, which meant there were no windows. Instead, dozens of sconces and candles lined the walls and table, casting everything in an orange glow. The queen was there already, seated at the head of the table. Farah, as heir to the throne, sat to her right.

Ellina's troop was not present.

"*Daughter,*" the queen said in elvish. Rishiana was dressed simply, white hair trailing down white robes, fingers and wrists free of ornamentation. Her ears, by contrast, were adorned in extravagant gold, bearing every one of the fifty rings that signified her rank as queen. "*Please. Sit.*"

But Ellina had halted. "*Where are the others?*"

"*Your troop?*" Rishiana's eyes were steady. "*They were not invited.*"

It was not unusual for the queen to open conversations in elvish. Unlike most elves, Rishiana did not merely use that language as a tool but generally preferred elvish over mainlander. Still, as Ellina glanced around the near-empty chamber, she knew the queen's choice of language could not be an accident.

Her nervousness returned.

"*I am surprised, Mother,*" Ellina said, careful to keep her tone light. "*I thought you would want to hear my troop's report.*"

"*I do. But that is not why I summoned you here tonight. Now please,*" Rishiana unfolded a hand and repeated her command, "*sit.*"

Ellina had no choice but to do as her mother asked. She urged her legs to move—one breath, two, before the muscles obeyed—and sat.

Mercifully, a row of servers appeared then, allowing Ellina a moment to compose herself. She smoothed the fabric of her trousers, touched a finger to the dagger hidden underneath. She let the motion calm her. She reminded herself again that, no matter what the queen had heard about her and Venick's battle in Kenath, no matter what she suspected, she knew nothing for certain. And Ellina knew how to play her own hand, did she not? She knew how to court certain questions and avoid others, how to twist the truth, even in elvish. She watched the servants ladle hot broth into golden bowls and prepared to steer the conversation in the direction it needed to go—one that avoided all questions of *why*, but instead focused on questions she could answer easily, in any language: *what* and *how* and *when*.

The servants withdrew, but the queen did not immediately speak, and so Farah and Ellina did not, either. The first course passed in silence, as did the second. Wine was served. Ellina accepted but did not drink. She toyed with the stem of her glass.

Only after the servants presented the third course did the queen speak again. "*As I said, there is a reason I summoned you here tonight, and it is not to hear your report.*"

Farah set her silverware down with a delicate clink. Ellina kept her eyes on her plate.

The queen said, "*I am leaving the city.*"

Ellina's attention snapped up. She was so surprised that she switched to mainlander without thinking. "What?"

"That is my reason for calling you here today," the queen continued, following Ellina into that language. "My sister, your aunt Ara, has fallen ill. A wasting disease. She has sent for me, and I will be journeying to the city of Lorin to see her."

Ellina gripped the edge of her seat. Relief—pure, like spun gold—poured into her, followed by quick confusion, then fear as she processed her mother's words. "No," Ellina finally replied. "You cannot go."

"Of course I can."

"It is not safe. We are at *war*. The queen remains in Evov during times of war."

"I am traveling north, not south. And Ara is family. She does not have long to live."

Ellina had never met her aunt Ara. She lived in the far northern reaches of the territory and never visited. From what Ellina knew, Rishiana and Ara had once been close, but soon after Rishiana became pregnant with her first daughter something had happened between the two sisters. A terrible fight, Ellina was told, though about *what*, no one seemed to know. After, Ara had left the city for good.

Ellina said, "Surely Ara could come here…"

Rishiana dismissed that idea with a wave of her hand. "She would not survive the journey in her condition."

"Let me come with you, then."

"No."

"But—"

"I need you here, with Farah," the queen said. "The two of you must govern in my place while I am away."

"The *two* of us?" Farah interjected. "Mother, *I* am your heir. Surely I do not require Ellina's help..."

"You will accept it nevertheless."

"She knows nothing about the court. She is rarely even *here.*"

"Ellina serves these lands, just as you do."

"Not in the same way."

"Is your pride truly so tender?" Rishiana asked coolly. Ellina imagined her mother arching an eyebrow, though of course the queen would never. It was perfect poise for her mother, perfect calm, as always.

Farah leaned forward, imploring. "This is not about pride. It is about trust."

"You are right. I trust you to respect my decision."

"But—"

"You are not queen yet, Farah," Rishiana interrupted, "and you will not become queen until I choose it. Until then, you and your sister will govern as equals. You will accept her help, and you will be grateful for it."

Which Farah clearly was not. She glared, her nostrils flaring in a rare show of emotion. But if Rishiana noticed Farah's anger, she ignored it. She sat back in her seat, hands folding with finality. "Ara's condition is only worsening," Rishiana said. "If I am to see her, I must go now. I will not be away long. A month. Two, at most. All arrangements have already been made. I leave at dawn."

TWENTY-EIGHT

The moon marked time.

As Venick went north, he watched night after night as the moon slowly inked away. He felt like that. Slivered, a shadow of who he had once been.

He had changed. Venick knew this without really understanding it. But he felt it. He felt how single-minded he had become. How easily he offered himself up, how his loyalty was branded into each of his choices.

He thought about Ellina. Her wounds would be healed by now. Her brethren would have tended them, perhaps wrapped them in the same leaves she had used on him. Her open flesh would heal quickly with the use of those leaves. But he wondered if the scars ached. He wondered if a phantom pain remained, if she could still feel the memory of how those scars had come to be, and why.

He wondered if she regretted it.

Venick imagined what he would say to her if he could. He wanted to tell her that he knew how it felt. That he understood how a scar could hurt long after it had healed. He wanted to tell her that *he* regretted her scars, all of them, not just the ones she'd earned on his behalf, and not just the ones he could see. That he would take them from her, if he could.

Venick pressed his palms to his eyes and felt a wash of remorse that he *couldn't* take them from her. Then, remorse for his own remorse, because he overestimated himself, and seemed unable to protect anyone he cared about.

That night he didn't light a fire. He lay on his back and gazed at the stars. Far away, a wanewolf called into the air. Her partner answered. Their mournful howls sang long and low.

• • •

He reached the edge of the forest.

He stood at the line of trees and marveled at the simple sight of open land. He saw the dim outlines of the northern mountains in the distance, the tundra reaching between them, its barren soil like an endless black lake.

• • •

He was hungry. He was thirsty. He broke the ice that frosted the ground and crunched it between his teeth. He hadn't seen a single sign of life since leaving the forest. Not an elf or human. Not a bird or hare. The Shallow Sea was still days away, and Venick began to worry at his own growing weakness. He had counted on his ability to hunt. Had counted on there being prey *to* hunt. But there was nothing. If the elves made this journey, they must come prepared, well prepared, perhaps with homing horses they could summon to cross the tundra faster. But Venick had no horse. He was not prepared.

He brushed his wet hands on his trousers and walked on.

• • •

He could smell the sea.

He knew that smell, a smell as old as his whole life. It was salt and sand and open water. Venick became eager. He put on a burst of speed. He crested a ridge and it came into view.

A thin fog hung over glassy grey water. The sky was peppered with clouds, and their shadows drew shapes on its surface.

He reached the shore. He stripped off his boots and stepped into the water. It was freezing, but he didn't pull away. The burn made him feel alive.

• • •

Venick was lucky.

He was lucky, to have spotted a glimpse of the fox as she left her den. He was lucky, that the cubs inside were too small to flee. He had not eaten anything but moss and ice in days. Venick was delirious with hunger.

And yet, as he gripped the cub around her neck, he felt odd. As if killing and eating the fox was wrong. As if some unknown force urged him not to.

He was not well, he thought, to think such strange things.

Certainly not, as he set the cub back in her den.

He stood. His head swam. He didn't know how far north he'd walked, only that he was deep in the heart of it. The Shallow Sea had been a constant presence to the east, but soon he would break away from the water towards the mountains. When he did, his chances of finding food would become even slimmer.

He looked again at the fox den and his stomach twisted in longing. But he did not eat a fox.

That's when he noticed the trail.

• • •

The path was stamped lightly into the earth, so lightly that it was hardly a path at all.

Venick did not remember choosing to follow it. Hunger turned his mind bright and shiny, and his thoughts were not his own.

He had waking dreams. He dreamed that his mother was there. She patted his cheek and smiled. But then his mother became his father, and the pat turned into a slap. Venick drew his sword. *You disgrace us*, his father said. *You will put a stop to this*. Venick stabbed, and saw his father die again, until he realized it was not his father at the end of his sword but Lorana. *Do not mourn me*, she said, clutching the hilt where it pierced her belly, blood running from her mouth. *Live your life, Venick. Be happy*.

He licked his chapped lips and gazed into the pale sky. He was aware that he was losing his grip on reality. When he saw the mountains looming overhead, it took him a full minute to understand that they were real. He must have walked a long way for the mountains to be so close. But he did not remember this, either.

• • •

It occurred to Venick, in a rare moment of clarity, that he was going to die.

There was no food and little water. Even if he evaded starvation, he could hear the wanewolves sing in the distance at night, and if they caught his scent he would not be able to evade *them*. Dourin's sword was no comfort. He was too weak to defend himself with it.

He drew the sword anyway. He was deep in the mountains. The image of them reflected on the glass's emerald surface.

. . .

The moon marked time, but Venick was no longer watching.

His hunger was gone now. His thirst was. He didn't feel tired or cold or afraid. He didn't *feel*. He didn't think much, either. His entire existence had narrowed into two feet moving him forward, step by step.

He wondered again, without being bothered by wondering, if he would die. He examined the idea, the words *if* and *die* like the links in the chain around his neck. They could be pieced together or taken apart. They were themselves but also part of each other.

He touched that necklace. It belonged to an elf he had cared about once. But this reminded Venick of another elf whom he cared about, too.

Feeling flooded him at the thought of Ellina, a painful spark of light in a dark room. It slapped him to life. He became hungry and thirsty and tired and cold all at once. He remembered where he was, and where he was going, and why.

He no longer wondered whether he would die. As long as he could fight for her, he knew he wouldn't.

It was with this promise in his mind that Evov came into view.

The city was not hidden. It was not even obscured. It opened to him the way a thought does, seemingly from nothing, magnificent and startling and in perfect view.

TWENTY-NINE

He was apprehended.

Venick expected this. He didn't think he would be allowed to wander Evov's streets unescorted, a lone human in a land of elves. He was surprised how long he did wander before he was finally spotted and ordered to halt. Four soldiers appeared above and below, peeling away from buildings to block his way. But no, not soldiers, not quite. They wore no armor. But they were *armed*, and they had that look about them. Stiff lips. White knuckles. Elven-still, elven-quiet, but elven-predatory, too, and ready for a fight.

Venick kept his hands open and loose. He greeted the elves in their language, then told them his purpose. He had practiced what he would say. Had expected to say it over drawn weapons, the words shouted in a rush before they could shoot him dead, but the elves did not draw their weapons. They were too surprised, it seemed. It was his fluent elvish, maybe. Or maybe it was simply his presence, as if they had never seen a human in their city, had no template for how to react.

Venick grabbed that hesitation and used it, pushing his own ideas into the empty space. "*I have been traveling through the southern forests*," he said. "*I have a message for Ellina*," he said. "*You must take me to her.*"

They seemed to come to their senses then.

They disarmed him and bound his hands. Venick let them. He told himself this was the best way. He told himself he had nothing to fear. He spoke elvish. That was its own sort of armor, a weapon more valuable than Dourin's sword. As long as they took him to Ellina, he could explain everything, explain it *fully*, and there would be no more need for threats or bound hands or violence. They would understand he was an ally. They would understand he could help.

Then they reached for his necklace.

Venick jerked back with such force that he was knocked off balance. He stumbled, then fell, nearly dragging another elf down with him.

"No," he said, shoving down a sudden surge of nausea. "Not that. It's mine."

He should have known better than to fight. He should have understood the precariousness of his position. He would have, had he not just spent a fortnight on the tundra, had he not been exhausted and travel-worn and out of his mind with hunger. But Venick did not understand this. All he understood was the ugly fear in his gut, the horror at what he knew would happen next.

Irritation flashed across the elf's face, then suspicion, which was not unlike the suspicion Venick had seen in Ellina that first day. The elf grabbed again for his necklace. Venick panicked. He kicked. Missed. More elves joined the struggle. Another hand reached for the chain. This time it was caught and pulled. It bit into his neck. It slipped over his head and was gone.

. . .

The necklace was not the worst thing.

This is what Venick told himself as the elves dragged him through the city. He was alive. He was upright and walking. He had not been blindfolded and so he could see paths in the golden light of dusk, could watch the city as it opened before them.

Evov seemed to grow larger the deeper they went. Venick had heard stories of the city, how elves shaped the stone by hand, carving the rock piece by piece in the way elves like to do, but he had not expected *this*. The city was impossible, a dizzying maze of walkways and bridges and spires, grey and gold buildings forged right into the side of the mountain. It was tall, too, the city built *up* as well as *out*, with narrow stairways and ladders stamped into the stone that guided elves off the main road and up into a web of storefronts and homes.

The paths became narrower the higher they climbed. Crowded, too. He guessed that whispers of *human* must have traveled fast because they were soon surrounded by golden-eyed gazes, elves looking on from above and below. Venick ducked his chin and tried to avoid those gazes. Tried to ignore the sound of their hollers, their questions raised into the air, voices echoing between high stone walls. *A human? Here?* And, less encouraging, *What are you waiting for? You know the law.*

Venick glanced at their hands, their faces, trying to calculate the risk. It would be easy for one of these elves to take matters into his own hands, to pull out a longbow or a sword and cut Venick down.

He bit down on the thought. When they took him to Ellina, he would set this right. He would explain everything. He would convey the danger they were in, the importance of securing the city. They would see that he was not a threat, that he was there to *help*.

Gods, let that be true.

• • •

They didn't take him to Ellina.

Venick knew the moment they entered the dim, cavernous web of rooms that this was not the sort of place the royal family greeted guests. He smelled the wet rock, the burnt oil lamps. He saw the tunnels swallowed dark where the light did not touch. This wasn't a council's chamber or a stateroom.

This was a prison.

"Please, listen to me," Venick said in elvish. More elves had joined them as they'd trekked through the city. He could hear the cat-quiet pad of more than a dozen feet behind him. He didn't dare turn to look, to count. He didn't want to know just how bad his odds were, or to startle them into drawing their weapons. But he risked a glance to the side, trying to catch the eye of the elf on his left and right. *"Please,"* he said again. *"There are southern forces gathering. You must tell—"*

"Enough," said the elf to his left. She didn't snap, didn't raise her voice. There was no inflection, just the cool tone of an elf who expected to be obeyed. The lamps were lit at long intervals, the dark reducing their group to shapes and sounds, but Venick could see she was small for an elf. She had a delicate nose, severe eyes. She glanced at him, and he remembered another elf's command, another elf's *enough.* Ellina had spoken that way to Dourin in Kenath. Ellina had the same eyes as this elf, the same voice.

"Queen Rishiana?" Venick asked, heart spluttering, daring to hope.

The elf's eyes slimmed. *"Farah,"* she corrected. So it *was* a member of Ellina's family. Farah was Ellina's second eldest sister. Venick could see the resemblance clearly now. The proud tilt to her chin, the way her hand rested on her sword.

"*I was traveling with Ellina,*" Venick said, grabbing the chance. "*I saw something in the south. An army.*" Venick relayed everything he had seen and learned. The words came out in a rush. They echoed breathlessly through the tunnels. "*They are preparing for war,*" Venick said. "*They will march north.*"

At some point, they had come to a stop. Venick was facing Farah. Her golden eyes reflected tiger-like in the dark. Dourin had not told Venick much about Ellina's sisters. Venick expected them to be like Ellina, and Farah was in some ways. And yet, there was an air to Farah that was different. A subtle taste of disdain that was absent in Ellina.

A long moment passed. Then: "I do not believe you."

Venick blinked. "I spoke in elvish."

"But who is to say the rules of elvish apply to *you?*"

It was as if the ground he was standing on shifted. It turned to ice, cracked and broke and sucked him under.

Reeking gods.

"But they do," he said. "You must know that they do."

"Let me tell you what I know." Farah clasped her hands behind her back. She wore black armor. The hammered iron made her skeletal. "I know that we have a border. I know that humans are not allowed *across* that border. And I know that a human has now appeared in our city with a stolen sword and an impossible story. He claims we are in danger. He claims the *southerners* are uniting. And then, there is this." She held up his necklace. "What is a human doing with Miria's necklace?"

Miria's necklace? Venick shook his head. "That necklace belonged to an elf named Lorana."

"No." Farah stepped closer. "This necklace belonged to our eldest sister Miria. She disappeared into the south eight years ago. *This* belonged to *her.*"

"That's—" But the words dried up as Farah reached a hand into her collar and pulled out her own nearly identical chain.

"Each of us three sisters has one," Farah said. "They were forged here together in the mountains. They were a gift from our mother. Do you see? They are the same."

They were. But it made no sense. What was Lorana doing with Miria's necklace? If Miria had disappeared eight years ago...

Eight years ago.

"No."

Eight years ago was his sixteenth nameday.

"No."

His mother had given him his first hunting knife. He remembered the day clearly. He had gone into the forest to practice. He threw the knife at a tree over and over, watching it chip the wood, carving patterns in the bark.

"*No.*"

He'd heard a noise behind him and dropped the knife. He remembered feeling more foolish than afraid, that at the moment he might truly need his weapon it had fallen from his hands.

Lorana stepped out of the shadows. It was the first time he'd ever laid eyes on her. He remembered the surprise, then the flush of embarrassment, because she was beautiful and he was young and it was all so unexpected. But then she gave a little smile. *I am Lorana,* she had said.

Venick saw the way the story went. He saw how he and Lorana met in the woods every afternoon. He practiced with his knife, and she practiced with him, and slowly they began to know each other. He saw their friendship bloom, a warm, lofty thing. He saw himself grow older, and his feelings began to shift. He was desperate to hide them. She was his friend, and she was an elf. Even then, he'd known the law. But some feelings are impossible to hide. Venick saw himself fall in love with the elf who lived among them.

But *why* did she live among them? Why had she chosen to come to the mainlands? And who had she been before?

Venick's mind revolted. It couldn't be. Lorana was not Miria. She was *not*.

But, the necklace.

But, Miria's disappearance.

Slowly, Venick's mind shaped a different story. He imagined that Lorana lied about her name. He imagined that it wasn't a coincidence that the same year Miria disappeared into the south was the year Lorana appeared in Irek. He imagined that Lorana, like her youngest sister, had black hair. That she could easily pass as a southerner. Could easily hide her identity.

And here, another memory. Venick saw Ellina in the forest. He saw the way she held his necklace, questioning him around the fire. This time, he made himself forget the lurch of anger at his necklace in her fist. He remembered only Ellina's eyes, her calculation, the answers she sought. *The elf who gave this to you. What was her name?* He had not thought anything of his answer, yet that answer spurred Ellina to save his life. Later, he remembered Ellina's confession. *I wanted to kill you when I saw you*, she had said. *I wanted to kill you, and maybe I would have, if not—*

If not for Miria.

This was Ellina's reason. *This* was why she wanted Venick to live. Dourin said that Miria mysteriously disappeared into the south, but what if she hadn't? What if she *ran away*, and came to live in a little human city by the water? What if Ellina knew the truth all along?

This is elven silver. Ellina's voice rang in his memory. *It belongs to an elf. Where is she?*

Gone.

Gone, or dead?

Ellina pushed Venick for answers, yet he realized now that she must have already known the truth.

Did you love her?

Ellina knew who Venick was. She knew who he and Miria had been to each other.

Venick was falling. He was standing at the edge of the cliff, and this time he did jump, and was speeding towards the earth, air screaming in his ears, his eyes. He had known Lorana. He had *loved* her. But she wasn't who he thought she was. Miria. Lorana was the lost princess Miria. And he hadn't even known.

His exhaustion hit him all at once. Farah was still waiting for a response, but Venick didn't see Farah. He saw Ellina. He saw everything he had never comprehended about her, every clue uncovered. The sudden rush of understanding gutted him.

"Well?" Farah prompted, but Venick hardly heard. He had the sensation that he was underwater, that everything sounded far away. "What have you to say?"

"I told you what I came to tell you."

"You have not told me what you are doing with my sister's necklace."

Venick laughed. The joyless sound of it was sharp in the small space. "Ask Ellina."

"Ellina is not here."

"Find her. She will explain." He was glad they were speaking in his language again. He didn't truly believe his words.

"Yes," Farah said slowly. "Perhaps Ellina *does* have some explaining to do. She told me about you. You are the one she was seen fighting with in Kenath. But I do not believe Ellina mentioned traveling through the elflands with you." She became still. The elves around them did. "You have erred by coming here, human. You have broken our laws. You have entered elven lands and infiltrated our hidden city with the intent of spreading lies. You have been found with the necklace of our missing sister. You claim *elves* are building an army."

"It's the truth."

Farah stiffened, and Venick knew he had misspoke. "Man knows no truth," she replied, "and cannot be trusted." She glanced at the guards. "I will speak to Ellina. In the stateroom, publicly, at dawn. Find her. And bring the human, too."

• • •

Venick was chained to the wall by one wrist. Then he was left alone.

Time passed. It was impossible to know how much time, but Venick found he didn't care. His mind wandered from thought to thought, dreams morphing into wakefulness morphing back into dreams until he didn't know what was imagined and what was real, only that he was lost in both.

At some point he was given food and water. Venick didn't even have the strength to feel grateful. He ate and drank everything. He didn't ask questions. Didn't think his questions would be answered, anyway. The elf who had brought him his food left, and he was alone in darkness once more.

• • •

Venick dreamed of Lorana.

In his dream, he relived past conversations. He picked apart gaps he had never before noticed, holes in the fabric of who she was. He remembered the way she had taught him elvish, her quick corrections. Once, she asked him to lie.

Say anything, she had said. *Pick something simple, but untrue. I want you to know how it feels.*

He tried to tell her he hated her. The words felt caught in his throat.

Try harder, she said. He did, but his mind became strange. The words seemed to drift away from him, sand falling through fingers. He closed his eyes, but suddenly he could not remember the elven word for *hate*. And who was he trying to hate, anyway? He opened his eyes.

I cannot.

Lorana nodded, pleased.

Now you, he insisted with a sly smile. *I want to see what you look like when you try to lie to me.*

I would never— But she blinked, her mouth popping open.

Interesting, he said, and laughed.

He woke. He remembered his dreams and relived them again.

In all her years in Irek, no elf came looking for her. No one recognized her. Even if elves knew what Miria looked like, they didn't *expect* to see her in human clothes doing human things in a human city. Her disguise was perfect because it was honest. She didn't try to hide. She didn't need to.

But Ellina knew. Somehow, she knew about Miria's secret life. She must know about Miria's death, too.

Venick felt unstrung to think of Ellina in this way. He was dizzy with it. He'd suspected, during their first few days together, that Ellina must have some hidden reason for saving him. What else could possibly explain it? Why would she risk herself for a human?

Then he'd gotten to know her a little, and he started to wonder if maybe there was no hidden reason. Wasn't it possible that Ellina had saved him for him alone? He'd even—he winced to think of it—convinced himself that she'd done it because there were feelings growing between them. He'd thought the attraction was mutual.

Gods, what an idiot he'd been.

Despite these revelations, there was still so much he didn't understand. He wanted to know why Miria had fled Evov, why she'd chosen to come to Irek. He wanted to know why Ellina had never told anyone, had instead allowed the north to believe Miria had mysteriously vanished. Most of all, he wanted to know why Ellina bothered saving him at all when instead she could have vindicated her sister with his death. Venick closed his eyes, but behind closed lids he saw Ellina's steady gaze, her wash of black hair, her prowess.

I wanted to kill you, when I saw you.

Because it was his fault, what had happened to her sister. Miria was dead because of *him*.

Sadness, then. It welled. He couldn't believe, after everything, that *this* was how it was going to end.

Really. After everything. He couldn't believe it.

THIRTY

Ellina pressed a hand to her temple.

She did not know how long she had been sitting in her reading room practicing her elven lies. Long enough for the moon to rise and then fall again. Long enough for the candles to burn low, their sides caked in dripped wax. The pressure behind Ellina's eyes was a distraction. So were the rugs, the windows, the entire *room,* spinning dizzily. But Ellina would not quit. Not yet.

Since her mother's leaving, Ellina had begun practicing her lies with a new, almost feverish determination. She understood now more than ever how vital it was that she master this craft. And she believed that she could. She, who had always had a gift for deception, who could unmake the truth with a simple twisting of words...surely *this* was not beyond her skill.

If it was possible at all.

Ellina had not believed that it was at first. Even as she attempted her first few lies in elvish all those many days ago, she had not believed it. But as Ellina continued to practice, pushing through the headaches and the dizziness and the blaze in her lungs, she began to feel the change. Felt, subtly, as if she was breaking through her own skin. Before, attempting a lie in elvish had been like knocking on a brick wall. Now the wall was made of wood. It was hollow. She could sense what was hidden on the other side.

It was meager progress. Still, Ellina was encouraged. She became convinced that lying in elvish *was* possible. That if she worked hard enough, practiced long enough…

A tap at the door interrupted those thoughts. Ellina blinked up, then glanced at the candle, marking the time. Late. Too late for visitors.

She answered the door to find a servant standing on the other side. "*Cessena*," he said, dipping a quick bow. "A human has entered the city. He is asking for you."

Ellina pulled back. "What?"

"A human. In the city." She stared as the elf continued speaking—*He came with a message. A southern army, he says, marching north*—but Ellina was hardly listening. Her eyes went to the window. She gazed through the black night towards the bay, the mountains, the city that lay beyond. Her heart began to pound. She could feel it beating against her ribs.

No, her heart said.

Impossible, it said.

"Princess, are you listening?" the servant pressed. "Please, he is in the dungeons. You must come at once."

• • •

The sight of him nearly undid her.

Ellina realized, only now, that she had not truly believed the servant or his message. When the elf had come to her suite and began explaining, it had sounded like a story. Even as Ellina had fumbled to dress and flown from her rooms, she imagined this was happening to someone else, that it could not be real, could not be *her* life, because there was only one human who would ever ask for her, and he was gone.

But he was not.

Two prison guards guided Ellina down the dark tunnel to where Venick had been chained. There were no windows here. Instead torchlight gleamed, turned the prison's murky puddles to glass. They cast shadows over Venick's hunched figure, transforming him into a mirage of light and dark. Ellina wanted to imagine that it was a trick of the light how gaunt he appeared, how pale, lips cracked, one manacled wrist bloody and bruised. It was difficult to look at him. Difficult, too, to stay still, to resist the urge to step forward, to demand to know how he had entered their city and what he had done and *why*.

His winter eyes lifted to hers.

"Leave us," Ellina told the guards. They hesitated.

"*Cessena*, it is not safe…"

"You think I cannot protect myself against a single, unarmed human?" She made her tone to bite. "Do as I say."

Another moment's hesitation, a pause that lasted just long enough for Ellina to sense their doubt—and their suspicion. But then they were bowing and murmuring more dutiful *cessenas* and leaving.

Ellina's eyes found Venick again. Her anger took a shape she did not recognize. It squeezed her chest, dug fingers through her heart. He frightened her. What he had done frightened her. That he had managed to cross the tundra on foot, unsupplied, following the path to their hidden city on what could have only been a *guess*… "You have lost your mind."

His smile had a hard edge. "You heard my message, then?"

Yes, Ellina had heard his message, and she could scarcely believe it. Or him. What he had done…what had he *done?* "Dourin said—I thought…" She made herself stop. Gather her composure. Try again. "You were supposed to return to the mainlands."

"I know. I didn't."

"You went south."

"Yes."

"And then you came *here.*"

"Yes."

"Fool." Ellina heard the tremor in her voice, which meant others would hear it too. It was a weakness she could not afford. She inhaled deeply, fighting for calm. "Elves will call for your death. A quick execution is the best you can hope for. That is what happens to humans who enter our lands." Another deep breath, another attempt to calm herself. Her heart was stammering in her ears. She could scarcely speak. "Trespassing in the forest was one thing, but this? Truly, Venick. What were you thinking?"

The way he looked at her then, how his eyes became winter frost. It cracked Ellina open. She had the sudden sense that she knew what Venick would say next, that he would tell her he did not care about his own life, that he could not, not given everything *else*. And she saw it. She saw how something in him had become blown and tattered, a torn sail unable to catch the wind. It frightened her all the more.

But there was something else. The cast of his gaze. How he looked at her like he was seeing her for the first time. He was altered, she could sense it, yet she had the feeling that it was not just the journey across the tundra that had changed him, not just his imprisonment. She did not know what it was.

"Venick?"

He hesitated. Ellina heard the steady drip of water down rock. The light ping of droplets into an unseen puddle, the silence in between, the anticipation for the next drop to fall. She felt like that. Suspended.

"I know who Lorana was."

Ellina felt the words more than she heard them. A flash of shock. Hand dug into sword's pommel.

Venick said, "She was your sister, Miria."

The world chilled. Impossible. It was not possible for him to know that.

"I know you recognized her necklace," Venick went on. His voice had quieted, the words hovering between them, but she felt his intensity, the way it grew and morphed into something fierce and final. "I know that's why you chose to save me. I didn't always know. But I wondered. And then I learned the truth and I understood. Farah recognized the chain. She told me the necklace belonged to Miria. And Miria disappeared eight years ago, the same year Lorana appeared in Irek. A coincidence, I thought, maybe. But it wasn't."

Ellina wanted to deny it but could not, because he spoke elvish and could demand the truth, and she could not anyway, because she was unable to speak at all. Her throat constricted. She felt suddenly, brutally choked.

"You could have told me," Venick said. His expression firmed, became glacial as he pushed himself to standing. The chain around his wrist clanked. "Why didn't you *tell me*?"

Ellina's hand fell from her sword. "I could not."

"Yes, you could have. At any point, you could have—"

"No, Venick, I *could not*. I promised Miria that I would keep her secret. I promised her in elvish."

Venick seemed to understand. Elves rarely made promises of secrecy in elvish, but when they did, those promises could never be broken, in *any* language. The power of elvish forced the speaker to tell the truth, but in the case of oaths, it bound those truths forward into the future. Ellina had sworn to Miria that she would tell no one of her escape, and she was beholden by the rules of their language to keep her word.

"You could have found a way," Venick said. "*You* could have."

Maybe. But Ellina had not wanted Venick to know. Not before, when she loathed him, and loathed herself for saving him. Not after, when she had started to know him, and began to question if she had been wrong about him. If she had been wrong about everything.

Venick seemed to sag, tipping his head back against the stone wall. He cast his gaze upward. "*She* could have told me. I don't—" A hard swallow. "All those years. I can't believe she never did."

"She wanted a new life," Ellina replied, knowing it was not enough, it was nothing, yet needing to explain anyway. "The throne was never meant for her. She would have hated it. So she left. If anyone knew about her escape, they would have come for her. Keeping that secret... it was the only way for her to be free."

"I *loved her.*"

Ellina swallowed. "I know."

"And then you..." He met her gaze. "You saved me for her. In her honor." His eyes became clear pools. "But you should not have. It was my fault, what happened to her. I blame myself."

Ellina had too, once. She remembered it: the hot spark of hatred. The way hatred made herself less herself. But Venick did not kill Miria. The southerners did that. *They* were the reason she was dead. And Ellina understood now, did she not? She understood how it was possible to forget yourself, to forget about their laws and the border. She remembered how it had been traveling with Venick, talking with him, sleeping side by side. The vulnerability. The inability to hide her thoughts. But also the strange realization that she did not *want* to hide. That she would not mind if he cracked into her very core.

It had hurt her to feel that way. Hurt more when Venick fled, and *that* hurt her too, because she was a fool, because she should have known better than to care what he did or where he went. Ellina had rejected those feelings. She railed against them. She convinced herself that Venick's abrupt departure was for the best. He would return to the mainlands where he belonged. No final words, no apologies or farewells. No question of whether or not to acknowledge everything that had happened between them. It was better this way.

But Venick had not returned to the mainlands. Had instead gone south to investigate the vanished cities and the southerner's growing power, and had uncovered their enemy's secret, and had come *here*. To warn her.

"Venick…" She took an unsteady step forward, searching for the right words to explain that yes, she *had* blamed him. But that was before she knew him. Before she understood.

"You were right about the southerners," he said flatly. "They are uniting. And if you saw what I had seen…they will *crush you*. Your sister doesn't believe the rules of elvish apply to humans. She doesn't believe my warning—"

"She will. She must."

"—but *you* believe me," Venick went on. "You have my warning. You can hold the army off if you gather your defenses now." His eyes seemed to shed some of their anguish, and in them was a glimmer of the eyes Ellina knew. The ones that had won her trust long before she understood how such trust was even possible. "Nothing else matters. None of this—*that* is what's most important. Stopping the army. You can survive an invasion. I know you can. No matter what happens to me now."

"Nothing will happen to you now."

"You said it yourself. A quick execution is the best I can hope for."

"I was angry. I did not mean it."

His expression turned inward, as if he was listening to an internal voice. "Maybe I deserve it."

Ellina became angry. "Listen to what you are saying."

"I know what I'm saying."

Yet before Ellina could tell him that no, he did not know, and he had no right, and how dare he, not now, after everything, the rough creak of a door echoed down the corridor and Ellina froze, all those thoughts lingering unspoken.

THIRTY-ONE

Venick watched Ellina catch her words. Stop, swallow, turn.

He saw her sorrow. He wondered what she'd been about to say before the sound of the opening door had cut her short.

You are right.

You killed my sister.

I should be glad for your death.

I am.

But if that was true, why was she gazing at him like that, eyes wide and full of concern?

The unseen door scraped closed. Venick could hear the hush of distant footfalls heading their way, the echo of them across cavern walls. Could hear, under that, the whispers. Terse. A little worried. A voice rose over the others and ordered silence. The hall fell quiet except for the blurry tremble of feet on stone. More than three, fewer than six. It was impossible to count for sure, with the echoes. Impossible anyway, given Venick's current state. His head swam, fuzzy. Blame the fatigue—

The heartache, Venick. Be honest.

—for his present condition. Venick felt like he'd marched across the tundra twice. Felt like his mind couldn't get a grasp on his own name. He'd felt this way before, right after Ellina had killed that southerner for him. Ears ringing, breath gone, a clammy mixture of shock and remorse both.

The dungeon grew lighter as those footsteps approached, the warm glow of a torch illuminating the path ahead. The elves appeared next, four silhouettes coming their way. Venick glanced at Ellina, who had shuttered her expression. She watched the elves without a trace of her earlier concern. Perfectly calm, perfectly elven.

Give it a try, why don't you?

But he couldn't. Could not even *attempt* it. Venick was too raw to hide his feelings. And what did it matter, anyway? These elves didn't care that Venick's heart had turned to ash, that his ruin was written clearly on his face. They approached without sparing him a glance. They were taller than most, broad in their backs and shoulders. The firelight threw their shadows long across the walls. *Soldiers*, Venick thought. True soldiers, unlike the elves who had apprehended him in the city.

At least Evov has soldiers.

He should be glad for it. He was. Only, maybe not so glad they'd come for him.

"*Cessena*," they said, bowing. "Farah has ordered a summons."

Ellina darkened. "Only the queen can order a summons."

"In the queen's absence, that power falls to Farah, and she wants to speak with you." A reluctant glance in Venick's direction. "Both of you."

Ellina opened her mouth, ready to argue.

She stopped herself. Emptied her expression again in the next instant, then gave Venick a glance he recognized but could not interpret. "Very well."

An elf reached for Venick's wrist and grabbed the manacle. Venick didn't pull away. Didn't grimace at the pain, either, where his skin was rubbed raw. A key was produced. It clicked into the lock. The chains fell to the floor.

Venick looked at the elves' weapons and thought—the thought impulsive, absurd—about making a run for it. He almost laughed at his own stupidity. *That* scenario ended only one way: with a sword through his back and him dying on the floor. He loosened his shoulders instead and allowed his hands to be rebound, then followed the elves as they led him out.

The walk back through the tunnels seemed shorter than the descent, and soon they emerged into open night air. The dark velvet sky spanned wide. The city lights twinkled, and it seemed to Venick that Evov had become a reflection of the stars. They were guided through narrow alleys and cool, damp tunnels cut into the mountain, staying mostly on the edge of the city. Venick found himself looking up again and again at the jigsaw of buildings and bridges scattered in the rock overhead. Doors and windows gaped down at him, mostly dark, a few lit with lamplight. There was no glass. There were hardly any curtains, either, as if the elves didn't fear what might come through those windows. As if they had nothing to fear.

And they didn't, Venick reminded himself. Evov was a hidden city. The city *itself* was a gatekeeper.

Let you in, didn't it?

Venick did not quite understand the magic that ruled this city, but he did know that if Evov wanted to remain hidden, he wouldn't have found her. That the city had appeared for him could only mean that she *did* want to be found. Before, he had thought the elves would value this. That to them, the city's good opinion would hold meaning.

How painfully naive of him.

The air warmed as they walked, the night's chill edging into the sticky balm of morning. Daylight would come soon. Venick imagined how the sky would brighten with it. He focused on this rather than the four elves who guided him, Ellina trailing close behind. She had grown quiet, eyes down, her fingers tracing a pattern on her sword's pommel. Thinking.

About what, I'm sure you know.

Hell. His impending death? His revelations about her sister? Or was it the secrets they shared?

Venick had replayed those secrets over and over in his mind. Their fight with the southern conjurors. The shaft of Ellina's arrow sunk deep into an elf's neck. After, how Venick had demanded answers, demanded to understand. The way Ellina looked right before he kissed her.

Those secrets must still be safe, or else Ellina would not be walking free. Venick knew this, yet was not comforted. He remembered the way Farah had peered at him in the dungeons, the way an idea seemed to gather behind her eyes. *Perhaps Ellina* does *have some explaining to do.*

They rounded a bend and the palace came into view. Venick had not been able to see it before, not from the belly of the city, but now he could see the castle in its entirety, appearing as if risen from the fog. It was massive, a claw reaching out of a black canyon. Venick peered into that void, blinking away the sudden vertigo. "Gods."

"I would not say that here," the guard beside him warned. "Elves do not believe in gods."

"I'm not an elf."

The guard's lip curled, just slightly. "I know."

There was a single bridge arching over the void that connected the castle to the rest of the city, which led them into the entrance hall. Despite the hour, the palace was brightly lit. Venick was immediately unbalanced by the arched ceilings, the spiraling mosaic that crowded every inch of the walls. Blues and greens and reds raced together, creating patterns that rippled between shining pieces of glass, each one fitting neatly into the others. Compared to the rigid stone exterior, the hall looked out of place.

It *was* out of place. It took a moment for Venick to remember that elves did not care for art. *They* certainly wouldn't have designed the inlaid stonework, the bold colors sweeping across the walls. His mind caught on the thought, momentarily distracted.

But that thought was lost as the guards pushed him onward through a series of rooms that, unlike the entrance hall, were bare-walled and dark-stoned. Venick was reminded of the sewers in Kenath, the coarse chill of them. But then, this chill wasn't just the walls, wasn't just the air. It was a slimy fear, one that had been building slowly for days—hell, *weeks*—and one that Venick pushed away *again*.

It was true, what he'd told Ellina in the dungeons. It shouldn't matter what happened to him now. She had his warning. *That* was what mattered. That, and what she did with the knowledge. Which was stopping the southern uprising. Which was preventing their enemy from invading both her country and his. These were the things that counted, and nothing else.

Nothing? Really?

Venick glanced back at Ellina. Felt his chest ache with everything he now knew about her. Felt a little pain there, too, where that knowledge settled. It shouldn't make a difference whether she'd saved him for him, or out of duty to the dead. It changed nothing.

Believe that.

She lifted her gaze to meet his eye, and he saw it again—that inexplicable concern. *No*, Venick wanted to tell her. *You've done enough*, he wanted to tell her. If Ellina was concerned, it could only be because she still felt she owed it to Lorana to protect him. But how could Venick explain? He wanted to tell Ellina that she had it wrong. He wanted to apologize for Lorana's death, to explain how much he regretted it, how he'd give anything to undo it. He wanted to both beg Ellina's forgiveness and then convince her that he didn't deserve forgiveness, because if not for him Lorana would still be alive.

And maybe part of him wanted to accuse Ellina, too. He wanted to blame her for lying to him, for confusing him, for digging her fists into his shirt when he kissed her and allowing him to believe so many ridiculous, impossible things.

But before Venick had a chance to say anything, they reached a double-wide set of doors and halted. One of the guards unbound Venick's wrists while another set both pale hands on the wood and *pushed*, using all his weight to reveal a long stateroom. Then they were guiding Venick forward and Venick, conflicted and resigned, allowed himself to be led through the doors.

THIRTY-TWO

Ellina felt as if she was seeing things clearly for the first time.

She had struggled so hard for clarity. Had sought the truth, and found it, and lost it. It slipped through her fingers, pooling in and around *other* truths, the ones she had ignored and misread and forsaken. Like: elves will kill other elves. Like: humans and elves can become allies. Like: a royal princess, raised a soldier, beloved by her country, can break the law.

As Ellina marched down the long stateroom floor—marking Farah there on the raised dais in the room's center, the rest of Ellina's troop fanning to either side, a nearly-full court filed in the gallery behind them—she thought of everything she had come to understand. That understanding settled into her. It was heavy and hard. A grounding weight.

She wondered, distantly, if she should be bothered. If she should be *shamed*, for what she had become and had done and was about to do. But

Ellina was not shamed. She was not thinking of things like shame. She was thinking only of what she now understood, and what she wanted, and what she was willing to do to get it.

The guards who had escorted them to the stateroom peeled away then, leaving Ellina and Venick to approach Farah alone. This was custom. Subjects summoned to the court—even the accused—never met the queen under guard.

But Farah was not queen, Ellina reminded herself. No matter how much her sister might wish it. No matter how satisfied she appeared standing on that dais, watching Ellina answer to her like a dog being whistled home. It was no secret that after Miria's disappearance, Farah had expected to be crowned immediately. The queen, however, had decided to wait. That was her right; Farah would only take the throne when Rishiana chose it. There were no rules as to when.

Yet it was no secret, either, that Farah was impatient with waiting. Ellina had always been aware of Farah's impatience. Had tucked the knowledge away, marked it as *to be expected* and *unimportant*. Many heirs were impatient. Many heirs wanted their turn at power.

But not many heirs attempted a shot at that power before their time. Not many heirs would stand so boldly on the stateroom's dais as Farah was doing now. And so it was only in this moment, as Ellina studied her sister, as she saw the gleam of some dark feeling lurking in Farah's eyes, that the knowledge of Farah's impatience became significant, somehow. Dangerous.

Ellina was not afraid of danger. She knew how to spot a threat, how to home in on its power and disarm it. To find the weakness, the places where the armor joined, and *stab*.

She knew, also, to allow no weaknesses of her own.

Ellina glanced in Venick's direction. He had been quiet during their walk from the dungeons. He was quiet now. And pale, and defeated, and just—*sad*. His sadness pulled at her heart. Twisted and stuck, there, deep inside.

But this was not a weakness, Ellina told herself. It was not the same. And indeed, knowing what she now knew, this made her strong. Strong enough to accept what she could now see clearly. Strong enough to pull her expression blank, to firm her jaw and lengthen her stride as she and Venick made the long, silent march down the stateroom floor.

"Sister," Farah said in greeting. Despite the hour, Farah was dressed in full guard's armor, white hair outlined against black iron, hands clasped behind her back. Her voice carried easily between high pillared walls. "You received my summons."

Ellina dropped her gaze deliberately to her troopmates organized by Farah's side—Branton, Artis, Kaji, Dourin and Raffan—then lifted her eyes to scan the onlookers in the gallery: a mix of courtiers and senators and citizens. "Yes," Ellina replied. "As did the rest of the palace, I see."

Farah might have smiled. "Word travels quickly within these walls."

"Then let word of *this* travel quickly." Ellina and Venick came to a stop before the dais. A beat of silence, the press of it on her ears, and then, calmly: "I received your summons, and I am here to decline."

A murmur from the audience. Shuffling robes, a stifled protest. Farah's brows lifted, just slightly. "You decline?"

"You had no right to order a summons." Ellina mirrored Farah's stance, hands clasped behind her back, spine stiff and straight. "You are not queen yet, and you do not command me."

More muttering. Farah's expression, which had been still, turned to ice. She was angry, and for good reason; Ellina had just made it impossible for Farah to argue without committing her own treason. What Ellina had said was true. Farah did not have the right to summon Ellina to the stateroom. Only the queen had that power. The mere attempt to do so was a dangerous overstep.

But Farah recovered quickly. She spread her hands. "Sister, you misunderstand. Of *course* I am not summoning you as a queen would her subject. Consider my summons a request. I only thought you would want to be present to hear the human's fate."

The court continued to whisper, differently now.

Ellina looked at Venick and felt it again: that tender tug on her heart. She forced herself to remember Kenath. The conjurors, the river, the storm. Venick's choices. How he was when he fought, the way his body became a wall built of his own will. She thought again about how he had disappeared after the whipping. Her own assumptions, and how wrong they had been. Venick had not fled back to the mainlands. He had gone south, for *her*.

Ellina thought of his life price. It was easy to believe that Venick risked his life for her out of duty or honor. He owed her a debt. According to the laws of man, his life belonged to her. Yet Ellina had become aware that this was not his *entire* reason. She understood—one of many new understandings—that there was an undercurrent to each of Venick's choices. Even when he tried to hide it, she could still see the truth's veiny skin, translucent when held up to the light. She saw how she could trace those veins, could feel the pulse of things.

An idea. It drove into her.

"A human has entered our city," Farah said, lifting her voice to address the room. "He has broken the law."

Ellina touched the edges of this new idea. She thought its shape was like the shape of her earlier anger: formless, yet quickly solidifying into something true and real.

"He aims to spread misinformation," Farah continued. "Rumors of the southern army have already leaked through Evov. Our citizens are confused. They are afraid."

Venick was not looking at Farah, either. His focus was fully on Ellina. His eyes were hard. Suspicious. As if he, too, saw this nameless idea forming in her mind and did not trust it.

"They do not understand how a *human* has entered our hidden city. It is worrisome and must be dealt with quickly."

Ellina looked back at her sister. She and Farah did not look much alike. Ellina was small and dark while Farah was silver, angelic—the very picture of an elven queen. Ellina and Farah shared their opinions on political matters, though. Or, they *had*.

It struck Ellina that when she looked at Venick she no longer saw what her sister saw. Not a threat, but an ally who risked his life to do what they should have done, to learn what they should have known.

What she should have.

The clay of her idea hardened to a firm shell.

"There will be no trial," Ellina interrupted. Her troop stirred. Farah turned to peer at her.

"Of course not," Farah agreed. "A human does not get a trial, merely a sentencing. And his sentence is death."

"His sentence is not for you to decide."

Her sister stared. "And why is that?"

"His fate belongs to me."

Venick's voice was rigid. "Ellina, no, you can't—"

Farah asked, "His fate belongs to you?"

"He owes me his life," Ellina explained. "I won his life price. He is mine now to do with what I will."

"Those are human laws."

"He is human."

"We do not honor human life prices."

"Yet we expect humans to honor our laws?"

"*Ellina.*" Venick's voice was strained. She ignored him.

"Yes, Ellina." Raffan cut in. "What are you doing?"

"Claiming what is mine."

"*Yours?*" Raffan's mask was perfectly mastered, his expression wiped clean. Even his voice, which usually betrayed him, held no inflection. He was trying, Ellina thought, very hard. Which meant he was furious. "His execution is well-deserved. And overdue."

"I disagree," Ellina argued. "Venick came to deliver a warning. We have all heard his message. The southerners are uniting. They are building an army. They will come north."

"Impossible," Raffan said.

"Is it? We saw how they infiltrated Kenath. We saw the vanished cities."

"The southerners are weak. They will never unite. And even if they did, to what purpose? Elves do not kill elves. The north and south both abide by those laws. The human is a liar."

Ellina bit back her retort. She breathed into her words. "He is not a *liar*. He is an ally. He risked his life to come here. And he can prove himself in elvish. When the queen returns, *she* will believe him."

The audience was abuzz now. There was a shift. A subtle change in the pitch of their whispers. Ellina could practically hear their denial morph into reluctant doubt...and more. Farah eyed them, surely sensing, as Ellina did, how the battle was tipping. Her expression seemed to sour. "But there are rumors," Farah argued. "It is said that the laws of elvish do not apply to all."

Ellina's heart gave a heavy thump. "That is absurd."

"Still." Farah drew her hands together. "It does create some doubts.

It is true that our language has held us to honesty for thousands of years, but men have been spinning their lies for nearly as long. The human cannot be trusted." A pause. Gathering ammunition, the draw of a bow, shot through teeth that peeled back and bared. "And if *you* trust a human, I wonder what that says about *you*."

Ellina flexed her hands. Checked herself as she started to reach for her sword. Replied, coolly, "If my trust is to be doubted, that is a matter for the queen to decide. When she returns."

"I could order his execution," Farah warned. "I could order it right now."

"Against *my* wishes, which means you would be acting against our mother's wishes."

"When the queen is absent, *I* am in charge."

"*Ellina.*" Venick sounded panicked. He seemed to know enough not to grab her, yet not enough to stay silent. She made the mistake of looking at him then. She saw his horror. "*Don't.*"

Ellina understood that horror. Venick was remembering the last time she had defended him. Ellina remembered it, too. She could still smell the wet forest, could hear the creak of trees in the wind. Could see her troop standing by, Raffan's rage, her choice that was not truly a choice, because despite the pain of Venick's lies uncovered, despite her anger, she could not bear the thought of Venick's death, or allow Raffan to kill him. She had accepted Venick's punishment instead and everything that followed: the kiss of air across her back. The peal of the whip.

This conversation was much like that whipping: a calculated risk. Ellina saw each move in play. She saw again what she wanted and how she aimed to get it. When she pulled her eyes off Venick and back to her sister, the heavy weight of her understanding cracked in two. She could hold the separate halves in her palms. Could read, scrawled there in the fissure, how this would end. How to *make* it end. Ellina spoke the words clearly. "When our mother departed, did she give you command of the city, or was that duty to be shared between us?"

Farah went rigid with anger.

"Venick lives," Ellina said. "We will wait for Rishiana's return so that she may hear his warning. Until then, the queen is the only one with the power to overrule me, and you, Farah, are not queen."

Farah's gaze promised revenge. "Not yet."

• • •

"What are you *doing?*" Dourin demanded as he pushed his way into Ellina's suite.

She stepped aside to make room, closing the door behind him. It was fully morning. Her receiving room was bathed in soft light. Ellina felt its warmth, which reminded her that she was not warm, that she was cold and had been cold for a very long time.

Dourin rounded on her. "You have taken things too far. Do you not remember the forest? Do you not remember what Raffan will *do to you?*"

Yes, Ellina remembered. Of course she remembered.

"Clearly you have forgotten," Dourin continued, "or else things in that stateroom would have gone very differently this morning. You would have allowed Farah to kill the human. You certainly would not have *claimed him.*"

"I had to."

"You *had to.*" She had never seen Dourin like this. "Tell me it is not what it seems, Ellina. Tell me you defended the human because of some sorely misplaced sense of duty, and that you are about to march back down to the stateroom and renounce him."

Ellina could. She could sooth Dourin with pretty lies, could deny his worries. The old Ellina would have. The old Ellina would have hardened herself, pulled on a face of steel and said what needed to be said.

She realized it was not true, when she imagined herself to be cold. Maybe she had been once, but she had changed. *He* had changed her. And so Ellina began speaking, softly at first, then gaining strength as she told Dourin everything. She started from the moment they found Venick in the elflands and talked until she had said it all. By the time she finished, Dourin was gazing at her in disbelief. "Ellina…"

"I know." She stopped him before he could continue. "But what else could I do?"

Dourin crossed his arms. Unconvinced. Unhappy. "So he remains a prisoner here until the queen returns to hear his warning, but what then? She might kill him anyway."

"Yes."

"Or Raffan might."

Ellina remembered Raffan's marble face, the way it showed his anger more fully. "Yes."

"And if Venick is lying about the southern army?"

"He speaks elvish, Dourin. The laws of our language have always applied to humans, no matter what Farah says. And he has no reason to lie."

Dourin spread his hands. "Does he not?"

Ellina thought about how Venick had been granted freedom twice, and twice he had thrown it away. She thought of how he had fought for her in Kenath, then killed for her in the forest. She remembered his winter eyes. How they warmed her.

He had smiled to hear her sing. The memory dug into her. Miria had taught her that song. Ellina wondered if Miria had ever sung it for

Venick. She wanted to know if he recognized the tune. She had been afraid to ask.

She understood why Dourin might think Venick's story was just a story, but Ellina knew better. "I believe him. If he says the southerners are building an army, then that is the truth."

Dourin said, "I hope, for all our sakes, that you are wrong."

THIRTY-THREE

It was dawn by the time the guards escorted Venick from the stateroom.

His mind was overfull. It held too much, as if his thoughts were a many-sided die. He turned that die over, but he could only see one face at a time. He thumbed the white porcelain. It was fragile. If he dropped it, it would crack.

Ellina had noticed. In the dungeons, she had peered into his eyes, saw the hazy gleam. She guessed the reason—

A fortnight on the tundra, a fool's journey to reach her.

—even if she hadn't said so. He'd seen her anger that was not anger but worry. He'd come to know it well.

He needed to speak with her. He must. What she had done—what had she *done*? Angst stitched up his spine. She had to take it back. All of it. He would *make* her. Yet after Ellina and Farah's argument, a trio of guards had materialized between them to shove Venick away.

Breathe, Venick commanded himself. *Wait*. Ellina would come. Later. When things were quiet. She would come for him then, and when she did he would explain everything in a way she would understand, would force her to see that he didn't need her claiming him, didn't need her protection. Reeking gods, this wasn't *about him*.

The guards moved him through the palace, but Venick hardly noticed. He was so caught in the web of his own mind that he was barely aware of the elves who guided them, their angry murmurs, disgust half-hidden. Barely aware, either, of the path they took: through hallways, an atrium, up a stairwell.

Up, Venick. That mean anything to you?

It might have. Had his mind been clearer, he might have questioned why they were going *up* when the dungeons were *down*. But Venick's mind wasn't clear. It was back in the stateroom with Ellina. It was listening to her claim him. It cupped around a frantic feeling. Barbed, like poisoned stingers.

One of the guards said something, which startled Venick. "What?"

"I *said*," the elf replied, "*move*."

He was pushed into the receiving room of a bedroom suite, which was expansive and far too rich. Venick looked around, peering up at the vaulted ceiling, the wide windows. "But, the prison…"

"This is your prison now." The elf crossed his arms over his hammered steel breastplate. He had high cheekbones, small eyes, a deep mouth. A pendant peeked over the elf's cuirass, black and red. "This door is iron-backed. You cannot burn it off. And we are in the palace's tallest tower. It is a long way down from the window."

"I don't understand."

"The only way *out* is through the window," the elf insisted. Hinting at something, Venick realized. Not that hard to guess *what*. "You might take a look. See if you can fly." The guard's mouth tipped, just slightly. A sneer.

They left, and locked the door behind them. Venick stared at that door for a long moment.

He forced himself to move.

He wandered from the receiving room into the sitting room into the bed chamber. He checked the drawers first—all empty—then went to the open window to peer down. He confirmed the guard's not-so-subtle suggestion: the tower was high and steep. If he fell from this height he would hit the rocks far below. His body would shatter.

He returned to the door. Solid, oak and metal. He tested the lock, which was bolted from the outside.

There would be no easy chance of escape, then. No weapons, either, except for a curtain rod he managed to unscrew from the wall. Venick hefted it in one hand. Heavy. Iron. A pointed whorl at the end like a spear.

He set the rod next to the bed.

He waited.

• • •

She didn't come.

Venick was restless. He should sleep, he knew that he should, but he couldn't. He paced the room. He tried to *think*, but he couldn't do that either. He could only replay in his mind a string of visions. Ellina in the stateroom. Ellina's eyes cutting to his. Ellina bargaining for his life—and in doing so risking her own.

A rush of anger. He beat it back, tried for calm. Managed it, mostly, until he remembered Ellina again, and his anger surged again, and he beat it back *again*. His thoughts eclipsed.

Venick considered his prison, the jeweled sconces, fireplace large enough to fit a grown man. This was undoubtedly Ellina's doing. He wondered if she'd argued for this change in accommodations like she'd argued with her sister in the stateroom. He wondered if word of his pampered prison would travel like murmurs of *human* had through the city. He thought of the guards who had led him here, their hands at their weapons, ready—no, *hoping*—for Venick to misstep, to give them a reason to strike. Their ears had been heavily adorned in gold, each ring significant. One elf had worn a pendant.

Venick glanced again at the door. Anxious. He was too anxious.

There was a writing desk. A hard-backed chair. He sat, and shut his eyes, and watched the morning ripen from behind closed lids. His body sank, muscles relaxing one by one. But still his mind could not. He scanned the events of the past day, raking his memory for the error, as if there was but one, and if only he could find that single, fatal mistake, he could undo everything that had gone so wrong.

But there was no single error. Or if there was, the error was *him*. A human in an elven city. A human meddling in elven affairs. A human who cared when he shouldn't.

He was fighting sleep now. Yet he thought if only he could stay awake a little longer, maybe the door would open and Ellina would come. In that final moment.

The door stayed closed.

• • •

The sky was clear and bright when Venick woke.

He was sore. There was a welt on his wrist from the shackle, a tight pain in his back from falling asleep in a chair. His head ached, and his lips were cracked and dry. He washed himself in the water basin. He rubbed the grime out of his skin, scrubbing until he was pink and raw.

A click at the door. The lock.

It wasn't her.

"You have a knack for getting yourself imprisoned," Dourin said as he strode into the room. He had traded his legion armor for silken tunic and trousers. A shortsword was belted to his hip in place of the standard legion-length broadsword. He caught sight of the downed curtain rod and lifted a brow. "Inventive."

"Where's Ellina?"

"Handling the backlash of your arrival, I am sure. Your presence here is not, shall we say, *celebrated*."

"I need to speak with her."

Dourin rolled his eyes. "Of course you do."

"It's important."

"More important than your impending execution? If I were you, human, I would be most worried about *that*."

Venick looked out the window. A breeze whined against the tower. "You think I'm lying about the army, too."

Dourin crossed to the writing desk and pulled out the chair. He sat gracefully, arms and legs folding. "What I believe is irrelevant."

"If an elf had come with my message, you would be preparing. You wouldn't be wasting time."

"Oh, I am not so sure about that," Dourin said. "Elves have not fought a true war since the purge. We have all but forgotten how. Where would we even begin?"

Venick shook his head. "It's not that hard to figure out."

"Says a human. Your race is made for battle."

"Elves train to fight, too."

"Not in the same way. We fight each other one-on-one, yes, but we know little about planning battles."

Which Venick knew already. Still. "It's beside the point," he said. "You can't do *nothing*. You should be recruiting soldiers, calling on the rest of the legion, preparing your arms. Evov might be a hidden fortress—"

"It let *you* in."

"—but there are cities to the south and east that would easily be crushed by the army I saw."

"And how, oh great warrior, would you suggest saving them?"

Venick hesitated. Dourin's tone was dry, but his eyes were steady, curious, in a way that suggested he might truly want the answer.

"I would start by slowing the southerner's progress." Venick moved to the desk where Dourin sat, rummaging for parchment and ink. "Part of an army's strength comes from its ability to move swiftly." He drew a rough sketch of the elflands. Forests to the south, mountains to the north, a tundra between them. "If the southerners reach the tundra, you will be disadvantaged. They have the numbers. They will be able to overwhelm an inexperienced army, especially if that army is smaller. But," Venick drew a circle around the mountains, then the forests, "if you pin them where they can't move, you'll have the advantage. The legion's strengths lie in small contingents, troops like yours of six or ten. You could perform targeted strikes. Take out their supply wagons, assassinate their leaders. Cut the legs off the beast and you stop it in its tracks."

"And if we cannot stop it? As you so studiously noted, the legion is small, and our troops are currently scattered around the elflands. What if the army reaches the tundra anyway?"

"Recruit more soldiers. Train them, arm them with green glass. Station them in the mountain pass. Don't meet the southern army in open battle on the tundra—lure them to you. You will need to evacuate exposed cities, but your soldiers will still have the advantage. The pass will bottleneck an army. You can pick the southerners off bit by bit."

Dourin looked skeptical. "Let us say, *hypothetically*, we did what you suggest. There is still the problem of gathering and training these soldiers."

Venick looked up at the vaulted ceiling. "I could do it."

"You."

"Yes." He drew his gaze back down. "I have the training. I have the knowledge."

"Have you forgotten that you are a prisoner? Northern elves will not follow you. You are not even supposed to *be* here."

"Then I'll advise in secret. I'll teach you and Ellina everything I know, and *you* will head our defenses."

"Ours, is it?"

Venick hesitated. "The mainlands are at risk, too."

"But you did not come here for the mainlanders."

Venick wasn't certain how to respond to that, so he said only, "Evov sits atop green glass mines. That's valuable. How large is your arsenal?"

Dourin uncrossed and re-crossed his legs. "A human, wondering about our arsenal."

"You'll need to arm your soldiers."

"Indeed."

Venick gave an impatient sigh. "So you don't know."

"Oh, I *know*."

"But you won't tell me? Fine. Take me there. *Show* me your armory. I'll take inventory."

Dourin laughed. "If I do not want to tell a human about our weapons, I certainly would not want to *show* him."

"What's the worst that could happen?"

"You will kill me as soon as we arrive."

"That wouldn't serve my purposes."

"You will escape."

"I wouldn't make it far if I did."

"Then you will make a fool of me, merely for agreeing to your pre-posterous plan."

Venick gave a hollow laugh. "Dourin," he said, "we both know, of the two of us, you are not the fool."

• • •

Dourin didn't take him to the armory.

Instead the elf departed with promises to send the palace *eondghi* in order that Venick's mental wellbeing might be checked since he had, in Dourin's words, clearly lost his mind. When he left, the click of the bolt rang loud. It seemed to echo through the room for a long time after.

Venick stared at the door. The handle, ornate. The keyhole was a lit-tle black eye. He shook himself, finally, and tried to arrange his thoughts. Which were a mess.

Venick became well-acquainted with his prison. He went through the drawers again, more carefully this time, checking for false bottoms, test-ing the strength of their handles. He learned the number of steps it took to cross between bed and dresser and fireplace, the size and position of each wall sconce, which of them burned oil and which burned wax. He discovered blind spots, places he could stand unseen with curtain rod in hand.

To do what, Venick? Launch an ambush?

If it came to that.

He developed a particular fondness for the locked door and its keyhole. Venick worked that keyhole with a quill from the writing desk, face hovering close, inhaling the scent of brass as he listened for the telltale click of a lock come undone. It was only after an hour of this that he discovered the keyhole was mere ornamentation. The real bolt must be higher up and inside the door. Unreachable.

He broke the quill in two and threw it across the room.

Resigned, Venick went to the window. He rested his elbows against the sill, leaned out and closed his eyes and tried to be still, to be calm.

But he couldn't be still or calm for long. Soon his eyes were open again and he was studying the terrain, imagining how an army might weave through the mountains, the way their metal bodies would gleam in the sunlight. He looked down and saw that the void below the palace was not, in fact, infinite, as he had believed on first sight. Water glinted far below, frothing white against the mountain base. The only way across that water was over the wide bridge that connected the palace to the rest of the city. That was good. The castle would be difficult to take by force.

But not impossible. Again, Venick contemplated the strength of the city's magic. He wondered—*really* wondered—how he had managed to enter Evov. Was it because the city had allowed him entrance, or because its magic was failing? Could enemy elves enter the city, too?

This made him think, oddly, of the sneering guard who had led him to his new prison. Venick felt a strange tug in his chest, a discomfort.

But of course that guard made him uncomfortable. Venick remembered the way the elf had warned him that the window was his only method of escape. The double meaning.

Venick dragged a hand across his mouth, felt the rough stubble. He was tired of the lies, the coded hints in every word elves spoke. Elves were known for winning wars with words, but language had it limits. Sometimes you had to *act*.

Worked so well for you, has it?

When things got messy, Venick was happy to give over to impulse, let his hands and body make the decisions. He fought that way. He loved that way. But *had* it worked for him? He thought of Lorana. Of his mother and Ellina. All his failures.

He pushed away from the window, swept his gaze again around his prison. Venick wondered if this was always the nature of redemption, or if it was merely the price one paid for murdering their own father. He wondered if it was his destiny to die here like this: alone, a thousand leagues from home, split between two worlds. Fighting for them both. Yet belonging, really, to neither.

THIRTY-FOUR

Ellina roamed the palace halls. She saw the familiar arched ceilings, the patterned stone, the bare walls, unadorned. Usually, when Ellina returned to Evov after a campaign it felt as if she had never left. It was easy to come here, to breathe in the cool air, to visit her suite and see that things looked exactly as they always had.

It did not feel that way now.

Ellina felt Venick's presence, the way it changed things. Even though he was not with her, she sensed him. She felt it in the way the servants whispered, the way the entire palace seemed too small. She saw it in the way Farah's guards watched her, their mouths tight, golden eyes following her every movement.

And indeed, it seemed as if the guards were *always* watching her. Ellina noticed how palace paths that were usually empty were now occupied, courtyards previously unguarded now patrolled, all by Farah's guard. Was it Ellina's imagination, or had Farah stationed more sentries here than before? They seemed to be *everywhere*, dozens more than Ellina remembered, posted on every corner, in the mouth of every hallway, at the top of each tower. They were all dressed in the same hammered armor, all carrying the same standard longsword, all watching the corridors with too-keen eyes.

Ellina did her best to avoid them. She avoided Venick, too. Since the stateroom meeting, Ellina had not gone to the north tower. She had not walked those winding stairs or opened the uppermost door. She did not step into the room, or sweep her gaze across the glittering suite, or meet the eye of the human within.

But she imagined it. Her mind was in those chambers, roaming those rooms. She wondered what Venick made of his new prison even as she knew he hated it. He would not like the ruse, the way the suite's elegance masked the reality. He might even prefer the dungeons because they were closer to the truth. No matter in chains or in comfort, Venick was a prisoner still.

"He asks about you," Dourin told Ellina one afternoon three days after Venick's arrival. They sat in her reading room at a pedestal table. Light streamed in through half-drawn curtains. "He wants to speak to you."

"I know."

Dourin reached for the hourglass sitting between them. He turned it over. Its wooden base clinked against the table. "What do you plan to do with him until the queen returns?" When Ellina did not reply, Dourin said, "You cannot ignore your little pet forever."

"He is not my pet."

"Call him what you like, but that is how everyone sees it."

"That is not how *I* see it."

Dourin shrugged, and Ellina went quiet. She watched the hourglass.

The sand piled onto itself, forming a little mound. She allowed it to mesmerize her.

In the three days since Venick's arrival, word of his warning had spread. The citizens, it seemed, were divided. Those who did not share Farah's misgivings could be heard whispering anxiously, discussing the possibility of a southern attack. The human had relayed his warning in elvish, they reasoned. And their hidden city had allowed him entrance. How else would he have found Evov if not because his purpose was pure? He *must* be telling the truth.

The other half wanted to see Venick's head on a spike.

"Farah is unhappy," Dourin said.

"Of course Farah is unhappy. She thinks Venick is lying about the southern army. She wants him dead."

"That is not what I meant. You humiliated her." Dourin frowned. He hesitated, visibly, before saying, "I saw her speaking to Raffan. Last night in the archives."

Ellina paused. "They could have been discussing anything."

"But they were probably discussing *you*."

Ellina understood Dourin's concern. An illicit nighttime meeting in the privacy of the archives between her bondmate and her sister? It was unusual. It *was* worrisome. Though Farah and Raffan were, by blood and bonding, both members of the royal circle, those two elves had never been anything more than cordial acquaintances. They were not friends. They had no business together, no reason to meet.

Dourin leaned forward. "I trust you, Ellina. Do you trust me?"

She lifted her eyes. "Yes."

"Then listen to what I am about to say to you. It is not good that Farah is angry. It is not good that Farah and Raffan have reason to make you their common enemy. You have played them both, but this is not the kind of game you can win. Abandon it now, before it is too late."

"Abandon Venick, you mean."

"If you continue to defend him, things will only become worse for you."

"And if I do not? If I pretend not to believe him, and ignore his warning, and call for his death, as Farah has? What *then*? How are we supposed to prepare to battle a southern army if we cannot even acknowledge its existence?"

"There are other dangers. More pressing dangers." Dourin's expression changed, became anguished. "You cannot fight the southerners if you are banished to the whitelands for your involvement with a human."

"It will not come to that." But Ellina thought of Venick hidden away in his prison. She thought of the way *other* rumors were spreading, and why she did not go to him now. She said, "I need more time."

Dourin sighed, rubbing his temple. "To do what?"

But Ellina had not told Dourin about her elven lies. She had not told anyone. The reason, she decided, was simple. Farah believed Venick could lie in elvish. But this was wrong. The wilding chieftain had been specific—only *conjurors* had that power, and human conjurors had been eradicated long ago. Still, if it became known that elves could lie in elvish, what was to stop elves from believing that humans could, too? Venick's warning would be dismissed. The queen would take Farah's side. Venick would be executed, and the enemy army would arrive uncontested.

This was the reason Ellina gave herself, yet perhaps it was not her only reason. She herself had need for secrecy. Learning to lie in elvish would do her no good if others *knew* she could lie.

Ellina looked at Dourin. Here was her friend. Her dearest ally. He would keep her secret if she told him the truth.

Do you trust me?

Yes.

And that was true. Ellina did trust Dourin. She trusted him enough to tell him her nakedly treasonous story about Kenath and Venick and the forest. She had confessed everything, confident that Dourin would not turn his back on her, would not call for her banishment. And he had not. Had instead done what she knew he would, which was to listen, and shake his head, and stand by her anyway.

Yes, Ellina thought. She trusted Dourin. But trust was not what kept her from telling him about her plans or her newfound power. Trust had nothing to do with it.

Dourin seemed to have forgotten his question. He was staring out the window. He said, "We should alert nearby cities of the danger. They should be evacuated. They can take refuge here, in Evov."

Ellina tapped a fingernail on the table. "I thought you did not believe Venick's warning."

"I never said I did not believe him."

"So you were just being difficult."

Dourin skinned a smile. "I am *being* pragmatic. I am trying to make the best of an impossible situation."

Ellina huffed. "As am I."

"You are not exactly equipped for pragmatism." Dourin squinted, twirling his finger at her. "Not where the human is concerned."

"Why? Because I—" She shut her mouth.

"Care for him?" Dourin supplied. "Yes, actually. Your insane performance in the stateroom is proof of that."

"I am not insane."

"In love. Insane." Dourin tilted his hands back and forth as if balances on a scale. "Same difference."

But his words brought Ellina up short. She drew back a little.

It was true that Ellina cared for Venick. After everything they had been through, after a bargain made by firelight, after Venick pulling her from a river and promising her safety, after watching him pummel Raffan because Raffan had hurt her, because Venick wanted to hurt whoever caused her pain, and especially now, after seeing what Venick had risked for her and her country—how could she not care for him? But *love?*

The word condensed like fog, blurred and chilled the air around her. No. She could not allow herself to believe that. Ellina shook her head. "I do not love him."

Dourin's smile became a mere crook of his mouth. He laid a gentle hand over hers. "Of course not."

THIRTY-FIVE

Venick lay on the floor of his prison-suite, staring at the ceiling. Unmoving. Unblinking. His eyes burned, but Venick refused to shut them. His vision became weird. The ceiling morphed and spun, light to dark to light again. A mirage.

The sound of footsteps approaching broke the trance. Venick blinked. Listened to the shift of feet halt outside his locked door. The *snick* of the bolt. The door swung wide.

It was Dourin. Venick knew it was without having to look. That elf had been his only visitor these past six days, besides the servant who brought him meals and the occasional guard come to taunt him. But it was too late in the afternoon for meals. And Venick knew those footsteps.

"Lazy," Dourin accused when he spotted Venick sprawled on the floor. The elf nudged him with the toe of his boot. "And I thought you were a tireless warrior. What will the queen think when I tell her how worthless you are?"

Venick closed his eyes. Tried—very deliberately—not to snarl in response. Deep breath, then letting it go, and *then*, calmly, "I wouldn't be worthless if you let me out."

Venick could hear the smile in Dourin's tone. "If I let you out you would surely do something foolish, and then what would the queen think of *me*?"

Venick rolled to his feet. "We've discussed this."

"Yes," Dourin replied. "We have."

It was an old argument, worn threadbare between them these past six days. Venick wanted out. Venick wanted to start planning. Venick was tired of *waiting*. While the southern army advanced, they did nothing. It was wearing away at his sanity. If he was to be a prisoner here, hell and damn, at least let him be useful. That was why he had come, wasn't it? To warn the north about the southern army and to help them prepare. He could be teaching Ellina and Dourin about possible scenarios for attacks and counterattacks. Could be discussing the southern army's next move, who was leading them, what they wanted and how they would aim to get it. They could be devising a series of plans, then redevising them based on the number of soldiers they could secure.

Which was currently zero.

His frustration grew.

"When will the queen return?" Venick asked Dourin for what felt like the hundredth time. Dourin threw him an annoyed look. He didn't know. Venick knew he didn't, yet couldn't help but press. "She is taking too long. *This*," he swept a hand around the suite, "is driving me mad."

"And I thought you enjoyed the pleasure of my company. Careful, or I will think you ungrateful."

"We should be doing more. *You* should be calling on the legion."

Dourin tsked. "You *are* ungrateful."

Venick stalked to the window, yet made no move but to brace his hands against the frame. Dourin wasn't wrong. Venick should be grateful. He was here, and alive, with only a few fading bruises to show for his struggles. Yet Venick couldn't ignore the sour taste in his mouth or will away the knowledge that the north was still woefully unprepared to face an attack.

"Rest assured, human," Dourin said lightly. "We are evacuating nearby cities, just like you wanted. Those elves will start arriving in Evov any day now. They will be safe here."

Venick spun back around. "And if Evov's magic fails?"

"Unlikely."

"In war, nothing is unlikely."

Dourin rolled his eyes, which rankled. Venick knew most elves did not take his warning seriously. Even those who did didn't, really. The northerners did not understand, because they had not seen the army, and because they had been taught to believe elves didn't kill other elves. That was old law. Deeply ingrained. Even those who believed the southern army was coming didn't *feel* it. They were unafraid, because they were used to being unafraid.

Venick needed them to be afraid.

"We are not completely without defense," Dourin said. "There are some legionnaires in the city."

"Not enough."

"There is Farah's guard."

But Venick had seen Farah's guard. Had gotten to know them, a little, when they came to goad him with insults and threats. Again, Venick mustered the effort to speak calmly. "Those elves aren't meant for war. They are *palace guards*. They are arrogant and ill-equipped. When the army arrives, they'll be the first to die."

Dourin crossed his arms. "Let's not be dramatic."

"Have you ever been to battle?" Dourin was silent. "Well?"

"No."

"I have," Venick said, "and I know what I saw. The southerners must have thousands of soldiers. They were well armed. With *cannons*. Do you know why an army would spend the effort to drag cannons a hundred leagues across a tundra?"

"That is not—"

"They do it so that they can blast through city walls. Avalanche a mountain. They will blow your citizens to bits."

Dourin pressed his lips together. "Even if you are right, do not forget that you are still a prisoner here. Your position is tenuous at best—as is your influence. Most elves want you dead. It is a surprise no one has tried to kill you already."

"I don't care."

"Ah, human, no one is asking whether you care."

"Let me speak to Farah again."

"No."

"Ellina, then."

"She does not want to see you."

Which Venick knew, which was impossible not to know. He hadn't seen Ellina since she'd claimed him in the stateroom. She was avoiding him. He didn't blame her. She *should* want to avoid him. He could admit this.

What he couldn't admit was how he watched his locked door at night, waiting for her to appear.

What he couldn't admit was the rough, clawing sense of abandonment that filled him every night she didn't come.

Nor could he admit his own feelings. His feelings were petty. Child-ish. He had no right to feel anything, given the larger scheme of things. Yet the truth was still there, small but bright, a lamp flickering in the last of its oil: her silence hurt him.

Dourin guessed his thoughts. "She is worried."

"I know."

"You have caused her enough problems by coming."

"I couldn't *not* come." Venick rubbed a hand across his face. The tundra, the stateroom, and now this purgatory. It left him feeling frayed, and *that* made him speak too honestly. "I would have regretted it for the rest of my life if I didn't."

Dourin's tone was dry. "How endearing." Venick dropped his hand and glared. "No, truly. Are all humans so transparent?"

"Enough."

But the elf merely smirked. "Patience, little human. I see no army knocking down our doors. You will have a chance to make your case, but until then, we move carefully."

• • •

When the elven assassin came to kill him later that night, Venick felt almost relieved.

Maybe it was because he had been locked in this prison-suite for six days, and the unbroken stretch of time was driving him insane.

Maybe it was because he, like Dourin, had been expecting an assas-sination attempt, and the suspense of waiting was worse than the attack itself.

Maybe. But that still didn't explain the greedy pleasure that sparked inside him as he listened to the slide of the bolt turning, the following silence that could only mean an uninvited visitor was easing his door open—and didn't want Venick to know it.

It was late, nearing midnight. Venick had been leaning out the window, studying a small balcony positioned several stories below, considering the drop. Too far. He'd break his legs if he attempted it. His back, if he landed wrong. And there was no telling where that balcony led, even if he *did* survive the fall.

Now, however, Venick stilled. Kept his back turned, hands steady on the windowsill. The moon was high and strong that night. Its muted light set the room aglow. Even without the moon, Venick would have felt ready.

He had practice fighting in the dark.

The silence went on. It caressed Venick as he carefully lifted his hands from the sill, as he closed his eyes and *listened*, with his whole body. He could hear nothing. Besides the slow undoing of the door's latch, an elf would make no noise. An assassin would give nothing away.

So Venick imagined it. He imagined how the assassin would slide through the receiving room, weapon out and at the ready. That weapon would be small, easy to conceal. A knife, perhaps, or a seax. The elf would creep into the bedroom expecting to find Venick asleep, would have to quickly recalculate when he discovered Venick awake and upright. The elf would not be prepared for a fight. If Venick was lucky, he would not be armored for one.

Venick conjured up the memory of the elves he'd fought in the forest storm. Later, when he'd battled that elf from the southern army. Both times his sight had been stolen from him, but Venick knew now that he did not need his eyes to guide him. He could close them, and breathe out, and let instinct take over.

So it was instinct that had Venick counting one, two, three slow breaths.

Instinct, that alerted Venick to a slight change in the air behind him, a denseness.

Instinct, the moment Venick chose to duck and dive for his curtain rod, that allowed him to catch the assassin off guard. It gave Venick the upper hand as he spun and swung that rod, as the elf materialized into his vision, a shadowed form in the night. Venick caught a quick glimpse of the elf's face—small eyes, cropped hair, a wide mouth—as Venick brought the rod down hard. Felt the impact, heard the satisfying *crack* as it struck the elf's wrist, fragile bones breaking, a dagger falling to the floor. But this elf was trained, he was good. He recovered quickly, tucking his damaged hand against himself as he produced a second dagger. And then things happened too quickly for Venick to follow as the assassin lunged forward, pulling the darkness around him. As Venick attempted to parry the attack with his curtain rod, as he came to understand how laughable that weapon was against this elf and his arsenal of green glass daggers. The elf batted the rod aside, slipping easily into range. Venick saw a shimmer of green and thought, oddly, *beautiful*. It was the elf's dagger. Green and black, short and elegant. Finely made.

Yes, beautiful.

And this, too. The elf. A master of his craft. There was beauty in the way he smoked forward, weapon-hand up, arcing down. His body drew lines Venick knew, could read well, and for a fleeting moment Venick understood its beauty.

Then the elf drove his dagger into Venick's hip, all the way to the hilt.

A flash of pain. A rush of heat.

Venick stumbled sideways. His leg gave out. He dropped to his knees with a cry.

The blade. The sight of it embedded deep in his flesh. It was shocking. Foreign. Venick's breathing went labored. His vision spotted white.

The elf loomed closer.

A long pause. A silence that spoke. It told Venick what would happen next. The first dagger was still there on the floor by the assassin's feet. The elf would grab it. He would finish what he started and cut Venick's throat.

But that wasn't what happened. The elf studied Venick, the dagger, the moonlit room. He said something low in elvish, quick words Venick didn't hear. Then he disappeared through the window.

Stillness.

Dread.

Because Venick was not dead, but still vulnerable.

Because an assassin wouldn't just leave the job unfinished.

Unless, of course, he hadn't.

Venick's hand fumbled until he found the dagger in his hip. He ground his teeth and yanked it out. Blood spurted. The smell of it assaulted him, sweet and sickly. Venick fought a wave of nausea as he brought the bloodied blade into the moonlight and found the groove forged into its edge. It was the kind of groove an elf might use to house poison.

Venick exhaled, almost laughing. The blade was poisoned.

He kept the dagger in his hand as he angled his body upright. He tripped more than once on his way to the still-open door of his prison-suite. The staircase just beyond was high and narrow. The steps spiraled down farther than he could see.

Venick understood now that the surge of pleasure he'd felt when he heard the assassin enter his room was because he had been angry, and he had wanted somewhere to aim that anger. He knew it was because he had been lonely, and sick of worrying over the southerners and Ellina and how she ignored him. How ignoring him and being ignored had become the new habit between them. He had wanted something to distract him. Had been itching for a fight, for *pain* even, if only because he knew it was the surest way to take his mind off everything else.

When the poison entered his veins, Venick understood exactly the kind of fool he was.

The tremors came first. They wracked his body. Venick shuttered and stumbled as he exited his prison and attempted to navigate the stairs. A cold sweat broke across his skin. His clothes became soaked with it, and with his own blood, which pulsed out of his hip and down his thigh. Twice, he stopped to vomit. He couldn't feel his lips anymore, his face, his hands. And still he forced himself to move, because if he could make it to the bottom of this tower, if he could find help—

That what you think you'll find, Venick?

—he could survive this.

You won't.

But he must. He *must*. Fear entered him at the thought of his own death, of dying before he had the chance to tell Ellina everything. That he was sorry. That he wasn't angry, not like before. After the stateroom, Venick had been furious with Ellina. He'd wanted to accuse her of everything she had done for him, to accuse her of lying to defend him when she shouldn't have, of taking the whip for him and lying to save him and then lying about her reasons. He thought of those reasons. The shock of discovering Lorana's identity. His renewed grief. A spill of memories, like water tipped from a cup.

The truth had hurt at first. Gods, how it hurt. The revelation of Lorana's lies and Ellina's lies split him open.

But then the pain had eased. He thought the pain of the truth was like the cut on his chest in Kenath. The sharp bite of the sword, the fear to look. Later, touching the cut tenderly. Relief when the wound turned out to be not so bad. Not so deep.

Before, Venick hadn't known if he could forgive Lorana for her lies. If he could forgive Ellina for hers. But as Venick collapsed onto the stairs, rough stone digging into his legs and back, poison pounding through him, he found that forgiveness came easily. And what was there to forgive, really? A promise between sisters? The desire for a better life? Venick understood promises. He understood wanting something better, something *more*.

His thoughts came slowly now, with the ragged waywardness of a mind almost asleep. He had kissed Ellina. He'd done it because he wanted her, wanted to feel her skin under his hands, and because he thought she wanted it, too.

Now he didn't know what she wanted, and as he blinked up at the dizzy spiral of stairs above, he realized he never would.

The thought seemed to shake him. He wouldn't die, not here, not like this. He fought to stand. Reeking gods, he would *make* his legs move.

But he couldn't. His boots scraped uselessly against the stone. His fingers sought purchase and were left wanting. He was losing blood. He had nothing to stanch the flow.

His mind was dimming again. And still, he begged the silence, the gods, himself: *please, not here. Not like this.*

He could hear the ocean now. The sound of it filled his ears. He saw Irek and its slow, sturdy people. He saw the market, the river where he had once roamed, his house by the water. He saw his mother, heard her voice.

You will always be my son, Venick.

My precious child.

I love you still.

Venick closed his eyes. Felt cool sand under his cheek. Sun on his skin. Saltwater and safety and a homeland there for him, waiting.

· · ·

Please.

A frantic voice broke through the darkness. A low throb of sound, a choked interval.

Please, Venick. Wake up.

Fingers fanned his face, his chest, his leg. They slid over his skin and his body responded, which made him think this must be real, even as he wondered how it possibly could be.

Do not die. You cannot.

Venick.

Someone was pulling at his arm, but it felt distant. Dreamlike. Was he dying? It was hard to know.

Please.

His thoughts were splintered. Stiff and painful. He remembered a dim room. The smell of blood. Someone was wounded. Him?

If you die…

Yes, him. He had been wounded. It explained that broken voice, which was cursing him now. Angry.

An anger, he knew, that was meant to hide her worry.

He wanted to tell her not to worry. He wouldn't die. He was a born fighter. He had survived battles, the tundra, exile. He was strong. He could be strong.

But he couldn't hold long to any one thought. Words glowed and then pulsed away, a firefly's light. He felt borne on silent black wings, and he drifted.

Venick thought of his exile. The mountains. The cruel chill of the wind. How he had climbed high just to find it. How he'd climbed and climbed, fingers aching, muscles on fire, higher than the clansmen or their goats until there was nothing but sun and sky. The wind howled around him. It tugged him forward. *Just a little farther*, the wind would whisper. *Just a step more.* He feared the wind. He feared what it tempted. And it would be easy, wouldn't it? He worried how easy it would be to step a little farther. No one would mourn him if he gave the wind what it wanted. No one would even know.

His pain had been vicious. He had known the price of killing his father was banishment or death. He had known he might spend the rest of his life an outlaw. He'd scraped together a meager living in the mountains, thought about ending that living—hell, he'd lost count how many times.

It was, he'd once thought, the price of his betrayal. He convinced himself that misery was no less than he deserved.

But *did* he deserve it?

Hadn't his father betrayed *him*?

And for what crime, but to fall in love?

Venick, came that voice again.

Wake up.

You must wake up.

He saw Ellina then in his mind. Her hard stare. The hardness of the whole of her, and how she softened for him. He remembered the way he had drawn her close, inhaled her scent, kissed her and claimed her. The grip of remorse, after, when his mind cleared and he saw what he had done.

He wondered if this was normal, the way his mind and body had two separate sets of intentions.

He wondered if he would ever escape these anguishes of his own making.

Please, Venick.

You have been poisoned.

You are injured.

Venick became more aware of himself. He tried to open his eyes. His lids were too heavy.

Do not die, she said to him. *Don't you dare.*

This felt familiar. Those words. Hadn't he heard them before?

A bear trap. He had been caught in a bear trap. He remembered this. A cave. A fire. But—poison? Was the bear trap poisoned? He could hear her fragmented pleas, a stream of them as she pulled and pleaded that he wake.

"I'm here," he mumbled, cracking open an eye. There was no cave. No fire. Only a dark stairwell and Ellina, who froze for a single beat. Her face came into focus, then blurred again. When she sprang back into action, the quality of her movements changed. A pant leg was ripped. Pressure applied. A high call for help, orders snapped in two languages.

Venick's country would be ashamed to see him now. Weak, vulnerable in the hands of their adversary. A good soldier did not allow himself to be captured. Hell, a good soldier did not willfully walk into enemy lands and *get* himself captured. He should have known better. This was no way to earn his mother's forgiveness, and it wasn't his place to meddle in elven affairs. Who was *he*, that he might both care for an elf and care for his people? Who was he, to think he could fight for Ellina and fight for redemption? Had he not killed his father because of an elf?

Had he not learned his lesson?

• • •

A dim white light. The smell of candles burning. A metallic clatter, the shuffle of robes.

Voices, too. Softer, growing loud. Angry words spoken in elvish.

I will not tend a human.

You will if I order it.

Cessena, please. He is not one of us.

Do as I say, eondghi.

Venick's hip felt hot and huge, but his head was worse. It pounded, agonizing. The angry voices battered. He wanted to say something to calm that anger. *The pain*, he would whisper. *Please. Don't fight.*

He wondered if he had spoken aloud after all because there was sudden quiet. Then: a warm hand on his forehead. Callused. A hand he knew.

Sleep, she told him.

And he did.

THIRTY-SIX

Ellina stalked through the palace halls. Shadows rippled across the flagstone, soft and blue and grey. Dawn was coming. Outside the glassless windows the sky was clean and new. When the sun rose, the day would be brilliant.

The promise of its brilliance mocked her.

Ellina's palm dug hard into her sword's pommel. She was not brilliant or new. She was a looming storm. Rigid with fury. She had never known such anger.

An assassin with a poisoned dagger. Despite her bargain for Venick's safety, despite the public stateroom agreement, someone had sent him. And Ellina feared she knew who.

"Where is my sister?" Ellina asked the first guard she could find. The elf turned, blinked once, then gave his answer. Ellina started to march away.

"If this is about the human," the guard said to Ellina's back, "he got what he deserved."

Ellina recalled, as a young elf, admiring the skill with which elder elves could shut down their emotions. It was an art, she had always thought, a gift, the way they wiped their faces as smooth and still as glass. The queen was particularly gifted. Ellina used to spend hours studying her mother's face, searching for even the slightest hint of feeling but finding only the queen's composure, the queen's control.

Ellina knew she looked nothing like that now. As she whipped around to face the guard, she could feel heat rising under her skin, the hot swell of it, the way it curled her lip in anger. In the tower, too, when she had found Venick dying on the stairs and ran to him and snarled at others to help, she knew how she must have looked: panicked, terrified...*human*.

Ellina understood the wrongness of this, yet she could not stop the rush of fury or the words that came next. "*Speak ill of the human again,*" she said, "*and I will have you banished to the whitelands. Do you understand?*"

There was no need for the guard to answer. Ellina had spoken in elvish; he knew her threat to be true.

· · ·

Ellina found Farah where the guard said she would be: in the archives.

The room was cold and echoing, stacked with row upon row of books and scrolls. Torches and lanterns were not permitted near the parchment; instead, tall windows filtered in grey morning light. It streamed down in soft beams. The shadows were dense where the light did not touch.

Farah was there, tucked away between the stacks. She was speaking to another elf Ellina could not see—at least, not until Ellina came closer and that elf was revealed to her from behind the shelves.

"Ellina," Raffan said when he spotted her. Surprise lifted his brows, smoothed his features. Gone in the next instant, settling back into the Raffan she knew best: flat eyes, flat lips, a hard stare. Haughty, around the edges. Maybe a little cynical, too, as he said, "To what do we owe this pleasure?"

The words dried on Ellina's tongue. They dissolved bitterly and were swallowed.

Farah turned, and of course *her* expression did not change. "Sister," she said, opening her palms in a gesture that might have been welcoming and was not.

And maybe it was that movement—the false warmth, the way the lie of it crawled over Ellina's skin—that had her tongue working again. Had her sucking in a breath and splitting a smile—just as purposeful, just as false—as she replied. "I need to speak with you. Alone."

"Alone?" Farah folded her arms. "I think whatever you have to say can be said in front of your bondmate."

"Not this."

"We are not children. What secrets must we keep among us?"

"You are heir to the throne," Ellina replied. An acknowledgement. And a threat: "Are you saying you have no secrets?" Ellina's smile was gone now. "None at all?"

Farah's expression remained impassive, but her lighthearted tone—the false one she had been using—dipped into something colder. "Say what you have come to say."

"You sent an assassin to kill Venick."

"Many elves want the human dead. What makes you think it was me?"

"You did it so that his death would not be tied to you."

"And yet here you are, tying it to me."

"Do you deny it?"

"Yes."

"*Say it in elvish.*"

Farah did not flinch at the insult. Did not even blink. She merely tilted her head. "You are upset. I can *see* that you are. I must say, Ellina, these newfound expressions do not suit you."

Ellina hardened. "Do not change the subject."

"Am I? I thought we were trading accusations. I have a few of my own. Apparently, you and the human had *quite* an adventure while you were in the south. Raffan has been telling me. How you bargained for the human's life. How you took his punishment rather than let him die. I wonder, why would you do such things for him?"

Ellina stared. She was silent.

"Or perhaps you would like to answer this," Farah continued. "How did the human wind up with Miria's necklace? You never did explain."

"I gave it to him," Ellina lied.

"*Did* you."

"To prove that I had won his life price."

Farah's mouth tipped up, just slightly, at the corner. "*Say it in elvish.*"

Ellina knew then that she had been wrong to come. Stupid, idiotic, to corner Farah when she herself had so much to hide.

And yet...a lie. If Ellina could meet Farah's challenge. If she could give her answer, in *elvish*...

Ellina tried to quiet her racing heart. She inhaled, summoning her energy as she did when she practiced, bringing the words to mind. She dragged the lie over herself, held its seams closed. And there, like a gathering wind, she *felt* it. Felt the breeze of the lie open in her chest. Felt goosebumps shiver across her skin as the words rose in her throat, coated her tongue…

And stuck, just out of reach.

The lie dissolved then, vanishing as quickly as it had come. Ellina's own frustration billowed in its place. Her anger—at her sister, at herself—swelled like a sail.

And it changed. It became the kind of anger that thinks, that *sees*. She saw the closeness of Farah and Raffan's stances, their shoulders almost touching. She saw how, twice now, they had been caught alone together in the archives. This made Ellina think of her trek through the palace, which made her think of Farah's guards stationed there, and how large their ranks had grown.

But Farah did not believe Venick's warning. She, like Raffan, did not think the southerners posed any risk. Why would Farah increase the castle's guard if not to protect them from a threat she did not believe was coming? And then there was Dourin's warning, Dourin's worry, singing in Ellina's mind. *Farah is unhappy. You humiliated her. It is not good that Farah and Raffan have reason to make you their common enemy.*

Ellina seemed to see all of this as if from outside herself. She saw in quick flashes the vision of Raffan uncoiling his whip, the way he put all his strength into those lashes. She remembered, after, how he had questioned her…yet also *not* questioned her. *You took the whip for the human. Would he have done the same for you?*

"Well?" Farah asked, but Ellina's mind was spinning, it was soaring away. It almost did not matter whether Farah had sent Venick's assassin. It was no secret that Farah wanted Venick dead. And the law concerning humans in elven lands was clear.

"Ellina." Farah was growing impatient.

Ellina saw again how the conjurors had hunted her through the forest. The storm. The impossibility of it, and of the conjurors' strength, which had grown into something monstrous. She saw her attempts to convince Farah and Raffan of the danger, and how easily they dismissed her worries. Neither could be persuaded to take the threat seriously. Neither would even *consider* it.

But why? *Why?*

"*Ellina.*" Farah's patience was at its end. "Answer me."

"No."

"No?"

Ellina's thoughts seemed to crackle and spark. Her vision shimmered with all these unanswered questions. Like moving pieces of a puzzle, they worked before her eyes, arranging and rearranging yet never aligning. "I have told you already," Ellina finally replied, pulling her gaze back to Farah, seeing her sister now as though for the first time. Golden eyes. A crown of white hair. That lip, curled in subtle victory. "I do not answer to you."

Farah and Raffan exchanged a glance. Something wordless passed between them. "No," Farah agreed. "And nor I to you."

• • •

Ellina was not being careful.

This was unlike her. When had she become so careless? Yet she thought of how she had stormed through the palace, threatening guards, confronting her sister, and she knew that she *had* been careless. Reckless, even, in her anger.

Ellina slowed. She was in a faraway corridor. There was a set of narrow doors. A balcony. She went to it and emerged into open air. The day was just as she knew it would be: brilliant. The sky was a wide canvas. The wind, high and strong.

Ellina dug a nail into the balcony's stone railing, let the wind toss her hair into her face. She remembered again how she had found Venick in the stairwell, felt again her terror. She had been avoiding him, but after a time avoidance had begun to feel futile…and cowardly. So she went to him.

And was met with a gruesome sight. Venick, there, seemingly dead on the stairs. His skin had gone grey. His blood was everywhere, but it was the smell of it—ashy, burnt—that alerted her to the poison. Ellina's heart plummeted as she ran to him. She was certain her screams could be heard throughout the palace.

That moment would cost her. Ellina could no longer pretend indifference. Her concern for Venick—not merely for his life price, but for *him*—was obvious to anyone who cared to look.

Farah should care. Raffan should. Ellina considered it again: why had they not insisted for the truth in elvish? What were they waiting for?

This thought seemed to open a corridor of other thoughts. What *were* they waiting for?

Ellina peered out across the rough landscape and decided that whatever their reasons, one lucky thing would come of it; it bought her more time to practice her elven lies. Clearly, she needed that.

And Venick. He was lucky, too. It was sheer, stupid *luck* that the assassin had not killed him outright. That the poison was slow-working, that Ellina had found him when she did. But Ellina was not so naive as to believe their luck would hold. Assassins could try again. Rumors could persist. Farah could decide to push for answers, or Raffan could, or her mother could, as they should have done from the start.

Ellina had been careless, had been a fool, to leave her fate up to luck. She would do better.

THIRTY-SEVEN

He woke in a bed in an unfamiliar room. Dark, because there were no windows. A fire crackled in a small fireplace, fanning warm light.

Ellina was there. She knelt at his bedside, arms cradling her head, which rested beside his chest.

Venick became very awake all at once. Ellina must have felt him stir, or else felt the sudden kick of his heart, because she lifted her head. There was an imprint on her cheek from where it had pressed into the folds of his bedsheets. Her eyes were hooded, sleep-heavy.

"Ellina." Venick swallowed thickly. His voice was hoarse. Snatches of the past few hours flashed by in a discordant stream. He cleared his throat and tried to say more, but his tongue felt strange. Too heavy. He tried again. "Ellina…"

"Shh." She moved her hand over his, and Venick felt the contact deep in his belly.

"I'm so sorry."

"There is nothing to be sorry about."

"There is. Everything." Venick wondered if some of the poison still lingered in his veins. His thoughts looped dizzyingly over one another. Yet he was lucid enough, and in the following silence his mind went where it always did: to Ellina and Lorana and all his deepest regrets. "I meant what I said. In the dungeons."

Her grip on his hand tightened. "We can talk about that later."

"No. Now."

"You need rest..."

"What happened to Lorana *was* my fault." Venick pushed himself up, then wished he hadn't. His head swam. A thousand little needles jabbed his eyes. He closed them, but this was no better, because behind closed lids he saw Lorana as she had been on the night of her death. The way he'd fought to reach her, the frothy terror. Her blood on his hands, caked into his clothing. "You cannot forgive me for it," Venick said, and hell, his voice was breaking, but that wasn't going to stop him because he needed her to listen, to *hear*. "There is no reason for you to forgive me."

Ellina leaned forward. Her face was all shadow, except for her eyes, which glowed. "*But I do forgive you,*" she said in elvish.

Venick froze. Those words.

She forgave him.

But—she forgave him?

He saw her expression, earnest and imploring. He saw the curve of her cheek, the set to her mouth, all the little details that made her. She'd spoken in elvish, but...that wasn't right. It couldn't be.

Because?

Because...

"I don't deserve your forgiveness."

Ellina's gaze dropped to their interlocked fingers. "I think…" She faltered. "I think you have held onto your guilt for a long time." Her eyes lifted. "I think you have always blamed yourself. But you are not to blame. I believe you, Venick. That Miria did not take her own life, that the southerners killed her. And it is terrible, what happened, but it is not your fault. Do you hear me? It is *not*."

Venick stared at her. He couldn't comprehend it. Not her understanding, or the way she was looking at him now: tenderly.

His eyes grew heavy again. He was so tired—and confused, and pained, and unable to piece it all together. He didn't know what he'd expected now that Ellina was here, speaking to him again for the first time in days, but it wasn't this.

Yet he felt it. Ellina's forgiveness was there. It blanketed him, and Venick knew that it was a gift, this moment was a gift, because he hadn't thought he would live to see it, or even if he *had*, he thought he had done too many things to push Ellina away, had wronged her too many times.

"I wish…" he started to say, but sleep was there again. It pressed him down. It was dark and warm as it pulled him back into unknowing, Ellina's hand still in his.

· · ·

The next time Venick woke, Ellina had put some distance between them.

She hovered by the fireplace, her fingers skimming a row of glass jars on the mantle. The motion was unhurried. Absentminded, which was unlike her, which made Venick realize that she wasn't even looking at the jars. Wasn't reading the labels.

What, then?

Gathering herself, if he knew her. Tucking away her feelings, burying her thoughts as she prepared to turn and face him.

Which she did, slowly. The tenderness he remembered from before was gone. Now there was only that elven mask, which he hated, and that cool gaze, which he also hated, so even and controlled and *false*.

"You know that doesn't work on me," he told her.

She hitched a smile. "No," she agreed. "I suppose not."

But even her smile was false. The lie of it nettled him. Venick wanted to tell her to cut it out. Stop pretending, be honest, and weren't they past that now?

He didn't say those things. Drew his eyes up and around the room instead, surveying the tall cabinets, the neatly made bed on the opposite wall. The former was filled with vials and plants and all manner of things Venick didn't recognize. The latter was empty.

A healer's room. Venick plucked this knowledge out of a tumbled wave of combating thoughts. That's where they must be, which meant that Ellina's cries for help—the ones he remembered, vaguely, from the stairwell—had worked. It meant that an *eondghi*, a real one this time, had agreed to come to his aid.

Ellina returned her attention to the jars. She picked one up, examined its contents. "I will set you free," she said. "As soon as you are strong enough, I will help you escape. There is only one path in or out of the palace, but it is not heavily guarded. If we are careful…" She set the jar back with an almost-silent *clink*, then turned to look at him. The mask had fallen away, though Venick wasn't sure he liked this alternative any better. Her expression had hardened with an emotion both darker and more familiar: remorse. "I should have done it before. You should never have been held prisoner here."

Venick managed a wry smile. "Is that what you want? For me to leave?"

"I want you to *live*."

"If I escape, they will know it was you who helped me." Ellina didn't deny it. Hell, she *nodded*, like she knew it and didn't care. Venick sat up a little straighter, ignoring the way his bandaged hip began to throb. Ignoring the bitter taste in his mouth, anger and argument both. "You have to stop. You cannot keep *risking yourself* for me."

"I will not see you killed at the hands of my country."

"It won't come to that."

Ellina gave a dry laugh. "Has the poison addled your brain? *Look* at you."

"I'm alive."

"Barely."

"I make my own choices."

"What are you saying? That you would choose to stay?"

His answer, despite all his earlier doubts, came easily. "Yes."

"*Why?*" Ellina took a step closer. "Why would you want that?"

He held her gaze. "I think you know why." But color rose in Ellina's cheeks, and Venick remembered the forest, their kiss, all his promises. He couldn't say things like that to Ellina. He shouldn't even *think* them. He quickly added, "I was raised a warrior. I know about battle. I can help you prepare. And my country is at risk, just as yours is." He told her about the southern conjuror's threats and how the southerners would likely attack the mainlands once the northern crown fell.

Ellina exhaled, hard and frustrated. "I think you are making a mistake." She cast her gaze upward. "I think you are a fool."

"That's nothing new."

"If you stay, I cannot promise that you will survive."

"I'm not asking for any promises."

"When my mother returns…"

"I will give her my warning, just like you said." Venick gathered his voice, tried to make the words stick. "She needs to hear it from me."

"You. Of course. And if she does not believe you?"

"She will."

Which he couldn't know for certain. Which was a madman's bet. Still, his words seemed to have their desired effect. Ellina's posture softened. He watched the anger drain out of her. She came to sit on the edge of his bed.

Not an agreement, no, but a truce.

Venick watched her tuck a stray piece of hair behind her ear. Her golden earrings winked in the firelight. He was reminded of their first days together in the forest. She had sat opposite him in a cave. Her armor had been propped on a nearby stone. He remembered thinking she had looked small without it. Delicate.

Though, maybe *delicate* wasn't quite right. If she had looked delicate to him then, it was the delicacy of a spider's web: beautiful, yet crafted to kill.

"I want to know something," Ellina said.

"Anything."

"Miria taught you elvish."

Venick was surprised. "Yes."

"That would have taken years."

"Not so long as that." Venick recalled the painstaking hours he and Lorana had spent together, the way she tutored him through the words. She used to tell him he had no natural talent for her language, but they both knew that was untrue. "Six months, maybe, to master the basics.

Another year to perfect them. She was a good teacher."

Ellina plucked at his bedsheets. "Will you tell me what happened to her?"

"It's not a nice story."

"I want to hear it anyway."

But still, Venick hesitated.

"I think—" Ellina fumbled. "I want you to be honest with me. I want to be honest with you."

Honesty. The opportunity to give Ellina all his truths. For her to give him hers. Venick realized he *did* want to tell Ellina about Lorana. He wanted to remember the elf he had loved with someone who loved her, too.

And so it was, finally, that they told each other everything.

• • •

Venick must have slipped back to sleep, because the next time he woke, Ellina was gone.

He sat up slowly. He was sore, he was stiff, but his head felt clearer than it had in—what? Days? How long had he been like this?

He swung his legs over the bed. His hip was thickly bandaged, the skin around the wound hot and swollen. Venick didn't like the smell coming from that bandage. Didn't like the way his bad leg trembled as he stood. He walked the length of the healer's room just to see if he could. By the time he made it back to the bed, that trembling had spread to his *other* leg.

Amazing, how easily his body could betray him.

Wouldn't be the first time.

No, not the first. Venick paced twice more to the fireplace and back.

By the fourth attempt, he was dizzy and nauseous. Well. He had never fully recovered from his journey across the tundra. Add a dagger wound and a poisoning to the mix, and no wonder he was in bad shape.

You'll die, you keep it up.

Maybe. But Venick had already made his choice to stay. He wasn't lying when he said the north could use him, or that he had his own reasons for wanting to stop the southern army. So what if it was dangerous? He'd come this far; he wasn't going to give up *now*. And anyway, better to die here, fighting for something that mattered, than alone in exile.

Something? Not someone?

Venick had worn smooth the memory of Ellina by his bedside, her fingers linked through his, the gentleness he'd found in her expression. Even through the haze of the poison's aftereffects, Venick remembered that moment. And changed it, a little, in his mind. In his version of the memory, he asked Ellina why she was looking at him in such a way. Was her tenderness for *him*, or what had happened to him, or...?

I could not let you die, this imaginary Ellina would tell him.

You still feel obligated, Venick would reply, *because Lorana...*

Not for her. Ellina leaned in, touched a hand to his cheek. *What I did, I did for you.*

Venick caught himself. He knuckled one eye with a fist, let out a sigh. He knew better than to do this. He had to constantly beat down the impulse to pick apart these past few days, to invent meaning where there was none. He knew what such fantasies could cost him. What they'd cost him already. And anyway, it shouldn't matter how these last few nights had changed his and Ellina's relationship, or where they stood now. Friends. Partners. Call them *allies in the war* and have done.

Frustrated, Venick crossed back to the bed and sat heavily on its edge, then began working light fingers over the bandaging around his torso and hip, trying to get a sense of the injury, how it was healing. Focus on *that*, why didn't he?

The door clicked suddenly; his only warning that someone was coming. No time to grab a weapon, no weapon to grab even if there had been, and how was he defenseless *again*?

But it was only Ellina coming through that door, a thick stack of books cradled in her arms.

He watched her approach. Shoulders back, chin up, that dark braid slipping over one shoulder. Venick couldn't have said why the sight of it touched him. Maybe it was because of where his thoughts had just been. Or maybe it was because all of this—her posture, her steady stride— was so familiar to him, so typically Ellina, and it pained him to realize how well he'd come to know her.

Yes, Venick thought. He knew Ellina. He often felt like he'd known her a lifetime rather than a few short months. Though, that wasn't to say she couldn't still surprise him. She surprised him now with a smile that was unlike any he'd ever seen on her. It was small, almost shy. And this, the way she came to sit beside him, how she dropped the books onto the bed between them, fussing unnecessarily with their covers. The thought came to Venick. Slow, sticky, yet gaining shape, gaining color. Was she—*nervous*?

"These are for us," Ellina explained, eyes still on the books. "You said you know about planning battles…"

Venick felt a surge of hope. "You want me to teach you."

"Well." Her eyes flicked to his. "You did offer." She sobered a little. "I have been thinking about what you said. And you are right. We are not prepared to battle an enemy army. I fear we are too late already, but…I want to learn what you have to teach, if you are still willing."

Relief. A surge of gladness.

Finally.

Venick couldn't quite help his smile. He motioned at the pile. "Show me."

She did. She separated the books into two stacks, then three, opening covers at random. "They are from the archives. I brought whatever I thought would be useful. Maps, mainly. A few books about war."

"Elves have books about war?"

"History books, mostly."

But elves had only ever fought one war. "Books about the purge, you mean."

Her eyes wavered. "There are other histories," she said smoothly. "The building of Evov. The discovery of green glass. And I think," she squinted, scanning the spines, "there is a recounting of the hundred childless years, and all the fledglings raised in this city since."

But that surprised Venick. "Are there children here now, in Evov?" He had not considered this. Venick knew elves came to Evov to raise their young, but he had not considered that if war reached the city, elven children would be at risk, too.

"There are children in the palace," Ellina replied.

"But I didn't see—"

"You did, probably. Our children age quickly. A fledgling of eleven or twelve will look just like me."

Venick made a skeptical noise. "I doubt they will look *just* like you."

"Oh?"

"You don't move like a child."

Ellina's laugh surprised him. He realized, too late, what he was saying. "How do I move?" Her tone was amused. Teasing. His cheeks warmed.

Like water. Like magic.

"Like a soldier," Venick replied. He forced a shrug. "Your training shows."

"Does it?"

"And the way you speak. You're—precise."

Ellina squinted, then laughed again. "Precise?"

"Direct."

She lifted a shoulder. "Like you said. A legionnaire's training."

Venick had always wondered. "Why did you join the legion?"

Ellina drew one leg up, wrapped her arm around it. "It was something I could call my own. With two elder sisters, I struggled to find my place here. And I was good at it." She studied him. "Like you are."

"I was never an elite soldier."

"But you were trained in battle. You know about war."

"All men know about war."

"Not all men fight as well as you. Not all men could journey through the elflands and live, as you did." Venick cleared his throat, uncomfortable under her sudden scrutiny. "Who were you, Venick, before you came across the border?"

"A lowlander."

"That is *where*, not *who*."

"I was a soldier, and then…" He shook his head. "What do you want to know?"

Ellina did not break his gaze. She answered that question, and the larger one contained inside it. "Everything."

So Venick told her. He told her about his homeland and its hardworking people. He described the fishing season, how the air always smelled of brine, boats docked and bobbing on the water. He told her about the surrounding lands, the trees and plants that stayed green year-round. He described his mother as he remembered her from his childhood, the woman who would place a warm hand on his cheek and ask him who he wanted to become, who would smile when he replied that he wanted to be a warrior, like his father.

And his father. Venick pushed aside the lingering resentment and described how he'd learned war at his father's knee. How eager he had been to learn. He told Ellina about the first time he'd gone to battle, and how he had been afraid, yet more afraid that his fear would make him a coward, so he drove into the front lines to prove that he was not. He remembered the look on his father's face after that battle was won. The pride of a father discovering his son had become a man.

As Venick talked, Ellina pulled the books closer, came to lean against the headboard beside him. Her thigh fit against his. Her soft warmth radiated. It almost had Venick dreaming again.

He cleared his throat instead, pulled the volumes from her hands. He flipped through the pages, and his story changed. He detailed the things his father had taught him, things he'd learned himself on the field. He talked Ellina through a dozen possible battle scenarios, explaining how a small force might take a city, how a large force might take a city, how *one elf* might take a city, if he was good enough. He discussed planning an attack, and how the plan often determined the outcome. He talked strategy, how the clever option was not always best, how timing and momentum could tip a battle.

He began teaching Ellina everything he knew. He wanted to leave nothing out.

• • •

When Venick was strong enough to walk, he was escorted back to his prison-suite. This was done under the watchful eye of the palace *eondghi*, who commented that the human had been lucky to survive. The elf didn't sound entirely pleased.

Venick was unbothered. His suite was a prison, but it was one he had chosen, and at least the suite had windows.

• • •

Venick and Ellina fell into a routine.

In the mornings, Ellina would meet Venick in his rooms for lessons. They pulled the writing desk off the wall, scattered books and maps across its wooden surface as they discussed the southerners, the army, the coming war. During those times, Venick could almost forget that he was a prisoner. Could pretend, for a little while, that he was allowed in this city, that he was *wanted* there.

A wasted sentiment.

But it became harder to believe that, the more time he spent with Ellina. It felt good to teach. To have a purpose. To be needed, if not exactly wanted. And the north did need him. This became apparent as their lessons wore on, heads bent close, him explaining what the north needed to know while at the same time wondering how he could ever explain *everything*.

In the afternoons Ellina would leave and Venick would browse the books on his own. He inhaled the scent of dry parchment, ran a finger along their spines, some so old he feared they would crumble at his touch. He touched them anyway, pulling them closer to study their contents. Most were written in mainlander, though a few displayed elven glyphs. A mix of hand-written and printed. A mix of cursive and block font, black ink and blue ink and rare red. As Venick shifted through them one evening, he came upon a book he had not noticed before. He felt mounting anticipation as he read the spine.

A compendium of elven queens.

He drew it out of the pile. The binding was loose, the lacquer cover peeling, pages well-worn. The elflands were thousands of years old, and as Venick flipped through he saw each queen of centuries past had been entered here, their faces drawn in painstaking detail. Sometimes, a description was added under the image. Almost always, miniature etches of the queen's bondmate and children—no less detailed—accompanied her on the page.

Venick found Rishiana easily; hers was the final and most recent entry. The queen's likeness stared back at him. She had sharp eyes, delicate brows, a pointed chin. And below her...

His heart stumbled. Lorana. Her picture was there, painted in crisp little lines, all the details he thought he had forgotten. Venick traced her image with a light thumb. Waited for the pain, the fury and anger and sorrow that always accompanied thoughts of Lorana. But it didn't come.

Surprised, Venick?

Confused, more like. But then, maybe he shouldn't be, because he had felt this in himself, hadn't he? The way his grief had slowly changed, burned low, crowded out by other emotions that flared bigger, brighter...

His eyes drifted to Ellina's image next. His fingers followed, brushing the ridges where the paint had dried thick. He didn't stop to examine the feelings *her* image invoked. Moved his eyes instead to Farah, then to the short paragraph written in the margin.

Venick almost didn't notice the fifth picture on the page. It had been sketched in pencil—hastily, uncolored. It was, Venick realized, Rishiana's bondmate. His image was so faded that Venick could not get a sense of the elf's true features. Merely a ghost of a face. The record bore no name.

Venick's curiosity piqued. He'd wondered about Ellina's father. Venick had never heard anyone mention Rishiana's bondmate. Had never heard anyone *not* mention him, either, the way sensitive topics are sometimes avoided. But now Venick wondered, who was Ellina's father? And where was he now?

Sudden movement in the doorway pulled Venick from those thoughts. He looked up to find that he was no longer alone.

"Hello, human," Raffan said from where he stood in the room's arched entry.

Venick shot to his feet, hand reaching for a weapon that wasn't there. Not his knife, not his sword. Hell and damn, not even his curtain rod, little help as it had been. Venick's outstretched hand made a fist as Raffan stepped forward into better light. No missing *his* weapons: a sword at each hip, another slung across his back. Daggers, likely, hidden under the clothing. "Ellina comes here so frequently," Raffan drawled. "I wanted to see *what* could possibly be drawing her attention."

Venick understood the accusation. He was rigid, went more rigid still. "What do you want?"

"Answers."

"Don't have any of those."

"No? I hear you speak elvish."

Venick let out a laugh. It sounded strained. It was the irony, he thought. The irony was going to strangle him. "Last I remember, you were on Farah's side. You think I can lie in elvish."

Raffan's answering smile was manufactured; a twitch of a mouth that rarely made the gesture. "Then maybe we can agree. I will tell the truth if you do. What? You do not want to *bargain*?" Raffan tutted. "You certainly did not seem to mind bargaining with Ellina."

Raffan was at the desk now. All that separated them, a few slices of wood. He set his hands on the surface. His eyes dipped to Venick's injured hip and his smile changed, became chiseled. "You are lucky to be alive. Humans are easy to kill, and our city wants you dead."

Stupid. It was utterly stupid to rise to Raffan's bait. To speak at all. But the words were already in Venick's mouth, angry and alive, and he couldn't have stopped them if he'd tried. "I don't know about that. Your bondmate seems to want me here."

Raffan's grin fell away. "A lapse in judgement. But Ellina will be made to see reason."

"And you'll be the one to convince her? I've heard she has a history of—" Venick looked the elf over, "refusing you."

Too far, Venick.

Which he realized, too late, when a vein appeared in Raffan's neck, a crack in the elf's careful composure. Raffan leaned forward. His voice went black with fury. "Do you know how many humans Ellina has killed? You should ask her. Ask her what we do to humans who cross into our lands. Or perhaps you should ask her about her bonding. To *me.* Do you know what it means for Ellina to be my partner? No? Well, let me tell you."

He did. In sickening detail, Raffan explained *exactly* what he could do to Ellina.

"Well," Raffan said softly, "this has been pleasant. I do hope that wound of yours heals quickly."

He left as quietly as he had come.

Venick stared at the door. And stared, and stared, trying to rein in his anger. It wasn't working. His rage ballooned, burning red-hot. Scalding.

Unbearable.

He snatched a glass paperweight from the desk and hurled it across the room. It hit the wall with a crash and shattered.

• • •

Ellina entered Venick's suite later that evening and saw the shattered glass. He spoke before she could ask. "Raffan came."

Ellina's brows went up. "Did he...what did he say?"

But Venick couldn't tell her. He was horrified.

She came closer. She looked concerned. "Did he threaten you?"

"He threatened *you.*"

Understanding washed over her. "I do not want you worried about Raffan. I know how he works." But this was too much.

"If he—if he ever—"

"He would never hurt me that way," Ellina said.

"But he *has* hurt you." Venick's throat closed. He thought of the scars sketched into her back. The ones she had taken for him. How they would not be silvery white yet. Still raw, still new. Raised flesh, knotted and red.

"Many soldiers face the whip," Ellina replied. Venick darkened. He wouldn't respond to that.

I will handle Raffan she had said outside of Kenath. She'd argued with Dourin about letting Venick stay. After: the scream of horses killed for his sake. The quick draw of the bow, the twang of the string. Dourin's sullen silence, and how Ellina accepted his silence without regret. Her sacrifice. Later: other sacrifices. Lies told to her brethren. A whip across white skin. A southern elf dead. A loyalty that he didn't ask for, didn't think he deserved.

And now. Murder rose in him at the thought of Raffan. His cruel eyes. That little clip of a smile. Other, unthinkable things. Things that might have happened. Things that might happen still. Venick couldn't bear the thought of what Raffan wanted. He couldn't bear that Ellina might be forced to give it.

She refuses him. Dourin's words, in his mind. *To be with him, to bear his child.*

He would never hurt me that way.

But Venick didn't believe it.

Ellina saw his expression. She read his thoughts. "I understand the consequences of my actions," she said.

"It is my choice," she said.

"I have a right to make my own choices," she said.

But she didn't have a choice. Her choices were an illusion. Venick had never understood the conviction by which elves held to their laws. It wasn't right, their blind devotion to something so immoral as forced bondings. Forced *intimacy.*

"Are you asking me to just accept this?" Venick asked. "I can't. I won't."

"It should not matter to you."

"Of *course* it matters to me." Dangerous words.

Take them back.

But he wouldn't, he wouldn't. Not anymore. Not now that he and Ellina had promised to be honest with each other, not after he'd won her trust, and lost it, and won it back again. Venick let out a hard breath. He pinched the bridge of his nose. "It matters to me because I'm making things worse for you by being here."

"That is not true."

"Isn't it?" Venick dropped his hand in time to see Ellina open her mouth, ready with another denial. He cut her off. "Thought we were done lying to each other."

But her eyes sparked, defiant. "I am glad you came. I need you here. That is not a lie."

Venick blinked. Her words sliced through him. They severed his anger, cut the fury right out of him. It was *glad* and *need*. That admission fanned a hope he hadn't even realized he still harbored. "But Raffan…"

"Ignore Raffan."

Venick gave her a rueful look. "You say that like it's simple."

"It is simple. Raffan wanted revenge for what happened in the forest. He wanted to make you angry. You gave him what he wanted. That was your mistake. To be expected, I suppose, since you are such a fool."

"It's not my fault that—" But he caught sight of her face then, the way her mouth twitched. "Oh. Real funny, Ellina. Like I haven't heard that one before."

"You looked like you needed reminding."

He muttered a curse, which got her smiling. "It's not funny." But her smile only grew. "Hell." He rubbed a loose hand down his face, but he was fighting his own smile now. "Insults. Great. Not exactly my brand of humor, but whatever works for you."

"It works for me."

He shook his head, aware of how she'd lightened the mood, a little awed by how she'd managed it. His hope—the one he thought he'd buried—sparked like a match. It flared to life. Venick looked at Ellina, her twisted smile, the mirth in her eyes, and his heart squeezed. "Forget Raffan. You'll be the death of me, you know that?"

"No," she replied. Her smile softened. "I do not think I will."

THIRTY-EIGHT

Ellina exited the palace.

She made her feet to be silent against the stone floor. She was not trying to stay quiet, not exactly, but a kind of softness had settled into her, and she had the desire to move softly, too.

She pushed through a side door meant for servants and out into open air. There was a cobblestone path, narrow, worn smooth with time. She followed it. The path led her under the castle's shadow, through a stone garden and to the palace bridge.

The bridge was a massive structure, wide enough to fit a dozen horses abreast. There was a railing on either side, hip-high, to prevent elves from tumbling over. Ellina stepped onto the bridge's even surface. She gazed across its gentle arch, then peered into the ravine below.

From this height the water below looked calm. Surreal. Yet Ellina knew that if she ventured closer the water's details would become revealed to her. She would see that the bay was not calm at all. It was choppy. Violent, even. Waves boomed against the mountain base, spraying high. If a boat were to try and dock near those crags, it would be tossed against them. Its hull would shatter. Even if a ship were to drop anchor farther out away from the hazardous rocks, swimming to shore would prove treacherous.

Not that any elves would ever attempt to swim.

Ellina had argued all of this to Venick during one of their recent lessons. He worried about stealth attacks. He worried about ships sailing from the east. *A large army will move slowly*, he said to her. His finger pinned down the map they had been studying. His eyes had been soft, then hard, growing harder. *But that does not mean the southerners will not send smaller contingents ahead. They could come by sea. They could climb those cliffs.*

Elves do not sail, Ellina had insisted. *Even if they did, Evov will protect us. This city will remain hidden to our enemies.*

Venick had given her a grim look. *Are you sure?*

There was a time when Ellina's answer would have come easily. *Yes, of course.* She could have spoken that answer in elvish, how certain she was of its truth. Elves did not swim. They did not sail. Evov was hidden. These things were known.

Yet Ellina knew better now than to trust anything she had once believed. She herself had broken laws. She was learning to break more laws still. And if *she* could cut the binds that had once bound her world, she knew the southerners could, too.

No, she had told Venick instead. *I am not sure.*

Then we must be prepared to face an attack on all fronts.

Ellina had come to this bridge with Venick's words in mind. She tried to study the canyon as he might. She gazed at the sheer rockface, the purples and blacks and blues of it. Across the void, she could not quite make out the bridge's other end. A white fog had descended, clouding the mountains and the city beyond.

But then, a figure. Lean, dark. Ellina watched as it materialized through the mist. She blinked, hand already at her sword.

And saw, in the next moment, that her reaction was unwarranted. The elf moving towards her was not a southern stranger come to kill her. He was not a stranger at all, but her troopmate Kaji.

"Expecting someone else?" Kaji asked as he approached, eyes dipping to Ellina's hand at her weapon. She made herself let go. She peeled back her fingers one by one.

"No. No one."

Kaji was the eldest member of their troop. He was slender, willowy in his movements, artistically built. He kept his hair cropped short at the shoulders and wore a single golden ring on his smallest finger. Both the hair and the ring were unusual, but they were accepted without comment because Kaji was an impressive archer and, like Dourin, gifted with horses. Ellina had always respected him.

Kaji paused beside her. "Are you heading into the city?"

Ellina hesitated, weighing several answers before deciding—uncharacteristically—on the truth. "I am contemplating the strength of this bridge. I am wondering what would happen if we were attacked here."

The elder elf allowed his brows to lift. "So now we must worry about enemy elves discovering our hidden city, too?" His brows lowered. His voice became dry. "Another one of your human's insights, I suppose."

Ellina did not like that shift in tone. She stiffened to hear Kaji criticize Venick, which was, she knew, also a criticism of *her*. Kaji had been there in the forest. He had been there in the stateroom. He knew what Ellina had done for Venick, and how she had chosen his side.

Yet Kaji had also seen the vanished city of Tarrith-Mour. He had seen the conjured storm. Surely those events meant *something* to him.

"The southerners are stronger than they once were," Ellina replied evenly. "We cannot assume anything about their power or their weaknesses; we can only accept the danger. Venick believes we should be prepared to face an attack here in the city, and he is right." She turned her gaze back to the castle: mountainous, carved from stone, and high, so high. Yet isolated, too, and therefore vulnerable. Again, Ellina looked at the palace as she imagined Venick might. "If this bridge were blocked or destroyed, the elves inside would have no way to escape. The queen would not. An enemy could trap us here. We would be easily overwhelmed. This palace is a fortress, but it could also be a prison."

Kaji followed her gaze upwards. He stared at the castle for so long that Ellina thought he would not speak again. When he finally did, his voice changed. "Maybe it is good that the queen left the city, then." He turned a pointed look at her. "Or maybe not. Elves are growing restless. The tension between those who think we are in danger and those who do not is only getting worse. If the queen was here, the matter would be decided already."

"If Farah had stayed *out of it*, the matter would be decided, too," Ellina retorted, then frowned, hearing her own words. She was suddenly filled with the same prickling unease that had gripped her during her last argument with Farah. But she did not have time to piece the feeling apart because Kaji was staring at her, bewildered by Ellina's sudden vehemence. She regretted the outburst. She fixed her expression and smoothly changed the subject. "What you do think?"

Kaji blinked. "What do I think?"

"About the southerners."

He slowly shook his head. "I do not know what to think."

"But you were there in the forest. You saw the conjured storm and the vanished city."

"Those things are not evidence of anything."

"Yes, they are." Kaji spread his hands in a way that showed his doubt, but Ellina persisted. "Perhaps you should speak to Venick. Ask him about the army yourself." Ellina paused. An idea. "Will you?"

"Will I what?"

"Visit Venick. Speak with him. Ask him what he saw."

Kaji seemed perplexed by the turn this conversation had taken. "I am not sure that is wise."

"Why not?"

"He might not like the intrusion. I heard about the assassination attempt."

"You are not an assassin."

"I am a stranger to him."

"I know," Ellina said. "That is my point." Kaji was still uncertain, but Ellina's idea was growing now. It seemed to lay a hand on her shoulder. Its grip tightened. "You have doubts. So go to him. Judge for yourself."

Still, Kaji hesitated. Ellina could order him to visit Venick. She could make it a command. She outranked Kaji, and he would have no authority to deny her. But Ellina did not want to command Kaji. She saw his resistance and remembered her own. She remembered how Venick had broken through every one of her defenses. "Please?"

Reluctantly, Kaji gave a nod. "If that is what you wish."

Ellina's idea seemed to smile at her.

After they parted ways, Ellina went to the kitchens, then the scullery where servants were working. She spoke to each of them, asking for small favors. More water for Venick's basin, and soap, and fresh linens, please, would you mind? Venick would be grateful.

"The *human* would be grateful, you mean," one elf corrected.

"His name is Venick," Ellina replied gently.

No elf refused her outright. They understood the consequences of such a refusal. Still, elves were wary. They knew there was a human in their midst. They might even believe his warning. But this, going to him, speaking to him...they were unprepared. Many servants attempted to make excuses. Others nodded, looking hesitant, and agreed.

In the end, they all agreed. Ellina, feeling satisfied, watched them go.

THIRTY-NINE

Venick wasn't sure what to make of the flurry of visitors.

Elven servants filed into his suite, sometimes alone, more often in pairs, bearing gifts, all of them. By the time the week was over, Venick had enough new books to fill a small library. Had, in addition to that, enough dried goods to stock a household, and enough fresh linens, and soap and ink and a dozen other things he didn't need or know what to do with.

He accepted the gifts anyway. Warily at first, because he wasn't certain how to handle the unexpected influx of gracious elves.

Forced elves, you mean.

And they *were* forced, hell and damn, no need to guess by *whom*.

But as the days wore on, the meetings got easier. Elves would deliver their gifts, lingering afterwards, curiosity getting the better of both sides. They would ask Venick about his homeland or his journey or the army he had seen, and Venick would answer, then ask his own questions, *can you fight?* and *will you fight?* and *you know war is coming, don't you?*

To this, the elves' responses were mixed. Some nodded easy agreement, but others were still uncertain. In those times, Venick would repeat his warning in elvish. He'd watch the elves go wide-eyed, their façades cracking, weeds of doubt poking through the fissures. He saw skepticism melt into belief. Hearsay was one thing, but this, hearing Venick's warning face-to-face, *feeling* the raw truth of his elvish...

No one could deny his words then.

When Dourin came, he brought a sword.

"Don't lose this one," the elf warned.

"Dourin." Venick gripped the scabbard between surprised fingers. "There's no way you aren't breaking some rule by giving this to me."

"Oh, I am." Venick peered at him, but Dourin only shrugged in that showy way that was becoming part of him and said, "Ellina seems to trust you. And despite my own good judgement, *I* trust *her*."

"Enough to arm your enemy?"

"You," Dourin replied, "are not my enemy."

But Venick was surprised. He couldn't help but remember Kenath. The sewers, two elves, the wail of the alarm bells in the distance. After they had escaped that city, there was a moment when Venick thought Dourin would kill him. All it would take: a hand at his dagger, two steps and *done*. Venick remembered Dourin's disgust, the black anger that had shimmered and smoked, ready to erupt at the smallest spark.

Only, Dourin wasn't looking at him like that now. The elf's posture was easy. His expression was open. He noticed Venick's scrutiny and arched a brow.

"You learned that from me," Venick said.

"Learned what?"

Venick repeated the gesture—brow arched, mouth quirked—and

Dourin laughed.

"See?" Dourin said. "Look at us, the best of friends."

Venick smiled.

• • •

When Ellina came, she bore a gift of her own.

She pulled the chain from her pocket. It shimmered, and its shimmering seemed to reach all the way to his core.

Lorana's necklace.

"It belongs to you," Ellina explained without quite meeting his eye.

Venick took the cool silver into his palm. He lifted the chain to thread it over his neck, then paused. He saw Ellina's not-quite-gaze. Saw—or *thought* he saw—some feeling she was trying to hide.

He lowered his hands. He changed his mind and pocketed the necklace instead.

• • •

Venick was alone again. He'd stayed up to watch the setting sun. Its colors had dazzled him. He'd looked at the sky, and closed his eyes, and tried to name the feeling that claimed him.

He couldn't. Not as he watched the sun's final rays vanish behind black ridges. Not as darkness settled over the palace. Not as he'd doused each of his lanterns and watched his suite fade to black.

Not now, as he heard voices outside his open window.

He paused.

Slowly, on his toes, he returned to the window. He shifted so that his body was angled sideways across the sill. He peeked over to peer down.

The land below the palace was quiet. That single balcony beneath his window—the one he'd considered using to escape—was quiet, too. Empty.

Or *was* it? Venick caught the flicker of a shadow on the balustrade. Another, just there, on the tiled floor. His pulse quickened, ears straining against the silence. If he had to name his earlier feeling, he would have said it felt like this: a dark resonance.

Then, movement. A huddled lump hidden beneath too-dark shadows. A second form moving to join the first.

Raffan and—Farah?

It was. Raffan said something low. His voice was smooth. The light was too dim to see, the balcony too far to hear, but Farah turned slightly. A slice of light from the adjoining room cut across her face. Venick could see her eyes, her thin lips. They formed a loose smile.

Odd, Venick thought. Unfitting.

Which made him think of the guard who'd escorted him out of the stateroom. His black and red pendant. That display of jewelry had also been odd. Also unfitting. Venick's mind kept jumping back to it as if it were a wrinkle he wanted to rub smooth. His thoughts closed around its memory. Others, too. The assassin who'd been sent to kill Venick in secret. Raffan appearing in his room to deliver dark threats. And now this: Farah and Raffan standing close. The silk of Raffan's voice. That smile.

Venick tucked it all away. He gathered these visions and closed them inside a box. He would take them out to examine. Later.

Suddenly, Raffan looked up.

Venick smoked away from the window. He held his breath. A long minute passed. When he looked back over the window's ledge, the balcony was empty.

. . .

Morning came. Venick welcomed it. He hadn't slept well. He had dreams that—though he forgot them instantly upon waking—left him feeling strange.

Ellina arrived earlier than usual. It surprised him. So did the robes she wore, which were different than her usual palace attire of tunic and trousers. The fabric was airy, trailing in gentle folds at her feet. The neckline dipped low.

Venick stared. He had wanted to tell her something. He couldn't remember what it was.

"I am glad to see you up," she said. "There is something I want to show you. Not a book."

"Oh?"

"It is outside, on the palace grounds."

Venick came closer. He cocked a half-smile. "I doubt I'm allowed outside the palace."

"You are if I say that you are."

"And you think *I'm* the fool."

Ellina made an impatient noise. "It is early. We will not be seen."

Venick's grin broke fully free. "And what will we be doing, while we're sneaking around the palace grounds?"

Ellina smiled in answer. "You will see."

. . .

It was a garden of stone.

Venick had seen similar such gardens sprinkled around the grounds from his window's vantagepoint. Paths were hammered into the earth at hard right angles, the rocks chiseled and arranged in geometric patterns. Some areas were flat, others sloped. Sand gathered in the corners where the wind blew it.

Venick looked back up at the palace. It was the first time he had seen it fully in daylight. The sun was low in early morning. It illuminated the castle, drawing the towers high and wide, the white-washed stone gleaming like torchlight.

They went deeper. Statues began to appear. There was a figure of a mother elf and her fledgling arm in arm. Another of a man holding something. A book, maybe. Yet another of a young woman with a crow on her shoulder, her stone face roughened by time. The palace sat silently in the distance. Everything was quiet. But peaceful, like the quiet of sleep.

They rounded a corner, and the ground became a mirror.

But *not* a mirror, not quite. Venick blinked, unable to understand what he was seeing. Until he did. It was a pond. The water was pristine, still as glass. It reflected the palace and the sky above in perfect clarity.

"It is an everpool," Ellina said. "You step inside and ask it your questions. Sometimes, it gives you answers."

"I've never heard of such a thing."

"You are human," she replied, not unkindly. "Come. Let me show you."

Ellina slipped out of her shoes, then shrugged off her robe. She wore only a thin shift underneath, cream-colored and ribbed. She looked down at herself, then gave Venick a glance. Heat fanned his cheeks, and he felt a sudden stitch of nervousness as he did the same, unbelting his sword and removing most of his outer layers.

"Like this," she said, and took his hand.

The water was warm despite the air's chill. It pulled on Ellina's shift.

The hem became sheer silk. Then she dipped under, and Venick could see nothing of her. The water's reflection was too bright.

She broke the surface and the pattern rippled. "Now you."

He waded in deeper. The bottom of the pond was smooth, like the scooped-out inside of an egg. He stepped slowly, then eased himself under. He opened his eyes underwater but saw only blackness. He resurfaced, pushing his hair from his face.

"There are everpools scattered all around the elflands," Ellina said. Her expression was measured, but her voice was quick. Excited. "No one knows where they came from. There is no record of elves digging them. And then there is this." Ellina cupped her hands together underwater and lifted them, but they came up empty. "It is impossible to take water from an everpool."

Venick mimicked the motion, watching the water run over the sides of his cupped hands, leaving their center empty. He met Ellina's gaze in fascination. "And my questions? You said the water would answer them."

"You have to ask them first."

He was aware of her nearness. He could count her spiky wet eyelashes. Her eyes were golden jewels. "Why did you bring me here?"

"Because you are going to teach me how to swim."

That surprised Venick. "Oh?"

"Yes."

But he was still unsure. "You haven't wanted this before."

"I want it now."

The world became small. The warm pond. The vast sky. Ellina's slender form, her dark hair, a black fabric on the water's surface. Venick moved toward her, reaching out an uncertain hand. All his hope—and his doubts—came rushing back. He searched her expression, expecting to see shyness or uncertainty, but she did not look shy or uncertain. She looked resolute. Venick slid his palm around her waist.

"Do you trust me?" he asked quietly.

"Yes."

He held her lightly, giving low instructions as he moved them deeper, showing her how to tread water, how to push and pull it around her. He spoke continuously, relaying the information, but his mind, like the water, was adrift.

"Are you afraid?" he asked.

"No."

They moved deeper. He showed her how to suck in a lungful of air, how to hold it. How to cup her hands, look for currents, feel them ripple and spread. Venick continued to speak, but he didn't know what he was saying. He couldn't concentrate, not with Ellina so close. The air around them became warm. His blood was alive in his veins. He was caught in the idea that Ellina had once been cold, the very picture of an elven soldier, but now she was not. Her skin was soft under his fingertips. Her lips looked full and round.

She caught his eye and saw his expression. It changed hers.

The water splashed around them as she came back to standing. He realized he wasn't speaking anymore. He didn't know when he had stopped.

She said the water would give him answers.

His question. He knew what he wanted to ask. But he was afraid. He felt as if he'd asked already and pushed a topic that he knew better than to push.

"Venick."

He remembered the sound of her voice in the forest when she sang. Lovely. A little hushed. He remembered how it was to hear her sing, the way it buoyed him. He felt like that now.

Her answers. He could have them.

But what were words, really? What were questions, when there was this soft silence that felt like knowing? Venick didn't need to ask for answers. He could reach out and *take* them.

He did. He lifted a hand. He brushed Ellina's bottom lip with a thumb. He watched, breath held, waiting for her to pull away, to tell him no, we can't, not like this, Venick, not again.

But she didn't do that. She didn't, and Venick was filled with sudden wonder, because he'd thought about this, and guessed, and second-guessed, and now...

Now her breath was changing. His was, too.

This time when Venick kissed her, he kissed her slowly. He felt the kiss everywhere, in his fingers, his belly. It swelled through him. He pushed a hand into her wet hair, despite his promises to himself, despite all the reasons he shouldn't.

This is what Venick wanted to ask her:

This was the question burning inside him:

When you killed that southern conjuror.

When you bargained for my life.

Did you do it out of love of Lorana, or maybe...was it out of love for me, too?

Venick's kiss became that question, and Ellina's body answered. She moved under his touch. Her form sealed against his, her fingers fanning across his skin. Her breath tickled. He pulled her closer. She breathed a word that might have been his name, her lips moving against his, faster now. He dipped his tongue into her mouth. His need pooled low, the sweet ache of it like a burning rope.

The water splashed. The image of them rippled on its glassy surface. A perfect blue sky. Flushed skin, bodies tangled. And a human who knew the consequences of falling in love, but did it anyway.

FORTY

Ellina surrendered to the kiss.

It moved through her, swelling into something full-bodied and deep. An ocean. She was floating in it. This feeling. Him.

He cupped her face in his hands. His thumbs pressed gently into her hairline, then harder, gaining urgency. He exhaled into her mouth. She breathed him in.

She became dizzy with sensation. It was all around her, the touch and smell and taste of him that blurred into something she could not name, became a mere swath of color. Ellina felt as she imagined a bird must feel, catching tendrils, spinning high on air. She felt what it was to soar.

She leaned into the feeling. If she really was a bird, she would stretch out her wings. She would climb into the sky, farther and farther until the whole world was laid out beneath her. Ellina envisioned what she would see: sloped northern hills, the ones near the border where the east became the west. Gentle knolls furred in grass. Spores drifting on a breeze.

The southern forests. Those trees, stoic and still. Among them: a clearing. Damp forest ground. A place where she had killed an elf, and saved a man, and changed.

Ellina could see all the ways she had changed. She understood how this—the way her entire being had become like a soaring, winged creature—was part of that change. The old Ellina would not have been capable of such feelings. She would have been closed to the emotions of this moment, would have locked them behind a door shut so tight as to become seamless. But that door was not closed now. It was wide open. From within, the truth of her heart came pouring out.

Venick moved his hands to her waist. He seemed to want to pull her closer, though she was already flush against him. There was nowhere left for her to go. His fingers dug into her skin, his mouth on hers, hard and insistent. He kissed her earnestly, fearlessly. It made her fearless, too.

Yet were they not forgetting? Ellina seemed to remember her fears as if from a distance. She remembered that this—kissing in a public garden—was so rash as to border on suicidal. What if they were discovered? Even if no one discovered them *now*, the mere fact of this kiss was a risk. What if the truth came out in some other way?

And if it did? Ellina could see this, too: the queen's hard stare. The frosted, barren earth of the whitelands. A sword driven through Venick's chest.

The thought seemed to shake her. Reality flooded back in.

Ellina broke away.

Venick gazed down at her, his breath a little uneven, his eyes still warm…yet quickly growing concerned, quickly growing confused. "Ellina?"

Her heart was stuttering. In her mind, Ellina saw the cold, empty eyes of Venick's death. She felt as if it had happened already, as if this kiss had been witnessed and reported, and Venick sentenced, and killed.

Ellina took a step back and Venick's expression closed. "No," he said. "Venick—"

"No," he repeated. "Just…" His eyes roamed up and around, searching for the right words. "I need to know—if you don't—if this—" He cut off. Heaved a breath, then spoke clearly. "My heart is yours, Ellina. I know I shouldn't say that. I know it's wrong. But I've lied for so long that I just—*can't* anymore. And I need to know if you feel the same."

Ellina's breath caught. It stunned her that he could speak so boldly. Did he not fear the consequences of his words?

"Please," he said.

Ellina suspected Venick did not care for consequences. She had seen this side of him. She knew he could be reckless. It was recklessness that drove him to hunt for an enemy army rather than return to the safety of the mainlands, that made him run into a swordfight with nothing but a dagger, that had him venturing across the tundra in search of a hidden city in a foreign land. Once Venick set his mind to something he saw it through, no matter the risk. Venick did not care for risks. He was rarely careful. Really, he was a little self-destructive.

He had been lonely. Ellina remembered his story told by the firelight of the healer's room; how he had known Miria, and loved her, and lost her. How he murdered his father for betraying their secret. Venick had been forced into exile as a consequence of that murder, and the loneliness of exile had shaped him. Ellina could see that after three long years of banishment, Venick was desperate to rediscover his place in the world, to put his loyalty where he thought it belonged. Which was, apparently, with *her*.

And she had allowed it. She accepted Venick's loyalty and returned it with her own.

"Please," Venick said again. "Tell me the truth."

How was it that the truth could be so two-sided? It tempted. Ellina was tempted to tell Venick what he wanted to hear, because it would be good to finally admit it, and because she now knew it was true. Yet she also understood the consequence of such a confession. The very thought paralyzed her. "Venick," she started. "I…"

But then, in the distance: a horn's low wail. It came from far away, somewhere beyond the palace walls. It was a single, baleful cry that seemed to go all the way to her bones.

The sound startled Ellina. She took another step back.

She recognized that horn. But her mind was slow. It was still caught in the grip of Venick's question. It took her a moment to place that sound, and when she finally did, she slipped quickly down into a dark canyon of fear, because that horn was not merely a horn, but a heralding.

The queen had returned to the city.

"Ellina?" Venick asked again, but Ellina was not listening. She scanned Venick's flushed cheeks, his dripping hair, clothing soaked. She glanced down at her own thin shift, then at her robes—so different from what she usually wore—heaped in a pile by the pool's edge. Panic bubbled. How must they look?

As if all the rumors were true?

If the queen did not already know of Venick's presence in Evov, she would learn of it quickly. She would order an immediate stateroom summons. But Ellina and Venick could not arrive in the stateroom looking as they looked now: drenched, disheveled. And guilty, so guilty.

"You need to leave," Ellina told Venick. Her voice went higher. "Go back to your suite. Change your clothing—"

"I'm not going anywhere." His expression tightened. "Not until you answer my question."

"You do not understand…"

"I know you're afraid. I am, too, but—"

"Venick." She cut him off, horror mounting. "There is not *time*. We cannot be caught here. The queen—"

"I don't care about the queen!"

His outburst, rather than halting her, only fueled her panic. Ellina glanced around the quiet garden, expecting to see the queen's summoners rush around the corner at any moment. She felt time slipping away. They needed to leave, *now*. She tried to step past Venick, but the attempt at escape seemed to light something inside him. His face became a mask of denial. He blocked her path, his hand coming to grip her arm. "Stop it, Ellina. Stop pretending to be cold."

"I am not pretending—"

"I *know* you. I know when you're trying to hide from me."

"Venick." Ellina strained against him. "Let me *go*."

Venick glanced at where he held her arm. He blinked, releasing her. "I didn't mean—" He took a startled step back. His face was awash in shame. "I'm sorry."

Later, in Ellina's mind, she did things differently. She explained the situation to Venick, who did not know what the horn meant and misunderstood her fear. She put aside the gnawing dread for just a few moments more so that she could tell him everything: her feelings, her heart. The way he had opened her eyes to the world, forced her to see the true color of things. In Ellina's version of that moment, she would reach out, place her palm to his cheek. *I love you, too*, she would say. She would tear down the last boundaries between them, and give him the whole of her, and be glad of the giving.

But that was fantasy, and this was reality: Ellina's fear made it impossible to think. Her urgency became all that she knew. She moved again to flee, and Venick, rejected and ashamed, let her go.

• • •

Ellina moved through the palace towards her suite. The hallways were eerily quiet. Farah's guards—inexplicably, miraculously—were nowhere to be found.

She felt something slipping from her grasp. It was something she had always held close. She was afraid to let it go. She tried to draw it back. It turned to liquid and poured through her fingers.

She rounded a corner, then another. Her heart beat too fast, hard and hurting. She buried her hands in the folds of her robes.

Those robes. She remembered donning them in the privacy of her suite. Then she had gone to find Venick. That invitation, his quick smile. She had asked him to teach her how to swim.

It was something she had thought about for so long, but it seemed insane now. Worse: what followed. Him, moving closer. Him, kissing her. She should have known this would happen. She *had* known. And if she could admit that, then she could also admit this: she had *wanted* it.

Was that the unnamed feeling slipping free? Was it Ellina's want, which she had always buried? It was not buried now. It pushed free. It dug through the earth and bloomed.

Ellina scanned the halls as she walked. The horn sounded again, closer now.

She quickened her pace.

FORTY-ONE

Venick returned to his suite. The sun was high now. It streamed through his window in garish beams.

He heard the horn again in the distance: a long, sorrowful wail. Venick ignored it. He kept at what he was doing, which was pulling on a fresh shirt. He didn't know what the horn meant. He didn't care to know.

Dourin found him like that, there in his bedroom. The elf pushed through the door without preamble. His face was grave. "The queen has returned," Dourin told him. "You are being summoned to the stateroom for your trial."

Surprise wasn't quite the right word to describe how Venick felt at that news. Acceptance, maybe. Resignation, because they'd been waiting for the queen's return, and he should have anticipated this.

Still, this moment felt a little like his dream from last night. There was a sense of things unremembered. The lingering glow of it.

Dourin had not come alone. He was flanked by six of Farah's guards, three on either side. They watched Venick with blank eyes as he gave a nod, then stooped to retrieve his sword. He took his time, belting the weapon deliberately, pushing the prong slowly through the leather hole, adjusting it until it sat exactly how he wanted.

By the time Venick straightened, the guards' expressions were no longer blank.

Dourin shook his head. *You idiot.* But he said only, under his breath so the other elves wouldn't hear, "Be careful." Then he turned and led the way.

• • •

Venick had not been back to the stateroom since his first night here.

It looked much the same now as it had then, besides the sunlight streaming in through tall, narrow windows, and the gallery seating, which wasn't just half-full of elves. No, this audience was packed shoulder-to-shoulder. It reminded Venick of the mainlands whenever there was a dispute between men. Fights in Irek were settled with fists. Someone would throw the first punch. A crowd would quickly gather, shoving and jeering, alerted to the smell of blood like wanewolves on a hunt.

Another difference, then: these elves didn't jeer. Didn't move much at all, except to lean towards each other as they whispered. Venick couldn't hear what they were saying. Couldn't even guess what they *might* be saying. Their expressions were too guarded, the murmurs too soft. They sounded like dried autumn leaves, skating and hissing around Venick's boots as the guards marched him towards the room's center.

The queen wasn't there yet. Farah was. She stood on the raised dais, silent and watchful. At her signal the guards and Dourin moved away, leaving Venick to finish the trek alone. Venick scanned the audience as he walked, seeing no one else that he knew, no one he recognized, except *there*, Raffan in the front row. Venick locked eyes with that elf, then let his gaze move on, searching for…someone.

Someone. Sure.

Venick no longer trusted himself to see things clearly. He had been so *sure*. In the forest when he'd kissed Ellina for the first time, he could have sworn he saw the same feelings in her that he felt in himself. He remembered listing his reasons, as if tallying them would amount to an answer. She broke her laws for him. She killed her kin for him. When he kissed her, she kissed him back.

Then he'd learned the truth, and he began rethinking everything he thought he knew. Ellina didn't save him for him. She did it for Lorana. She spared his life in honor of her sister's memory. It was as good an explanation as any…yet still Venick found himself doubting. Was that really the whole of it? Or was there something more there?

He couldn't seem to let go of his damned *hope*. He went around and around in his own head, questioning everything. He didn't know what to think, and that was worse, so he'd finally begged Ellina for the truth. In the everpool, he'd admitted his feelings. He'd asked for hers in return. She had pushed him away, and maybe that was answer enough…except he still didn't *believe it*.

The uncertainty of it all was maddening. He should have demanded Ellina's answers in elvish. He wished he had. Maybe then he'd be able to yank his mind out of the past and concentrate on what he *should* be concentrating on: the scent of cool stateroom stone, the clink and rattle of guards' armor, the soft buzz of conversation.

Venick tried. He brought his gaze back to Farah and did his best to focus on these things, and on what he knew would happen next. The queen had returned to the city. She would soon reclaim her place on that dais. Venick would be given a chance to repeat his warning in elvish, and the queen would hear him and—

Please, reeking gods.

—believe him.

And then they would do what they should have done already, which was to gather more soldiers. Start training their own army. Send scouts south to spy on the southern forces, to report back on their weapons and their position and their leaders.

This was what Venick expected. Hell, it was what they had been waiting for. A month of staring at the same vaulted prison walls, of recovering from a knife-wound to the hip, of squinting at books and maps until he was half-blind from it—all in preparation for the queen's return.

And so Venick was unprepared when Farah lifted her hands to draw the audience's attention. More unprepared for the words she spoke next, or for the way that no one—save Dourin and himself—seemed surprised that she was starting his trial without the queen. "I have summoned this court to bear witness to the sentencing of the human Venick," Farah began, "who has been brought to answer for his crimes—"

"Wait." Venick's voice sounded sharp, even to him. He glanced between Farah and the elven audience, not understanding. "The queen is back in the city now. She summoned this court. I will answer to *her.*"

Farah gave a huff of an almost-laugh. "No. *I* summoned this court, and you will answer to me for your crimes."

"But you and Ellina agreed—"

"Not those crimes," Farah said, and this time she did laugh, low in the back of her throat. "My mother might forgive you for entering our city, but not once she learns *why.* So tell us, human. Why did you come to Evov?"

But her question made no sense. "You already know why."

"Remind me."

Venick felt it then: a strange, simmering doubt. The way his mind stretched for an idea that hadn't quite formed, hovering there, just out of reach. Again, he glanced between Farah and the audience, seeking some hint, some clue that might reveal what he was missing. "I came to warn you about the southern army."

"But that was not your only reason."

"It was. It is." Venick worked his hand over the pommel of his sword like he'd seen Ellina do a thousand times. He realized what he was doing and forced his hand down. "I came to Evov because of what I witnessed in the south. The army. They are coming north. I came because I can help you prepare to fight."

"You *came* for Ellina."

Venick blinked. Felt the earth open under his feet. Felt the world fracture and shift, his thoughts rearranging at dizzying speeds. "No." Then, louder. "No. This has nothing to do with Ellina."

"A pretty sentiment, but not helping your case. Tell us, is it true that you two traveled the elflands together?"

"Yes, but that's not—"

"And is it true that when Ellina returned to Evov, you journeyed here so that you could be reunited?"

"No." Venick felt suddenly ill. "No. That's not why."

"And *Ellina*," Farah continued. "Why is it that when you assaulted her bondmate in elven lands, she took your punishment? Why is it that even now, when your crimes are obvious, she defends you?" Farah's expression shone with sudden emotion, a lightning-quick flash of pride and greed and anger. "Tell us, human; are you *involved* with our elven princess?"

Everything went white. Snowy, a haze of disbelief settling softly. Venick could hear the audience's appalled silence. Could hear his own heartbeat pounding in his ears. "*No.*"

"Say it in elvish."

But Venick couldn't do what Farah was asking. "You said you didn't believe the word of a human. You think I can lie in elvish."

"I have changed my mind."

"Farah." That was Ellina's voice. Venick spun to see her striding towards them. She had changed back into her legion armor, a sword at her hip, her bow slung across her back. Venick's heart gave a sore thump at the sight of her.

He saw other things, too. Elves on all sides. Farah's predator stance. Raffan descending from the gallery. Guards lining the walls, more guards than had been there before, more coming still.

Venick thought—suddenly, vividly—of the coup in Kenath. Keen eyes, rippling shadows, a hunch. He remembered the vanished tent-city, hunting for an army, finding it and racing here and not being believed.

The guards who had escorted him out of the dungeons. How he believed them to be soldiers because they seemed larger than most elves. Darker.

The assassin. There had been a moment. Right as Venick turned to meet that attack. He had missed it before, but he remembered it now; the assassin had pulled his own shadow around himself.

And Farah. Venick saw her again as she had been in the dungeons. He remembered how she'd studied him, her black silhouette, a halo of firelight behind her. Farah seemed ready to believe his elvish *now*, yet he could still remember the way he'd given her his warning in that dark tunnel, the sting of her words when she claimed she did not believe him.

When she *pretended* not to believe him.

The thought came haltingly. Venick paled. He could think of only one reason Farah would pretend not to believe a warning like that—if she knew about the southern army, and didn't want others to know.

Venick realized, too late, what this was.

"Ellina." She was halfway down the stateroom floor. Venick started towards her, but a band of guards materialized between them. They formed a circle around Venick. He tried to break through. Trapped. His nightmare. It was there, prickling under his skin. It was *here*, in the scene before him. He saw in his memory Lorana surrounded by enemy elves. His fight to reach her, too late, watching her die. His fight to reach Ellina now, his sword useless and forgotten on his hip, the horror of his nightmare come back to life. A band of nausea circled his throat. "Ellina, *don't.*"

But she already had. It was too late.

FORTY-TWO

Ellina strode through the stateroom.

"Farah." She spoke her sister's name again. Listened to it echo between high stone walls. The silence that came after seemed to ring. It was a glass orb that held everything else she would say, every moment that was to come. Later, when Venick was gone and Dourin was gone and Ellina betrayed, she would imagine she held that orb in her palm and could undo everything that had gone so wrong. That she could turn back time, see the trap and avoid it.

The stateroom was full of elves. They crowded the gallery, lined the walls. All eyes were on her, a few hostile, a few anxious, all the rest shut down to blank-eyed nothing. Ellina lowered her voice. The room was pitched to carry. "What are you doing?"

"Holding a trial." Farah's voice was like Ellina's. Calm, certain. But her gaze sparked in delight.

Ellina said, "I thought we agreed. For a trial, the queen must be present."

"The queen has just returned. She is coming."

"But she is not *here*."

Farah ignored that. "I was just wondering, what are the human's feelings for you?"

It was only then that Ellina noticed just *how* crowded the room was, and mostly with Farah's guard. Those elves seemed huge in their metal armor, some wearing full helms so that only their eyes were visible. A group of them formed a barricade around Venick who stood in the stateroom's center, who had been trying—unsuccessfully—to break through to her.

"We have all heard the rumors," Farah continued. "A human, following you through the elflands. Fighting for you. *Defending* you. What are his motives, I wonder?" Farah's tone changed. "What are *yours*?"

Ellina's eyes snapped back to her sister. "We have discussed this already. I thought I made myself clear."

"It is illegal for elves and humans to fall in love."

"He does not love me."

"No?" Farah gestured around the stateroom. "We are all gathered. Why not ask for the truth in elvish?"

"How will that help? You think he can lie in elvish."

"Maybe," Farah agreed as if she had not just suggested otherwise, "but *you* cannot."

Ellina's understanding was cruel for coming so late. She spotted Raffan moving towards them. She saw Venick, face white. And Dourin, who had shuttered his expression, but who broke that mask for the slightest second to aim a warning. *Close yourself, Ellina. How could you forget?*

She did. She shut her eyes briefly, willing her body to stone…yet felt, despite her efforts, the way heat slowly crept into her cheeks, blazing them red. The sensation held her still. There was no help for it, no way to hide it, and Ellina thought—judging by Farah's next words—that her sister knew it, too.

"Do you think we have not noticed how different you have been acting?" Farah asked darkly. "We have been watching you, Ellina. We have seen how you treat the human, how you care for him. How...*emotional* you have become. It is time now that you explain yourself."

It gave Ellina no pleasure knowing that she had been right. All along, she had suspected that Farah and Raffan were biding their time, gathering evidence, waiting for the right time to bring Ellina before the court so that her confession could be heard by all. Ellina had planned for this, practiced for it, yet she realized now that she had never truly believed this moment would come.

There were a lot of things she did not believe. She was beginning to despise herself for that.

She concentrated on this. She honed that anger until it was ground to a sharp edge. Deadly. Like her. She reminded herself that despite all her beliefs about the world, despite her insistence that they could never change, *she* had changed. She broke laws. She killed elves. And she was a liar.

She was very good at lying. Language need be no barrier.

"Name your accusations," Ellina demanded.

"You have fallen in love with a human."

"Untrue."

"In elvish, little sister."

The court muttered at the insult, but of course Ellina had expected this. She inhaled slowly, trying for something simple, something that still held a thread of truth. "*What you believe about us is false.*"

Farah was not fooled. "Be more specific."

Ellina thought about how she had begun practicing her lies with renewed vigor. She sought that feeling, pulled the sensation of it over herself, pushed all her weight against it as she formed the words...

And there, as before, she *felt* it. That subtle change, that slight loosening in her chest and throat. Ellina grabbed the feeling and harnessed it as she imagined the lie she wished to speak, felt it burn and gather and then softly, softly, "*I do not—love Venick.*"

A moment of nothing. A tantalizing bite of blue sky through the clouds.

Then: agony.

The backlash of pain was worse for being unexpected. Ellina's muscles seized, her lungs constricting as a column of fire shot up her spine and into her skull. She blinked dizzyingly. Her vision spotted. For a moment she thought she might black out. Yet she had said the words aloud, and in *elvish*.

The realization steadied her. She heard the crowd murmur again, differently now. She was certain they could see her effort to hide the pain, but she played that pain for anger, which she lashed at her sister. "*I do not—care about him at all.*"

Farah's cool confidence was gone now. "Have you ever loved him?"

"*No.*"

"*Could* you ever love him?"

"*No.*"

It went on. Each lie brought a fresh wave of pain, but Ellina pushed through it, and as she did the words seemed to come easier, as if smoothing a path for each other.

Venick stood frozen at the edge of her vision. She could not look at him, *would* not, because if she did she would certainly snap this small thread of power she had discovered within her. And yet, even without looking at him, she could feel him. She could feel the way he stood stat-ue-still, staring at her. She could hear how his breathing had changed. She could sense his fighter's stance, his hurt and anger that he had no-where to aim. And worse, perhaps worst of all, she could tell that he believed her.

Of course he believed her. Ellina had never told Venick about her conversation with the wildings, or explained how she was learning to lie in elvish. She remembered Venick's confession in the everpool, how she had left him there with nothing but her own silence. That memory churned and blackened in her gut. She should have told him the truth then when she had the chance...

And maybe she still could. The thought filled Ellina with savage de-termination. She could do this. She could harden herself, forge her will in steel, say what needed to be said to save them both. Later, when this trial was over, she would find Venick. She promised herself she would tell him everything.

Finally, Farah shook her head. "You do not care for the human at all?"

Ellina waved a careless hand. She saw it tremble and clenched it shut. *"Kill him, if it truly matters that much to you. What do I care? He is human."*

Farah glanced around the room. Word of this interrogation must have spread through the palace, because in addition to the full gallery, elves now hovered in the doorway and around the room's perimeter. Legionnaires, courtiers, senators; it seemed as if every high-ranking elf in the city had appeared to witness the spectacle.

"If you do not care about him, then why fight for him?" Farah asked. "Why try to protect him?"

"I used him to learn about war," Ellina replied in elvish. *"He was a tool. Nothing more."*

Farah was still staring at Ellina, who watched, and felt the dark pull of dread as a decision seemed to form in her sister's mind. "Very well. Since you have no issue that I call for his execution—"

"Stop."

The word came quietly, smoking through gallery, up the dais. Ellina spun to see the queen striding across the stateroom, her long robes sweeping behind her. "Stop," Rishiana said again. Her expression was calm. Her voice was calm. She gave no indication that she was angry, no hint of her inner feelings. Yet the mood in the room quickly darkened. "Farah. What are you doing?"

Farah motioned around the stateroom. "Holding a trial."

"I warned you." Rishiana's voice was a lick of lightning: innocuous, seemingly harmless. But with the power to instill fear. "I warned you. You are not queen yet. You do not have the authority to hold a trial, and you are overstepping grievously."

"Grievously? Mother, please." Farah clasped her hands behind her back as Rishiana reached the room's center. Farah was standing in the queen's place yet made no move to step aside. "I am doing you a favor. And I think you will agree with my verdict. The human should be sentenced to die."

Rishiana shot a glance at Venick. Ellina had no idea how much her mother knew about Venick's presence here, and it was impossible to tell what she thought at the sight of a human in their midst. Yet the queen's answer surprised Ellina. "Whether the human lives or dies is irrelevant."

"Are you suggesting that he will live?"

"I think it is clear what I am suggesting. You do not have the authority to summon a stateroom audience in this way. Not until you are queen."

There was a shift in the crowd. Was it possible that even *more* elves were appearing? Ellina's skin felt hot, the room suddenly stifling. Too full. Her eyes darted around the stateroom, and she noticed it. On all sides: dark eyes, dark armor, dark hair.

Dark hair?

"But *when* will I become queen, mother?" Farah asked. Her voice was low now, almost a whisper. Her hand came to rest on her sword.

"As soon as I choose it."

"And when will *that* be?"

"As soon as you are ready."

Ellina pulled her eyes back to Farah. A thought. A terrible realization…

Farah's face was a void. "I am ready now," she said, and drew her sword, and stabbed.

The world went silent. Ellina's ears rang. Rishiana looked down at the green glass in her belly. She staggered, wrapping a hand around the hilt. Her body thumped as it hit the floor.

Chaos erupted.

FORTY-THREE

Venick's mind was split into pieces.

The first piece was a vicious, bloodthirsty thing. Elves seemed to pour out of nowhere. Venick couldn't tell at first where they came from or what was happening, but then he saw their faces, and focused, and understood. Farah's guard—yet not quite. They were *dressed* like Farah's guard, but these elves were taller than most, dark hair, hard eyes, some wearing black and red pendants around their necks.

Venick remembered it then. He understood why these colors seemed so familiar. A banner. A raven between twin flames. Black and red.

The southerners.

Venick killed without care. He poured his soul into the bloody work of it, opening throats and bellies and spilling elven blood across the floor. He hardly saw what he was doing, hardly thought. His carelessness was dangerous. As he brought his sword down over and over, tearing flesh, ripping muscle, he paid no attention to how far he stretched, the angle of his body. It would be easy for an elf to break past his non-existent defenses, to step into the wide openings he allowed to appear at his shoulder, his back, his neck, again his shoulder, his ribs.

He half-wished someone would.

The second piece of him was calculating. It examined the elves like players on a board game. He saw again his story, but this time it was complete. He understood why Raffan had not seemed bothered by the vanished cities or the southerners' growing power. Why Farah had not believed Venick's warning—had *pretended* not to believe it.

The answer, now, seemed obvious. It was because they knew. About the southern army. About the plot to overthrow the queen. Hell, they had *planned* it. They had stalled to buy themselves time while they smuggled southerners into the city, feigned indifference to gain the advantage. Farah had wanted Venick dead, had tried to have him killed, because she knew his warning was real and did not want the queen to hear his revelations in elvish. And then when Farah couldn't kill him she changed her strategy. This summons, which brought the queen and the legion and Farah's guard together under one roof. Which left the rest of the city vulnerable. This coup, the queen's death. It was of *their design*.

The final piece, the piece he held close to himself, was falling. It was toes over the edge of a mountain ledge. It was closed eyes, dark imaginings.

Ellina was a liar.

She was the punishing grip of a hand over a windpipe. She was the slide of a knife between ribs.

The truth Venick had long sought was finally there for the taking. The question he'd wondered had been answered. Ellina did not love him. Did not—apparently—care about him at all.

She fought her own battle at the far end of the hall. Through the haze of shock and hurt and chaos, Venick caught glimpses of her fighting, *truly* fighting, with the intent to kill. Ellina moved like she was made of her weapon. She shifted exactly in time with the thrusts and swipes of her attackers, striking and ducking and parrying with grace. Killing—despite all her resistance to it—appeared to come effortlessly to her. It was a dance, the cries of fallen elves the merry tune. She drove her sword into elf after elf, moving so quickly it was impossible to see every attack clearly, to separate Ellina from the blur of green glass around her.

Yet it was impossible not to notice—the vision unexpected, unwelcome—how uneven the battle was. How easily the southerners surrounded her. The few loyal northerners battling by Ellina's side began to fall. A space appeared at her back, undefended. Venick started towards her, intending to cover that gap. His body pulled him in her direction. But her words reverberated through his mind—*I do not love Venick. Kill him, if it truly matters that much to you. What do I care?*—and he felt gutted all over again, like the blood pooling on the floor was *his*, and his heart was flailing uselessly in his chest, pounding furiously even as his lifeblood left him.

She had tried to tell him. He had asked, and Ellina had answered, but he hadn't believed her. Part of him still couldn't believe her. After everything, it seemed impossible that he could have been so wrong about her. As the battle raged around him, Venick's mind reached for some explanation, something that might explain how she had said such things in elvish...

And he remembered Lorana instead. Venick remembered how he had loved her, had spent years loving her, yet he hadn't ever really known her. Lorana wasn't a common elf. She wasn't even a southerner. She was the lost heir to the northern throne, yet she'd managed to keep the entire truth of that identity hidden from him. Venick had always thought there were no secrets between him and Lorana and had been so, critically wrong.

He thought of his father. The clues had been there, but Venick ignored them. *Loyalty to family first*, his father used to say. Venick had always thought that even if his father discovered the truth about Venick and Lorana's relationship, he would never betray them. But he had.

Maybe it was Venick. Maybe he was the kind of person who saw only what he wanted to see. He'd wanted to believe Ellina loved him, so he convinced himself that she did. He invented meaning where meaning didn't belong. But this wasn't a story, and Venick was too old for fantasies.

It was time he stopped pretending.

He'd lost track of the fight. Venick blinked back into his own body as he spun and drove his sword into flesh. Saw it split, felt warm blood splatter his face. He yanked the sword out and swiped again at another southern elf, this one short and wiry. She wore a belt of throwing knives, mostly gone, two left. She skirted backward out of range, threw the first. Missed. Threw the second. Venick brought his sword up, deflected it. He heaved his weapon up and over, flat-side down. Into the elf's skull. Smashed it, the dent fracturing her forehead. Venick stepped over the body, raising his sword to parry another attack.

But he wasn't watching his flank. He saw the sharp slide of green glass coming in on his exposed side, too late to block, to dodge, and *finally* someone had noticed the opening.

Venick waited for the blow, for the clean hand of death to finally take him.

It never came.

Dourin was there, turning away the attack, thrusting his own sword into the elf's gut. He ripped his weapon free with a huff, moving so that he was back-to-back with Venick. He looked how Venick felt: wild, brutal, alive with the fight. "We are outnumbered," Dourin said over his shoulder.

"I noticed."

"We have been betrayed."

"Noticed that, too."

"The southerners are winning."

"Are you going to—" a grunt as Venick blocked a mace, then *kicked*, sent the elf flying "—continue to state the obvious?"

"We need to retreat. *Now.*"

Venick scanned the stateroom. Elves were dead and dying all around, but there seemed to be more coming, and endless amount of *more.* Somewhere in the chaos, Venick had lost sight of Ellina.

Dourin was right. This was not a fight, it was a slaughter. And now they were outnumbered, a few loyal northerners battling to hold off the southern attack. They would not win this fight. There was no hope of it.

"*Venick,*" Dourin snapped.

"I hear you."

"Then *do* something."

But all Venick did was rake his eyes across the hall for Ellina. He'd lost sight of her. The wall of enemy elves had become too thick. And then Dourin was cursing him, invoking gods he didn't believe in as he growled at Venick and grabbed his arm and dragged him away.

FORTY-FOUR

Ellina stared blankly at the walls of her makeshift prison. Pasty silver rugs, a wide-open window. The books of her childhood lining the shelves.

Her bedroom, turned dungeon.

Her wrists were bound. Her ankles. She had taken a knife to the thigh. The wound had not been tended. It burned, bleeding freely into her bedsheets.

Farah was there. Raffan, too. They were speaking, but Ellina was not listening. She closed her eyes.

Their betrayal numbed her. Her mother's death did.

And Venick.

Ellina dipped her head. She remembered his unsteady breath as she spun her lies. After, she had sought him across the room. She had tried to reach him through the fighting. She struggled, and was reminded of how she had struggled in the river in Kenath. She felt like that: the spinning terror, clawing for breath. Frantic kicking that got her nowhere. And yet, in the river—though she had not understood this then—there was a feeling. A warmth. But small, like a candle.

Later, she would remember the feeling and understand it. It was the certainty that Venick would come for her. That she was not alone, that he would not let her die. Even as she clung to the sewage grate, teeth clattering, limbs locked, she had known he was coming. And he had.

She did not feel that way in the stateroom.

She tried to battle through to him. Her sword into an elf's neck. Torn out. Up, shearing another's arm off at the elbow. The gush of blood. A cry that might have been her own. Her eyes were only half on the fight. She scanned the room. She spotted Venick fighting his own battle on the other side. She saw him see her.

And realized that *he* was not trying to reach *her*. The cruel truth of it. Ellina had frozen. She tried to speak. *No*, she wanted to say. *Listen*, she wanted to say. But Venick was not listening. And then it was too late.

Raffan had come for her instead. She watched him stalk across the stateroom, dodging swords and daggers and axes. Their gazes locked. She had thought, *now*. She had thought, *yes*. Murder pulsed through her. She would kill him.

She had not.

He overpowered her. Maybe it was his size and strength, the many hours they had trained together, how he knew her tricks. Or maybe it was her own wretched heart, still reeling from Venick's broken trust and what she had done to deserve it. Raffan disarmed her, then forced her to the ground. *It is over*, he had said. *It is over, Ellina.*

She thought he would kill her, but instead he bound her hands and dragged her away. Ellina struggled. The fighting was mostly finished. It had been swift. Even if the north had heeded Venick's warning, even if they had prepared their defenses, no amount of planning could have prepared them for *this*.

Ellina came to learn the truth in pieces. The southern conjurors had entered their hidden city through shadow-weaving. It was a loophole, a way around Evov's magic. Enemy conjurors threaded their shadows onto Farah and her guard and were guided inside. They then used that power to guide *more* southerners inside. Those elves posed as members of Farah's battalion. They gathered in the palace, waiting for the moment when they would strike.

And what a strike. Farah had made mistakes early on—summoning Ellina to the stateroom, attempting to kill Venick in secret—but she had recovered. And she was clever. She saw Venick's trial as an opportunity to stage the coup she had been planning since—*when*? Since Miria's disappearance? Before then? When had Farah allied with the southerners? How long had she been plotting her rise to power?

When Raffan had come to haul Ellina away from the stateroom, she had not expected to escape, but she dug in her heels and frantically scanned the room for Venick. And then, unwillingly, almost as if it was not *her*, she moved her eyes to the bodies on the floor, searching for a dark-haired human, that strong face, those winter eyes. Nothing.

Ellina's hope was nearly as fierce as her despair. He had survived. Dourin, too.

"—use her. We need the unwavering support of the city." Farah was saying now. Sunlight streamed in through her bedroom windows. Somewhere in the courtyard on the grounds far below, Ellina could hear the muffled sound of boots on the pavement, elves storming the palace armory. The city's store of green glass weapons would now be in the southerner's hands. The knowledge was a bitter fruit. "We cannot risk revolt."

"We will kill any living witnesses who do not side with us," Raffan soothed. "For the rest of Evov, we are spreading the rumors of Rishiana's ill ability to rule." He smoothed back Farah's hair. Ellina was too numb to feel surprised by the intimacy of the gesture. Instead, her mind worked like a lock, the key sliding through the pins, the click of the tumbler as the lock released.

"You love him," she said. Two pairs of golden eyes cut to her.

"Excuse me?" Farah asked.

"You love Raffan. You are in love with my bondmate." Ellina was startled by her own words. She was surprised she was speaking at all. "Is that why you did it?"

Farah's tone was flat. "No."

"You did not have to kill our mother for him. You can *have him.*"

"Rishiana's death was unavoidable," Farah said evenly. "I regret that it had to happen this way. But her death was a mercy."

"A mercy," Ellina repeated.

"Yes."

"And now you will give *me* your mercy."

But Farah surprised her. "No."

"No?"

"I have a proposition."

Ellina glared. "My answer is no."

"You have not even heard my terms."

"I will not bargain for my life."

"Not *your* life," Farah corrected. Ellina stiffened.

"I told you already," Ellina said slowly. "I do not care about Venick. You cannot use him against me."

But Farah suspected. Maybe she knew the secret Ellina had learned from the wildings in the southern forests. Maybe she recognized Ellina's pain in the stateroom, her breathlessness as she lied in elvish. Or maybe Farah was simply guessing. Ellina would gladly give her own life rather than agree to anything Farah wanted. But Venick...

"Does that mean you have no objection if we hunt him down?" Farah asked coyly.

"No."

"What about his family? I hear he comes from a city called Irek. I hear his mother still lives there. Are you saying you would not mind if we burned the town? If we killed every single human left in it?"

All the blood seemed to rush to Ellina's ears. She thought of Venick's banishment. He had had a home, and fought for it, and lost it. He dreamed of one day redeeming himself and returning to that place... which would not be possible if Farah made good on her threat. Ellina's voice came out strangled. "You would not."

"We did once before, during the purge. We could again."

"That makes no sense. What would it gain you?"

"I think it will gain us your cooperation." Farah clasped her hands behind her back. "Your human did nicely, discovering our secret allies, spreading his warning around our city. There are elves who believed him, who knew the throne was in danger. There are elves who will follow you if they believe *you* are in danger, or if they think this alliance— and my initiation as queen—is not what you want. They might rebel. We do *not* want a rebellion."

Ellina looked out the window. Little motes of dust floated on the air. She could count them clearly.

"I would prefer to conquer Evov as we did Kenath," Farah said. "Smoothly, and with few civilian casualties. So here is what I need you to do now: snuff out any northern resistance. Pledge me your allegiance. No more fighting. No more games. Give our citizens no reason to doubt your loyalty to me. Do this, and I will instruct my soldiers to leave Irek unharmed."

Ellina wondered if those dust motes were like little worlds. She wondered if this world was a mote of dust in someone else's universe. If everything was just an invisible speck on a beam of sunlight.

"You have a strong sense of honor," Farah continued. "You know lives—human and elven—are at stake. I think you will take this deal."

It struck Ellina that her sister had not planned for her to survive the southerners' invasion. Farah thought, in the stateroom, that Ellina would be unable to deny her feelings for Venick. That she would be handed grounds for banishment, or worse. But Farah and Raffan *were* clever. They had found a way to salvage the pieces of that ruined plan. A better way, even, with Ellina as their pawn.

"Be grateful," Farah said. "It is better this way, little sister." And then, quietly, as if she had read Ellina's thoughts, "You could be dead."

FORTY-FIVE

Venick tipped his head back. He gazed into a candy sky. In the distance, the mountains were a faded smear. He could not see Evov. Even if he was closer, he knew he would not see the city. Since their escape, it had become hidden from them once more.

Venick thought he had forgotten this feeling. The helplessness, the misery. The burn of it in his chest, a hot coal on his heart. Or, if he hadn't forgotten, he thought he had tucked it away, buried it so deep that he would never find it again. Now, however, Venick felt it starkly. It was the feeling of loss. The grip of disbelief, of mistakes too severe to be unmade. Longing. Regret.

The pain of a broken heart. He thought he had forgotten that, too.

He'd been wrong about a lot of things.

Venick told himself that he was lucky. Yes, *lucky*. He was alive. He was free. And what had happened with Ellina…really, it was expected. The truth had been there all along, and Venick was getting better at seeing the truth for what it was. Ellina saved him in honor of Lorana's memory, then kept him around so that he could teach her about war. And it made sense. He knew Ellina's mind, how she strategized, how she drew her hand and calculated her next move. If she believed Venick could be valuable in the coming fight, why *wouldn't* she use him to teach her battle strategy? Why wouldn't she keep him as a tool to be honed and commanded, especially when he'd practically begged to do it? Ellina was sworn to her country. She made her choices for herself. Not for him. Not for *love*.

Be serious, now.

"Venick." Dourin appeared. The trek through the mountains had been eerily uneventful. They had seen no sign of the southern army or its conjurors. But now the mountains were behind them and only uncertainly lay ahead. "The path will soon split."

It was a conversation worn old between them these past three days. Dourin wanted Venick to stay. Dourin wanted Venick to fight. Dourin wanted a human ally in the war that was to come.

And war *was* coming. The southerners undoubtedly had elves in each major city from here to Tarrith-Mour. With Evov's supply of green glass, they would be able to arm those elves. When Farah took the throne, the execution would be swift. The only question now was how strong the northern resistance would be.

Not strong, judging by what Venick could see.

"We need you," Dourin said.

"I've made my opinion clear. And you don't need me."

"Yes, we do." Dourin motioned at him with a hand. "*You* are the one who discovered the southerners' plots. *You* have the mind for excellent military strategy. You and Ellina—" But he broke off.

Venick could point out that he had already told Dourin everything he knew about the southerners. He could point out that his *excellent military strategy* hadn't won them anything. But it wouldn't be true for him to say that they couldn't use him. They could. Still: "I want nothing to do with your war."

"*Our* war." Dourin corrected. "*Ours.* The southerners just secured a critical northern city. A northern city halfway between the Shallow Sea and the mainlands, *your* home. If you were them, where would you strike next?"

"The southerners have no interest in the mainlands."

"Are you sure?"

"Yes."

"Sure enough to risk your family's life? Your own?"

Venick shrugged, but his lies were quickly unraveling. It was true, what Dourin suspected. The southerners *would* come for the mainlands, eventually. Venick remembered stumbling upon the southern army and cornering a conjuror, his sword held against the elf's pale neck. *We are not coming for the mainlands*, the southerner had said. *At least—not yet.*

Venick thought of his mother. He thought of his hunting knife that had been a gift. How losing that gift felt like losing a piece of her. She was innocent. All the people of Irek were. Humans were people of war, but the southerners had conjurors. They had a massive army. If the southern elves overtook the north and then invaded the west, his mother would die. They all would.

"Help us," Dourin said.

Venick adjusted the sword on his hip and made no reply.

"What will you do otherwise? When the world is at war, where will you go?"

More silence.

"It is not like you to run." Dourin narrowed his eyes, then let out a long sigh. "We need each other."

Venick gazed back towards Evov. Though he couldn't see the city, he imagined that he did. He imagined that he could see right through to the palace. He saw Farah on the throne. He saw the quick cunning she and her sister shared, the mind for lies, the willingness to do anything to get what they wanted. Venick saw Rishiana's lifeless body. He saw Raffan.

And Ellina.

Venick thought of his homeland. His dreams of one day returning there, all the sleepless nights he'd lain awake contemplating the price of his redemption, the sacrifice it would take to absolve himself in the eyes of his mother. If Venick ever wanted to return home, there must first be a home for him to return *to*.

He could do what he yearned to do, which was to turn his back on the elves and their war, to forget everything he'd heard and seen and felt, to return to the mountains and the clansmen and forget the world, forget his hope of redemption, forget Ellina.

Or he could stay and fight. Could aid the northern elves. Could save his homeland and maybe earn himself a place back in it.

Venick remembered Ellina insisting that she made her own choices. How he believed her choices were an illusion. He thought maybe his were, too. War was coming. He was in it whether he wished it or not.

"For *my* people," Venick finally replied. "For them, I will join you."

Dourin touched a hand to his own chest, then reached out and placed that hand on Venick's shoulder. It was a symbol of elven friendship, and of thanks. Venick hesitated. There was a time when such a gesture would have warmed him. Now, though, he was tired of elves and their laws and lies and language. He was tired of wanting their acceptance. He did not want to fight for a race who regarded him as an enemy.

Dourin had, once. But Dourin wasn't looking at him with an enemy's eyes now. Dourin was his friend. Venick thought about that. He wondered when he and Dourin had become friends. He realized he was glad for it.

Venick gripped Dourin's shoulder in return.

They walked back to camp together. The air was quiet, broken by the soft sounds of elves clearing the ground, the muffled stomp of a horse, low chatter. Venick scanned their uncertain faces. Only a handful of elves had managed to flee the palace. Branton and Artis from Dourin's troop. A legion patroller named Lin Lill and her battalion. A few citizens, several senators, most of whom Venick didn't recognize. Those elves were still distrustful of him. And yet, there seemed to be a silent expectation, too. Venick knew what they said about him. Battle-born. A human ally. Friend of elves. Maybe more than friends, with a certain highborn elf...

"I know you do not want to talk about it," Dourin said, "but, Ellina..."

"You're right," Venick replied. "I don't want to talk about it."

"She was captured in the fighting."

"You don't know that."

"I know she did not escape with us."

"Ellina is a better fighter than any of those southerners." She was also outnumbered. Venick remembered the way elves had swarmed around her. But he didn't mention that. He pushed away any thought of it. He damned himself for the way his mind snagged on it, the growing worry. Reeking gods. Ellina wasn't his to worry about anymore. "She wasn't captured."

"It has been three days. If she escaped, she would have caught up with us by now."

But Venick thought again about Ellina's many schemes, and his mind offered him another reason why she had not yet come. "Maybe she chose to join a different side."

Dourin rounded on him. "She would never." He looked the way he had after Ellina slaughtered his horses. His expression twisted in anger. "Farah killed her mother. Raffan and Farah plotted against *our own country*. Ellina would never side with them. You know her better than that."

"I don't think I know her at all."

"You do," Dourin insisted. "She trusts you." Venick paled at the accusation, then hardened, suddenly angry.

"I trusted her, too."

"She is the same elf she has always been," Dourin said. "That has not changed. She needs us. She needs *you*."

Venick looked away. His jaw ached, locked against words he didn't want to speak, not really, and yet in this, too, he knew he had no choice. "We'll send a small force back into the city. If she is being held against her will, we'll break her free."

Dourin nodded, softening a little. "Thank you."

"You have no reason to thank me."

"I know this is not easy for you." His next words held no anger, no blame. Dourin spoke them gently. "I know how you feel about her."

"You don't know anything."

"She cares for you, too."

Venick stared at Dourin, then laughed at the utter absurdity of that claim. It rang through the camp, joyless and flat. Dourin had heard Ellina's profession as clearly as Venick had. And it was obvious. Venick should have known it was. Ellina was a liar. It was what drew him to her, what first sparked his attraction. Her cunning. Her sharp mind. He thought he'd seen her feelings grow for him the way his had grown for her, but he was wrong. He might not have believed it, had tried to see a way around it, but he knew better now. And anyway, there was no deny-ing the truth. When she said she did not love him, wouldn't even mind his death, she'd spoken the words in elvish.

FORTY-SIX

War was coming.

It settled over Evov like a hand over a mouth. Stifling. Ellina watched from the palace's highest tower as the southern army arrived at last, as it snaked its way up the mountain pass and conjurors guided the soldiers into the city streets, over the palace's wide bridge, through her home. They stationed themselves in Evov, set claws into the earth, filled the air with their cannon powder-and-metal stink. They razed the green glass mines, sending elves in droves to haul out the precious glass. The city's smithies came alight with their work. Weapons were produced in mass numbers. Handed out. Passed around until every soldier was armed and ready.

Farah orchestrated the plans. Together, she and Raffan promised the southerners everything they desired. *We killed the queen for you,* Farah told them. *We band together with you. Once the north and south are united, we will conquer the world with you.*

Ellina saw it all, heard it all, yet seemed unable to grasp this new reality. To think of her mother's death, the stateroom slaughter, Venick… the pain hit fresh every time, so raw and real that it threatened to overwhelm.

So Ellina did not think of it. She tucked away all memories of the stateroom. Raffan and Farah's plots. Dourin…and Venick. She did not think about their parting. She did not think about her lies or his broken trust or all the things she wished could be undone.

She thought only about what she would do next.

She would escape. She was being watched, but loosely. After pledging loyalty to Farah, Ellina had been put under a kind of house arrest. She was stripped of her weapons, ordered out of her armor. Farah's guards all knew to be aware and wary of her, not to trust her. It did not matter that Ellina had made her pledges to Farah in elvish; Farah *was* suspicious. Whether or not Farah knew about Ellina's ability to lie in elvish, she *did* know about Ellina's ability to twist the truth, how Ellina could muddy elven words in order to trick and deceive. Ellina had been enlisted as a legion spy for that very skill, and Farah had no intention of trusting Ellina on her pledge alone.

"You are not to leave the palace grounds," Farah had told Ellina. "I have positioned a brigade of guards on the bridge. They have been instructed to prevent you from crossing it. They will use force, if necessary." Farah had paused then, waiting for a reply, but when Ellina said nothing Farah merely nodded. "I hope you give them no reason to harm you."

Farah was not wrong to block the bridge. If she wanted to prevent Ellina's escape, that was the most obvious path out of the castle.

But not the only.

One morning, Ellina slipped outside. A pair of guards stationed at the palace entrance saw her leave. They exchanged a glance but made no move to stop her. Where, after all, could she possibly go? The bridge was blocked. The castle was surrounded by water. This prison was an isolated island.

It was a half-day's journey to the base of the mountain. There had been a path here once, crumbled now, huge sections missing where the rock had eroded or fallen away. The trek was exhausting, all rocky handholds and unsteady footing. When Ellina finally reached the water, she stood there, staring into the foamy white waves. They roared against the mountain. Saltwater sprayed. Gulls cried and swooped and dove.

Ellina was not a strong swimmer. Her only practice had been in a calm everpool, and as she gazed out across the bay, Ellina knew this water would be different. More dangerous. Deadly, even. But that was not what held her back.

She watched the waves gather and fold. Pound the rock, spray high, retreat. At a glance, the cliffs seemed impenetrable. The water was no match. But Ellina knew how over time the water would wear the rock. The waves would erode it, break it into sand and dust. This brought to mind one of Venick's lessons. She remembered him leaning over the writing desk, tapping a finger to a page. The force of an attack was not what mattered most, he had said. Planning mattered. Patience and persistence mattered.

Ellina knew she could brave the freezing water and escape. She could do it *now*. Once out of the city, she would find Venick and Dourin and continue what they had started. They would form a plan and gather their own soldiers. They would stop her sister and the southerner conjurors. The vision was tantalizing. Painful, even, the way she ached for it.

Or she could stay.

As Ellina stared at the waves and thought of things like *patience* and *persistence*, she realized how unique a position she was in. A mole in an enemy's kingdom. It was a spy's dream. She could listen and watch and wait. She could gather and relay information about Farah's plans, her motives, her line of attack. Ellina had observed the southern army. She had seen what the conjurors were capable of. The northern resistance was weaker, but Ellina could tip the coming war in their favor. With the right information, they could *win*.

Ellina would find a way to make contact with the northern resistance. She thought of the everpools, the many secrets of those waters, and a plan began to form. She would pass her information to Dourin. And Venick…

Ellina squinted up into the bright sky. Venick might be a problem. If he ever learned what Ellina had done—that she had joined her sister in exchange for Irek's safety, that she was planning on risking herself *again*—he would never accept it. Ellina doubted he would care that her position as a spy here was valuable. Venick's honor would never allow it, especially when he had begged her, again and again, to stop endangering herself for him. If Venick knew what Ellina planned, he would come for her. And then Farah would kill him.

No. Venick could not be allowed to know. For the first time, Ellina thought kindly on the lies she had told in the stateroom. It was better if Venick believed them.

She turned away from the ocean. She barred her heart against the desire to dive into that freezing water and swim until she reached Venick or swim until she drowned. As Ellina climbed the steep rock back up to the palace, she held him in her mind. *I am sorry*, she said to him. *Forgive me*, she said to him. One day she would escape. Maybe, one day things would even be righted between them. But not yet. Her position here was a gift, a *weapon*, and she knew just how to wield it.

Acknowledgements

To my editor Susanne, who saw the plot when it was ugly, and knew where I wanted to go, and helped me get there. To Damon and Chrissy and their fantastic design work. To my parents (all of you guys) who have been reading my novels since the first, who have seen my writing grow. And of course, to my husband. My husband, who watched me go again and again into my own head, who would lose me for weeks, sometimes months as I locked myself away to write this book, who would tease me and call me a "dreamy butterfly," but who knew that I'd always come back to him, and when I did, that I'd want him to read it first.

Made in United States
Orlando, FL
01 December 2021

11012609R00217